MODERN ARABIC SHORT STORIES

Ronak Husni & Daniel L. Newman

MODERN ARABIC SHORT STORIES

A Bilingual Reader

SAQI

ISBN 13: 978-0-86356-436-9

Manufactured in Lebanon

SAQI

26 Westbourne Grove, London W2 5RH
825 Page Street, Suite 203, Berkeley, California 94710
Tabet Building, Mneimneh Street, Hamra, Beirut
www. saqibooks. com

Contents

Introduction

The short story (*qiṣṣa, uqṣūṣa*) is a particularly fruitful genre in contemporary Arabic literature, and almost all major authors have at one point or another in their careers ventured into this field. The present collection provides the reader with a taste of the prowess of the masters of the modern Arabic short story. All except Najīb Maḥfūẓ, Yūsuf Idrīs, Muḥammad Shukrī and Muḥammad al-Zafzāf are active to date.

Naturally, when putting together a reader of this type, it is not always easy to decide whom to include and exclude. The selection process involved many an hour vividly discussing the multitude of stories from which we had to choose. At the same time, we did not focus exclusively on an author's most recent work; instead, we chose to include those stories that were most appropriate for the reader, and which had not been translated.

All too often, works of this kind, though claiming to represent Arabic literature in general, are decidedly "Eastern-centred" inasmuch as the focus is on Middle Eastern authors. As one of the aims of the present book is to provide readers with a sample of the best in modern Arabic short stories, we wanted to make sure that all areas of the Arab world would be represented, from Morocco to Iraq and the Gulf. Similarly, we also aimed to include both male and female authors. However, this was never intended to be an exercise in "political correctness"; rather, the objective was to provide as complete a picture of the modern Arabic short story landscape as possible.

The potential readership for this book is varied. Though the primary target audience consists of students of Arabic, the fact that each story is accompanied by an English translation makes the book accessible to all those interested in contemporary Arab fiction but who lack the language skills to read the stories in the original. There are ample notes following each story in which relevant language and cultural points are discussed, making this reader eminently suitable for both home and classroom use. The stories in the book can be used in core language classes as well as in a Modern Arabic Literature course at all levels. Although some of the texts may be too challenging for novices, they will provide good practice for more advanced students. We have taken this into account by arranging the texts in order of difficulty, the easier ones first. The added advantage to this graduated approach is that it enables students to chart their own progress and proficiency.

Anyone dealing with Arabic texts has to confront the issue of language variety in view of the diglossic nature of the language, i.e. the fact that there are competing varieties, linked to register, many of which are mutually unintelligible. As this is neither the place nor the occasion to enter into a disquisition on this controversial topic, suffice it to say that we have decided to include only stories written in the normative (supranational) variety, known as Modern Standard Arabic (MSA), or *fuṣḥā* (فُصْحَى). At the same time it is, of course, impossible to exclude the colloquial altogether, since no Arabic speaker has MSA as his or her mother tongue, so it is only natural that in dialogue most authors render the language that is actually spoken. In those cases, the vernacular expressions are fully glossed in the notes with their equivalents in MSA. As a result, the book also offers highly interesting insights into the sociolinguistics of the colloquial and the interaction between MSA and the vernaculars, while containing interesting samples of colloquial expressions from all over the Arabic-speaking world.

All words in the language notes – including the titles of the books mentioned – are fully vowelled, whereas the conjugation vowels of the imperfect tense (المُضارِع) of form I verbs are added in brackets, e.g. عَسَّ (u). If there is more than one possibility, both are given, e.g. نَفَثَ (i, u). So-called diptote forms are marked by a *damma* (ُ), e.g. العَواصِمُ. In all other cases, declension vowels are omitted, as is the "nunation" (تَنْوين) – the regular indefinite inflectional noun endings – except for the accusative singular in certain words, e.g. عَفْواً, but عاصمة (rather than عاصمةً).

As texts and translation appear together, the language notes are, quite naturally, much shorter than they would have been had we opted for a traditional reader with only the original texts. Here, too, we have been led by a commonsensical and pragmatic approach, in that we have excluded comments on language points that the learner can easily find in standard translating dictionaries. Indeed, there is little point in simply repeating the translations that appear opposite the text! Notes were added for unusual meanings and/or cultural or intertextual references that were thought to be unfamiliar to our target readership. In this, we have been guided by our extensive joint teaching experience. At the same time we are fully aware that this process is to some extent subjective, and the results open to debate.

As far as the translations are concerned, we have taken into account the fact that the reader will primarily be used as a teaching and learning resource; as a result, an attempt was made to provide both an idiomatic translation and a crib for the student. All the translations are ours, except for the Qur'ān translations in the notes, which are those of M. Pickthall (1996).

The original texts appear in the way they do in the original publications, i.e. without any post-editing on our part. For instance, we have omitted or retained the vowel and declension markings that were present in the original texts.

Each story is preceded by a brief biography of the author, his or her key works and a brief background to the story.

Finally, we should like to thank the authors and others who have kindly granted permission to include the stories in the book. We are especially indebted to Salwā Bakr, Idwār al-Kharrāṭ, Fuʾād al-Takarlī, Zakariyyā Tāmir and Laylā al-ʿUthmān, who offered very useful advice on a number of issues and also provided us with biographical details.

Ronak Husni & Daniel L. Newman

Note on Transliteration

The transliteration used in this book is that of the *Encyclopaedia of Islam*, with the following deviations: <u>kh</u> = kh; ḳ = q; <u>dj</u> = j; <u>sh</u> = sh; <u>dh</u> = dh.

The transcription does not reflect the regressive assimilation (إدْغام) of the lateral in the definite article *al* with the so-called "sun letters" (t, th, d, r, z, s, sh, ṣ, ṭ, ḍ, ẓ, n), e.g. *al-Ṣaḥrā'* rather than *aṣ-Ṣaḥrā'*.

In line with common usage, *hamza* is not transcribed in word-initial positions, whereas the "nunation" (see the Introduction, above) is dropped throughout.

In the narratives of the short stories themselves, proper nouns and technical terms appear in their "recognized" – i.e. "broad" – transliteration forms in order to minimize "exoticness" in the narrative.

Abbreviations

CA	Classical Arabic
coll.	collective noun
dial.	dialectal
ECA	Egyptian Colloquial Arabic
ICA	Iraqi Colloquial Arabic
fem.	feminine
Fr.	French
It.	Italian
LCA	Lebanese Colloquial Arabic
masc.	masculine
MCA	Moroccan Colloquial Arabic
MSA	Modern Standard Arabic
pl.	plural
pron.	pronoun
sg.	singular
SCA	Syrian Colloquial Arabic

ʿIzz al-Dīn al-Madanī

Born in Tunis in 1938, al-Madanī is one of Tunisia's leading literary figures, and has been active in many different genres; his oeuvre includes novels, short stories, literary criticism and theory (see, for instance, his seminal essay الأَدَب التَّجْريبيّ, "Experimental Literature") and plays. He has been particularly prolific as a playwright, and one may cite, for instance, ديوان ثَوْرة الزَّنْج (*The Revolt of the Zanj*, 1983), set against the backdrop of the black slave revolt in ninth-century Baghdad; قَرْطاج (*Carthage*); مولاي السُّلطان الحَفْصِي (*The Ḥafṣid Sultan*), about one of Tunisia's mediaeval dynasties; رِحْلة الحَلّاج (*Al-Ḥallāj's Journey*), about the famous Persian-born mystic theologian al-Hallāj (857–922); and على البَحْر الوافِر (*On The Overflowing Sea*). He has also published a number of short story collections, the most famous of which are من حكايات هذا الزَّمان (*Tales of Our Time*, 1982), خُرافات (*Legends*, 1968) and العُدْوان (*The Aggression*).

In addition to having been a special advisor to Tunisia's minister of culture, al-Madanī has also been editor-in-chief of a number of Tunisian dailies and magazines. In 2006, he was awarded the Theatre prize for his entire dramatic oeuvre at the Doha (Qatar) Cultural Festival.

Al-Madanī frequently uses Arab history, folklore and classical Arabic literary genres as a spectrum through which he addresses contemporary issues such as governance and power. One such example is the story presented here, حكاية القِنْديل ("The Tale of the Lamp"), which appears in the above-mentioned collection من حكايات هذا الزمان. The story contains all the author's hallmarks inasmuch as it is an allegorical tale inspired by classical literature and loaded with intertextual references revealing al-Madanī's wide reading. At the same time, the language used is sparse and formal, devoid of the embellishments one would normally associate with the genre. In spite of its setting, the events depicted in the story clearly have an underlying link with issues bedevilling present-day society.

حكاية القنديل

The Tale of the Lamp

"I found myself in Baghdad, yearning for the *azad* date ..."
They claimed – and God knows it was true – that it was a year
of drought and famine (may God preserve us all!), which had
struck like lightning in one of the ancient capital cities of the
Maghrib such as Qayrawan, Fès, Sijilmasa, Gafsa or Mahdia.

Food had run out, and people went into the desert to look
for cacti and grass to assuage their hunger. After their hopes had
been dashed, they preferred death over life. May God preserve
us from oppression, evil and hunger! The drought lasted for
seven years until the camels knelt down, too weak even to carry
the humps on their backs. God is kind to the Believers! The
people always remembered the horrors of these dark years,
which became a milestone in their history from which they
counted events and feasts.

Once upon a time, there was a man who lived in one of
these ancient cities. He was extremely clever. Living in a time
of plenty and opulence, he believed that contentment was an
everlasting treasure. The story goes that during the day this man
repaired sandals in a nice shop located next to the Abu 'l-Inaya
school, although some people claimed it was next to the shrine
of al-Sayyid al-Sahib. Still others said that the man's shop was
close to the black-roofed gallery that had been built by the
caliph Isma'il al-Mansur al-Shi'i. At night, our protagonist
would busy himself with his family – his women, sons and
daughters. His life and those of other people were filled with
such contentment that not even a cloud on a summer's day
could spoil it. However, when he was struck by catastrophe, and
had to face crises from all sides, his heart and mind deserted
him, and when he saw the camels kneel out of sheer weakness,
his deep-rooted belief in contentment being an everlasting
treasure vanished. His conviction wavered and then faded away.
There was nothing left for him to hold onto! He flew into a
wild rage, but to no avail.

اشتهيت الأزاد١٠٢ وأنا ببغداد عفواً٣، بل زعموا، والله أعلم٤، أن سنة من الجفاف، والقحط، والمحل، والمجاعة٥، والمسغبة، عفانا الله٦ وأيام، قد نزلت نزول الصاعقة على إحدى العواصم٧ المغربية٨، كأن تقول القيروان٩ أو فاس١٠، سجلماسة١١ أو قفصة١٢ أو المهدية١٣ في العهد القديم الغابر. فانعدم القوت، فخرج الناس إلى الصحراء١٤ يطلبون الصبّار والحشائش١٥ البرية لسدّ الرمق، فلم يجدوا شيئاً. فأكلوا الطحلب والحجر، وآثروا الموت على الحياة بعد انقطاع آمالهم. وقانا الله١٦ وإياكم سنوات الظلم والشر والجوع، آمين! وتوالت سنوات الجدْب سبعاً إلى أن بركت الجمال وصارت لا تقوى حتى على حمل سنامها. الله لطيف بعباده المؤمنين! وما زال الناس يذكرون أهوال تلك السنوات المظلمة، فيؤرّخون بها أيامهم، وأحداثهم وأفراحهم...

وكان يعيش في تلك المدن العريقة رجل من أعقل الرجال، قد آمن– أيام العيش الرغيد– بأن الرضى كنز لا يفنى١٧. وكان هذا الرجل، يشتغل في النهار بإصلاح النعال١٨ وترقيعها في دكان ظريف يقع بجانب مدرسة أبي العنانية١٩ حسب رواة٢٠، وبجانب زاوية٢١ السيد الصاحب حسب فريق ثان من الرواة. ومن الرواة من كان يقول إن دكانه كان يقع بجوار السقيفة٢٢ الكحلاء٢٣ التي بناها أمير المؤمنين٢٤ اسماعيل المنصور الشيعي٢٥، والله أعلم. أما في الليل، فكان صاحبنا يشتغل بنسائه، وأبنائه، وبناته، وباتت حياته وحياة الناس راضية مرضية٢٦ لا تكدّرها حتى سحابة صيف! لكن، لما ألمَّ به الخطْب، ذُعر، ولما نزلت عليه الكارثة، فزع، ولما حاصرته الأزمة، انخلع عقله وقلبه وفؤاده. وحين رأى الجمال باركة من شدة الضعف تساقط إيمانه الراسخ بأنّ الرضى كنز لا يفنى، وتهافت اعتقاده، وغاض. ولم يعد الرجل يقبض على شيء! فثارت ثائرته، لكنّ ثورته٢٧ لم تُجْد نفعاً.

He said: "I've got to get food for my family. I just have to, even if it means going out stealing or killing!"

So, early one morning he left his house, armed with a knife. He walked close to the houses, looking around intently. The only thing he saw were the bodies of starving people piled up along the street, hordes of flies hovering around them. The red-hot sun beat down from a clear blue sky, while a scorching wind was blowing hard. What a horrendous sight! Look at this miserable humanity! The poor man cried and wept. Was there any point to any of this? None!

So what was he going to take back home? Wax? Was he going to turn wax into food for the children? Were they supposed to chew on it until it melted in their mouths? Damn this age of injustice!

The man threw the wax into the house, and the mouths caught it. Then he returned to his shop, took a large sack and filled it with everything he owned: sewing needle, thread, some nails, a hammer, knife and the lamp that hung from the ceiling. He locked the door to the shop, secured it and said to himself: "Let me get out of this place and explore the wide world." As the poet says:

> *Alexandria is my home*
> *If that is where I am.*

The man left his native land and everyone in it and embarked upon his journey, travelling day and night, week after week, month after month, not knowing what he would come across. He crossed deserts, wastelands and oases, encountering neither flowers nor animals. Then, he disappeared ... However, according to some storytellers, the man saw the walls of the city of Ghadamis appear before him, while others say that he continued on the Golden Road. The storyteller Abu Shu'ayyib Muhammad Bin Sulayman was certain that the man died of

فقال: «لا بدّ من القوت للعيال[28]، لا بد من ذلك ولو بالسرقة، والسطو، والقتل!».

فخرج الصباح الباكر مسلحاً بشفرته، وهو يحاذي جدران الشوارع، ويتلصص، فلم ير إلا جثث الجياع على قارعة الطريق متراكمة، وجحافل الذباب تطير عليها، والسماء زرقاء صاحية دائماً، والشمس حمراء حادة دائماً، والريح قوية لافحة دائماً. هذا المنظر البشع هذه البشرية التعسة! فبكى المسكين، بكى، وشهق وناح. وهل هذا يجدي نفعاً؟ كلّا وألف كلّا! وبماذا سيعود إلى البيت؟ بالشمع! فلتجعل العيال الشمع طعاماً لها. تلوكه، تلوكه، تلوكه حتى يذوب في أفواهها. فلعنة الله على هذا الدهر الظالم!

ورمى الرجل بالشمع في بيته، فتلقفته الأفواه. ثم عاد إلى دكانه، فتناول جراباً كبيراً وألقى فيه كلّ ما كان يملكه: إبرة الخياطة وبكرة الخيط وبعض المسامير ومطرقة وشفرة، وذاك القنديل المعلق في السقف. أغلق باب الدكان، أحكم غلقه وقال: «فلأرحل عن هذه البلاد، فأرض الله واسعة»[29].

إسكندرية داري
لو قرّ فيها قراري[30]

وترك الرجل الدنيا ومن فيها، وسلك الجادة، وسار ليلاً ونهاراً، أسبوعاً وشهراً، وهو لا يدري ما سيلاقيه، وهو يقطع القفار[31] والبراري[32]، ويجتاز الوديان[33] والصحارى[34]، ولا نبات يعترض سبيله، ولا دابة يأنس بها. ولا طائر يوحي إليه بالحياة، حتى غاب... ويقول بعض الرواة: إنه ظهر أمام أسوار غدامس[35] بينما يذهب رواة آخرون إلى القول: إنه سلك طريق الذهب. لكنّ الراوي أبا شعيب محمد بن سليمان يؤكّد أن الرجل مات جوعاً وعطشاً في الصحراء الكبرى. إلا أن صاحب الطير أبا البركات يثبت: أن الرجل قد لمحته حمائم[36] مدينة طمبكتو أمام أسوارها. ومهما يكن من أمر، فلننقل إن الرجل واصل طريقه رغم الجوع، والعطش، والتعب الشديد،

hunger and thirst in the Great Desert. However, Sahib al-Tayr Abu al-Barakat asserted that the man was observed by the pigeons of the city of Timbuktu in front of its walls. Whatever the case may be, let us assume that the man continued his journey, despite severe hunger, thirst and fatigue, since we do not want our story to end here ...

It was only with great difficulty that, on a crystal-clear night, the traveller reached the walls of a city made of red clay which had suddenly appeared in the bleak desert, much to his surprise. Excited, but perhaps also fearful, he knocked on the gate. A guard appeared, who said: "Welcome to the city of Timbuktu. You are among brothers."

This allayed the man's fears; he regarded this welcome as auspicious. He asked the guard for some water – for water means salvation – to wet his parched mouth. The guard said:

"Drink! However, one of the conditions of entry into the city is that you spend the night outside its walls. On the morrow, you may enter, provided you have a gift for our ruler, the Sultan."

Then the guard disappeared, and the man remained alone all night. He wondered what he was going to do about this gift for the Sultan, since he had nothing in his bag that he could give. What could he do? Damn this age of injustice!

When the voice of the *muezzin* calling the faithful to the dawn prayer resounded, the guard came out of the gate and hurried to rouse the man, who was purposefully very slow in waking up. The guard took him first to the mosque, where the traveller performed his ablutions, which he also stretched out for a very long time. Then, he prayed, taking his time with the genuflections and prostrations and stalling his prayers. His heart was throbbing like mad, the pulses reverberating like a drum.

The guard offered him some dates and milk. After having eaten, the man was finally led to the palace. He felt as though

لأننا لا نريد ألا تقف حكايتنا عند هذا الحدّ...

لقد بلغ الرجل بشق الأنفس في إحدى الأمسيات الشفافة مثل البلور أسوار مدينة طينية حمراء، قد قامت فجأة بين السباسب[37] الجرداء، فاندهش لذلك. ومن شدة الفرح، أو ربما من شدة الخوف، دق باب السور، فبرز له عساس[38] وصيف.

فقال له: «مرحباً بك في مدينة طمبكتو، أهلاً وسهلاً بك بين إخوانك!».

فهدأ روع الرجل، واستبشر خيراً بهذا الترحاب، فسأله شيئاً من الماء، والماء أمان، حتى يبل ريقه.

فقال له العساس الوصيف: «إشرب، لكنّ من شروط الدخول أن تنام الليلة خارج السور، ثم أن تدخل صباح غد بهدية على مولانا[39] السلطان».

ثم غاب العساس الوصيف، وبقي الرجل طوال الليل يسأل نفسه عما يهديه إلى السلطان، بينما هو لا يملك شيئاً في جرابه يستحق الاهداء! كيف يفعل؟ لعنة الله على هذا الدهر الظالم!

ولما أذن المؤذن صلاة الفجر، خرج له العساس الوصيف مهرولاً ليوقظه. فاستيقظ على مهل، ثم أدخله العساس أولاً إلى المسجد، فتوضّأ[40]، وأطال في الوضوء[40] وصلّى، وأطال في الركوع[41] والسجود[42]، وسبّح، وأطال في التسبيح[43]، وسلّم، وأطال في التسليم[44]، وذكر الله تعالى[45]، وقلبه يخفق كالبندير[46] الرنان من الضرب. ثم قدم له العساس التمر والحليب[47] فتناول تمرة، وشرب شربة. وأخيراً قاده إلى القصر. فأحس الرجل بأنه سجين هذه الملاطفة، هذه المجاملة، هذه الضيافة القاسية على القلب. ماذا سيهدي إلى السلطان؟ المطرقة! سيهشّم بها رأسه! الشفرة! سيذبحه بها! إبرة الخياطة؟ سيخيط بها جفنيه، وشفتيه! البكرة ! سيوثقه بها خلافاً وسيقول: «يا كلب

he were a prisoner of this kindness and courtesy, this merciless hospitality.

What would he give to the Sultan? The hammer? He would use it to smash his head in! The knife? He would slaughter him with it! The sewing needle? He would use it to sew his eyelids and lips! The thread? He would use it to truss him, saying: "You dog! You dare present me with wretched thread after we have treated you as our guest, honoured you and elevated you above ourselves! You dog!"

To which the traveller would retort: "May God protect me from the Devil!"

Finally the man found himself in front of the Sultan, who was surrounded by his retinue of servants. The Sultan rose from his throne and descended the dais to welcome his guest, saying: "Greetings. Welcome in our midst, esteemed guest." The Sultan then embraced his guest and kissed him, as though he was greeting a dear friend he had not seen in a long time. He bade the man sit next to him on the throne. The man continued to clutch his bag close to his chest, whereas the Sultan did not take his eyes off it. Suddenly, the ruler asked:

"Is that our present you've got in that bag of yours?"

All the members of the Sultan's entourage fell silent, agog in anticipation to see the wonderful gift for the Sultan.

The man mumbled: "Yes, my lord, this is your gift in the bag."

The Sultan shrieked with joy, while the man imagined his head on the chopping block. He put his hand into the bag, and hit upon the lamp. He took it out and gave it to the Sultan, who looked at it in wonder:

"What's this?"

The man said: "It's a lamp."

The Sultan was speechless, while everyone in his entourage craned their neck to get a better look at the object. Then the Sultan said: "A lamp?"

تهدي إلي بكرة من الخيط الحقير بعد أن استضفناك وأكرمناك وجعلناك فوق رؤوسنا! يا كلب؟! يا لئيم!» فقال الرجل: «أعوذ بالله من الشيطان الرجيم»٤٨.

وإذا به أمام السلطان وفي حضرة حاشيته٤٩.

ونهض السلطان من عرشه، ونزل ليقبل ضيفه أحسن القبول.

فقال له: «مرحباً، مرحباً، حللت أهلاً، ونزلت سهلاً!»٥٠.

وعانقه وقبله واحتضنه، كما لو احتضن صديقاً عزيزاً عليه لم يشاهده منذ زمان. وأجلسه بجانبه على العرش. وظل الرجل متماسكاً بجرابه لا يفارقه. وظل السلطان يديم إليه النظر، فقال: «هذه هديتنا في الجراب؟».

فسكت أفراد الحاشية مترقبين الهدية السلطانية الفاخرة.

وهمهم الرجل فقال: «نعم يا مولاي السلطان، هذه هديتكم في الجراب».

ففرح السلطان فرحاً شديداً. ورأى الرجل رأسه يطير تحت ضربة الجلاد! فأدخل يده في الجراب، فاصطدمت بالقنديل فتناوله، وأعطاه إلى السلطان.

فتعجب السلطان: «ما هذا؟»

فقال الرجل: «هذا قنديل!».

فبهت السلطان، واشرأبت أعناق أفراد الحاشية مستطلعين....

فقال السلطان: «قنديل؟».

فقال الرجل: «نعم، يا مولاي السلطان إنه والله٥١ قنديل من النحاس».

فقال السلطان مستفسراً: «وما معنى قنديل؟».

فأجاب الرجل: «هو آلة من النحاس، فيها فتيل وشيء من الزيت».

فسأله السلطان: «وما وظيفته؟».

"Yes, my lord – a lamp made out of copper."

"What does 'lamp' mean?" enquired the Sultan.

The man replied: "It is a device made of copper, with a wick and a little bit of oil."

The Sultan asked: "What does it do?"

"It gives light."

With increasing amazement, the Sultan asked: "It gives light just like the sun or the moon?"

"It lights up the world when the sun has disappeared and it is cloaked in darkness."

The Sultan was quite taken aback. "So, this is a piece of live coal from the sun?"

The man replied: "If you wish, my lord."

As the Sultan gazed at the lamp, turning it every which way, he said: "Does it give light at this moment?"

The man replied: "No, it's not giving off any light at the moment, my lord. Let me light it."

With a magical movement the man ignited the lamp, and light suddenly began to spread across the hall, leaving the Sultan quivering, almost fainting with joy and glee. The members of his entourage were clapping their hands and cheering, praising God for His munificence. The Sultan took the man to his side, grabbed the lamp and proceeded towards the window looking out onto the streets of the city. Lo, the streets were crowded with people eager to know about the Sultan's gift. Then, the Sultan cried out:

"This is the lamp!"

The crowd cheered, their eyes glued to the lamp:

"Long live the lamp! Long live the Sultan! Long live the lamp! Long live the Sultan!"

The Sultan then kissed his guest and said to him: "We didn't know about the lamp, and thanks to you, our esteemed guest, we've learned something that we didn't know. You've lit up our darkness. You've let the sun into our world, and for this, I'll make you a minister!"

فأجاب الرجل: «وظيفته أن ينير!».

فزاد تعجب السلطان: «أن ينير مثل الشمس أو القمر؟».

فأجاب الرجل: «أن ينير الدنيا حين تغيب الشمس ويعمّ الظلام الدنيا».

فانخلع السلطان: «إذن، هو قبس من الشمس؟».

فأجاب الرجل: «إذا أردتم ذلك يا مولاي السلطان!».

ثم قال السلطان وهو يقلّب القنديل بين يديه: «وهل هو ينير الآن؟».

فأجاب الرجل: «إنه لا ينير الآن يا مولاي السلطان ها إني سأوقده».

وبحركة سحرية أوقد الرجل القنديل. فشعّ النور فجأة فاهتزّ السلطان بذلك، وكاد يغمى عليه فرحاً وسروراً وانشراحاً. وصفق أفراد الحاشية وهللوا٥٢، وكبروا٥٣، وحمدوا الله على نعمته. فأخذ السلطان الرجل إلى جانبه، وتناول القنديل، وتقدم نحو الشباك المطل على شوارع المدينة، وإذا الجماهير مكتظة وهي تتشوق إلى معرفة الهدية.

فصاح السلطان: «إنها قنديل!».

فهتفت الجماهير٥٤، وأبصارها معلّقة بالقنديل."يحيا القنديل، يحيا السلطان! يحيا القنديل، يحيا السلطان !».

ثم أقبل السلطان على ضيفه فقال له: «إني لم نعرف في حضرتنا السلطانية القنديل. وبما أنك أيها الضيف المبجل العظيم قد عرفتنا بما لم نكن نعرف، وقد أنرت ظلمتنا، وقد أدخلت الشمس في دنيانا، فإني أجعلك وزيراً!!».

فقال الرجل: «يا مولاي السلطان أنا رجل من العامة٥٥، من أهل البر والتقوى، أحب العافية والطمأنينة، ولا أعرف تدبير السلطان."

فألح عليه السلطان إلحاحاً شديداً، فقال له الرجل: «أعفني يا مولاي السلطان من هذا المنصب أكن لك خادماً أميناً، وصاحباً ودوداً».

The man said: "My lord, I am but a commoner, a God-fearing man. I enjoy peace and tranquillity and wouldn't know how to advise a Sultan."

However, the Sultan insisted, upon which the man said: "My lord, I implore you to relieve me from this post. I'll be a faithful servant and devoted friend."

The Sultan exclaimed: "Outstanding! Bravo!"

Then the Sultan ordered the Treasurer to come to him. When he arrived, the three of them went to the Treasury.

The Sultan said to the traveller: "Take what you like from these worldly goods and improve your situation with it!"

The man grabbed as much jewellery, pearls, diamonds and other precious stones like coral as his bag could take. Then the Sultan bade the Marriage Judge of the city of Timbuktu to come to him immediately. When he arrived, the Sultan said to him:

"I am going to wed this man to my daughter Zubeida. I want you to write the marriage contract, and be quick about it!"

The Sultan then dressed the traveller in a gold-embroidered silk robe of honour and guided his guest to the princess in the presence of the courtiers. When the man saw his bride-to-be, he thought she was the most beautiful girl his eyes had ever beheld. She brought to mind the words of the ancient poet:

٩

> *My night, this bride is one of the Zanj*
> *Adorned with pearl necklaces.*

The Marriage Judge said: "Forsooth, I've never seen anyone as beautiful as Zubeida, nor anyone as tender, fragrant, slender or more delicate. She is like musk and amber, silk and velvet, like a flower and jasmine. It is time to draw up the marriage contract!"

The man made thousands of lamps for the Sultan, his courtiers and all the people. He hung them everywhere: in the palace, the mosques, the schools, streets, squares and houses.

فقال السلطان: «بخ بخ ثم بخ!»

ثم أمر السلطان بإحِضار صاحّب بيت المال. فلما حضر، ذهب ثلاثتهم إلى الديوان[56].

فقال السلطان للرجل: «تناول ما شئت من وسخ الدنيا فأصلح به حالك!!».

فغرف الرجل الجواهر واللؤلؤ والجمان والماس والزبرجد والمرجان بكلتا يديه حتى ملأ جرابه. ثم أمر السلطان بإحضار قاضي الأنكحة[57] بمدينة طمبكتو العامرة على الفور.

فلما حضر قال له: «هذا الرجل أزوّجه ابنتي زبيدة. فاكتب عقد النكاح على عجل!».

ثم خلع عليه السلطان خلعة من الدمقس والحرير مُوشّاة بالذهب، وأدخله نفسه وبحضور الحاشية على ابنته. فوجدها الرجل عروساً من أجمل ما رأى... فهي كما قال الشاعر القديم، لله دره[58]:

ليلتي هذه عروس من الزّنج[59]
عليها قلائدٌ من جُمانٍ[60]

وقال قاضي الأنكحة: «والله إني لم أر أجلّ من زبيدة، ولا أرخص منها، ولا أعطر، ولا أضمر، ولا أرق، فهي مسك وعنبر. وهي حرير ومخمل. وهي ورد وياسمين. والله لقد تنهدت وقت كتابة العقد!»

وصنع الرجل للسلطان وللحاشية وللناس أجمعين ألف ألف قنديل، علقها جميعاً في قصر المدينة، وأسواقها، ومساجدها، ومدارسها، وشوارعها، وسطوحها، وبيوتها. ووظّف عليها ألف وقّاد من الزنوج المرد حتى غرقت المدينة وسكانها في النور ليلاً ونهاراً. وعاش صاحبنا في النعيم والسعادة، وطابت له الحياة سنوات طويلة لا يعلم عددها إلا الله تعالى، إلى أن... نعم، إلى أن بدأ يحنّ إلى وطنه، ويشتاق إلى رؤية عياله وأهله. ورأى

He employed one thousand black men to light the lamps until the entire city and its inhabitants bathed in light night and day. As for our traveller, he enjoyed a life of comfort and happiness for many years, though only God knows for how long, until... yes, until he began to yearn for his native land, and to see his children and people again. He realized that the lean years must have ended by now, and that the fat years must have started, bringing with them prosperity and blessings. Yet, who knows? He asked the Sultan for permission to travel to his native land. The Sultan agreed, and the traveller began to prepare a caravan of camels, horses, donkeys and mules carrying rugs from Kairouan, mastic from the Yemen, teak from Niger, amber from the Sudan, ivory from Ghana, and other fineries.

And so the traveller left the bright lights of Timbuktu for his native land, under the protection of God the Almighty. As soon as he and his caravan arrived in his native city, people began crowding around him to grab his possessions; soon fights erupted over them, and they even began to kill each other. The mob attacked the camels, the horses, mules and donkeys with knives and ate them all. The traveller enquired what was happening, and was told: "The people in the city haven't had anything to eat for about twenty years."

He remembered his famous saying and former indignation, and said: "Damn this age of injustice!"

There was another man there, sitting motionless, observing the dreadful spectacle. Then he looked at the traveller. His eyes alternated between the terrible scene and the traveller, who was still sitting on his camel and staring at the humanity milling around like a swarm of locusts. Finally, the man got up and greeted the traveller. He said:

"I know you. You used to work as a cobbler, and your shop was next to the shrine of Moulay Muhammad al-Dakhil. My shop was opposite yours. I used to repair sandals. My shop used to be next to the shrine of Moulay Muhammad al-Kharij.

أن السنوات العجاف لا بد أنها أنتهت وأن السنوات السمان لا بد أنها حلت، حاملة معها الخير والبركة لكنّ من يدري؟ فاستأذن السلطان في الرحيل إلى بلده. فأذن له فتأهب وجهز قافلة من الجمال والخيل والبغال٦١ والحمير حمّلها زرابي٦٢ القيروان، ولبان اليمن، وساج النيجر، وعنبر السودان، وعاج غانة... وبارح مدينة طمبكتو السعيدة الآمنة بأنوارها المشرقة الساطعة، وقصد وطنه على بركة الله.

دخل الرجل بقافلته إلى المدينة. وإذا بالناس ينتشرون حوله، وإذا بهم يفتكون البضائع، وإذا بهم يتخاصمون وإذا بهم يتقاتلون، وإذا بالسكاكين ينحرون الجمال والخيل والبغال والحمير، ويأكلون، ويأكلون. فسأل «الرجل»، فقيل له: «أن أهالي المدينة لم يأكلوا شيئاً منذ زهاء عشرين سنة، وتذكر قولته الشهيرة ونقمته القديمة فقال: «لعنة الله على هذا الدهر الظالم».

وكان رجل آخر قابعاً في مكانه لا يتحرك، ينظر إلى المشهد المريع، ثم ينظر إلى «الرجل». ثم ينظر إلى المشهد المفزع، ثم ينظر إلى «الرجل «الراكب على راحلته، المتعجب من هذا الخلق المنتشر كالجراد ثم ينظر إلى المشهد المهول. وأخيراً، نهض، وأقبل على «الرجل».

فقال له: «لقد عرفتك، كنت تشتغل إسكافياً. ودكانك كان بجانب زاوية مولاي محمد الداخل. وكان دكاني قبالة دكانك. وكنت أشتغل بترقيع النعال. ودكاني كان بجانب زاوية مولاي محمد الخارج. لا بد أنك عرفتني الآن. لكن، قل لي، بالله عليك٦٣، كيف صنعت لتحصل على هذه الثروة؟ وماذا فعلت؟ قل لي فإني زميلك في الحرفة، وجارك في السوق، وقرينك يوم بدأت المحنة. وإلى أي بلد رحلت لتجمع هذه النعمة؟ قل لي إني مشتاق

You must remember me by now. Tell me, honestly, how did you manage to acquire such wealth? What have you been doing? Tell me, since we work in the same trade. I was your neighbour in the *souk*, and your companion on the day you started in the profession. Which country did you travel to in order to collect all these fine things? Tell me, for I am keen on bread and meat, silk, women, gold, tranquillity and sweet dreams. Save me from the pain and misery of this age of injustice!"

The traveller replied: "Leave this land, my friend, and follow the road until its end. There, you will find a city, and one of the conditions for entering it is that you offer a gift – any gift – to its Sultan. And the strange thing is that they reward you for it, too! As you can see, it is quite simple."

So the other man left his country in search of the good life, meat, silk, women, gold, tranquillity and sweet dreams. He travelled until the end of the road and crossed the desert until, one clear night, he arrived at a city made of red clay, like Marakkech or Tozeur, which had suddenly sprung up in the middle of the desert.

He knocked on the gate, after which a guard came out and greeted him in the most splendid fashion. The following morning, the guard woke him up and said: "Do you have a gift for our lord the Sultan?"

The man immediately answered: "Yes, I've got a gift in this bag."

The man quickly went through his ablutions and prayers and hastened to the palace, hurrying in to meet the Sultan and his entourage. He quickly prostrated himself and kissed the ground before the Sultan. When he raised his eyes he saw that the Sultan was barefoot, as were all the courtiers, including the guard who had brought him in. He rose from the ground, slipped his hand into the bag, and took out one of the most beautiful and best sandals that had ever been made in the city of Fès since its foundation.

إلى الخبز، واللحم، والحرير، والنساء، والذهب والراحة، والأحلام اللذيذة. أنقذني من آلام هذا الدهر الظالم!».

أجابه الرجل: «ارحل يا أخي عن هذا البلد، واسلك الجادة إلى منتهاها، وهناك تجد مدينة، من شروط دخولها أن تقدم هدية- أياً كانت- إلى سلطانها. فإذا ما أعجبته فإنه يجازيك. فالأمر سهل يسير كما ترى!».

ورحل الرجل عن وطنه طلباً للخير، واللحم، والحرير، والنساء، والذهب، والراحة، والأحلام اللذيذة. فسار إلى الجادة حتى منتهاها، واجتاز الصحراء، حتى بلغ إحدى الأمسيات الشفافة دائماً إلى مدينة حمراء طينية مثل مراكش[٦٤] أو توزر[٦٥] قد قامت فجأة بين السباسب. دق باب السور، فخرج له العساس الوصيف ورحّب به أجل الترحاب دائماً. ثم أيقظه في الصباح، وقال له: «هل لك هدية لمولانا السلطان؟». أجاب الرجل على الفور: «نعم لي هدية في هذا الجراب». ثم توضّأ الرجل متعجلاً، وصلى متعجلاً، وأكل متعجلاً، وسار نحو القصر متعجلاً، ودخل على السلطان وعلى حاشيته متعجلاً، فقبل الأرض بين يديه متعجلاً. وحين رفع عينيه وهو ما زال ساجداً، لاحظ أن السلطان حافي القدمين وأن أفراد الحاشية حفاة، وأن العساس حافي القدمين. فقام من سجوده وأدخل يده في الجراب، فتناول بلغة من أجمل البلغات وأحسنها، وأبدعها ولعلها من أروع البلغات التي صنعتها مدينة فاس منذ تاريخ تأسيسها إلى اليوم.

فقال له السلطان مبهوراً: «ما هذا؟».

فأجابه الرجل: «هذه بلغة هدية إليكم يا مولاي السلطان».

فقال السلطان: «وما وظيفتها؟».

فقال الرجل: «وظيفتها أن ننتعلها هكذا."

ومشى الرجل بها خطوات ففرح بذلك السلطان فرحاً شديداً، وصفّق

Surprised, the Sultan asked him: "What's this?"

"This sandal is a gift for you my lord."

The Sultan asked: "What's it for?"

The man answered: "It is to be worn as follows."

Thereupon the man took a few steps in the sandals. The Sultan was extremely pleased with this, and the courtiers all applauded.

They called out:

"Long live the sandal! Long live the Sultan! Long live the sandal! Long live the Sultan!"

The Sultan then went up to the man and said: "This is a most wonderful present you've given me, and it merits the greatest reward!"

The Sultan then ordered the Treasurer to come, and when he arrived, the Sultan told him: "Return whence you came."

The courtiers were surprised at this.

The Sultan said: "This man deserves a better reward than mere filthy lucre."

He turned to the man, and said: "Esteemed guest, please raise your eyes towards the ceiling."

The man lifted his head.

The Sultan asked him: "What do you see?"

The man replied: "I see a lamp."

"Behold the reward for your gift!"

أفراد الحاشية.

فهتفوا: «تحيا البلغة! يحيا السلطان! تحيا البلغة! يحيا السلطان!».

ثم أقبل السلطان على الرجل فقال له: «هذه أبدع هدية أهديت إليّ، فلا بد أن أجازيك خير الجزاء!».

ثم أمر بإحضار صاحب بيت المال. فلما حضر، قال له السلطان: «عد من حيث أتيت».

فتعجبت الحاشية.

فقال السلطان عندئذ: «هذا الرجل يستحق جزاء أعظم من وسخ الدنيا!».

ثم خاطب الرجل: «أيها الضيف المبجّل العظيم ارفع رأسك نحو السقف».

فرفع الرجل رأسه.

فقال له السلطان: «ماذا ترى؟».

فقال الرجل: أرى قنديلاً».

فقال السلطان: «هو لك جزاء على هديتك!».

Language Notes

1. ‏اِشْتَهَيْتُ الأَزاد وأنا بِبَغْداد‎: extract from the opening line of the so-called ‏مَقامة بغداد‎, composed by the Persian-born Fāris al-Hamadhānī (968–1008), who is credited with the invention of the ‏مقامة‎ genre (lit. "standing", but usually translated as "session" or "assembly"), which consists of social vignettes recounted in razor-sharp, eloquent rhyming prose (‏سَجْع‎). The ‏مقامات‎ are also a cornucopia of rare and archaic words. The genre was further developed by Abū Muḥammad al-Qāsim Ibn al-Ḥarīrī (1054–1122).

2. ‏الأَزاد‎: also known as ‏الزِّنْبِيق الأَبْيَض‎ ("the white lily"), it is a type of date (‏تَمر‎) known for its exquisite taste.

3. ‏عَفْواً‎: the usual meaning of this term is "Excuse me!" or "Don't mention it!" (in response to ‏شُكراً‎, "Thank you"). However, it can also mean "of one's own accord", and "spontaneously" (cf. ‏عَفْويّ‎, "spontaneous" and ‏عَفْويّة‎, "spontaneity").

4. ‏واللهُ أَعْلَم‎: this formula, which literally translates as "God knows best" or "(Only) God knows", is traditionally used to express doubt regarding the veracity of a statement.

5. ‏المَحْل والجَفاف, والقَحْط‎: in this example of lexical repetition all three words denote "drought", with ‏قحط‎ having the additional connotation of "dearth", or even "famine".

6. ‏عَفانا الله‎: lit. "May God spare us"; it is used when someone is faced with a particularly dire prospect.

7. ‏العَواصِمُ‎: sg. ‏عاصمة‎; the modern word for "capital (city)", but used in the past for any major urban centre.

8. ‏المَغْرب‎: this term, which currently refers to "Morocco", used to denote the Islamic lands in the west (‏المَغْرب‎, "the place where the sun sets"). Note that in English, "Maghrib" tends to be synonymous with "North Africa" (i.e. Morocco,

Tunisia, Algeria and Libya).

9. القَيْرَوان: a town (and governorate capital) in central Tunisia, approximately 150 km from Tunis. An old centre of Islamic learning, Kairouan is the site of the first mosque in northern Africa (or إفْريقيا), and was the first Islamic capital of the region (and a base for military expeditions).

10. فاس: the traditional capital of northern Morocco, Fès (or Fez) boasts the oldest university in Morocco, dating back to the mid-ninth century and the famous قَرَوِيِّن mosque. Between the twelfth and fifteenth centuries, Fès was the undisputed political, economic and intellectual centre of the entire region. The town also achieved great fame as a religious centre.

11. سجلماسة: the ancient capital of the تافَللْت district, situated some 300 km from Fès, it acted as the gateway to the desert and was also the centre for a number of Moroccan dynasties. Today, only ruins remain of this most evocative of sites.

12. قَفْصَة: a town in Tunisia some 350 km southwest of Tunis. Its name is derived from the Arabicized form of Capsa, which was the name of the Roman settlement on that site. After playing a considerable part in the country's history, (even including a short independent spell in the eleventh and twelfth centuries), Gafsa (its current Latinized form reflecting the local pronunciation of ق as /g/) dwindled into oblivion.

13. المَهْديَّة: a Tunisian town and provincial capital (named after its founder, عُبَيْد الله مَهْدي, d. 934 AD), located on the coast some 200 km south of Tunis.

14. صُبّار: "cactus", "Indian fig" (or "tamarind"). However, there is also a possible play on the homographic صُبار (or صَبار ، صِبار), meaning "(smooth) stones" in Classical Arabic.

15. الحشائشُ: حَشيش sg. (coll.), which, in addition to "herbs" or "grass", also denotes "hemp" (cannabis).

16. وقانا الله وإياكم: lit. "May God preserve us and you (from imminent evil)."

17. الرِّضى كنز لا يَفْنَى: this is a reference to the fixed expression القَناعة كنز لا يَفْنَى ("contentment is an everlasting treasure"), which is attributed to 'Alī Ibn Abī Ṭālib (d. 661), the Prophet's cousin and son-in-law, who was also the fourth caliph in Islam.

18. النِّعال: sg. نَعْل (pl. also أَنْعُل), originally denoted "sole".

19. مَدْرَسة أبي العنانية: this Fès-based school was founded in the fourteenth century.

20. رُواة: sg. راو (<رَوَى, "to report, narrate"). Also related are رواية ("novel") and روائيّ ("novelist").

21. زاوية: lit. "corner" (of a building), it originally denoted the cell of a Christian monk (also صَوْمَعة). In Islam, it refers to a small mosque (which in many cases houses a saint's tomb), prayer room or (especially in the Maghrib) a building for members of a صُوفي brotherhood (طريقة).

22. سقيفة: pl. سَقائِف; originally the roofed portion of a street.

23. كَحْلاء: this is the feminine form of أكْحَل ("black", especially referring to eyes, with the plural form كُحْل being homonymous with "antimony"; "kohl" (pl. أكْحال).

24. أمير المُؤْمنين: this was the traditional title of caliphs in Islamic history.

25. اسماعيل المنصور الشيعي: Mawlāy Ismā'īl b. al-Sharīf Abū 'l-Naṣr, the second sultan of the Alawid dynasty, who reigned for fifty-five years, between 1672 and 1727.

26. راضية مَرْضية: this is a Qur'ānic phrase: إرْجعي إلى رَبِّك راضيةً مَرْضيةً ("Return unto thy Lord, content in His good pleasure"; 83:23, الفجر).

27. فثارت ثائرته، لكنّ ثورته: this is a typical example of a type of word play in Arabic, in which the same root reappears in different guises.

28. العِيال: sg. عَيِّل (pl. also عالة); lit. "dependents".

29. أرض الله واسعة: lit. "God's Earth is wide", this expression

is commonly used in the sense of "There is plenty of opportunity elsewhere." (Note that أَرْض is feminine!)

30. الاسكندرية داري: this is another extract from a *maqāma* by al-Hamadhānī (see above), i.e. from the so-called المقامة الجَاحِظِيَّة, which has the following famous opening lines:

اسْكَنْدَرية داري   لَوْ قَرَّ فيها قَراري
لَكِنَّ بالشَّام لَيْلي   وبالعِراقِ نَهاري

31. قِفار: sg. قَفْر, "desert" or "wasteland" (also, see below, صَحْراء).

32. بَرار: sg. بَرِّية, "open country".

33. وِدْيانٌ :واد sg.

34. صَحَاري: pl. of صَحْراءُ (indef. pl. صَحار), which, depending on the location, can be translated in English as "desert" or "Sahara" (also in Arabic الصحراء الكُبْرَى). Note that صحراء is grammatically feminine.

35. غَدامِس: a small oasis in the Libyan Sahara, near where the Libyan, Algerian and Tunisian borders meet. It owed its former prosperity to its position as a hub in the trans-Saharan trade.

36. حَمائمُ: pl. of حَمامة, which can denote either "pigeon" or "dove".

37. سَباسِبُ: pl. of سَبْسَب. Also قَفْر سَبْسَب.

38. عَسَّاس: (عَسَّ< (u) "to patrol by night") Although this form can only be adjectival (meaning "spending the night patrolling"), it is nominalized here to "one who patrols at night", i.e. a "guard" or "night watchman". This also betrays the author's origins, as the private guard to the Tunisian ruler, the Bey (باي), was known as العَسّة المَصُونة.

39. مَوْلانا: lit. "our lord"; a variant of Mawlāy (مَوْلاي, "my lord") – commonly transliterated in Morocco as Moulay – the honorific title borne by Moroccan sultans.

40. وُضُوء: lit. "cleansing" (cf. تَوَضَّأ); the obligatory (minor) ablution to be performed by Muslims prior to prayer. It generally involves washing the face, hands and feet, rubbing

the head, rinsing the mouth and washing the ears. This is contrasted with the "major" ablution (in order to remedy a state of "major" impurity such as after intimate relations, menses), i.e. غسْل, which refers to washing the entire body in ritually pure water. The full ablution is also performed on corpses.

41. رُكوع: the verbal noun (مَصْدَر) of رَكَعَ (a), "to bow", "kneel down". The individual acts of bending are known as رَكْعة (pl. رَكَعات).

42. بَسْمَل: verb denoting the uttering of بسم الله الرَّحْمَن الرَّحيم ("In the Name of God, the Beneficent, the Merciful"). The formula is normally used at the beginning of the recitation of the Qur'ān or any activity. Other such formula-based verbs include حَوْقَلَ, "to say لاحَوْلٍ ولا قُوّة إلا بالله ("There is no power and no strength save in God"); حَمْدَلَ, to say الحمد لله ("Praise be to God"); سَمَّى, to say بسم الله ("In the name of God").

43. سَجَدَ> (u) "to bow down", "prostrate oneself" during prayer; it is also the plural of ساجد ("prostrate [in worship]"). The individual prostration is known as سَجْدة (pl. سَجَدات).

44. تَسْبيح: this is the مَصْدَر of سَبَّحَ, and refers to the part of the prayer during which the worshipper utters the phrase سُبْحانَ الله ("Praise the Lord!").

45. ذكر الله تَعالى: lit. "mention of God the most High"; in prayers and worship, it refers to the repetition of the phrase الله تعالى. In a *ṣūfī* context, ذكر is associated with the constant repetition of words and formulae, often accompanied by dancing, which induces a trance-like state.

46. بنْدير: (pl. بَنادير), a musical instrument resembling a tambourine.

47. التَّمْر والحَليب: this is the traditional offering to welcome a guest (especially in North Africa).

48. أَعوذُ بالله من الشَّيْطان الرَّجيم: this formula is used when faced

with a particularly heinous sight or occurrence. It may be compared to the English "Get thee behind me, Satan!".

49. حاشية: (pl. حَواش) in addition to the meaning in this text, this word also denotes "commentary" (in the margin) of a book.

50. حَلَلْتَ أهلاً ونَزَلْتَ سَهْلاً: an expansion of the traditional greeting أهْلاً وسَهْلاً (said by the host), which literally means "(you are among) kinfolk and on level (i. e. hospitable) land". The expression here literally means "you have stopped among your people and you have descended upon a plain". There are a number of variants, the most common ones being أَتَيْتَ قائماً أهلاً ومَوْضِعاً سَهْلاً ("You have come to a people who are like kinsfolk and to a place that is smooth and plain") and قَدِمْتَ أهلاً ووطِئْتَ سَهْلاً ("You have come to your people and you have tread onto a level plain").

51. واللهِ: lit. "by God" (in the sense of "I swear"), this expression is used profusely in Arabic in a wide variety of contexts, e.g. "I swear"; "Believe me"; "No kidding".

52. هَلَّل: to say لا إله إلّا اللهُ ("There is no God, other than God").

53. كَبَّرَ: to say اللهُ أكبَر ("God is great"). Also see note No. 41.

54. جُمْهُورِيَّة, جُمْهُور, sg. :جَماهير "group" (which gave us "republic"), it initially denoted "a group of people" or "main part of the people" (or, indeed, the chief part of anything).

55. العامَّة: lit. "the common folk", vs. الخاصّة (lit. "the special ones"), "the elite".

56. ديوان: "chancellery" or "council of state"; ديوان originally referred to official records or register (< دَوَّنَ, "to record"), and then to the place where the records were kept). The same word also denotes a poetry collection.

57. أَنْكِحَة: sg. نكاح ("marriage"), with عَقْد النِّكاح denoting "marriage contract" (in the East, the usual expression is عقد الزَّواج).

58. للهِ دَرُّهُ: lit. "his achievement is due to God" (دَرَّ,

"achievement", but also "milk"!).

59. الزَّنْج: (pl. زُنُوج), this term usually denoted the black peoples of the east coast of Africa. In Arab history, however, زنج usually refers to the rebel slaves who rose against their Arab masters in Abbasid Iraq (in 689–90, 694 and 869–83).

60. هذه لَيْلَتي...: these are two lines from a poem by the famous Abbasid poet أبو العَلاء المَعَرِّيّ (973-1058).

61. البِغال: sg. بَغْل (pl. also أبْغال).

62. زَرابي: sg. زُرْبية. This word is more common in North Africa than in the Middle East, where the usual term for "carpet" is سَجّادة (pl. سَجاجيد).

63. بالله عَلَيْك: lit. "as God is your witness". It is used in the sense of an oath to assert one is telling the truth, or as an entreaty, i.e. " I beg you".

64. مَرَّاكش: town in Morocco about 220 km south of Casablanca (الدَّار البَيْضاء). It was the capital of the Almohad dynasty (المُوَحِّدُون), which ruled over Muslim Spain (al-Andalus) and North Africa in the twelfth and thirteenth centuries. Afterwards, it continued to be one of the official residences of Moroccan rulers.

65. تُوزَر: town in southwest Tunisia. As an oasis, it once served as a transit point for caravans plying the Sahara. Today, Tozeur is perhaps best known as a popular tourist destination.

Zakariyyā Tāmir

Zakariyyā Tāmir (Zakariya Tamer) was born in 1931 in
Damascus, Syria. One of Syria's most famous writers, he is
particularly renowned for his short stories, many of which have
been translated into numerous languages. In addition, he is also
one of the Arab world's leading authors of children's stories.

Tāmir's stories often deal with injustice and opposition to
social and political oppression in society. He was forced to leave
school in his early teens to support his family, and continued
his education at night school. The hardships he experienced in
his early life no doubt provided inspiration for his literary work,
in which he gives a voice to Syria's poor and dispossessed.

He published his first collection of short stories, صَهيل الجِواد
الأبْيَض (*The Neighing of the White Steed*), in 1960, while working
as a blacksmith in a foundry in Damascus. The immediate
success of the book allowed him to embark on a new career
as a government official, while editing several periodicals like
al-Mawqif al-Adabī (*The Literary Stance*), *al-Maʿrifa* (*Knowledge*)
and the children's magazine *Usāma*.

Tāmir was one of the co-founders of the Syrian Writers'
Union in 1968, and its vice president for four years. After losing
his position at *al-Maʿrifa* following the publication of politically
controversial extracts from works of the famous nineteenth-
century reformer ʿAbd al-Raḥmān al-Kawākibī, Tāmir left his

homeland in 1981 and settled in London, where he edited a number of publications while writing articles for the newspaper *al-Quds al-Arabi* (1989–94).

Among his many collections of short stories, one may cite ربيع في الرَّماد (*Spring in the Ashes*, 1963); الرَّعْد(*The Thunder*, 1970); دمشق الحرائق (*Damascus Fire*, 1973); لماذا سَكَت النَّهْر (*Why the River Fell Silent*, 1973); قالت الوَرْدة للسنونو (*The Flower Spoke to the Bird*, 1978); النُّمُور في اليوم العاشر (*Tigers on the Tenth Day*, 1978; English trans. 1997); نِداء نوح (*Noah's Summons*, 1994); سَنَضْحَك (*We Shall Laugh*, 1998); and القُنْفُذ (*The Hedgehog*, 2005).

The following story is an example of how superstition sometimes serves as a tool to dominate and exploit women in traditional societies. Aziza is a beautiful, naive young woman who is concerned that her husband is on the verge of remarrying another woman. In desperation, she resorts to visiting a *sheikh* who pretends to know how to undo the magic spell Aziza is allegedly under. This is a tale of deceit and a loss of innocence.

امرأة وحيدة

A Lonely Woman

Aziza was a beautiful girl with a fear of black cats. She looked worried the moment she sat down in front of Sheikh Said. His eyes were jet-black and fiery. They closed in on Aziza, who was trying to ward off an ever-increasing panic, exacerbated by the smell of incense rising from a copper dish, which filled her nostrils and slowly numbed her body.

Sheikh Said said: "So, you want your husband to return to you?"

"I want him to return to me," Aziza replied, hesitantly.

Sheikh Said smiled as he added, mournfully: "His family wants him to get married again."

He threw bits of incense into the dish filled with live coal, and said: "Your husband will return to you, and he will not take another wife." His voice was sedate and soft, and soothed Aziza, who heaved a deep sigh of satisfaction. The Sheikh's face lit up. "However, my work doesn't come cheap," he said.

Aziza's face dropped. Staring at the gold bracelet on her wrist, she said: "I'll pay you what you want."

The Sheikh guffawed, and said: "You will lose a little, but you will regain your husband. Do you love him?"

Aziza angrily muttered under her breath: "No, I don't."

"Did you have a fight with him?"

"I quarrelled with his family."

"Do you feel that your chest is tight?"

"I sometimes feel as if I have a heavy weight on my chest."

"Do you have any disturbing dreams?"

"At night I always wake up from my sleep, frightened."

Sheikh Said shook his head several times and said: "Obviously, your in-laws have bewitched you."

Aziza was gripped with fear and shouted: "What can I do?"

عزيزة[1] صبية جميلة، تخاف القطط السوداء، ولقد كانت مضطربة لحظة قعدت قبالة الشيخ[2] سعيد، وكانت عيناه قطعتين من السواد المتوحش، تحاصران عزيزة التي كانت تحاول الافلات من هلع ينمو ويتزايد رويداً رويداً بينما رائحة البخور المتصاعدة من وعاء نحاسي تفعم أنفها وتخدر لحمها ببطء.

ويقول الشيخ سعيد: «اذن تريدين أن يرجع إليك زوجك؟».

أجابت عزيزة بتردّد: «أريد أن يرجع إليّ».

فابتسم الشيخ سعيد بينما أردفت قائلة باكتئاب: «أهله يريدون تزويجه مرة ثانية».

قال الشيخ سعيد وهو يرمي في وعاء الجمر نتفاً من البخور: «سيعود إليك زوجك، ولن يتزوج مرة ثانية».

وكان صوته وقوراً هادئاً منح عزيزة الطمأنينة، فندّت عنها آهة ارتياح طويلة، ابتهج لها وجه الشيخ وقال: «ولكنّ عملي يتطلب مالاً كثيراً». فاكتأب وجه عزيزة، وقالت وهي ترمق سواراً ذهبياً في معصمها: «سأدفع لك ما تريد».

ضحك الشيخ ضحكة قصيرة حادة ثم قال: «ستخسرين قليلاً ولكنك ستربحين زوجك. أتعينه ؟».

غمغمت عزيزة بسخط :«لا أحبه».

«ــ اختلفت معه ؟».

«ــ تشاجرتُ مع أهله».

«ــ هل تشعرين بضيق في صدرك ؟».

«ــ أشعر أحياناً كأنّ حجراً ثقيلاً على صدري».

«ــ أتشاهدين أحلاماً مزعجة أثناء نومك ؟».

«ــ أستيقظ دائماً في الليل وأنا مرعوبة».

فهزّ الشيخ سعيد رأسه عدة مرات وقال: «لا بدّ أن أهل زوجك قد سحروك».

ارتاعت عزيزة وهتفت: «ما العمل ؟!».

"To end their magic spell would require ten pounds' worth of incense."

Aziza was silent for a moment. She raised her hand to her chest, and took out ten pounds from her dress. She handed the money to Sheikh Said, and said: "That's all I have."

Sheikh Said got up and closed the black curtains in front of the two windows overlooking the narrow winding alley. Then he came back and sat in front of the copper dish in which the embers were glowing over smooth white ashes. He threw in some more incense, and said:

"My brothers, the *jinn*, hate the light and love darkness because their houses are underground."

Outside, the day was like a white-skinned woman. The sun's yellow rays burned down on the streets and fused with the murmur of the crowds. Sheikh Said's room, however, was dark and quiet.

"My brothers, the *jinn*, are kind. You'll be lucky if you gain their love. They love beautiful women. Remove your wrap."

Aziza took off her black wrap, revealing her full-shaped body, enveloped in a tight dress, to Sheikh Said. The Sheikh started to read from a book with yellow-stained pages in a low, mysterious voice. After a while, he said: "Come closer ... Lie down here."

Aziza lay down near the incense dish. Sheikh Said put his hand on her forehead while he continued reciting strange words. Suddenly, he said to Aziza: "Close your eyes. My brothers the *jinn* will arrive shortly."

Aziza closed her eyes and the Sheikh's voice rose, in a harsh commanding tone: "Forget everything."

The Sheikh's hand touched her smooth face. She remembered her father. The Sheikh's hand was rough, and had a strange smell. It was a big hand, no doubt with many wrinkles. His voice, too, was strange; it rose gradually in the quiet room with its dust-coloured walls.

The Sheikh's hand reached Aziza's neck. She remembered

«(– فسخ سحرهم يحتاج إلى بخور ثمنه عشر ليرات)».

فوجمت عزيزة لحظة ثم مدّت يدها إلى صدرها، وأخرجت منه عشر ليرات، وأعطتها للشيخ سعيد قائلة: «(هذا كلّ ما أملك)».

فنهض الشيخ سعيد، وأسدل ستائر قائمة على النافذتين المطلّتين على الزقاق الضيّق المتعرّج، ثم عاد إلى القعود أمام الوعاء النحاسي الذي تتقد فيه الجمرات فوق رماد أبيض ناعم، فأخذ يلقي البخور وهو يقول: «(إخوتي[3] الجان[4] يكرهون النور ويحبون العتمة لأن بيوتهم تحت الأرض)».

وكان النهار خارج الغرفة امرأة لحمها أبيض، والشمس يتوهج ضياؤها الأصفر في الطرقات ويمتزج بصخب الناس غير أن غرفة الشيخ سعيد كانت مظلمة ساكنة.

«(– إخوتي الجان لطاف. ستكونين محظوظة إذا نلت حبهم. إنهم يحبون النساء الجميلات. انزعي ملاءتك)».

وتخلت عزيزة عن ملاءتها[5] السوداء. فبدا لعيني الشيخ سعيد جسدها الناضج في ثوب ضيق، وابتدأ يقرأ في كتاب أصفر الأوراق بصوت خفيض غامض النبرة، ثم قال بعد حين: «(اقتربي. تمدّدي هنا)».

واضطجعت عزيزة بالقرب من وعاء البخور[6]. فوضع الشيخ سعيد يده على جبهتها وهو مستمر في تلاوة كلمات غريبة الرنين وبغتة قال لعزيزة: «(أغمضي عينيك. سيحضر إخوتي الجان)».

أطبقت عزيزة عينيها. وصعد صوت الشيخ خشناً آمراً: «(انسي كلّ شيء)».

يد الشيخ تلمس وجهها الناعم. تذكرت أباها. يد الشيخ خشنة، ورائحتها غريبة. يد كبيرة، ولابد من أنها كثيرة التجاعيد. وصوته غريب يعلو شيئاً فشيئاً في الغرفة الصامتة ذات الجدران الترابية.

وتبلغ يد الشيخ عنق عزيزة. تذكرت عزيزة يد زوجها. يده ناعمة طرية

her husband's hand; it was soft and tender, like a woman's. He worked as a clerk in a grocery shop owned by his father. He never once attempted to caress her neck with tenderness; instead, his clawing fingers would grope the flesh of her thighs.

The Sheikh placed both his hands on her. His hands gently ran across her full breasts, and then moved down along the rest of her body, only to return once more to her breasts. This time, however, they were less gentle and began to squeeze her breasts ferociously. Aziza moaned. With difficulty, she opened her eyes, gazing at the wisps of smoke spreading through the room.

Sheikh Said took his hands away from Aziza. He continued his reading, added some incense on the burning embers in the dish, and said: "My brothers the *jinn* are coming ... They're coming."

A sharp jolt spread through Aziza's body, and she closed her eyes. With a voice that seemed to come from the other side of the world, Sheikh Said intoned:

"My brothers, the *jinn*, love beautiful women. You're beautiful, and they'll love you. I want them to see you naked when they come. They'll take away all the magic spells."

Panic-stricken, Aziza whispered: "No ... no ..."

The *sheikh* replied sternly: "They will hurt you if they don't love you."

Aziza remembered a man she once saw in the street. He was screaming like a wounded animal before collapsing, white foam forming on his mouth, kicking with his hands and legs as if he was drowning.

"No ... no ... no."

"They're coming."

The smell of incense grew much stronger. Aziza started to breathe loudly. Sheikh Said shouted: "Come, blessed ones, come!"

Aziza heard faint, joyful laughs and words she could not understand. She sensed the presence in the room of a large

كيد المرأة. وهو يعمل كاتباً في دكان البقالة التي يملكها والده. و لم يحاول في أي مرة أن يداعب عنقها برقة إنما كان يعتصر بأصابع شرهة لحم فخذيها. الشيخ يلمسها بكلتا يديه. يداه على صدرها تربتان على نهديها الناضجين برفق وتنحدران إلى بقية الجسد ثم تعودان إلى النهدين وقد فقدتا رفقهما فضغطتا عليهما بضراوة، فتأوهت عزيزة، وفتحت عينيها بصعوبة لتشاهد دخاناً خفيفاً منتشراً عبر فراغ الغرفة.

وأبعد الشيخ سعيد يديه عن عزيزة، ومضى يقرأ ويرمي البخور فوق الجمر المتقد في الوعاء النحاسي ثم قال: «سيأتي إخوتي الجان. سيأتون».

فسرت في جسد عزيزة قشعريرة حادة، وأغمضت عينيها، وسمعت الشيخ سعيد يقول بصوت تناهى إليها كأنه آت من آخر العالم: «اخوتي الجان يحبون النساء الجميلات. أنت جميلة وسيحبونك. أريد أن يروك عارية عندما يقبلون، وسيبعدون عنك كلّ سحر».

همست عزيزة بذعر «لا لا».

فجاءها تواً صوت الشيخ كصدى صارم: «سيؤذونك إذا لم يحبوك».

وتذكرت عزيزة رجلاً أبصرته مرة في الشارع، وكان يصرخ كحيوان جريح ثم ارتمى على الارض والزبد الأبيض على فمه وأخذ يحرك ذراعيه وساقيه كغريق.

«— لا. لا. لا».

«— سيأتون».

وازدادت رائحة البخور وتكاثفت، وراحت عزيزة تتنفس بصوت مسموع. وهتف الشيخ سعيد فجأة: «تعالوا تعالوا يا مباركين تعالوا»

وسمعت عزيزة ضحكات خافتة مرحة وكلمات غير مفهومة، وأحسّت أن الغرفة اكتظّت بمخلوقات قزمة[7] كثيرة العدد لم تتمكن من فتح عينيها

number of dwarf-like creatures. She could not open her eyes in spite of repeated attempts to do so. She felt the creatures' hot breath on her face. One of them grabbed hold of her lower lip, and greedily squeezed it.

The carpet felt rough under her naked back. The incense fumes gathered and turned into a man who held her in his arms and anaesthetized her with his kisses. A wild fire erupted in her blood as the mouth left her lips and moved to the rest of her body. Aziza was panting, too afraid to move. Then her fear subsided, and she slowly began to experience a novel sense of ecstasy.

She smiled as she looked at white stars, a dark-blue sky, yellow plains and a fiery red sun. She heard the murmur of a river in the distance. However, the river would not remain remote. She laughed with joy. Sadness was a child that was running away from her. Now she was an adolescent. The neighbours' son kissed and embraced her. No ... No ... This was shameful. Like when the baker's assistant gave her some bread while she was standing at the door of her house; then, suddenly, his hand shot out and pinched the nipple of her small breast. She was hurt, angry and confused. Where is his hand? Ah, here it is. His hand once again touched her body. *On her wedding night she had screamed in pain, but now she does not scream. She saw her mother holding up a handkerchief, soaked with blood, while her relatives looked on, curiously. Her mother was shouting, her face beaming with joy: "My girl is the most honourable! Let our enemies die of envy!"*

Aziza returned to the dry, yellow fields. The clouds were high in the sky. The heat of the sun was close to her. She twisted and turned, flushed, her body burned by a fierce heat. The sun was a fire closing in on her, sneaking into her blood. Aziza resisted peaking. At that moment, the rain poured down, and her entire body shuddered.

After a short while, Sheikh Said moved away from Aziza's naked body and headed towards the window. He drew back the curtains. Daylight flooded the room, setting Aziza's white flesh aglow.

على الرغم من محاولاتها المتكررة، ولفحت وجهها أنفاس حارة، وأطبق فم واحد على شفتها السفلى واعتصرها بنهم.

وكانت السجادة خشنة تحت ظهرها العاري، وكان البخور يتجمع ويتحول إلى رجل يحتضنها بين ساعديه ويخدّرها بقبلاته. وشبت نار جائعة في دمها بينما كان الفم يترك شفتها وينتقل إلى بقية الجسد. عزيزة تلهث ولا تتحرك. خوفها يضمحل. وتتذوق على مهل نشوة ذات طعم جديد.

أوه تبتسم. تضحك. أبصرت نجوماً بيضاء وسماء زرقاء قائمة وسهولاً صفراء وشمساً من نار حمراء. وتسمع عزيزة خرير نهر بعيد. النهر. إنه ناء. لن يظل نائياً. تضحك.مرح. الحزن طفل يركض مبتعداً عنها. إنها الان طفلة كبيرة. قبلها ابن الجيران وعانقها. لا لا. هذا عيب. وعندما كان أجير الخباز يناولها أرغفة الخبزوهي واقفة على باب البيت، مديده وقرص حلمة نهدها الصغير تألمت. غضبت. ارتبكت. أين يده؟ها هي يده تمتلك جسدها ثانية. وفي ليلة العرس أطلقت صرخة، والآن لا تصرخ. أبصرت أمها تمسك منديلاً مبتلاً بالدم⁸ يتفرج عليه أقاربها بفضول، وتصيح أمها ووجهها يبوح بفرح طاغ: «بنتي من أشرف البنات. ليمت الأعداء غيظاً».

وتعود عزيزة إلى حقول صفراء. حقول بلا ماء. الغيوم في الأعالي. الشمس نار تدنو من عزيزة. تتلوى عزيزة وتتهالك منتشية تحرقها حرارة قاسية. الشمس نار تقترب وتتسلل إلى الدم ولا تحاول الذروة، وعندئذ هطل المطر، وارتعد جسدها كله.

وابتعد الشيخ سعيد بعد قليل عن جسد عزيزة العاري، واتجه نحو النافذتين وأزاح عنهما الستائر، فتدفقت في الحال شمس النهار إلى الغرفة، وتألق لحم عزيزة الأبيض مغموراً بالضوء الساطع.

Aziza fidgeted, and opened her eyes slowly and carefully, surprised at the brightness of the sunlight. She got up, dismayed. Sheikh Said said: "Don't worry. My brothers, the *jinn*, have left."

Aziza bent down, weary and ashamed. She picked up a piece of her clothing. She wished she could have lain there for a long time, motionless, eyes closed.

Sheikh Said wiped his mouth with the back of his hand, and said to her: "Don't be afraid ... They've left."

Tears ran down her cheeks. At that moment, she heard the cry of a hawker in the alley. It sounded to her like the weeping of a desperate man who would not die. A few minutes later, Aziza was walking alone in the narrow twisting alley. She raised her head expectantly, but there was no passing bird. The sky was blue and empty.

وتململت عزيزة، وفتحت عينيها بتؤدة وحذر، ففوجئت بضياء الشمس، ونهضت مذعورة، فقال لها الشيخ سعيد: «لا تخافي، إخوتي الجان رحلوا».

وانحنت عزيزة بإعياء، وكانت متعبة، وخجلة، والتقطت أول قطعة من ثيابها، وتمنت لو ظلت أمداً طويلاً مستلقية دون حراك مغمضة العينين.

ومسح الشيخ سعيد فمه بظهر يده، وقال لها ثانية «لا تخافي. رحلوا».

فترقرقت الدموع في عينيها بينما تعالى في تلك اللحظة في الزقاق صياح بائع متجول، وتناهى إلى سمعها بكاء رجل يائس لن يموت.

وبعد دقائق كانت عزيزة تمشي وحيدة في الزقاق الضيق الطويل المتعرّج. وحين رفعت وجهها إلى أعلى متطلعة بلهفة، لم تعثر على أي طائر عابر إنما كانت السماء زرقاء خاوية.

Language Notes

1. عَزِيزَة: this is an old-fashioned, traditional name that derives from the male name عَزِيز, which is also an adjective meaning "precious" or "dear". It is worth pointing out that many Arabic and Muslim names have adjectival meanings and most of them are used for both sexes, e.g. سَعِيد(ة) ("happy"), سَلِيم(ة) ("sound"), جَمِيل(ة) ("beautiful"), رَشِيد(ة) ("rightly guided").

2. شَيْخ: (pl. شُيُوخ), variously transcribed in English as *Shaikh, Sheik, Shaykh* or *Sheikh*, the word initially meant "old man" (this meaning is also used in the Qur'ān). Later on, the term became a title referring to a leader, noble or elder. It is also a term of address for an Islamic religious or legal scholar, while it is often extended to those purporting to have this expertise, as is the case in this story. Sheikh Sa'īd in this story is not a genuine Islamic scholar, but someone who pretends to have the power and knowledge to undo magic spells.

3. إِخْوَة: this is one of the plurals of أَخ ("brother"), the other one being إِخْوَان. Note, however, that there is a difference in meaning; the latter plural is used in the sense of 'brethren', as in, for instance, الإِخْوَان المُسْلِمُون, "The Muslim Brotherhood".

4. جِنّ: (*coll.* cf. جَانّ;sg. جِنِّي) "Genie" (*djinn, jinn*) refers to ghosts or spirits created out of fire (cf. Qur. 15:26–7), which are frequently mentioned in the Qur'ān (*sūra* 72 is almost entirely devoted to them) as well as in many folk tales (not least of which in *The Thousand and One Nights*). Often said to be endowed with magical powers, the *jinn* of folklore can take on many shapes, while many people believe they are much like humans, capable of being good and bad. The *jinn* are part of popular beliefs mainly in North Africa

and Egypt. The same root has also given us مَجْنُون, "mad" or "madman" (i. e. one possessed by a *jinn*).

5. مَلايَة: this is a large cloak or shawl often made of wool, wrapped around the top half of the body with one end tucked in under the arm and enveloping the body.

6. بَخُور: in some Arab countries incense is used to keep the evil eye away from the sick. In the United Arab Emirates, for instance, guests are usually provided with coffee and the smell of incense as soon as they arrive. In recent years there has been an increase in the varieties of incense aroma. They come in the shape of sticks or powder, or the raw ingredient is grated.

7. مَخْلُوقاتٍ قَزْمَة : small ghostly creatures (here referring to *jinn*); قَزْم (pl. أَقْزام): lit. "dwarf".

8. مِنْديلاً مُبْتَلاً بالدَّم: this is a reference to an old tradition, which is still alive in some areas (especially in the countryside). After the consummation of the marriage on the wedding night, a white sheet or cloth with the bride's blood on it is paraded as a sign that she was a virgin, and thus an honourable girl from an honourable family.

Muḥammad al-Zafzāf

Born in 1942 in Sūq al-Arbaʿa al-Gharb (Souk Larbaa El Gharb), near Qunaitra in Morocco, Muḥammad al-Zafzāf studied philosophy at the University of Ribat (Mohammed V) before becoming a secondary-school teacher in Casablanca, which would remain his home until his death in 2001 after a long-suffering illness.

Considered the master of the Moroccan short story, al-Zafzāf is held in the greatest esteem all over the Arab world. He produced an impressive body of work, including many novels as well as plays and criticism. His short story collections include حِوار في لَيْل مُتَأَخِّر (*Late-night Dialogue*, Beirut, 1970), بُيُوت واطئة (*Low Houses*, Casablanca, 1977), الأَقْوَى (*The Strongest*, Damascus, 1978), غَجَر في الغابة (*Gypsy in the Forest*, 1982), الشَّجَرة المُقَدَّسة (*The Sacred Tree*, 1980) and مَلك الجِنّ (*King of the Jinn*, 1984; Spanish trans., 2002). Interestingly, in the West al-Zafzāf is mainly known as a novelist thanks to translations into French and Spanish of some of his novels, such as المَرْأة والوَرْدة (*The Woman and the Rose*, Spanish trans., 1997), بَيْضة الدِّيك (*The Cock's Egg*) and الثَّعْلَب الّذي يَظْهَرُ ويَخْتَفِي (*The Fox Who Appears and Disappears*, French trans., 2004). The French translation of بيضة الديك, *L'oeuf du Coq*, received the prestigious Grand Atlas Prize in 1998.

Like others in his generation (such as Muḥammad Shukrī),

al-Zafzāf gave a voice to ordinary Moroccans, especially
those living on the margins of society. His is a literature of
social realism, arguing the cause of those who cannot express
themselves, often doing so in the local vernacular. The story
presented here, *The Sacred Tree* (taken from the homonymous
collection), provides a good example of both the type of
prose and subject matter tackled by al-Zafzāf. The language
is Standard Arabic, yet clearly Moroccan (or North African)
in the way it is used, with a number of peculiarly Moroccan
usages. This fits in well with the subject, which, despite certain
universal features, is quintessentially Morrocan and reveals a
great many things about that country's contemporary society.
At the same time, al-Zafzāf is not a "political" author, as such;
this is no pamphlet or treatise dressed up as a work of fiction.
Rather, it is fiction with a social conscience, drawn from real-
life events; the realism is palpable and the narrative enthralling,
with tragedy often commingled with comedy.

The Sacred Tree

Some youngsters who had enjoyed some education simply smiled with derision and contempt. What did it matter to them if they cut down a tree in an abandoned place? What did it matter to them, even if it was a towering tree in a garden heavy with delicious fruit that fell because it was ripe or rotten, or remained hanging from the branches?

They were stretching themselves, craning their necks, the better to look at the crowd milling around. They did not pay any attention to the work that was going on in the middle of this clearing where there was nothing but a tree. Behind it, there were panels of reinforced concrete that were being carefully and slowly erected. Behind the high-rise panels, there were darkly coloured buildings in which the window frames had not yet been installed, the giant gaps redolent of the gaping maws of mythical animals. A cordon of auxiliary security forces formed a tight circle, preventing anybody from approaching the clearing where the tree stood on a brown sandy hillock.

A crowd gathered behind the hedge made up of the auxiliary troops, who responded violently, flailing their batons at shoulders and knees. One could hear the laments – perhaps it was a child being trampled underfoot, desperately clinging to its mother, barefoot and covered in rags. Behind, some youngsters with a modicum of education continued to crane their necks. One of them said to his neighbour:

"That's what the state does best."

"What's it to you what the state does? What do you care if they cut a tree? The day after tomorrow they'll build a modern building, and that won't have anything to do with you either! The money for the rent won't go into your pocket!"

"Fair enough, but this magical nonsense should be rooted out. They continue to worship this tree."

الشجرة المقدّسة

بعض الشبان الذين تعلّموا قليلاً اكتفوا بالابتسام علامة السخرية فقط والاستهزاء. ماذا يهمهم في شيء، قطع شجرة في مكان خال؟ ماذا يهمهم حتى ولو كانت سامقة في بستان، وقد تدلت منها ثمار شهية، تتساقط بفعل نضجها أو فسادها، أو تظل معلّقة على الفروع والأغصان[1]؟ وقف بعضهم يطلون مشرئبّين ينظرون إلى الناس المتزاحمين، لا إلى العملية التي تتمّ وسط تلك البقعة، الخالية إلا من شجرة.

وراء الشجرة، هناك ألواح من الإسمنت المسلح تركّب ببطء وإتقان. امتدت، خلف تلك الألواح، التي ترتفع في السماء، عمارات أخرى داكنة، لم تركب بعد رتاجات نوافذها، فبدت مفتوحة كأفواه حيوانات خرافية.

كان هناك سياج من رجال القوات الاحتياطية، يشكل دائرة متينة متماسكة، يمنع الناس من الاقتراب من الوسعة، حيث تشمخ الشجرة، فوق مرتفع أرضي بُنّي اللون.

الناس يتزاحمون خلف سياج رجال القوات الاحتياطية، الذين كانوا يردون بعنف، بضربات على الأكتاف أو عند الركب، فتسمع أنات، وقد يسمع زعيق طفل، تحت الأرجل، تشبث بأمه الحافية الممزّقة الثياب.

أعناق بعض الشبان المتعلمين، في الخلف، ما تزال تشرئبّ. قال أحدهم للذي بجانبه:

ـ هذا أحسن ما فعلت الدولة.

ـ ماذا يهمّك، أنت، ممّا تفعله الدولة؟ قطع شجرة لا يهمنا في شيء. بعد غد سوف تبنى، في مكانها، عمارة جديدة، لن تهمنا أيضاً في شيء، ولن تضع ثمن كرائها[2] في جيبك.

ـ على كل، يجب القضاء على مثل تلك الخرافات. لقد ظلوا يقدسون تلك الشجرة.

"They'll worship it even more once it's been cut down!"

"Quite the contrary, they'll forget all about it."

The crowd around the clearing continued to grow, with plenty of jostling forwards and backwards. Some rifles and thick-ended batons were raised into the air and then swooped down hard on arms and bodies. A woman pulled back her snotty-nosed child and said to another woman, who completely ignored her:

"What's that tree got to do with us? This government wants the curse of Sidi Daud to descend upon it. Believe you me, not one of them will be able to sleep tonight without something bad happening to them."

"What does the government care?" said the second woman, without even turning around.

"It's the poor devils that are cutting the tree that'll be hit by the curse. The *makhzen* keeps well clear of it. They're always making people dig their own graves, while they make sure they're out of harm's way."

The woman realized that it was dangerous to talk like that, and she started to tremble with fear, anxiously looking around. She was scared that one of the *makhzen* agents might be behind her and would take her down to the police station, where she would be flogged and hung like a sheep from a butcher's hook in one of the cells. She thought about the three children she had to feed after her husband had passed away.

She continued talking to the woman next to her: "The government know what they're doing. They wouldn't cut the tree if there wasn't a good reason."

The other woman asked: "So, you're not afraid of the curse of Sidi Daud? Shut your mouth or he'll come to *you* when you're asleep tonight!"

"And what am I supposed to have done to Sidi Daud? I'm just a poor widow, trying to make ends meet and care for my children as best I can!"

The woman left the crowd. She didn't want any problems,

– سوف يقدّسونها أكثر عندما تقطع.

– بل سوف ينسونها.

كثر الازدحام حول الوسعة، وكثر التدافع إلى الأمام وإلى الخلف. بعض
البنادق وبعض العصي الغليظة الرؤوس كانت ترتفع في السماء، وتهوي
على بعض الأذرع أو الأجسام. جرّت امرأة طفلها الصغير، ذا الخطم[3]
الملطّخ بالمخاط، وهي تقول لامرأة لم تهتم بها:

– ما لنا ومال الشجرة[4]؟ هذه حكومة تريد أن ينزل بها بلاء «سيدي[5]
داوود». والله، لن يستطيع أحد منهم أن يغمض عينيه الليلة حتى تحصل له
مصيبة.

وقالت المرأة الثانية دون أن تلتفت إليها:

– الحكومة مالها؟ أولئك الرجال المساكين، الذين يقطعون الشجرة، هم
الذين ستصيبهم اللعنة. المخزن[6] بعيد كلّ البعد عن ذلك. إنّهم يدفعون الناس
إلى حتفهم دائماً، ويبقون في الخلف.

أدركت المرأة أنها تقول كلاماً خطيراً. ارتعدت من الخوف، التفتت
حولها. خافت أن يكون، أحد المخزنيين[7] خلفها، فيأخذها إلى المقاطعة[8]،
حيث تُجلد وتعلق مثل شاة في أحد الأقبية. فكرت أن عليها أن تعول
أطفالها الثلاثة، الذين تركهم لها الزوج وانتقل إلى حيث سيذهبون جميعاً.
وعادت تقول للتي بجوارها:

– الحكومة تعرف ما تفعل، لو لم تجد مصلحة في قطع تلك الشجرة لما
فعلت ذلك.

قالت المرأة الأخرى:

– ألا تخافين من لعنة سيدي داوود؟ أغلقي فمك، وإلا، وقف عليك
هذه الليلة في المنام.

– وماذا فعلت لسيدي داوود؟ إنني مجرد أرملة فقيرة، أعول ثلاثة أولاد
بكل الوسائل.

انسحبت المرأة من الزحام. لا تريد مشاكل مع المقاطعة، ولا مع سيدي

either with the police or with Sidi Daud. What's more, she did not even know Sidi Daud. She had never seen him, and his grave was not in the clearing. People said he had planted the tree where his soul had migrated. It was also said that nobody had planted this tree, but that it had just appeared one day in the clearing, as though it had been there for years. She had only appealed for his help once, when her husband had been on his deathbed for more than two years. However, a few days after visiting the tree, Sidi Larbi – or Sidi Daud – had taken her husband's soul.

The sun seared the bodies in the crowd, while the people had become unrecognizable because of the dust and debris flying around. All that could be seen were the drops of sweat glistening on their noses. The noise of the bulldozer in the clearing continued unabated. A few of the workmen were whiling away the time by playing with the ropes attached to the tree trunk. Behind them, the rifles were still trained on the crowd. A government order must be enforced to the letter. Then, the trunk and branches could be heard to crack, and the tree fell to the ground. Some of the workmen let go of the ropes and ran off. Behind them, the policemen also beat a hasty retreat. None of them felt like having their eyes poked out by a falling branch. The security cordon began to disintegrate, and once again rifle butts and batons were raised. Crooked arms were flailing about in empty space. Voices of protest rose, both muffled and loud. One of the onlookers said:

"Tomorrow or the day after, a building will be constructed on the resting place of Sidi Daud's soul."

"I'm afraid that these people will call it 'Sidi Daud's Building', and that they'll hang candles and amulets along its walls."

"Anything is possible."

The jostling around the clearing increased. People had left their small, pokey shops, rushing to see what was going on. Others preferred to observe the scene from a distance. Two cars drew to a halt in front of the crowd. The police chief got out

داوود. حتى سيدي داوود، لا تعرفه ولم تره قط في حياتها. لايوجد له قبر في الوسعة. قالوا هو الذي زرع الشجرة وتقمّصت[9] روحه.

قالوا أيضاً، لم يزرعها أحد. لكنّ الناس فوجئوا، ذات صباح، بتلك الشجرة في الوسعة، وكأنها بنت سنوات. هي لم تتبرك[10] بها إلا مرة واحدة؛ عندما ظل زوجها في فراش الموت أكثر من عامين. لكن، بعد الزيارة بأيام، أخذ سيدي لاربي أو سيدي داوود روح زوجها.

تلفح الشمس بشدة أجسام المتزاحمين، التي لا تعرف من جراء الأوساخ، فلم تلتمع سوى حبات من العرق على أنوفهم. هدير الجرافة في الوسعة ما يزال مستمراً... بعض العمّال تسللوا بالحبال المربوطة على جذع الشجرة. وراء ظهورهم كانت البنادق مُشرعة. يجب تنفيذ أمر الحكومة، بدون توانٍ أو تخاذل. بعدها سمعت طقطقة الجذع والفروع، فخرت الشجرة علىَ الأرض. ترك بعض العمال الحبال وركضوا إلى الخلف. الحرس من خلفهم أيضاً تراجعوا. لم يكن واحد منهم يوماً يتمنى أن يفقأ عينه غصن شجرة.

اختل نظام الدائرة فارتفعت أعقاب البنادق ورؤوس العصي في السماء من جديد. التوَت الأذرُع وتخبّطت في الفراغ. وسمعتُ أصوات الاحتجاج مكتومة وعلنية[11].

وقال أحدهم:

— غداً أو بعد غد سوف ترتفع عمارة فوق روح سيدي داوود.

— أخشى أن يسميها هؤلاء عمارة سيدي داوود ويعلقوا عليها الشموع والتمائم[12].

— كلّ شيء ممكن!

ازداد الازدحام حول الوسعة. بعض الناس ركضوا من حوانيتهم الضيقة ليروا ما يحدث. البعض الآخر فضّل أن يراقب الأمر من بعيد. توقفت سيارتان قرب المزدحمين. نزل قائد المقاطعة من إحداهما، وسبقه بعض

of one of them, preceded by a few of his men, who set about clearing a path for him. At first, the people were shocked to see him. Some began to curse him under their breath, while the policemen lashed out in every direction.

The party was surrounded by a cloud of dust. Only the police chief knew how important it was to appear cool and indifferent. The slightest movement could trigger no end of unrest and chaos, especially in matters as sensitive as this one. Dust flew up. Then, there were cries, and the fleeting movement of batons and rifle butts. All this was necessary at such a time. The greatest ruler in the world only has to do one thing – to keep his nerves under control. The greatest head of government, minister, police chief, or whatever, all of them have to make sure of only one thing, namely to keep themselves under control.

However, those who receive orders do not control themselves. Sometimes they, of their own accord, think they are enforcing an order that has come down to them. Any head of state is capable of receiving a slap in the face and still continue smiling in front of television cameras. People will admire him precisely because he did not react the way they would have done – indeed as they do for the slightest thing. However, when the camera lights are not trained on him, that very same leader can just as easily give the order to destroy tens of cities. Afterwards, he will hold grand speeches, cloaking himself in the innocence of one who respects his fellow man.

Arms and voices rose, rifle butts pierced the sky, sometimes hitting a baton or a skull. There were screams, faces oozing with blood, bodies collapsing to the ground. The police chief never made the slightest movement; he tried to prepare himself for when he would become a minister, standing in front of a television camera. (*Stand firm! The hour of vengeance is near, and you will be able to destroy tens of cities.*)

Some of the rifle butts inadvertently brushed against him because of the thickness of the crowd, those people who

الحرس، يوسعون له الطريق. أصيب الناس أول الأمر بذهول عندما رأوه. أخذ بعضهم يشتمه بصوت منخفض. الحرس يضربون في كلّ اتجاه.

تطاير الغبار حول الموكب الصغير من كلّ الجهات. القائد وحده كان يعرف معنى أن يتظاهر الإنسان بالثبات واللامبالاة. أدنى حركة تثير شغباً وفوضى لا حل لهما، خصوصاً في أمور ذات حساسية مثل هذه. الغبار يتطاير، والصراخ والعصي وأعقاب البنادق تتطاير، كلّ ذلك شيء ضروري في لحظة مثل هذه. ما على أكبر رئيس دولة في العالم إلاّ أن يتمالك أعصابه. ما على أكبر رئيس حكومة، أكبر وزير، أكبر وال، أكبر عمدة، أكبر قائد مقاطعة، أكبر فلان إلاّ أن يتمالك نفسه. لكنّ الذين يتلقون الأوامر لا يتمالكون أنفسهم. يعتقدون أحياناً أن أي تصرف فردي، يأتي منهم، هو تلبية لأمر سام. إن أيّ رئيس دولة في العالم يمكنه أن يتقبل صفعة ويبتسم أمام كاميرا[13] التلفزيون. سوف يقدره الناس لأنّه لم ينفعل مثلهم لأتفه[14] شيء. لكنه في الخفاء، يستطيع أن يعطي الأوامر لتهديم عشرات المدن. لأن كاميرا التلفزيون ليست موجّهة إليه في تلك اللحظة. بعد ذلك سوف يخطب في الناس مظهراً براءة الإنسان تجاه أخيه الإنسان!

الأذرع الآن ترتفع، والأصوات ترتفع، وأعقاب البنادق تتراشق[15] في السماء، تصطدم برؤوس العصي أحياناً، وبرؤوس البشر أحياناً أخرى. تصرخ الأفواه وتنزّ الوجوه دماً، وتسقط الأجسام أرضاً. لكنّ القائد دائماً لا يتحرك. إنه يحاول أن يعود نفسه على أن يصبح وزيراً، أمام كاميرا التلفزيون. (أثبت. سوف تأتي لحظة الانتقام، في حينها، عندما تستطيع أن تهدم عشرات المدن).

أعقاب بعض البنادق تناوشه، عن غير قصد، بفعل زحام الجماهير، التي

worshipped this tree. Yet, he did not flinch. He retained his stern smile, despite the dust that covered his face and a large part of the crowd. However, one of those receiving orders had lost his self-control. Thrown from God knows where, a large stone landed on the police chief's head, fracturing his skull. He sank into the dust, his smile still fixed on his lips, covered in a pool of blood and soil. The troops opened fire. Stones were flying through the air, heavy with dust. Shots rang out, though no one knew where they were coming from. Bodies fell; others fled, scattering in every direction, pushing and shoving one another. A cloud of dust rose up. It was a fully-fledged battle, total chaos.

Feelings of anger, fear, hatred, courage and cowardice enveloped the tree that lay lifeless on the ground. Bullets were flying everywhere, ripping everything in their path. Everything became blurred: the laments, the weeping and dying screams. The police chief's lips still had a smile on them, despite the blood and soil, as though tens of cameras were crowded around him in order to get a shot of him.

The people began to disperse. The narrow streets became empty as the doors and windows dotted along the haphazardly built walls were shut. Eyes appeared through the chinks and crannies in the walls, windows and doors. However, these eyes did not see anything except the troops, spread out across the clearing or posted at the entrance of the maze of squalid alleyways in which the sewage and garbage had amassed.

Some shopkeepers, greengrocers, spice merchants and other small traders left their goods in order to take shelter wherever they could. A few old women who sold henna, herbs, locally produced soap and various magic paraphernalia such as rats' tails, and crows' heads, scattered in every direction, abandoning their wares on the pavement. The policemen approached their chief, who signalled to them to take him to one of the cars. One of the policemen was struck by the chief's extraordinary strength of character when he saw him lying there, still smiling as though nothing had happened.

تقدّس الشجرة. لكنّه لا ينفعل. ابتسامته صارمة وجادة، رغم الغبار الذي يحجب وجهه عن كثير من المتزاحمين. غير أن أحد الذين يتلقّون الأوامر لم يتمالك نفسه.

من مكان ما هوت قطعة حجر كبيرة على رأس قائد المقاطعة فشجّت رأسه. سقط على التراب، وظلت الابتسامة أبداً مرسومة على شفتيه اللتين ظلتا تسبحان في بركة من الدم والتراب. أطلق الحرس الرصاص. تطايرت أحجار في الفضاء المغبر، فتلتها رصاصات لم يكن أحد يدري من أي مكان كانت تنطلق. أخذت الأجساد تسقط، تهرب وتشتتّت، وتتفرق وتصطدم بعضها. ارتفع الغبار. معركة حقيقية فعلاً. لم يعد هنا نظام لأي شيء. عواطف من الغضب والخوف والحقد والشجاعة والجبن، كلها تحوم حول شجرة مقطوعة. الرصاص ينطلق من كلّ مكان ويخترق كلّ مكان. اختلط كلّ شيء. العويل والبكاء وأنين الاحتضار الأخير. ابتسامة قائد المقاطعة كانت ما تزال مرسومة على شفتيه، رغم الدم والتراب، كأنّ عشرات الكاميرات تتزاحم حوله، لتلتقط له صوراً.

تفرّق الناس خلت الشوارع الضيقة، وأغلقت النوافذ والأبواب، المركبة تركيباً عشوائياً على جدران، بنيت كيفما اتفق. كانت بعض العيون تطل من ثقوب أو شقوق في الحيطان والنوافذ والأبواب لكنّ تلك العيون لم تكن ترى سوى حرس غير منتظمين، في الوسعة وفي رؤوس الأزقة القذرة المتفرعة، التي تجمعت فيها القاذورات والأوساخ.

أصحاب بعض الحوانيت، من خضّارين وعطّارين وأشباه بقالين، تركوا سلعهم واختفوا في أماكن ما. بعض العجائز اللواتي يبعن الحنّاء والعطر والصابون البلدي ولوازم السحر، كذيول الفئران ورؤوس الغربان، تفرقن وتركن سلعهُن على الطوار. اقترب بعض الحرس من القائد. أشار إليهم بيده فحملوه بسرعة إلى إحدى السيارات. تعجب أحد الحراس من شدة صبره عندما رآه ما يزال يبتسم، كأن شيئاً لم يقع.

Language Notes

1. أَغْصان: غُصْن .sg = فَرْع (.pl فُرُوع).

2. كِرَاء: MCA "rent (money)" (.pl أَكْرِية), < أَكْرَى, "to rent out" (اكْتَرَى, "to rent", "hire"). In MSA, the usual term is إيجار (أَجَرَ <> اسْتَأْجَرَ, "to rent", "hire").

3. خَطْم: lit. "muzzle", "snout".

4. ما لَنا ومال الشَّجَرة: dialectal phrasing common in a large number of dialects (e. g. Egyptian and Iraqi as well as Moroccan). It is important to note that مال here does not refer to "money" or "wealth"; rather, it is a particle used to denote possession. MSA: ما لَنا وللشَّجرة.

5. سيدي: strictly speaking سَيِّدي ("Mister", "Sir"), the form here is pronounced *sīdī* and is used in North Africa for people enjoying a high social or religious status. It is also the usual epithet for saints, as is the case here: سيدي داوود. It is sometimes abbreviated to سي: e.g. سي مُحَمَّد.

6. مَخْزَن: lit. meaning "storehouse" (< خَزَنَ, u, "to store"), the word is used here in the peculiarly Moroccan sense of "the authorities" (formerly only the Treasury, i.e. "the place where the money is stored").

7. مَخْزَنِيّ: "a *makhzan* man" (see above مخزن), i.e. "government official".

8. المَقاطعة: MCA "district office". In MSA this word denotes "district".

9. تَقَمَّصَ (الرُّوح): "to transmigrate (the spirit)"; cf. تَقَمُّص, "metempsychosis". Note that تَقَمَّصَ شَخْصية فلان means "to pretend to be someone else", "to take over someone else's personality".

10. تَبَرَّكَ ب: "to seek a blessing (بَرَكة) from a saint.

11. عَلَنِيَّة: = عَلَناً, سِرّاً, سِرّيّاً <> في العَلَنِ ('secretly').

12. تَمائِمُ sg. تَميمة.

13. كاميرا: this borrowing is increasingly used, at the detriment

. مُصَوَّرة or آلة التَّصْوير of the homegrown coinings

14. أَتْفَه: superlative of تافه ("insignificant").

15. نَتَراشَقَ: MCA; MSA تُرْشَقَ ("are thrown").

Ibrāhīm al-Faqīh

Aḥmad Ibrāhīm al-Faqīh was born in 1932 into a middle-class family in Mizda, a small village in the famous macadam hills of الحمادة الحمْراء (Hamada Hamra), about 100 miles south of the Libyan capital Tripoli. After completing his secondary education in Libya, he went to Egypt in 1962 to study journalism. When he returned to Libya, al-Faqīh worked briefly as a journalist before moving to London to study theatre. Resettling in Libya in 1972, he became head of the country's National Institute for Music and Drama. In the 1980s, during his stay in Britain as a diplomat attached to the Libyan embassy, he completed a PhD at the University of Edinburgh.

Together with Ibrāhīm al-Kūnī – a fellow member of the so-called "Sixties Generation" – al-Faqīh is undoubtedly one of the most famous and influential Libyan authors of the present day. He has published the following collections of short stories: البَحْر لا ماء فيه ارْبَطوا أحزمة المقاعد (The Empty Sea, 1966); (Fasten Your Seatbelts, 1968); اخْتَفَت النّجُوم فأيْنَ أنْت (The Stars Disappeared, and Where Were You?, 1985); امْرأة من ضَوء (The Lady of Light, 1985); خمس خنافس تحكم الشَّجَرة (Five Beetles Are Ruling the Tree, 1998); and مَرايا فينيسيا (Reflections of Venice). In addition, al-Faqīh has also been prolific as a journalist and critic, playwright and novelist. Several of his works have been translated into English, including غَزالات حُقُول من الرَّماد (Gazelles, and Other Plays, 1999);

(*Valley of Ashes*, novel, 1995); تشارلز وديانا)(*Çharles, Diana and Me, and Other Stories*, 1999); and مَنْ يَخَافُ أَجَثَا كريستي (*Who's Afraid of Agatha Christie?*, novel, 1999). Al-Faqīh also edited a volume of translated short stories written by Libyan authors that had originally appeared in the London-based magazine *Azure* under the title *Libyan Short Stories* (1999).

Probably his most ambitious project to date is the prize-winning trilogy (translated as *Gardens of the Nights*, 1995), consisting of سأهبك مَدينة أُخْرَى (*I Shall Offer Another City*); هذه تُخوم مَمْلَكتي نَفق (*These Are the Borders of My Kingdom*); and تُضيئه امرأة واحدة (*A Tunnel Lit by a Woman*). Like the Egyptian Yaḥyā Ḥaqqī's قِنْديل أمّ هاشم (*The Lamp of Umm Hashim*, 1944) or the Sudanese al-Ṭayyib Ṣāliḥ's مَوْسِم الهِجْرة إلى الشمال (*Season of Migration to the North*, 1969), al-Faqīh's trilogy highlights the alienation of Western-educated Arab – in this case, Libyan – intellectuals, on the cusp between the Western temptations to which they at some point give in and the realization that salvation can only come from within.

The present story, extracted from اختفت النجوم فأين أنت؟, is to some extent also preoccupied with alienation, albeit not in the traditional sense inasmuch as it depicts the protagonist's inability to deal with changes in tradition for reasons rooted within himself rather than being based on experiences outside his native society. The result, however, is no less dramatic and tragic, and at times even comic, all of which is powerfully conveyed by al-Faqīh's tight, polished prose style, which, as the story develops, is increasingly at odds with the protagonist's mental disarray.

Excerpt from
The Book of The Dead

At first he thought that they had all, for some reason, decided to play truant that morning. On his way to class, the teacher, Mr Abd al-Hafiz, had walked past the teachers' room. He, too, had got into the routine of taking roll call. He continued his journey to the classroom through the long hallway, the walls of which were covered with notices and students' drawings.

When he saw that the door at the end of the hallway was closed, without a sound emanating from inside the room or any of the usual racket that could be heard every morning, he knew that the little devils had invented some excuse for not turning up for class that day. It also meant that he had to return to the school office to have it out with them about this recurrent absenteeism. He swore that he would record any student's unauthorized absence, whatever their excuse or reason.

As if to remove all doubt he opened the door, and without so much as glancing inside he closed it again. He considered going back to the school office, were it not for the faint whisper he had heard when opening the door. He looked inside again and, much to his surprise, he discovered that they were all there. They were sitting properly in their seats, quietly opening their copybooks and silently studying or writing. They behaved as though they had suddenly transformed into grown men.

Abd al-Hafiz entered the classroom, completely dumbstruck. He immediately started looking around to see whether the 'fat cat' from the Ministry was lurking somewhere. Indeed, the only possible explanation for this eerie calm that pervaded the class was that one of the ministerial inspectors had arrived before him to conduct an inspection round in order to embarrass him in front of the students and record that he had arrived late for

صفحة من
كتاب الموتى

ظنّ للوهلة الأولى، أنهم جميعاً، ولأمر ما، قد تغيبوا عن الحضور إلى المدرسة هذا الصباح. كان الأستاذ عبد الحفيظ قد مرّ وهو في طريقه إلى الفصل بحجرة المدرسين وأخذ كما هو الروتين سجلّ الحضور وسار يقطع ممراً طويلاً تملأ جدرانه الصحف الحائطية ورسوم التلاميذ، إلى حجرة الدرس.

وعندما رأى الباب في نهاية الممر مغلقاً، ولم يسمع للطلبة صوتاً، ولم يتناه إليه ضجيجهم وعراكهم كما هي العادة كلّ صباح، أدرك أن هؤلاء الشياطين قد تدبروا عذراً للهروب من الدرس هذا اليوم. وأن عليه أن يعود إلى الإدارة ويسألها بحزم أن تجد حلاً لهذا الغياب المتكرر، وأقسم بينه وبين نفسه أن يسجله عليهم غياباً غير مشروع مهما كان العذر أو السبب.

ولمجرد قطع الشك باليقين فتح الباب ودون أن يهتم بإلقاء نظرة إلى الداخل أعاد قفله، وهمّ بالرجوع لولا أن تناهت إليه عند فتح الباب همهمة ضعيفة، فأعاد فتحه من جديد واكتشف لدهشته الكبيرة أنهم جميعاً هناك، يجلسون في أدب إلى مقاعدهم ويفتحون في هدوء كراريسهم، وينكبون في صمت على المطالعة أو الكتابة، ويتصرفون كأنهم تحولوا فجأة إلى رجال كبار.

دخل الأستاذ عبد الحفيظ وقد عقدت لسانه الدهشة إلى الفصل، فتش أول ما فتش عن (القط الذي جاء من الوزارة)، فليس هناك من تفسير لهذا الهدوء العجيب الذي يعم الفصل إلا أن مفتشاً من مفتشي الوزارة قد سبقه إلى هنا، اختار هذا الوقت المبكر لجولته التفتيشية كي يحرجه أمام الطلاب ويسجل عليه مرة أنه جاء إلى الدرس متأخراً، نظر إلى ساعته واطمأن إلى أن

class. But then Abd al-Hafiz looked at the clock, and was fully reassured that he was on time, no doubt about it. He would defiantly raise his head to this inspector, whom he imagined standing alongside the blackboard. However, there was nobody there. What kind of prank was this? He knew about the cat-and-mouse game these inspectors were so proficient at, and inflicted upon him.

He walked around the blackboard and the desk, in case the inspector was hiding behind one of them, but there was no cat or mouse. He stopped for a minute, baffled and at a loss to explain what was going on. His gaze wandered around the room in search of something out of the ordinary, but everything was the way it should be: each boy was sitting at the desk which had been allocated to him at the beginning of the year; the window was still the same; the mulberry tree behind it, which had recently sprouted leaves, still stood proud and tall; the drawings on the wall were the same feeble and primitive scribblings that had always been there; the blackboard had not moved an inch from its place. This was definitely his classroom and these were definitely his students, with their usual faded, grimy features. He had not taken the wrong route into work, nor had he entered a school on another planet, in another country or city. Everything inside the classroom was as it should be, except, that is, for this eerie calm, which he had never witnessed in any classroom for as long as he had been a teacher.

His attention was drawn to a previously empty seat at the back of the class which was now occupied by one of the students whom he was used to seeing in front of him, at the first desk on the left. He was about to ask him for the secret behind this change, but his attention was drawn to the student's former seat, where he suddenly discovered a *demon* – God help us! – sitting quietly. There was no doubt that this was a demon who had taken on the guise of a girl, and was sitting in this seat, close to him, impudently and shamelessly. It was against all the laws of nature!

ميعاد حضوره في التمام والكمال، ورفع رأسه في تحدّ يواجه ذلك المفتش الذي تصور أنه يقف الآن بمحاذاة السبّورة. لم يكن هناك أحد، ما هذا الهزار[1] الثقيل؟ إنه يعرف لعبة القط والفأر التي يتفنن هؤلاء المفتشون في لعبها معه.

طاف بالسبّورة والمنضدة عساه الآن يختفي خلف إحداهما، لم يجد قطاً ولا فأراً فوقف لدقيقة مندهشاً، عاجزاً عن تفسير ما حدث، أجال بصره داخل الحجرة عله يجد شيئاً غريباً قد حدث، كان كلّ شيء كما هو، كلّ ولد يجلس إلى مكانه الذي تعود أن يجلس إليه منذ بداية العام، النافذة هي النافذة ومن خلفها شجرة التوت التي اكتست حديثاً بالورق تقف في زهو وكبرياء، والرسوم على الحائط هي نفس الرسوم بدائية وركيكة تعود أن يراها دائماً، والسبّورة لم تتزحزح قيد أنملة[2] عن مكانها والفصل هو فصله، والتلاميذ هم تلاميذه، بسحناتهم الترابية الباهتة، فهو لم يخطىء الطريق ولم يدخل خطأ إلى مدرسة في كوكب آخر، أو وطن آخر، أو مدينة أخرى غير مدينته، كان كلّ شيء في داخل الفصل عادياً وطبيعاً، ما عدا هذا الهدوء الغريب الذي لم يره طيلة عمر أمضاه في التدريس يحدث في فصل من الفصول الدراسيّة.

استرعى أنتباهه أن مقعداً مهجوراً في آخر الفصل جلس إليه الآن واحد من الطلبة ممن تعود أن يراهم أمامه في أول مقعد على الشمال، همّ بأن يسأله عن سرّ هذا التغيير لولا أن حانت منه التفاتة إلى مكانه السابق، فإذا به يكتشف فجأة أن – عفريتاً – يجلس في هدوء إلى ذلك المقعد، تعوّذ بالله من الشيطان الرجيم، إنه دونما شكّ عفريت، تنكر في صورة بنت من البنات وجاء في صفاقة وقلة أدب وذوق مخترقاً كلّ النواميس في الدنيا، ليجلس إلى ذلك المقعد قريباً منه.

He looked at her with consternation as she sat among his male students as if she was one of them, as if she had known them, and they her, for ages; as if this was a perfectly normal and natural thing to do; as if there was nothing wrong with the fact that a girl was present in a school for boys and in a class devoted to the teaching of boys. He continued to stare at her, both in terror and astonishment, as though he had seen a corpse in his class.

How could Mr Abd al-Hafiz bear a sight of this kind, knowing full well that this was not a girls' school, but a boys' school, where all the teachers and students were male? How could this girl have ended up here, and what right did she have to come here and sit down, in front of him, on this morning? He was never going to allow any creature to catch him unawares like this. He had got up that morning, done his prayers, had breakfast, shaved, corrected his students' assignments, put on his coat and come to school without even the slightest inkling that there would be a demon in the shape of a girl brazenly sitting in front of him. He could never have imagined that this was going to happen to him!

He had always imagined that girls had to study other things, that they were taught by female teachers and surrounded by girls in schools especially for them, which had big iron gates and high walls and were filled with mystery and secrecy.

He thought that what was taught to boys was for males only, and any female ought to be embarrassed and ashamed to hear it. He could never have imagined that any girl would depart from the principles of decency and modesty and sit down in class together with boys, with a total lack of shame and morals; to listen to the things the boys listened to, to write down what they wrote down and to be examined on the things they were examined on. As for this girl, she must surely be lost – either that, or she had slipped into the school through the window. She was clearly engaged in some plot against him, and he was not going to treat her like the

نظر إليها مذعوراً وهي تجلس بين طلابه الذكور كأنها واحد منهم، كأنها تعرفهم ويعرفونها منذ الأزل، كأنه شيء عادي وطبيعي ولا غبار عليه أن تكون في مدرسة للبنين وفصل من الفصول المخصّصة لتدريس الأولاد بنت. استمر ينظر إليها في ذعر واندهاش كأنه يرى في فصله قتيلاً.

إذ كيف للأستاذ عبد الحفيظ أن يستوعب مشهداً كهذا وهو يعلم تمام العلم[3] أن هذه ليست مدرسة للبنات، إنها مدرسة للأولاد كلّ مدرسيها رجال، وكل طلابها ذكور، كيف إذن تسللت هذه البنت إلى هنا وبأي حق جاءت وجلست، ليجدها قبالته هذا الصباح، إنه لن يسمح أبداً لكائن من كان أن يأخذه هكذا على حين غرة، لقد قام اليوم من نومه، وأدى صلاته، وتناول إفطاره، وحلق ذقنه، وصحّح كراريس تلاميذه، وارتدى معطفه وجاء إلى المدرسة دون أن تكون له أدنى فكرة أن عفريتاً تنكر في صورة بنت وجاء يجلس في صفاقة أمامه، خالي الذهن تماماً من كلّ هذا الذي يحدث الآن.

لقد تصور دائماً أنّ للبنات دروساً أخرى يجب أن يتعلمنها، على أيدي مدرسات من بنات جنسهن داخل مدارس خاصة بهن، مدارس لها بوابات حديدية كبيرة ولها أسوار عالية ولها تكتم وسرية.

وأن كلّ ما يقدم من دروس للأولاد هو شيء خاص بالرجل يجب أن تستحي وتحتشم أي امرأة من الاستماع إليه، لا أن تخرج عن كلّ أصول الأدب والحشمة وتجلس في تهتك وفجور ودونما خجل أو حياء مع الأولاد في الفصل، وتستمع إلى ما يستمعون إليه، وتكتب ما يكتبون، وتمتحن فيما يمتحنون فيه، وأن هذه البنت لابد قد أخطأت طريقها، أو تسللت إلى المدرسة من الشباك، وأنها مدسوسة عليه دسّاً، وأنه لو سمح لنفسه أن يعاملها كغيرها

other students, even if it was a sin or a crime under the law for which he would be made to appear before a judge.

He was afraid that the students had noticed the terror and turmoil that had gripped him, so he pulled himself together, straightened his posture, knitted his brow and addressed the girl formally, trying to conceal any trace of the excitement he felt within.

"Stand up."

She stood up. How shameful! ... She was indeed a woman, with a build and height similar to his. She had bulging breasts and long black hair that ran down to her shoulder blades. She was a woman who had blossomed, and the time had come for her to get married rather than mix with boys who had recently reached maturity at a secondary school. Surely this was a trap.

"Name?"

Before she could open her mouth, the boy who had given up his seat for her and sat at the back of the class volunteered the answer:

"Her name is Zahra, Sir."

He was infuriated by the intrusion of this boy who, as he only just now discovered, had a physical deformity, in addition to being ugly. His clothes were filthy, while his teeth were yellow-stained and worn. He knew that this boy scoured the streets for cigarette butts.

Pretending not to have heard the boy, Mr Abd al-Hafiz repeated the question angrily, quickly running out of patience:

"Name?"

"Zahra Abd al-Salam."

He sensed both defiance and superiority in her voice. So, this Abd al-Salam allowed his nubile daughter to leave the house and brazenly go to a boys' school, sit down with them and mix with them? What father in the world could possibly allow that?

He looked for her name on his attendance sheet. It was there, written in pen, added to the list, which had been typewritten.

من الطلاب لكان في ذلك إثم، أو جريمة يعاقبه عليها القانون، ويساق بسببها إلى القضاء.

خشي أن يكون التلاميذ قد لاحظوا ما أصابه من ذعر وارتباك، فتدارك نفسه وشد قامته، وعقد ما بين حاجبيه، وخاطبها بلهجة رسمية حاول أن يجعلها خالية من أي أثر لما يعتمل في صدره من انفعالات.

ــ قيام.

وقفت. إنها يا للعار° امرأة قامتها في حجم قامته، صدرها نافر، وشعرها طويل أسود يغطي الكتفين، امرأة نضجت ثمارها وحان أوان ذهابها إلى بيت الزوجية لا الاختلاط مع الأولاد الذين وصلوا حديثاً سن البلوغ في مدرسة ثانوية. إنّ في الأمر مكيدة.

ــ اسمك؟

وقبل أن تفتح شفتيها أسرع الولد الذي ترك لها مقعده وجلس في آخر الفصل، متطوعاً للإجابة.

ــ اسمها زهرة يا أستاذ.

أغاظه تطفل هذا الولد الذي اكتشف الآن فقط كيف أنه ممسوخ القامة، وأنه قميء. متسخ الثياب، وله أسنان متآكلة صفراء، وأدرك أن كلّ ما كان يلقاه متناثراً فوق أرض الحجرة من أعقاب السجائر إنما دخنها هذا الولد. أعاد السؤال بغيظ ونفاد صبر متجاهلاً ما قاله الولد.

ــ اسمك؟

ــ زهرة عبد السلام.

أحسّ في صوتها نبرة تحدّ واستعلاء، أي عبد السلام هذا الذي يسمح لابنة في سن الزواج أن تخرج من بيتها، وتأتي دون حياء إلى مدرسة للأولاد تجلس معهم وتختلط بهم، أي أب في الدنيا يسمح بذلك؟

فتش عن اسمها في سجل الحضور، كان اسمها هناك مكتوباً بالقلم، أضيف إضافة إلى القائمة التي كتبت بالآلة الكاتبة، التبس عليه الأمر، إذن

This made the entire matter even more obscure to him. So the school management knew about this. There was no doubt that the girl was party to the scheme that was being plotted against him. Mr Abd al-Hafiz thought about all his enemies among the inspectors, who hated his frankness and time and again conspired against him, sometimes blocking his promotion. They were also behind his having been transferred to another school, and now they could not find anything to do to him except if they broke every law and decree in the land. They plotted against him by putting a girl in one of the classes that he was teaching; indeed, this trap could not have been set for anyone except him.

He had forgotten whether he had finished his preparation, just as he no longer knew whether he was supposed to teach Arabic or Religious Education that day. With a trembling hand, he picked up the chalk and went to the blackboard in order to write something down. He wrote down the date and then stopped, as if he realized for the very first time that it was the Seventies now, and that he had started working as a teacher twenty years earlier. Suddenly he felt weak and exhausted, and sat down again in his chair, feeling totally worn out. He noticed that the girl was still standing, and so he made a gesture with his hand, not knowing himself whether it meant that she should leave, sit down, disappear or die.

However, she quietly sat down, raised her small head and looked at him, defiantly. At that moment, he decided that he would hand in his resignation that day, without any hesitation or regret. He sat down without saying a word and buried his head in his hands, oblivious to the probing eyes that surrounded him. He thought about this heresy ... this deviation ... this abomination. He had lived his entire life in piety, complying with the boundaries laid down by God, believing that women are inviolable and must be protected, and that their place is in the home, far from the gaze of men. He knew that when a man

فالإدارة على علم بالموضوع، بل هي لاشك شريكة في المؤامرة التي تدبر ضده، فكر الأستاذ عبد الحفيظ في كلّ أعدائه من مفتشين كرهوا صراحته فصاروا يكيدون له مرة وراء الأخرى، يعرقلون أحياناً ترقيته، يتسببون في نقله من مدرسة إلى أخرى، وهاهم اليوم لا يجدون ما يفعلونه به إلا أن يخترقوا كلّ ما في الدنيا من سنن وقوانين، ويدسّون عليه في فصل من الفصول التي يقوم بتدريسها بنتاً، إنهم لا يقصدون بهذه المكيدة أحداً سواه.

نسي ما قد أتم تحضيره، نسي إن كان درس اليوم في اللغة العربية أم في الدين، أمسك بيد مرتعشة إصبع الجبس، اقترب من اللوحة ليكتب شيئاً، كتب التاريخ، ووقف عنده، كأنه يكتشف لأول مرة أنها الآن السبعينات، وأن أكثر من عشرين عاماً قد انقضت من عمره مدرّساً، أحسّ فجأة بالوهن والإعياء، فجاء وجلس متهالكاً على كرسيّه، اكتشف أن البنت ما زالت واقفة فأشار لها بيد إشارة لا يعلم إن كان معناها أن تخرج أو تجلس أو تختفي أو تموت.

لكنها في هدوء جلست ورفعت رأسها الصغير تنظر إليه في عناد، في حين قرر هو أن يقدم اليوم وبلا تردد ودونما ندم استقالته، جلس و لم يقل شيئاً، دفن رأسه بين يديه، نسي العيون التي تحاصره. فكر في هذه البدعة، هذه الضلالة، هذه النار، لقد عاش طوال عمره ورعاً شريفاً مستقيماً يراعي حدود الله ويعرف أن للمرأة حرمة يجب أن تصان، وأن مكانها داخل البيت بعيداً عن أعين الرجال، وأنه ما التقى رجل وامرأة إلا وكان الشيطان ثالثهما[٦]،

and a woman are together, Satan is never far away. So, when a woman meets thirty men, or a thousand men, there must be devils everywhere, enough to fill the universe; a catastrophe will befall this world, while Judgment Day will be nigh.

Mr Abd al-Hafiz dictated a sentence the students had to parse, as he sat immersed in thought. As soon as he finished the lesson, he would go to the school management and hand in his notice. This was the last time they would try to make him resign. This was exactly what they wanted. They had put this girl in front of him in a desperate attempt to make him do it. But he would not resign. He was not going to allow them to win just like that. The wisest course of action for him was not to rise to the bait and remain a thorn in their side.

When he finished the lesson, Mr Abd al-Hafiz angrily went to see the head teacher. It was clear that he was going to feed him some story or other. As it turned out, the girl's father was a government official who had recently been transferred to this remote part of the city, where there was no other secondary school except this one. Lest the girl be prevented from getting an education, the school had been obliged to accept her. The Ministry had agreed, and the girl was placed in the school. So, it was clearly a legal matter. However, he was not going to be deceived by this ruse, since he knew all the tricks of these youngsters who all of a sudden called the shots at the Ministry's Centres for Educational Management and Orientation. He was going to fight them, by himself; he was going to show them the extent to which this entire business was crooked.

The next day, he decided to ignore the girl. There was no doubt that the best thing to do was to pretend to forget about her, to ignore her and to teach his class as though she was not there at all. Mr Abd al-Hafiz made up his mind that he would not direct any question to her, nor would he collect her copybook or refer to her presence or absence. He would disregard her and treat her with contempt until either she or whoever brought her here became ashamed, and she returned whence she had come, humiliated and defeated.

فما بالك[7] إذا التقت امرأة وثلاثون رجلاً، لا بل ألف رجل، فمعنى ذلك أن الشياطين سيملأون الكون، وأن كارثة ستحلّ بالدنيا، وأن يوم القيامة بات وشيكاً.

أملى على الطلاب جملة ينشغلون بإعرابها، وتفرغ هو لأفكاره، ستنتهي الحصّة وسيذهب إلى الإدارة يقدم استقالته، هـا هم يدفعونه أخيراً إلى الاستقالة، إن هذا بالضبط ما يريدونه، فهم ما جاءوا بهذه البنت ووضعوها أمامه إلا لحمله على الإتيان بفعل يائس كهذا، لكنه لن يستقيل، لن يمنحهم أنتصاراً مجانياً كهذا، وأن الحكمة كلّ الحكمة هي أن يفوّت عليهم هذه الفرصة وأن يبقى لهم كالشوكة في الحلق.

عندما أنتهت الحصة وذهب الأستاذ عبد الحفيظ حانقاً يقابل مدير المدرسة، كان على ثقة من أنه سيلفق حكاية ما، وكانت الحكاية هي أن للبنت أباً يعمل بالحكومة انتقل حديثاً إلى هذه الضاحية البعيدة من ضواحي المدينة، ولأنه ليس بالضاحية مدرسة ثانوية غير هذه المدرسة، ولكي لا تحرم البنت من تعليمها، فإن المدرسة لا تجد غضاضة في قبولها، وأن الوزارة وافقت وأنّ وضع البنت في المدرسة، وضع قانوني ولا غبار عليه.

لن ينطلي عليه الأمر فهو يعرف كلّ أحابيل هذا الجيل من الأطفال الذي قفز فجأة إلى مراكز التوجيه والإدارة في التعليم، وسيدخل معهم الصراع وحيداً، وسيريهم كيف أن الأمر مليء بالغبار.

في اليوم التالي، قرر أن يتجاهل البنت، فلا شك أن أبلغ رد هو أن يتناساها وألا يعمل لها حساباً على الإطلاق وأن يقدم درسه غير شاعر بوجودها، كأنها ليست هناك أصلاً، وصمّم الأستاذ عبد الحفيظ بينه وبين نفسه أنه لن يوجّه لها سؤالاً ولن يلمس لها كراساً ولن يؤشر على اسمها بالحضور أو الغياب وأن يهملها ويحتقرها إلى أن تستحي على نفسها أو يستحي من جاء بها على نفسه وتعود ذليلة، مهزومة، من حيث أتت.

He entered the class, once again surprised at the strange silence he had thought exceptional the day before. Suddenly the disputes, fights and din had disappeared. The boys were like beings from another planet, one where there were no cattle pens, forests, monkeys or sand. The dirt had disappeared from their faces, which gleamed like lamps. They had made an effort with their appearance; their hair was combed, while they were wearing elegant, clean clothes. The poor among them had suddenly become rich, their humble dwellings transformed into castles, their ignorant peasant mothers into sophisticated, learned ladies. It was as though this was the first time he had seen them. A new spirit, one which he had never experienced in the whole of his teaching career, pervaded this class that day; a perfume he hadn't smelled before was spreading through the air. It occurred to him that this was the first time that everyone had actually been present. And when he asked for an answer to a question, he found that all of them, without exception, had a written reply. What had happened to them, and what miracle had brought about this dangerous revolution?

During the lesson, Mr Abd al-Hafiz gradually discovered the strange transformation that had taken place in those students. Whereas once most of them had been apathetic, dim and distracted during lessons, they had now suddenly become hardworking, eager to reply. It was then that he had an epiphany, for that was really what it was; the fact that answers appeared on their lips with the kind of fluency and eloquence he had never witnessed in a class up until that moment made him realize, for the very first time, the importance of his teaching. Students listened to his words as though what he was saying informed them about what was going on in the world, and held the mysteries of existence. This was something he had never experienced before in his twenty years of teaching. Without realizing, he found himself looking at the girl, taking in her cockiness and the diabolical power she was endowed with. She

دخل إلى الفصل، دهشه أن يرى مرة أخرى هذا الهدوء العجيب الذي
ظنه أمس حالة استثنائية، اختفى فجأة الخصام والعراك والضجيج، الأولاد
كائنات من كوكب آخر، كوكب ليس فيه زرائب ولا غابات ولا قرود
ولا رمال، اختفت من فوق وجوههم الأتربة فصاروا يتألقون كالمصابيح،
اعتنوا بهندامهم وتصفيف شعورهم، وارتدوا ملابس نظيفة، أنيقة، فقرهم
صار فجأة غنى، وبيوتهم القميئة الملتصقة بالأرض صارت فجأة قصوراً،
وأمهاتهم القرويات الجاهلات صرن فجأة سيدات علم وذوق وثقافة،
بات يتأملهم كأنه يراهم لأول مرة، روحاً جديدة لم يعرفها طوال حياته في
التدريس تعمر اليوم هذا الفصل، وعبير لم يعهده من قبل ينتشر في الجو،
وتنبه إلى أن حضورهم كامل للمرة الأولى، وعندما سأل عن الواجب وجد
أنهم جميعاً وبدون استثناء قد كتبوا واجباتهم، ما الذي حدث في الكون
وأي معجزة هذه التي جاءت بهذا الانقلاب الخطير؟

وعندما مضى مع الدرس كان الأستاذ عبد الحفيظ شيئاً فشيئاً يكتشف
التحول العجيب الذي أصاب هؤلاء الطلبة، إن أكثرهم خمولاً وغباء
وسرحاناً أثناء الدرس صار فجأة يشتعل حماساً للإجابة، فالعبقرية هبطت
عليه الآن وفي هذه الساعة، والغريب أنها حقاً كذلك، فها هي الإجابة تأتي
على ألسنتهم سهلة مرنة يقولونها بفصاحة وقدرة على التعبير لم يعهدها في
فصل من فصول الدراسة قبل الآن، بل إنه هو نفسه يحس الآن ولأول مرة
بأهمية الدروس التي يقدمها، إنهم ينصتون إليه ويتابعون كلماته كأن ما
يقوله صار فجأة أخطر ما في الدنيا، وأن بحوزته كلّ أسرار الكون، حالة لم
يعرفها طيلة العشرين عاماً في التدريس إلا هذا اليوم، ودون أن يدري وجد
نفسه يسترق النظر إليها، أي سطوة تملكها، أي قوة جهنمية جاءت تحملها

was sitting innocently in her chair, as though this sorceress did not know the extent of the power she wielded, as though what was happening had nothing to do with her. What demonic land did she come from, that she was able to succeed where all the educational books and Ministries of Education in the world had failed?

However, it is not books and ministries, nor countries, organizations, equipment or fleets that fail to make students, but students themselves; they are inhabited by evil spirits, filling the world with unrest, tumult and strife. Their greatest amusement is not to study, but to engage in fighting, resistance and disruptive activities. Rather than studying, their biggest joy is being annoying, stubborn and fractious. Then, *she* came and brought Satan's trickery to mankind. It was this trickery that turned their poverty into wealth, their stupidity into intelligence, their ugliness into handsomeness. Mr Abd al-Hafiz was certain that she was able to wave a magic wand over the Earth and make it come alive, or conjure up a flock of pigeons or a colony of rabbits from her sleeve. She could produce any miracle if she wanted. There was something strange and terrifying in all of this which he, as a mere mortal, was incapable of fathoming.

Once again he glanced over at her, and noticed something in her features that shed light on what had baffled him; it was that everything about her was normal. It was clear from the very first time he had laid eyes on her that she could not have been anything but Libyan. There was something deep-rooted in her "Libyan-ness" that was reflected in her features. He saw it in the slight yellowness that the signs of wealth and prosperity could not conceal. In spite of the yellowness, beauty emanated from her face, the kind of beauty of oases filled with date palms, quiet and unassuming. He did not see anything in her features that was extraordinary, that betrayed the power she held. Yet Mr Abd al-Hafiz kept thinking she was a devilish being that belonged to a world other than our own …

معها، إنها تجلس في براءة إلى مقعدها، كأن هذه الساحرة لا تعلم بمدى القوة التي بحوزتها، كأن ما يحدث يحدث بمعزل عنها ولا دخل لها فيه، من أي بلد من بلاد الجان جاءت لتفلح فيما فشلت كلّ كتب التربية ووزارات التعليم في العالم؟

بل ليست الكتب والوزارات وإنما هي دول وأنظمة وأجهزة وأساطيل لم تفلح في أن تجعل الطلبة، غير أنهم طلبة، تسكنهم روح شريرة فيملأون الدنيا شغباً وضجيجاً وعراكاً، تسليتهم الكبرى ليست الدراسة بقدر ما هي هذه المناكفة والعناد وأعمال الشغب، فتأتي هي لتحيلهم من شياطين إلى أوادم، وتحيل فقرهم إلى غنى وغباءهم إلى نبوغ، وقبحهم إلى وسامة. تأكد لدى الأستاذ عبد الحفيظ أنها تستطيع أن ترمي فوق الأرض عصا وتجعلها حية تسعى، وأن تخرج من كمّها أسراباً من الحمام أو قطعاناً من الأرانب. وتأتي بأي معجزة لو أرادت، وأن في الأمر شيئاً مهولاً عجيباً هو لاشك أعجز وأصغر من أن يعرف له تبريراً، أو تفسيراً.

عاد من جديد يسترق النظر إليها عله يجد شيئاً في ملامحها يضيء ما اعتراه من حيرة وذهول، كان كلّ شيء فيها عادياً، بنت تحس فيها منذ النظرة الأولى أنها لا يمكن إلا أن تكون ليبية، شيء موغل في ليبيته تنطق به تقاطيع وجهها وتراه في هذه الصفرة الخفيفة التي لم تفلح في إخفائها كلّ دلائل الرخاء والنعمة في ملامحها، ولكنّ برغم الصفرة فإن جمالاً يفيض به وجهها، جمالاً كجمال واحات النخيل ليس فيه إثارة، وليس له صخب أو ضجيج، لم ير في ملامحها شيئاً خارقاً ينبئ بهذه القوة التي تملكها، ومع ذلك فإن الأستاذ عبد الحفيظ ما زال يعتقد بأنها شيء شيطاني ينتسب إلى عالم غير عالمنا.

Suddenly, all his suspicions were confirmed when he glanced at the bottom of her chair and saw that her feet were like donkey's hooves. He nearly uttered a shriek loud enough to shatter all the walls of the school, but then he realized that it was simply the heels of her shoes. He was afraid she could now read his thoughts, become angry with him and decide to use her tricks to transform him on the spot into a pillar, a tree, a frog or a meowing cat. The thought of this danger sent shivers throughout his body – God protect us from Satan! Then, he closed the religion book and left the class before the lesson had ended.

When he got home, Mr Abd al-Hafiz was still shaking. He felt an overwhelming fear, as though he had committed some crime, and some terrifying punishment would inevitably befall him. He imagined her following him everywhere with her donkey's hooves. Sometimes she would be sporting two scary wings like those of a bat, or she would be a dragon, fearsome flames spewing forth from its mouth. Other times, he imagined her with claws like those of a mythical animal, or she would appear to him as Satan, chasing him wherever he went. He had to force himself more than once not to repeat her name in a loud voice, out of sheer fear and terror.

After his morning prayers he discovered one of her notebooks. He had forgotten his promise not to take it together with the other students' copybooks. He sat down, turning it over with trembling fingers. However, contrary to what he thought, there was nothing strange or bizarre about the copybook; it did not contain any magical words or riddles such as those found in the Book of the Dead. Everything was normal, just as in all the other copybooks, except that her handwriting was better and more beautiful. He made up his mind; with the obstinacy of a child, he grabbed hold of his pen and gave her a low mark despite the fact that all her answers were correct. He would engage her in battle. He would not flinch before the oppressive kings that served her.

وتأكدت فجأة كلّ ظنونه عندما التفت إلى أسفل المقعد الذي تجلس فيه فرأى أن قدميها كأنهما حافرا حمار وكاد أن يطلق صرخة تهدّ جدران المدرسة كلها لولا أن تنبه إلى أن هذين هما كعبا حذائها، وخشي أن تكون الآن قد قرأت أفكاره، وغضبت منه، وقررت أن تحيله على الفور إلى مسخ، إلى عمود أو شجرة، أو ضفدعة، أو قطة تموء، أحس برعشة تسري في كلّ بدنه لهذا الخاطر، تعوّذ بالله من الشيطان، وأقفل كتاب الدين، وخرج من الفصل قبل أن تنتهي الحصة.

اكتشف الأستاذ عبد الحفيظ وهو يصل إلى البيت أنه مازال يرتعش، وأن خوفاً غريباً يسيطر على كلّ مشاعره، كأنه اقترف جريمة ما، وأن عقاباً مروعاً مهولاً سوف يحل به لا محالة، ورأى أن صورتها وهي بحافري الحمار تلاحقه في كلّ مكان، أحياناً ترتدي جناحين مخيفين كجناحي خُفّاش وأحياناً يراها كالتنين تقذف لهباً هائلاً من فمها.

وأحياناً لها مخلب كوحش خرافي، تجسدت له شيطاناً يطارده أينما ذهب، وضبط نفسه أكثر من مرة يردّد اسمها بصوت عال في خوف ورعب.

وعندما اكتشف بعد صلاة الفجر أن لها كراساً قد نسي وعده وأحضره مع كراريس الطلبة، جلس إليه يقلبه بأصابع مرتعشة وبعكس ما كان يظن لم يجد في الكراس شيئاً غريباً أو عجيباً ولم يجدها تستعمل في الكتابة طلاسم أو أحاجي كما في كتاب الموتى، كان كلّ شيء فيه عادياً كغيره من الكراريس، عدا أن خطها أكثر تنسيقاً وجمالاً. قرر في ذهنه شيئاً، وبعناد كعناد الأطفال أمسك القلم وكتب لها درجة ضعيفة برغم صحة إجاباتها، سيدخل الصراع معها ولن يخشى كلّ الملوك المسخرين لخدمتها.

In class he awaited her reaction, expecting to be turned into a mouse, cat or frog. He would neither yield nor scold, as the question was one of principle and dignity, life or death. He saw that she was distressed as she compared her copybook with her neighbour's. She was about to say something when he peevishly silenced her so she would cry, commit suicide or throw herself out of the window. He would not be fooled by her wiliness and cunning; he would fight this black magic that she had brought with her until his dying breath. Lesson after lesson went by, and he continued to provoke her, taking every opportunity to rebuke her; despite her zeal, he consistently gave her the lowest mark.

As for her, it was as though she was not party to the fight; she sat calmly in her chair, while her warm fragrance spread throughout the classroom. She took a strange interest in her lessons, as if the entire thing did not concern her. There was no doubt that this calm was entirely feigned, and this composure artificial; no doubt she was preparing something dreadful for him. Every day he imagined that this dreadful thing would take place; he would find the school turned into a pile of ashes or the students transmogrified into monkeys. He imagined waking up one day and finding that he had become a rabbit, a hedgehog or a pig. One day after another passed as he awaited the catastrophe that lay in store for him – an earthquake or the arrival of Judgment Day. But neither the earthquake nor Judgment Day came. If something was going to happen, it would no doubt become clear to him very soon.

When one day he entered the classroom and did not find her there, he felt as though the thing on which he had built his life had suddenly collapsed. The magic that had filled the classroom had vanished, as had the perfume. He was once again faced with the boys' ugliness, poverty and stupidity as they all reverted to their previous despicable state. The classroom had become darker and gloomier; the sun that had risen along the ceiling of the room was extinguished that day.

ووقف عندما جاء إلى الدرس ينتظر رد فعلها لتمسخه فأراً أو قطاً أو
ضفدعة، فهو لن يستسلم أو ينهار فالمسألة مسألة مبدأ وكرامة، حياة أو
موت، رآها وهي مهمومة تقارن كراسها مع كراس زميلها في المقعد. همّت
بأن تقول شيئاً فأسكتها بشراسة، لتبك أو تنتحر أو ترم نفسها من الشباك،
فلن ينطلي عليه مكرها ودهاؤها، وسيحارب إلى آخر رمق فيه هذا السحر
الأسود الذي جاءت به معها، مضى حصة وراء الأخرى يتحرش بها، يتحين
الفرصة لتقريعها، يمنحها برغم اجتهادها أقل الدرجات شأناً وقيمة.

وهي كأنها ليست طرفاً في الصراع، تجلس هادئة إلى مقعدها وتنشر
داخل الفصل عطرها الدافئ، وتهتم اهتماماً غريباً بدرسها كأن الأمر كله
لا يعنيها، إنها بلا شك تتصنّع هذا الهدوء وهذه المسكنة تصنعاً، وأنها تبيّت
له أمراً فظيعاً، وتصور كلّ يوم أن يرى ذلك الأمر الفظيع يحدث. أن يأتي
فيجد المدرسة قد صارت كوم رماد، أو أن طلابه تحولوا فجأة إلى قرود. أو
أنه صحا من النوم فوجد نفسه قد صار أرنباً أو قنفذاً أو خنزيراً، مضى يوم
وراء الآخر وهو ينتظر حدوث الكارثة، أو قدوم الزلزال أو مجيء يوم القيامة
لكنّ الزلزال لا يأتي، والقيامة لا تقوم وإن في الأمر شيئاً سيفصح عن نفسه
قريباً دون ريب.

وعندما جاء يوماً إلى الفصل ولم يجدها هناك أحس كأن الشيء الذي
بنى عليه حياته فجأة ينهار. اختفى السحر الذي كان يملأ الفصل واختفى
العبير، عاد إلى الأولاد قبحهم وفقرهم وغباؤهم ورجعوا مرة أخرى أنذالاً
كما كانوا، صار الفصل أكثر تعتيماً وإظلاماً، فالشمس التي كانت تشرق في
سقف الحجرة انطفأت اليوم.

He always imagined that the girl's disappearance from school would constitute a victory for him, and fill his heart with joy and pride. He felt that he had lived on the edge of his nerves these past days; he had fought her magic to get this result. However, this was not a sweet victory. Instead, he felt that a strange sense of grief had gripped his heart, while his throat was as dry as tinder. He felt he had lost something very precious that had filled his heart every morning – a driving force and a challenge. For the first time, he began to reflect on the entire episode, and was left with a feeling of remorse. Spiders were weaving their webs inside his chest. He had been mean in his treatment of her. He had been unfair to imagine her as Satan, a demon or a dragon, when in fact she was only a small, innocent child. If he had married young, he could have had a daughter her age. He stared into the classroom, which looked as deserted as a ruin, inhabited by the diabolical boys. He seriously thought of going to look for her to ask for her forgiveness. He would talk to her father, humbly requesting the latter to send his daughter back to school, where he would treat her like a princess or a queen. He resolved to do this at the earliest opportunity; but then the next day she was back, and returned the students' wealth and handsomeness to them as her warm perfume once again wafted through the classroom.

The sun once more shone in class, and Mr Abd al-Hafiz noticed with joy that a flock of sparrows now rested in his heart. The tree stretched its branches and blossomed inside his chest. For the first time, teaching was the most beautiful profession in the world. It was no longer a heavy chore to come to class; rather, it was a feast that was repeated each day. The girl was no rebel, foreigner or dragon; she was a pretty little girl, who radiated, and to whom he showed love and affection. He was generous in his marks for her. He would grow worried if she was only one minute late. He missed her from the moment he left the classroom until he returned the next day.

لقد تصور دائماً أن اختفاء البنت من المدرسة سيكون انتصاراً يملأ قلبه فرحاً وزهواً، وأنه عاش على أعصابه كلّ الأيام الماضية وكافح سحرها وناضل ضدها من أجل هذه النتيجة، لكنه لا يجد لهذا الانتصار طعماً، بل هو على العكس من ذلك يحس بكآبة غريبة تعتصر قلبه، ورماداً يملأ حلقه، وأن حياته فقدت شيئاً جوهرياً كان يملأ قلبه كلّ صباح تحفزاً وتحدياً، ولأول مرة بدأ يراجع نفسه ويحس بتأنيب الضمير، عناكب تنسج شباكها داخل صدره، لقد كان شرساً في معاملتها، وأنه كان ظالماً عندما تصورها شيطاناً أو عفريتاً أو تنيناً في حين كانت هي مجرد طفلة صغيرة بريئة، كان من الممكن لو تزوج مبكراً لأنجب بنتاً في سنها، وتأمل الفصل وقد صار موحشاً كأنه خرابة والأولاد كأنهم شياطين تسكن هذه الخرابة.

وفكر جدياً في أن يذهب للبحث عنها ليسألها الصفح والغفران، سيستجدي والدها صاغراً أن يعيدها إلى المدرسة وسيعاملها كأميرة أو ملكة. وصمّم على أن يفعل ذلك في أول فرصة، لولا أنها في اليوم التالي جاءت، تعيد إلى التلاميذ الغنى والوسامة وتنشر عطرها الدافئ داخل الحجرة.

وتزرع الشمس مرة أخرى في قلب الفصل ورأى الفرحة سرباً من العصافير تحط الآن في قلبه، وشجرة ييست أغصانها[1] تخضوضر وتزهر الآن في صدره، ولأول مرة صارت مهنة التدريس أجمل مهنة في الدنيا، والمجيء إلى الفصل ليس واجباً ثقيلاً وإنما عيد يتجدد كلّ يوم، والبنت ليست مارداً ولا جنية ولاتنيناً، وإنما أنثى صغيرة جميلة، مضيئة، وهو يتودّد إليها، يمنحها الدرجات بسخاء، يقلق إذا تأخرت عن المجيء دقيقة واحدة ويشده الحنين إليها منذ أن يغادر الفصل وحتى يعود في اليوم التالي.

Throughout all this, Mr Abd al-Hafiz did not realize that he was increasingly paying attention to his appearance. He started wearing the suit he used to save for *Eid*, every day. He started to shave every morning and put cologne on, whereas previously he would forget to shave once or twice a week. For the first time, he reflected on his past life. He realized that he had prematurely entered a phase in his life, believing, wrongfully, that he was nearing the age of retirement when in reality he was only forty-five or forty-six. Despite the fact that he had a wife, whose body had withered, and children who milled about like ants inside the house, he was still in the prime of life. Most of life's goodness and sweetness still lay ahead of him. He would be unjust to himself, to his age and youth, if he were to think of himself as an old man. Did he not have a grandfather who married his eighth or ninth wife while he was in his seventies? He again felt like a boy, the same age as his students, new blood rushing through his veins. He saw a beautiful carpet on which boats, gardens, birds and butterflies were painted, and which stretched between his house and the school; every morning he walked upon this carpet. No sooner did he see the girl sitting calmly in her seat, spreading her light like a lamp, than his body would be immersed in a delicious daze. He knew that the remit of her magic had increased and that he, like the students, had fallen under her spell. He would get through the lesson feeling happy, finishing up very quickly. He would be seized by a passion for her and wait impatiently until he saw her again the next day.

Mr Abd al-Hafiz did not know why, afterwards, he came to hate staying indoors, as if there was something inside him that was restricted by the houses, rooms and places that had ceilings, walls and doors. So he began to increase the frequency of his walks outside, in squares and public gardens. He would look at the sea, addicted to thinking about this girl who had suddenly entered his life just as she had entered his classroom, out of the blue. Over time he began to experience a strange feeling

وفي أثناء ذلك لم ينتبه الأستاذ عبد الحفيظ إلى أنه صار يعتني بمظهره أكثر من ذي قبل، وأن البدلة التي كان يدّخرها للعيد[8] قد نسي العيد وصار يرتديها كلّ يوم، وأنه صار يهتم بحلاقة وجهه ووضع الكولونيا فوقه كلّ صباح بعد أن كان يهمل حلاقته إلا مرة واحدة أو مرتين في الأسبوع، ولأول مرة يفكر في هذه الأعوام التي انقضت من عمره ويدرك أنه دخل مجال الحياة مبكراً حتى ظن زورا وبهتاناً أنه قد اقترب من سنّ التقاعد في حين أنه لم يتجاوز الأربعين إلا بخمسة أو ستة أعوام، وأنه برغم الزوجة التي جف عودها والأطفال الذين ينتشرون كالنمل داخل البيت مازال في نضج رجولته وعنفوانها وأن الحياة ما زالت أمامه عريضة بكل لذائذها وطيباتها، وأنه كان يظلم نفسه ويظلم عمره ويظلم شبابه عندما يتصور أنه صار عجوزاً وينسى أن له جداً تزوج امرأته الثامنة أو التاسعة وهو في سن السبعين، فيحس كأنه عاد ولداً صغيراً في عمر تلاميذه وأن دماء جديدة تجري كالنسغ في عروقه، ويرى بساطاً جميلاً نقشت فوقه قوارب وحدائق وعصافير وفراشات قد امتد بين بيته والمدرسة يمضي كلّ صباح فوقه، وما إن يراها تجلس في هدوء إلى مقعدها وتنشر كالقنديل ضوءها، حتى يغمر جسمه خدر لذيذ فيدرك أن دائرة سحرها قد زادت اتساعاً وشملته كما شملت الطلبة، ويمضي مع درسه سعيداً، وينتهي الوقت سريعاً، فيعاوده الشوق إليها وينتظر بفارغ الصبر أن يراها في اليوم التالي.

ولا يدري الأستاذ عبد الحفيظ لماذا- بعد ذلك - صار يكره البقاء في البيت كأنّ في صدره شيئاً تضيق به البيوت والحجرات والأماكن التي لها سقف وجدران وأبواب فصار يكثر الذهاب إلى الخلاء، والميادين الرحبة الفسيحة، والحدائق العامة، وتأمل البحر وإدمان التفكير في هذه البنت التي دخلت فجأة حياته كما دخلت فجأة حجرة درسه. وصار يوماً وراء الآخر يحس بشيء غريب نحوها، شيء ينكره ويخشاه ويخافه ويملأ قلبه

towards her, which filled his heart with fear. It was a sensation he did not want to express or acknowledge, except to himself. It was a strange creature that reared its head from under the ice mounts and appeared detached from the mind and will, defying all the rules and laws of one's being, challenging all the customs and traditions in which he believed, all the high ideals to which he had devoted himself. He refused to recognize or believe this, since to do so would bring about the disaster he was expecting.

Every morning he saw her sitting in her seat, innocently and meekly as though she was unaware of the odious struggle raging inside of him, which emitted a terrible deafening noise. While these light, unknown threads tied him so strongly to her, he resisted and fought as though allowing his heart to give in would result in his falling into a dark, bottomless abyss. If he gave his thought free expression it would hover around her and give rise to a frightful, massive shock that would cause all the buildings in the world to come crashing down on him. The blaze burned his heart; it was the first time in his life that he had felt this kind of inflamed passion, as though it had always been there, covered by a huge pile of ashes, until the arrival of this girl rekindled the cinders and they grew into a blazing inferno raging within him.

The biggest tragedy was that she had begun to come to him in a dream. It was not a dragon spewing fire, or a mythical creature with batwings; it was a beautiful young girl with an inviting glow who came to him in his sleep. He would meet her in a wide, open space, as though they were Adam and Eve suddenly fallen down to Earth, meeting up after having lost each other for many years. However, the meeting was a shock – a terrifying, sweet, horrible, beautiful and loathsome clash. Mr Abd al-Hafiz would awake from his sleep in a panic, begging God for forgiveness. He would stumble along to school, ashamed and confused. He did not have the strength to look at her, or at anyone else for that matter, as though anyone looking into his eyes would immediately discover a loathsome deed.

رعباً، شيء لا يريد أن يفصح عنه أو يعترف به حتى بينه وبين نفسه، كائن غريب يرفع من تحت أكداس الجليد رأسه ويطل بمعزل عن العقل والإرادة متحدياً كلّ سنن الكون وقوانينه، متحدياً كلّ التقاليد والأعراف التي آمن بها، وكل المثل العليا التي كرّس نفسه لخدمتها، وهو يرفض أن يعترف به أو يصدقه، لأنه لو انصاع لأمره واعترف به أو صدقه لحصلت الكارثة التي كان يتوقعها.

إنه يراها كلّ صباح تجلس في براءة ووداعة إلى مقعدها كأنها لا تعلم بهذا الصراع البغيض الذي يدور في نفسه ويصدر دوياً هائلاً يصم أذنيه، وهذه الخيوط الخفية المجهولة التي تشده بقوة إليها وهو يرفض ويقاوم كأنه لو طاوع قلبه لوجد نفسه يسقط في هاوية مظلمة عميقة مخيفة ليس لها قرار ولو سمح لفكره أن يمضي حراً طليقاً يحوم حولها ويلتقي بها لأحدث ذلك اللقاء صداماً هائلاً مروعاً تسقط له كلّ الأننية في الدنيا، والوهج يحرق قلبه، شعور ملتهب يحس به لأول مرة في حياته، كأنه كان دائماً هناك، تغطيه أكداس هائلة من الرماد إلى أن جاءت هذه الصغيرة تنفخ عنه الرماد حتى صار جحيماً يحرق صدره.

والمصيبة الكبرى أنها صارت تأتيه في الحلم، ليست تنيناً يقذف اللهب، أو كائناً أسطورياً يرتدي أجنحة خفاش، كانت تأتيه في النوم أنثى صغيرة، جميلة، مضيئة شهية، ليلتقي بها في أرض خلاء كأنهما آدم وحوّاء هبطا فجأة إلى الأرض، وتاها عن بعضهما سنيناً، ثم جاء اللقاء، على حين غفلة جاء اللقاء، بل هو الصدام، صدام مروع هائل لذيذ بغيض جميل كريه، فيستيقظ الأستاذ عبد الحفيظ من نومه مذعوراً، ويستغفر الله كثيراً، ويذهب إلى المدرسة خجولاً مرتبكاً، متعثّر الخطى، لا يقوى على رفع بصره إليها، أو إلى أحد غيرها، كأن أحداً لو رأى عينيه لاكتشف فيهما على الفور فعلة نكراء.

As the days went by, he became increasingly convinced of the fact that he was the victim of a secretly hatched conspiracy, and that he had been right from the start in seeing something diabolical in this scheming girl. She had begun to deceive him with her innocent and meek appearance, and she had caught him in her net. She had cast her black magic on him and masterfully ensnared him, and he now saw himself stumbling like a blind man towards a terrifying quagmire filled with turpitude, debauchery, godlessness and filth. He had become the victim of satanic, demonic or magic designs and actions. This feeling grew like a satanic flower within him, against all intelligence, logic and will. It grabbed hold of him, mocking ideals, traditions, morals and virtue. This feeling could not have come to him out of the blue; it had to be by design or as a result of some magical power. From the outset, he had imagined that something dreadful would come to pass. If it was an earthquake or Judgment Day, it did not happen. Instead, something more dreadful and terrifying happened. It had brought him to this chasm and made him – a teacher and educator – think about this girl in this shameful and terrifying way, which was devoid of morals, dignity and virtue. She was the age his daughter would be if he had one, and he would be her Religious Education teacher.

The only way to resist her spell would be to fight magic with magic. And so Mr Abd al-Hafiz began to delve into old, yellow-stained books with a frenzy that bordered on hysteria, in the hope of finding something that would counteract the effect of her book, which she had brought from the world of the dead and ghosts. Much to the surprise of his wife and children, he turned the house upside down searching for a trace of this magic. He began to dig up the threshold to the house with a pickaxe, given to the illusion that they had buried something for him there. He ripped the covers of the copybooks and schoolbooks in search of something the size of a safety pin hidden in one of them. He did

ويوماً وراء الآخر نما في ذهنه يقين كامل بأنه ضحية مؤامرة دبرت في الخفاء، وأنه كان على حق عندما رأى في هذه البنت منذ أول يوم شيئاً شيطانياً مدسوساً عليه دسّاً، إذ مضت تخدعه .بمظهرها الوديع البريء، وترمي شباكها حوله، وتنفث⁹ سحرها الأسود في ضلوعه، وتتفنن في غوايته، حتى رأى نفسه يمشي كالأعمى ليقع في بئر مظلمة مخيفة تمتلئ فسقاً وفجوراً وإلحاداً ورجساً، وأنه الآن ضحية عمل شيطاني من أعمال الجن أو السحرة، فهذا الشعور الذي نما كالنبات الشيطاني في صدره .بمعزل عن العقل والمنطق والإرادة، وأخرج من تحت الجليد رأسه هازئاً وساخراً من المثل والتقاليد والأخلاق والفضيلة، لا يمكن أن يأتي عفواً ودونما تدبير أو عمل من أعمال السحر.

لقد تصور منذ البداية أن شيئاً فظيعاً سوف يحدث، وإذا كان الزلزال لم يأت، والقيامة لم تقم، فإن شيئاً أكثر فظاعة وهولاً هذا الذي يحدث الآن، ويجره إلى هذه الهاوية ويجعله وهو الأستاذ والمربّي يفكر في بنت بحجم ابنته لو كانت له ابنة، وتتلقى دروس الدين على يديه، بهذه الصورة المخجلة المرعبة المجردة من الخلق والشرف والفضيلة، وأن لا خلاص له إلا بسحر يقاوم سحرها، فبدأ الأستاذ عبد الحفيظ من فوره ينقّب بحماس أشبه بالهستريا في المجلدات التي اصفرّ لونها عله يعثر عندها على حل يبطل مفعول كتابها الذي جاءت به من عالم الموت والأشباح، ومضى لدهشة الزوجة والأطفال يقلب البيت رأساً على عقب عله يجد أثراً لهذا السحر. ويأخذ فأساً ويحفر عند عتبة الباب علهم دفنوا له شيئاً هناك. ويمزق أغلفة الكراريس والكتب المدرسية عل شيئاً بحجم الدبوس مدسوساً في أحدها،

not hesitate to cut off all the hair on his head, since he thought that an alien body the size of a grain of dust had insinuated itself in his hair. He was convinced that all around him people were looking at him and whispering. He saw the school head threatening to dismiss him. He saw his wife take her children and leave for her family's home. He saw his students laughing disdainfully and rudely when he arrived. All his suspicions had been confirmed. He had uncovered all their tricks. He knew that they were all plotting against him and using this girl to destroy his life. He was also convinced of the fact that his wife, students, the school head and teachers, the inspector from the Ministry and its directors, were all part of this conspiracy. Nothing could quench his thirst for revenge except to set fire to his home, the school and the Ministry without further ado. Mr Abd al-Hafiz resolutely proceeded to carry out this plan.

و لم يتردّد في حلاقة شعر رأسه كله عندما ظن أن جسماً غريباً بحجم ذرة الغبار قد غافلوه ووضعوه في شعره، وتأكدت كلّ ظنون الأستاذ عبد الحفيظ عندما رآهم يتهامسون في كلّ مكان من حوله، ورأى مدير المدرسة يقدم له إنذاراً بفصله من العمل، ورأى زوجته تأخذ أطفالها وتذهب إلى بيت أهلها، ورأى التلاميذ يضحكون في حضوره باستهتار وقلة أدب، تأكدت كلّ ظنونه وانكشفت أمامه كلّ ألاعيبهم وأدرك أنهم جميعاً قد تآمروا ضده واستعملوا تلك الصبية لتدمير حياته، وأن زوجته وطلابه ومدير المدرسة ومدرسيها ومفتشي الوزارة ومدرائها كلهم شركاء في هذه المؤامرة، وأن لا شيء يشفي غليله إلا أن يحمل الآن ناراً ويذهب ليشعل الحرائق في البيت والمدرسة والوزارة. فمضى الأستاذ عبد الحفيظ من فوره ينفذ هذه الرغبة بحزم وتصميم.

Language Notes

1. الهزار: interestingly enough, this is primarily used in ECA; MSA مَزْح, نُكتة. Note that in the text, the phrase الهزار الثَّقيل refers to a bad joke, whereby ثَقيل does not have its usual meaning of "heavy"; rather, in this context it refers to "difficult to laugh with". In this context, one may refer to the Arabic expression دَمّ ثَقيل, meaning "very serious" (of a person), as opposed to دمّ خَفيف, "light-hearted".

2. قَيْدَ أنْملة = قَيْدَ شَعْرَة.

3. يَعْلَمُ تَمام العلْمَ: this expression, which consists of a finite verb followed by تَمام ("complete") + مَصْدَر of the same verb indicates that something is done to the fullest extent. Note, however, that this construction only occurs with verbs of realization and knowledge such as عَرف and أَدْرَكَ.

4. عفْريت (also عَفْريت, pl. عَفاريت): this refers to a class of fantastic beings from the netherworld, known for their power and cunning. In contemporary folklore, they are regarded as a type of جنّ (see حكاية القنديل) or demon (while in Egypt it can also denote the ghost of a deceased person). The word عفريت is also commonly used to denote naughtiness, e.g. أنت عفريت, "you little devil" (e. g. to a child).

5. يا للعار: lit. "oh, the shame" (< عار, "shame", "dishonour"). This expression is commonly used with reference to acts that are considered shameful. Also note the ل after the vocative patical يا is pronounced لَ. This construction (which is highly classical) can also be used with a proper noun: e.g. يا لَمحَمّد (meaning "come and help Muḥammad")

6. الشَّيْطان ثالثُهُما: this is part of a common saying (ما اجْتَمَع رَجُل وامرأة إلا وكانَ الشَّيْطان ثالثُهُما), according to which the Devil is always the third person present (a metaphor for temptation and evil) when a man and a woman are alone

together. The saying is based on the famous *ḥadīth* (saying of the Prophet Muḥammad): ما خَلا رَجُل بامْرَأة إلاّ وكان الشَّيْطان بَيْنَهُما.

7. ما بالك: note that this expression can also (more rarely) mean: "What do you think?"

8. عيد: pl. أعْياد; though strictly meaning any "feast day", it is often used to refer to the most important Muslim feast, the عِيْد الأضْحَى or "Feast of Immolation", which takes place at the end of the pilgrimage (Ḥajj), on the tenth day of the month ذو الحجّة.

9. نَفَثَ (سحرها) (u,i): the use of the word (lit. "to spit") here is a reference to the نفَّاثة, a sorceress who ties knots in a cord and then spits on them while uttering a curse (cf. Qur'ān, *sūra* 113:4).

Najīb Maḥfūẓ

Najīb Maḥfūẓ (Naguib Mahfouz) (1911–2006), is widely considered one of the most prolific and accomplished Arab writers of the twentieth century. He was awarded the Nobel Prize for Literature in 1988 and wrote a total of thirty-five novels, fourteen collections of short stories and plays, as well as three collections of journalism.

Maḥfūẓ was born in the working-class district of Al-Jamaliyya in Cairo where he lived until the age of twelve, when his family moved to the ʿAbbasiyya suburb. Both districts provided the background for much of his writing.

After studying philosophy at Cairo University, he worked as a civil servant for many years alongside his journalistic activity, which included contributions to many Egyptian publications (e. g. *al-Risāla*, *al-Hilāl* and *al-Ahrām*).

Thoroughly grounded in both classical and modern Arabic literature, Maḥfūẓ was also very familiar with, and influenced by, European authors such as Tolstoy, Dostoevsky, Maupassant, Chekhov and the French philosopher Henri Bergson. Critics traditionally classify Maḥfūẓ's work into four chronological phases: historical, realistic, modernist and traditional.

Maḥfūẓ's literary career began with short stories, which he initially published in literary Egyptian magazines and then later as a collection of stories entitled همس الجُنون (*The Whispers of Madness*, 1938). Despite his great literary success, Maḥfūẓ continued to work as a civil servant in various government departments until his retirement in 1971.

After his early "historical" period, which included the novels لُعْبَة الأَقْدَار (*The Game of Fate*, 1939), رادُوبِيس (*Rhodopis*, 1943) and كفاح طيبة (*The Struggle of Thebes*, 1944), Maḥfūẓ's interest in the 1950s shifted to the situation of the modern Egyptians and the impact social changes were having on the lives of ordinary people. His main work of this period is undoubtedly the so-called "Cairo Trilogy", which consists of بَيْن القَصْرَيْن (*Palace Walk*, 1956), قَصْر الشَّوْق (*Palace of Desire*, 1957) and السُّكَرِيَّة (*Sugar Street*, 1957). All three are set in the Cairo of Maḥfūẓ's youth and depict the vicissitudes of the family of al-Sayyid Aḥmad 'Abd al-Jawādī over three generations, between World War I and 1950. This work is regarded by many critics as the pinnacle of the author's realistic period.

After President Nasser's death in 1970, Maḥfūẓ wrote the novel الكرنك (*Karnak*, 1974), in which he attacked the police state and its nefarious effects on the population. Among Maḥfūẓ's other works one may mention أولاد حارتنا (*The Children of Gebelawi*, 1967); اللصّ والكلاب (*The Thief and the Dog*, 1961); ميرامار (*Miramar*, 1967); and رحْلة ابن فطومَة (*The Journey of Ibn Fattouma*, 1983). His creative imagination is most vivid in ملحمة الحرافيش (*The Harafish*, 1977) and ليالي ألف ليلة (*Arabian Nights and Days*, 1982).

Despite being Egypt's most popular writer and a national institution, Maḥfūẓ's views did not meet with everyone's approval, and in 1994 he narrowly survived an attempt on his life when he was stabbed by an unidentified attacker, thought to be a religious fundamentalist. The attack had a huge impact on his health and all but ended his writing career.

Thanks to the Nobel Prize, Maḥfūẓ was the first Arab author to gain popularity in the West, and nearly all his books have been translated into many languages.

The current story is taken from the collection رَأَيتُ فيما يَرى النائِم (*I Saw, in a Dream*, 1982) and is a typical example of Maḥfūẓ's fascination with magical realism. A tale of conjoined Siamese twins is turned almost into a kind of tragic comedy. The descriptions of each twin, their preoccupations and moods, bear witness to Maḥfūẓ's vivid imagination and creative prowess. In more ways than one the story may also be regarded as an allegory of the relationship between individuals whose lives are inextricably (literally, in this case) linked with one another, and the contradictions and struggles that ensue from that bond.

قسمتي ونصيبي [1]

Qismati and Nasibi

God had given Mohsen Khalil, the spice seller, everything his heart desired, except, that is, children. Many years went by, and still there were no children. Yet Mohsen Khalil tried very hard to be satisfied with what God had chosen to bestow upon him.

He was of medium height, which was fitting for one who believed in moderation in all things. He was overweight, but maintained that this was an attractive feature in both men and women, as well as a sign of prosperity. He was proud of his huge nose, his strong jawline and the mutual love that existed between him and other people.

Fate had smiled upon him by granting him Sitt Anabaya. In addition to being an excellent housewife, she was a buxom, fresh-looking beauty with luscious, rosy skin.

Chickens, geese and rabbits roamed freely atop their one-storey house. Devotees of Sitt Anabaya's cooking never ceased to wax lyrical about her splendid dishes and pastries made with lashings of traditional butter.

Life had been good to the couple in every respect, except in stubbornly denying them the joy of having children. They had tried everything, but to no avail. Sitt Anabaya had sought the advice of loved ones as well as fortune-tellers, soothsayers and the like. She even visited shrines. Eventually, she went to see medical doctors. Unfortunately, their verdict was not encouraging in that the problem lay with both husband and wife. They added that there was hardly any hope left for them. And so, a dark cloud of sadness settled above the couple.

But just as Mohsen approached his forty-fifth birthday and Sitt Anabaya turned forty, their prayers were finally answered. When Sitt Anabaya was certain she was pregnant, she cried out: "Thank God and Sidi al-Kurdi, I'm pregnant!"

Mohsen was overjoyed and full of gratitude. The news soon circulated throughout al-Wayliya, the area near the Abbasiyya district where the couple lived and where Mohsen had his shop.

عمّ[2] محسن خليل العطار[3] أجزل الله له العطاء فيما يحب ويتمنى[4] ماعدا الذرية[5]. دهر[6] طويل مضى دون أن ينجب مع مجاهدة للنفس لترضى بما وهب الله وبما منع[7].

كان متوسط القامة ممن يؤمنون بأن الخير في الوسط. كان بديناً وعنده أن البدانة للرجل كما للمرأة زينة وأبّهة[8]. وكان يزهو بأنفه الضخم وشدقيه القويين وبالحب المتبادل بينه وبين الناس.

وحباه الحظ[9] بست[10] عنباية ذات الحسن والنضارة والطيات المتراكمة من اللحم الوردي الناعم، إلى كونها[11] ست بيت ممتازة.

يغني سطح بيتها المكوّن من دور واحد بالدجاج والإوزّ والأرانب، ويلهج عشاق مائدتها بطواجنها[12] المعمرة وفطائرها[13] السابحة[14] في السمن البلدي[15].

دنيا مقبلة في كلّ شيء ولكنها ضنّت بنعمة الإنجاب في عناد تطايرت دونه الحيل. نشدت شورى[16] الأحبة، ولجأت إلى أهل الله[17] من العارفين والواصلين[18]، وطافت بالأضرحة[19] المباركة، حتى الأطباء زارتهم ولكنهم أصدروا فتوى غير مبشرة شملت الزوجين معاً عمّ محسن وست عنباية وقالوا إن الأمل الباقي أضعف من أن يذكر. ووقفت في سماء النعيم الصافية غمامة حزن مترعة بالحسرة لا تريد أن تتزحزح.

ولما شارف عمّ محسن الخامسة والأربعين وست عنباية الأربعين تلقيا من الله رحمة. هتفت ست عنباية بعد تدقيق وعناية «يا ألطاف الله[20]! إني حامل وحق[21] سيدي الكردي[22]!».

كان عمّ محسن أول من طرب وشكر. وتردد الخبر في الوايلية[23] على حدود العباسية[24] حيث يوجد بيت الأسرة ومحل العطارة.

The wondrous nine months of waiting finally passed, and then came the hour of childbirth, with the cries of labour turning into a chant of joy for the couple.

As soon as the midwife picked up the baby, she stared at the infant in astonishment and bewilderment, and began to intone the traditional religious formulae. She hurried to the luxurious east wing of the clinic to look for Mohsen. When he saw the anxious look on the midwife's face, he murmured in a worried tone:

"May God have mercy on us! What's happened?"

She hesitated, and whispered: "It's a strange creature, Mr Mohsen."

"What do you mean?"

"The lower body is joined, but the upper half is split!"

"No!"

"Come and see for yourself."

"How is Sitt Anabaya doing?"

"She is fine, but unaware of what is going on around her."

Filled with anxiety and disappointment, Mohsen rushed towards the baby. He stared at the strange creature, the bottom half of which was indeed joined, with two legs and an abdomen, whereas the top half consisted of two parts, each with its own chest, neck, head and face. The twins were screaming together, as if each of them was protesting against his situation or demanding complete independence and freedom. Mohsen was overwhelmed by a variety of emotions – confusion, bewilderment, embarrassment, a sense of foreboding about the problems that lay in store – all of which gathered around him like dark, heavy clouds.

Inwardly, he began to repeat the traditional phrase that he normally used in business after a failed deal: "May God grant me profit!"

Indeed, he wished it were possible to get rid of this defect, so that he could have peace of mind. Going about her routine

وانقضت الأشهر التسعة في انتظار بهيج، وجاء المخاض٢٥ يهزج بالأنين السعيد.

ولما تلقت الحكيمة٢٦ الوليد حملقت فيه مذهولة مبهوتة. وراحت تبسمل٢٧ وتحوقل. وهرعت إلى الصالة الشرقية الوثيرة فوقفت أمام عم محسن مضطربة حتى تمتم الرجل خافق القلب:

– ربنا يلطف بنا٢٨، ماذا وراءك؟

همست بعد تردد:

– مخلوق عجيب يا عم محسن.

– كيف؟

– أسفله موحد وأعلاه يتفرع إلى اثنين !

– لا !

– تعال انظر بنفسك.

– وكيف حال الست؟

– بخير ولكنها غائبة عما حولها!

وذهب في أثرها مضطرباً خائب الرجاء. وحملق في المخلوق العجيب. رأى أسفله موحّداً ذا رجلين وبطن واحد، ثم يتفرع بعد ذلك إلى اثنين لكل منهما صدره وعنقه ورأسه ووجهه. وكانا يصرخان معاً وكأنَّ كلاً منهما يحتج على وضعه أو يطالب باستقلاله الكامل وحريته الشرعية. هيمن على الرجل شعور بالارتباك والحيرة والخجل وحدس المتاعب تتجمع فوقه كالسحب المليئة بالغبار.

وترددت في داخله العبارة التجارية التقليدية التي يحسم بها الموقف عند فشل صفقة من صفقات العطارة وهي «يفتح الله»٢٩. أجل ودّ لو في الإمكان التخلص من هذه العاهة٣٠ التي لن يذوق معها راحة البال. وقالت

duties, the midwife said:

"The baby's in good health. All vital functions are totally normal."

Mohsen retorted: "Both of them?"

Confused, the midwife said: "They are not twins; this is *one* baby!"

Mohsen wiped the sweat that had appeared on his face and forehead as a result of his inner turmoil as well as the summer heat, and asked: "Why can't we consider them two babies?"

"How can there be two of them when it is impossible to separate one from the other!"

"It is indeed a problem. I wish it had never been born."

The midwife said, in a preaching tone: "Whatever the case may be, it is God's gift, and it is unwise to question His wisdom."

Mohsen sought forgiveness from God. The midwife continued:

"I will register the baby as one person."

Mohsen sighed, and said: "We will become a laughing stock, and the talk of the town!"

"Patience is a virtue!"

"But wouldn't it be better to consider the child as two, with a single abdomen?"

"He can't deal with life except as a single person."

They stood in silence, exchanging glances, until she asked him:

"What do you want to call him?"

As he kept silent, she said: "Muhammadayn! Do you think this is a suitable name?"

He did not utter a word, shaking his head in resignation.

Sitt Anabaya was shocked when she realized what was going on. She wept for many hours until her beautiful eyes were all red. She felt just like her husband. However, this situation did

الحكيمة وهي مستغرقة في عملها الروتيني:

– صحة جيدة، كأن كلّ شيء طبيعي تماماً...

فتساءل عم محسن خليل:

– الاثنان؟

فقالت الحكيمة بحيرة:

– ليسا توأمين... هذا وليد واحد!

فجفّف الرجل عرق وجهه وجبينه المتصبب من داخله ومن جو الصيف وتساءل:

– ولم لا نعتبرهما اثنين؟

– كيف يكونان اثنين على حين أن انفصال جزء عن الجزء الآخر مستحيل!

– إنها مشكلة، ليتها لم تكن أصلاً!

فقالت الحكيمة بلهجة وعظية:

– إنه منحة من الله على أي حال ولا يجوز الاعتراض على حكمته...

فاستغفر الرجل ربه فواصلت الحكيمة:

– سأسجله باعتباره واحداً.

فتنهد عم محسن قائلاً:

– سنصبح أحدوثة ونادرة!

– الصبر جميل!

– ألا يستحسن اعتباره اثنين ذوي بطن واحد؟

– لا يمكن أن يتعامل مع الحياة إلا كشخص واحد.

وتبادلا النظر صامتين حتى سألته:

– ماذا تسميه؟

ولما لازم الصمت تساءلت:

– محمدين[31] !... ما رأيك في هذا الاسم المناسب؟

فهز رأسه مستسلماً دون أن ينبس[32]. ولما انتبهت ست عنباية لما حولها صعقت، وبكت طويلاً حتى احمرّت عيناها الجميلتان. وشاركت زوجها

not last long, as both Sitt Anabaya and her husband responded to their parental instincts.

She started breastfeeding the baby on the right, and when the crying stopped, she fed the one on the left. Instinctively, she started calling the baby on the right "Qismati" and the one on the left "Nasibi", as these were the two names by which the newborn had been called since the first week.

Each child had his own individual personality; Qismati would be asleep while Nasibi remained awake, babbling, crying or suckling. As time went by, the astonishment waned, except outside the home. What was once odd and weird soon became familiar.

Both Qismati and Nasibi received their fair share of care, love and tenderness.

When family members came to visit, the mother would say: "No matter what, he is my son," or, "They are my sons."

As for Mohsen, he began to reiterate the phrase: "Ours is not to question the wisdom of God!"

Realizing that childhood does not last long, he thought about the future with worry and trepidation. Sitt Anabaya, for her part, was completely absorbed by her twin burden, as she had to breastfeed, change and raise not one but two children. She had to control her nerves when one of them slept and needed silence, while the other woke up and wanted to play.

Thank God, they had different features; Qismati had a deep brown complexion, with soft lineaments and hazel eyes, while Nasibi had a white complexion with black eyes and a large nose.

The twins began to crawl about on their two feet and four hands, uttering one word after another, and trying to walk. It became clear that Qismati learned to speak more quickly, but had to yield to Nasibi when it came to crawling and walking, or playing with things and destroying them.

Nasibi remained the dominant one in their early years,

عواطفه. غير أن ذلك لم يستمر طويلاً فاستجابت ست عنباية في النهاية إلى عاطفة الأمومة وعم محسن للأبوة. وراحت ترضع الأيمن فما سكت البكاء حتى أرضعت الأيسر. وبعفوية جعلت تنادي الأيمن بقسمتي والأيسر بنصيبي فمنذ الأسبوع الأول عرف الوليد باسمين.

وتميز كلّ بفردية فربما نام قسمتي وظل نصيبي صاحياً يتناغى أو يبكي أو يرضع. ومع الزمن خفّت الدهشة وإن لم تخف أصداؤها في الخارج، وألفت الغرابة، وزالت الوحشة.

ونال قسمتي ونصيبي حظهما الكامل من الرعاية والحب والحنان. ومضت الأم تقول للزائرات من أهلها:

– ليكن من أمره ما يكون فهو ابني، أو هما ابناي.

واعتاد الحاج محسن– فقد أدى الفريضة٣٣ بعد التجربة– أن يقول:

– لله حكمته!

وعلم بفطرته أن الطفولة ستمر كدعابة ولكنه فكر في المستقبل بقلق واختناق. أما ست عنباية فاستغرقتها متاعبها المضاعفة. كان عليها أن ترضع اثنين، وأن تنظف اثنين، وأن تربي اثنين. وأن تملك أعصابها إذا نام أحدهما واحتاج للهدوء وصحا الآخر ورغب في الملاعبة. واختلفت بقدرة قادر٣٤ صورتاهما، فبدا قسمتي عميق السمرة رقيق الملامح عسليّ العينين، أما نصيبي فكان ذا بشرة قمحية وعينين سوداوين وأنف ينذر بالضخامة. وأخذ الوليد يحبو على القدمين وأربع أيد، وينطق كلمة بعد أخرى، ويحاول المشي. ولوحظ أن قسمتي كان أسرع في تعلم النطق ولكنه كان يذعن لمشيئة نصيبي في الحبو والمشي، وفي العبث بالأشياء وتحطيمها. لبثت القيادة طيلة تلك الفترة المبكرة بيدي نصيبي واتسمت بالعفرتة٣٥

which were marked by naughtiness, destruction, the chasing of chickens and the torturing of cats. Thanks to Qismati's submissiveness to Nasibi, the boys did not quarrel, except on those rare occasions when Qismati would want to rest and Nasibi would prod him with his elbow, making Qismati cry continuously.

When they turned four, or just afterwards, they began looking out the window at the children outside. They would raise their eyes towards the sky from the rooftop and ask a multitude of questions:

"Why does each boy have only one head?"

Confused, Sitt Anabaya answered: "God creates people the way He sees fit."

"Always God ... God ... Where is He, this God?"

Mohsen answered: "He sees us, but we do not see Him. He can do anything, and woe unto those who disobey Him!" He told them what they needed to do in order to gain His approval. Qismati grew worried and told Nasibi:

"Listen to *me*, or I will hit you ..."

They would watch the moon during the summer nights, and extend their arms towards it. While Qismati sighed with resignation, Nasibi would erupt with anger. This prompted Mohsen Khalil to ask:

"Do we imprison them in the house forever?"

Sitt Anabaya said: "I am worried they'll be abused by other children ..."

Hajj Mohsen decided to carry out an experiment. He sat on the doorstep of the house on a wicker chair, and placed his children on another chair beside him. Children of all ages soon gathered around them to take a closer look at the strange creature, and no manner of rebuke or reprimand could stop them. The father had no alternative but to pick them up and carry them back into the house, whispering with grief: "The problems have started."

والتدمير ومطاردة الدجاج وإيذاء القطط، غير أن خضوع قسمتي لنصيبي أعفاهما من الشجار عدا الأويقات[36] النادرة التي كان يميل فيها قسمتي للراحة فلا يتورع نصيبي عن لكزة بكوعه حتى يسترسل في البكاء. ولما بلغا الرابعة من العمر وجاوزاها، أخذا ينظران إلى الطريق من النافذة ويشاهدان الأطفال، ويرفعان أعينهما نحو السماء من فوق السطح فانهمرت الأسئلة مع اللعاب:

− كلّ ولد ذو رأس واحد، لماذا؟

فتجيب ست عنباية مرتبكة:

− ربنا يخلق الناس كما يشاء...

− دائماً ربنا. ربنا. أين هو؟

فيجيب عم محسن:

− هو يرانا ونحن لا نراه وهو قادر على كلّ شيء، والويل[37] لمن يعصيه! ويحدّثهما الرجل عما يجب ليحوزا رضاه فيخاف قسمتي ويقول نصيبي لقسمتي:

− اسمع كلامي أنا وإلا ضربتك...

ويريان القمر في ليال الصيف فيمدان نحوه أيديهما. يتنهد قسمتي مغلوباً على امره ويثور نصيبي غاضباً. ويتساءل الحاج:

− هل نحبسهما في البيت إلى ما شاء الله[38]؟

فتقول ست عنباية:

− أخاف عليهما عبث الأطفال...

وقرّر الحاج أن يقوم بتجربة فجلس أمام البيت على كرسي خيزران[39] وأجلسهما إلى جانبه على كرسي آخر. سرعان ما تجمّع الصغار من مختلف الأعمار ليتفرجوا على المخلوق العجيب ولم ينفع معهم زجر أو نهر حتى اضطر الرجل أن ينسحب من مجلسه وهو يحملهما على ذراعه، وتمتم في أسى:

− بدأت المتاعب.

However, an idea came to Sitt Anabaya by divine inspiration. She suggested that she could convince her neighbour to send her son Tariq and daughter Samiha to play with Muhammadayn. The neighbour, Mashkura, agreed. So Tariq and Samiha came over; Tariq was a year older than Muhammadayn, whereas Samiha was the same age.

At first, they panicked and did not want to become friends with Muhammadayn. Sitt Anabaya bribed them with presents until they became used to them. The neighbour's children were also led by their curiosity and sense of adventure.

In the end, Qismati and Nasibi were pleased with their new playmates, but the fact that they greatly loved having them around did not mean that their love was returned.

They talked about many things, played various games and invented lots of stories. And so, they found others to whom they could throw their football and with whom they could play tug-of-war.

Samiha became the object of their desire, with each of them wanting to keep her for himself. When they watched television, they would argue about who would sit next to her.

It was because of Samiha that they had their first real fight in front of their family, which led to a bloody lip for Qismati and black eyes for Nasibi. This incident marked Qismati's freedom from Nasibi; thenceforth, he felt an individual in his own right. From that moment on, both of them could agree and disagree.

One day, Hajj Mohsen said: "They are now at an age that they should go to school." Sitt Anabaya frowned, her face showing the guilt she felt inside. Then he said: "This is not open to discussion!" After thinking for a long time, he added: "I will bring them teachers. They should at least learn to count so that they can take my place in the shop."

Teachers came and instructed the boys in the basics of religion, language and mathematics. Qismati's response to learning was very encouraging. Nasibi, on the other hand, had

ولكنّ الله فتح على ست عنباية بفكرة فاقترحت أن تقنع جارتها بإرسال ابنها طارق وبنتها سميحة للعب مع محمدين. ووافقت الجارة مشكورة فجاء طارق وسميحة، وكان طارق أكبر من محمدين بعام أما سميحة فكانت تماثله في عمره.

وقد فزعا أول الأمر ونفرا من الصحبة غير أن ست عنباية استرضتهما بالهدايا حتى زايلتهما الوحشة وجرفهما حب الاستطلاع والمغامرة.

وسعد قسمتي ونصيبي بالرفيقين الجديدين، وأحبا حضورهما حباً فاق كلّ تقدير، رغم أنه لم يفز بحب في مثل قوته. وتنوع الحديث واللعب وابتكرت الحكايات. وجدت الكرة الصغيرة من يتبادل رميها، ووجد الحبل من يتصارع على شدّه، وباتت سميحة هدفاً وردياً كلّ يرغب في الاستحواذ عليه، وكل يدعوها إلى الجلوس إلى جانبه إذا جمعهم التلفزيون. وبسبب سميحة نشبت بينهما أول معركة حقيقية على ملأ من[٤٠] الأسرة، فدميت شفة نصيبي وورمت عين قسمتي، وبها تحرر قسمتي من الذوبان في نصيبي وأخذ يشعر بأنه فرد بإزاء آخر فتبادلا من الآن فصاعداً التوافق كما تبادلا التنافر. وقال الحاج ذات يوم:

ـ جاءت السن المناسبة للمدرسة.

فتجهّم وجه عنباية وارتسم في أساريره الشعور بالذنب فقال الحاج:

ـ إنه باب مغلق[٤١]!

وتفكر ملياً ثم قال:

ـ سأجيء لهما بالمعلمين، يجب أن يعدا على الأقل ليحلا محلي في الدكان...

وجاء المعلمون، ولقنوهما مبادئ الدين واللغة والحساب. واستجاب قسمتي للتعلم بدرجة مشجعة أما نصيبي فبدا راغباً عن العلم متعثراً في الفهم

no desire to learn, and hence was slower in his understanding. As a result, he resented his brother and disturbed classes by singing, playing and childish teasing. The difference was especially irritating during the religious education classes, which Qismati took to with enthusiasm while Nasibi displayed total indifference. The teacher was doubly annoyed by Nasibi's stubbornness. Mohsen reprimanded Nasibi on many occasions, but could not bring himself to hit him.

At the age of eight, Qismati wanted to pray and fast, and despite the fact that Nasibi was not interested, the latter found himself participating in the ablutions to a great extent, while being more or less forced to bow and prostrate. Realizing the weakness of his position, he had no choice but to resign himself to the facts. At the same time, he became consumed with anger.

Nasibi was ordered by his father to fast, but he tried to break his fast in secrecy in order to allay his hunger. Qismati, however, was quick to protest, saying: "Don't forget that we share one abdomen. If you take a single morsel, I'll tell Father." Nasibi was patient on that occasion, but it did not last, and he started to cry. His mother took pity on him, and told her husband:

"'God only demands of a soul what it can bear.' Let the boy be until he's one or two years older."

Confused, the father replied: "If he breaks his fast, he will break the fast of the other as well!"

The problem was only solved by the Imam of the Sidi al-Kurdi mosque, who claimed that it was the intention that counted. So Qismati's fast was lawful even if it was broken by Nasibi. And so Qismati continued to fast even if Nasibi did not.

Each of them had now developed his own personality. They increasingly grew to dislike one another, and the moments in which they got on became few and far between. Tearfully, their mother said: "My God, they cannot stand each other, yet neither can live without the other. How can they go through life like this?"

والاستيعاب، ومن أجل ذلك حنق على الآخر، وكدّر ساعات مذاكرته
بالعبث والغناء والمعاكسات الصبيانية، وبدا الخلاف مزعجاً في تقبل التربية
الدينية التي أقبل عليها قسمتي بقلب مفتوح على حين وقف فيها نصيبي
موقف اللامبالاة. وضاعف زجر المعلم من عناده، ونهره أبوه كثيراً ولكنه
أشفق من ضربه.

وعند بلوغ الثامنة أراد قسمتي أن يصلّي ويصوم. ومع أن نصيبي لم يمل
إلى ذلك إلا أنه وجد نفسه يشارك بقدر لا يستهان به⁴² في الوضوء، وأنه
يركع تقريباً على الركوع⁴³ والسجود⁴⁴. ولشعوره بضعف مركزه أذعن
للواقع وهو يمتلئ حنقاً وغيظاً. وأمره أبوه بالصيام، وحاول أن يشبع جوعه
في الخفاء ولكنّ قسمتي احتج قائلاً:

– لا تنس أن بطننا واحد، وإذا تناولت لقمة واحدة أخبرت أبي...

وصبر يومه حتى نفد صبره فبكى فرقّت له أمه وقالت للحاج:

– الله لا يكلّف نفساً إلا وسعها⁴⁵، دعه حتى يكبر عاماً أو عامين.

فقال الأب في حيرة:

– ولكنه إذا أفطر أفطر الآخر!

وهي مشكلة لم يحلها إلا إمام سيدي الكردي فقال إن العبرة بالنية
وأن صيام قسمتي صحيح حتى لو أفطر نصيبي. وصام قسمتي رغم إفطار
نصيبي مستنداً إلى نيته أولاً وأخيراً. وتوكد لكل شخصيته، وحال بينهما
نفور دائم آخذ في الاستفحال، وندرت بينهما أوقات الصفاء. وقالت الأم
بعين دامعة:

– يا ويلي، لا يطيق أحدهما الآخر، ولا غنى لأحدهما عن الآخر،
فكيف تمضي بهما الحياة؟!

She went through hard times as the twins argued about everything and anything. Qismati loved cleanliness, while Nasibi hated the very idea of bathing unless he was obliged to do so. Their parents mediated between them, asking Qismati to give up some of the cleanliness while in exchange Nasibi would become a lot less dirty.

Nasibi was a glutton and never had enough, which caused Qismati indigestion.

Qismati was fond of love songs, while Nasibi loved loud music. The major source of disagreement, however, was caused by Qismati's increasing love of reading and knowledge. When Qismati was reading, Nasibi preferred playing out on the terrace and annoying passers-by and neighbours.

Nasibi could tolerate Qismati's reading for a while, but then he would spoil his concentration, after which they would engage in a fight that usually ended in victory for Nasibi. Qismati would try to use negotiation rather than senseless violence: "I've got my hobbies and you've got yours; but my hobbies are more suited to our unnatural circumstances."

Nasibi replied, severely: "This means that life will become a permanent prison."

"But we have no part in the outside world."

"On the outside, there's happiness, whereas in this room there's only grief."

"You always annoy people, and so they mock us."

"I can't but behave like that. I am even thinking about flaunting myself in the street."

"You will turn us into a laughing stock."

At this point, Nasibi shouted: "I hate being imprisoned. I envy the stars."

Qismati replied, derisively: "You're out of your mind."

Nasibi's reply came fast and hard: "There's no way we can ever agree."

مضت على الشوك، وشمل الخلاف أشياء وأشياء. قسمتي يحب النظافة ونصيبي يكره فكرة الاستحمام إلا أن يضطر إليه اضطراراً، وتوسط الوالدان على أن ينزل قسمتي عن شيء من النظافة نظير أن ينزل نصيبي عن كثير من القذارة.

ونصيبي نهم لا يشبع فكثيراً ما كان يصاب قسمتي بالتخمة. ولقسمتي ولع بالأغاني العاطفية على حين يعشق نصيبي الأناشيد الصاخبة. أما ذروة الخصام فقد احتدمت لحب قسمتي النامي للقراءة والاطلاع، يحب أن يقرأ كثيراً والآخر يفضل اللعب فوق السطح ومعاكسة السابلة والجيران. ونصيبي يمكن أن يصبر ساعة على إنهماك الآخر في القراءة ولكنه عند الضرورة يعرف كيف يفسد عليه تركيزه واستغراقه حتى يشتبكا في معركة تسفر عادة عن أنتصار نصيبي. وقال له قسمتي مجرباً المناقشة بدلاً من العنف غير المجدي:

– لي هواياتي ولك هواياتك ولكنّ هواياتي أنسب لظروفنا غير الطبيعية.

فقال نصيبي بحدة:

– معنى ذلك أن تتحول الحياة إلى سجن دائم.

– لكنّ لا نصيب لنا في الدنيا الخارجية.

– السعادة في الدنيا والكآبة في الحجرة.

فقال قسمتي:

– إنك تعاكس الناس فينهالون علينا بالسخرية.

– أموت لو فعلت غير ذلك. بل إني أفكر في اقتحام الطريق.

– ستجعل منا أضحوكة وفرجة...

فصاح نصيبي:

– إني أكره السجن وأحسد النجوم.

فقال قسمتي برجاء:

– يلزمك الكثير من العقل.

فقال نصيبي بازدراء:

– لا سبيل إلى الاتفاق.

"But as you can see, we're one, despite the fact that there's two of us!"

"That's the problem! But you have to submit to me without resisting."

"You're stubborn and you love to argue."

Their parents called them into the living room for a meeting. They no longer had any peace of mind, and their happiness was ruined. They believed that tragedy would strike the household if they did not remedy the situation quickly. Sitt Anabaya kissed them both, and said: "You have to love each other; if you do, all problems will vanish."

Nasibi said: "He's the one who hates me!"

But Qismati retorted: "You're the one who hates *me*!"

Despondently, Sitt Anabaya said: "You're two in one, inseparable, and there must be love."

Hajj Mohsen then said: "Reason demands that you get on, otherwise your life will become hell. It is not acceptable for one of you to oppress the other. It is possible to live together in harmony. Nasibi should be patient when Qismati wants to read, and in return Qismati should willingly agree to play with Nasibi. You also have to accept to listen to different kinds of songs so that each can enjoy his favourite music. As for religion, that's not open for discussion!"

Qismati said: "I'm all in favour of harmony, even if it will cost me dearly." Nasibi kept silent, and Qismati added: "He's the one who doesn't like harmony, nor will he be ready for the day you ask us to work in the shop!"

The father replied firmly: "There's no escape from the unavoidable!"

Sitt Anabaya implored with vehemence:

– لكننا واحد كما ترى رغم أننا اثنان!

– هذه هي المصيبة ولكنّ عليك أن تذعن لي دون مقاومة.

– إنك عنيد وتحب الخصام.

ودعاهما الوالدان إلى الاجتماع في حجرة المعيشة. حقاً إنهما فقدا الشعور براحة البال وتنغص عليهما صفوهما. وآمنا بأن كارثة ستحل بالبيت إن لم يسارعا إلى حسم الداء. قبلتهما عنباية وقالت:

– فليحب أحدكما الآخر، إن وجد الحب تلاشت المشاكل!

فقال نصيبي:

– هو الذي يكرهني!

ولكنّ قسمتي بادره قائلاً:

– بل أنت الذي تكرهني!

فقالت ست عنباية متأوهة:

– إنكما اثنان في واحد لا يتجزأ ولا بد من الحب.

وقال الحاج محسن خليل:

– الحكمة تطالبكما بالوفاق وإلا انقلبت الحياة جحيماً لا يطاق، ذوبان أحدكما في الآخر مرفوض، والوفاق ممكن، فليصبر نصيبي عندما يرغب قسمتي في القراءة، وفي مقابل ذلك على قسمتي أن يرحب بالحركة واللعب مع نصيبي، وليكن كلّ غناء مقبولاً ليستمتع كلّ بأغانيه المفضلة، أما الدين فلا مناقشة فيه.

فقال قسمتي:

– إني على استعداد طيب للوفاق رغم ما يكلفني من ضيق.

ولاذ نصيبي بالصمت فرجع قسمتي يقول:

– إنه لا يحب الوفاق، ولا يعد نفسه ليوم تدعونا فيه إلى العمل في الدكان!

فقال الأب بحزم:

– لا بد مما ليس منه بد!

وعادت ست عنباية تقول بحرارة وضراعة:

"You must love each other, as this is your salvation."

However, the parents still did not have any peace of mind. They looked on, fraught with worry and grief.

Nasibi hesitantly tried to change for the sake of harmony, which involved a constant fight to overcome his indomitable instincts. Qismati, for his part, embarked upon the new path with greater determination and will in order to put an end to his ordeal, appealing to his parents for help when necessary.

As they reached the age of reason and were on the verge of adolescence, their problems reached a peak. Their suppressed dreams began to manifest themselves, threatening to explode. Each of them developed his own way of thinking, and regarded the other as a threatening intruder, an enemy that must be defeated. They were both fed up with the hateful unity that fate had inflicted upon them and from which there was no escape. They would clash in a vortex of fiery and crazed outbursts. A raging wave would emerge from the depths, removing any sense of shame, while impetuosity superseded regret.

Their anger would grow and they engaged in battle, exchanging the harshest of blows. Afterwards the hostilities would die away, with the combatants becoming immersed in silence and distress. This lasted for a long time, until Qismati said: "Because of this curse, life cannot go on peacefully."

Calmly but petulantly, Nasibi replied: "But it will go on like this anyway!"

Qismati's hazel eyes grew darker, and he said: "We're condemned to be without the harmony that the rest of mankind enjoys."

"You're sick, and so are your ideas."

Qismati replied sarcastically: "It is clear that one of us is sick."

Defiantly, Nasibi retorted: "I will no longer give up any of my rights. There will be no more truce from now on."

"But I've got rights, too!"

– عليكما بالحب ففي رحمته النجاة.

ولكنّ الوالدين لم يصفُ لهما بال. وتابعا ما يحدث بقلق وأسى.

وبذَل نصيبي في سبيل الوفاق جهداً متردداً لغلبة الأهواء الجامحة عليه على حين مضى قسمتي في الطريق الجديد بإرادة أقوى ورغبة أنقى مستأنساً بعواطفه الصادقة وميله المخلص لوضع حد لعذاباته، ومستعيناً عند الضرورة بوالديه. ولما ناهزا الحلم وشارفا المراهقة تصاعدت أزمتهما إلى الذروة. احتدمت الأحلام المكبوتة منذرة بالانفجار. وتبلورت لكل منهما ذاتية مستقلة فبدا الآخر غريباً مهدداً للأمن، وعدواً يجب أن يقهر. ضاق كلّ منهما بالرابطة القدرية[٤] التي فرضت عليهما وحدة كريهة لا فكاك منها. وتلاطما في دوامة من الانفعالات المحرقة الجنونية. وفارت من الأعماق موجة عمياء جرفت ستر الحياء، فارتطم الاندفاع بالندم، واشتعل الغضب فانخرط الاثنان في معركة وتبادلا الضربات القاسية. وهمدت الحركة غائصة في الصمت والشجن. استمرت فترة غير قصيرة إلى أن قال قسمتي:

– إنها لعنة لا يمكن أن تمضي معها الحياة في سلام...

فقال نصيبي بهدوء عنيد:

– لكنها ستمضي في طريقها على أي حال!

فأظلمت عينا قسمتي العسليتان وقال:

– قُضي علينا بالحرمان من الانسجام الذي تحظى به جميع المخلوقات...

– إنك مريض ذو أفكار مريضة...

فقال قسمتي بسخرية:

– أحدنا مريض ولاشك!

– فقال نصيبي بتحدٍّ:

– لن أنزل عن حق من حقوقي... فلا مهادنة بعد الآن.

– لي أيضاً حقوقي.

They looked at each other, defiantly, sorrowfully. All dialogue thus ended on the worst possible terms.

It was then that they saw Samiha, their childhood friend, in a new light. From the window, they would watch her come and go, either on her own or in the company of her mother, which awakened past memories that soon faded.

That day, however, they saw another Samiha. The flush of youth had matured her, adding even more radiance and increasing her desirability. Qismati got drunk on the nectar of temptation, while Nasibi's wild imagination got the better of him. Qismati's heart was touched by a ray of beauty, just as a flower is touched by a ray of sunlight and opened up by it. He wished she were next to him, instead of that wretched Nasibi, and for the first time he felt that Nasibi was not only a physical burden but also an insurmountable obstacle to his true happiness.

Nasibi continued to shake his head in bewilderment, and when he saw the girl waiting next to the entrance of her house, he rushed to the street, dragging Qismati with him. Samiha saw them shooting across the street, then took a few steps back and smiled. Nasibi lunged towards her, extending his hands to her chest, which caused her to panic and run inside her house. This animalistic attack drew the attention of some passers-by in Wayliya Street, and so they returned home, with Qismati berating and cursing Nasibi, who had come to his senses and grown quite submissive.

Qismati's fury bore down heavily on his brother: "This is scandalous! You're nothing but a lunatic ...!"

Nasibi was at a loss, and did not reply. Their mother knew what had happened, and was distressed. When Qismati told her the truth, she said to Nasibi: "You will destroy yourself one day ..."

Qismati lashed out: "And he will destroy me along with him, through no fault of mine!"

Nasibi said, boldly: "We need a wife!" The mother was

وتبادلا نظرة متحدية وبائسة، فانقطعا عن الحوار على أسوأ حال.

وفي ذلك الوقت رأيا سميحة زميلة الطفولة بعين جديدة. كانا يريانها من النافذة وهي تذهب وتجيء منفردة أو بصحبة أمها فتوقظ ذكرى عابرة ثم تختفي. أما ذلك اليوم فرأياها بعين جديدة. رأياها وقد أنضجتها شعلة الصبا فأضفت عليها بهاء وأثرتها بشهد الرغبة. أترع قلب قسمتي برحيق الفتنة فثمل على حين جنّ نصيبي بالأخيلة الجامحة. تلقى قلب قسمتي شعاع الحسن كما يتلقى البرعم شعاع الشمس فيتفتح. تمنى لو تحل محل نصيبي من وجوده التعيس، ولأول مرة يشعر بأن نصيبي ليس قيداً فحسب ولكنه سدّ منيع في طريق السعادة الحقيقية. أما نصيبي فظل رأسه يتحرك في اضطراب، ولما وجد الفتاة واقفة من مدخل بيتها تنتظر اندفع إلى الطريق جاراً معه قسمتي. مرق من الباب إلى الطريق فرأته سميحة فتراجعت مبتعدة باسمة. ولكنه اندفع نحوها مسدداً يديه إلى صدرها ففزعت ووثبت داخلة إلى بيتها. ولفتت الهجمة الحيوانية أنظار بعض المارة في شارع الوايلية ولكنّ قسمتي رجع إلى بيتهم بسرعة وهو يسب ويلعن والآخر مستسلم، له بعد إفاقة مباغتة. وغضب قسمتي وصاح به:

ـ إنها فضيحة وما أنت إلا مجنون.

فلم يجبه نصيبي مغلوباً على أمره. وعلمت الأم بما حدث فجزعت، ولما عرفت الحقيقة من قسمتي قالت للآخر:

ـ ستهلك نفسك ذات يوم.

فهتف قسمتي:

ـ وسوف يهلكني معه دون ذنب.

فقال نصيبي بجراءة:

astonished, at a loss for words. Nasibi continued:

"Since you gave birth to us, you're responsible for getting us married to a nice girl."

Qismati said: "No girl will agree to marry both of us!"

Nasibi replied, defiantly: "Then look for two wives for us!"

Qismati replied, with sadness: "We are doomed to live by ourselves!"

Nasibi said: "Then let us consider ourselves a single individual, as this is, after all, how we are registered on the birth certificate."

Ruefully, Qismati retorted: "An object of fun, not for marriage."

Their mother was unable to stay in the room: "The Hajj may have the solution!"

Nasibi erupted in anger, and said to his brother: "The only solution is the one we find by ourselves. Let's wait until midnight, when there are fewer passers-by. Then we will go out into the darkness to look for prey."

Qismati shouted: "Your imagination is running wild!"

"Don't be a coward."

"Don't act like a madman!"

Hajj Mohsen said to his wife: "This issue has never been far from my mind, but there is no family that would happily offer us their daughter."

"So what's the solution?"

The father said, his voice fading away:

"A needy woman in her fifties will come and look after

– نحن في حاجة إلى زوجة!

فبهتت الأم ولم تدر ماذا تقول فواصل نصيبي:

– كما ولدتنا فإنك مسؤولة عن تزويجنا من بنت الحلال[47].

فقال قسمتي:

– لن توافق بنت على الزواج من اثنين!

فقال نصيبي بتحد:

– ابحثي لنا عن زوجتين:

فقال قسمتي بحزن:

– قُضي علينا أن نعيش وحيدين!

فقال نصيبي:

– فلنعتبر شخصاً واحداً كما نحن مسجلون في دفتر المواليد.

فقال قسمتي بأسى:

– شخص للفرجة[48] لا للزواج.

واضطرت الأم أن تغادر الحجرة وهي تقول:

– قد يكون عند الحاج الحل!

وثار غضب نصيبي، وقال للآخر:

– لا حل إذا لم نعثر عليه بأنفسنا، فلننتظر حتى ينتصف الليل ويندر المارة ثم ننطلق في الظلام وراء أي صيد يقع.

فهتف قسمتي

– خيال جنوني....

– لا تكن جباناً.

– لا تكن مجنوناً.

وقال الحاج محسن لزوجته:

– لم يغب عني هذا الموضوع، ولكنّ لا توجد أسرة ترضى بمصاهرتنا.

– والحل؟

فقال الرجل وصوته يخفض.

– ستجيء امرأة مسكينة في الحلقة الخامسة لتقوم على خدمتهما!

them!"

Such a wretched creature, in both looks and circumstance, indeed came to the house. They fed her and cleaned her up so as to make her agree to what they wanted her to do. This was followed by a period of calm, at least on the surface. In reality, Nasibi mistreated the woman during the daytime, to compensate for his nocturnal torments. Qismati, for his part, appeared gloomy and disgusted. He asked Nasibi: "What have I done to deserve this?"

Nasibi answered, fretfully: "Is it my fault, then?"

Qismati did not reply. He remembered Samiha, who had stolen his heart, and his suppressed emotions exacerbated his grief. The truth is that both of them felt lost and worthless, but neither felt the pain of the other. Quite the contrary! Each accused the other of being responsible for their hardship, and each wished he could get rid of the other at all cost.

Their father asked them to work with him in the shop, if only for the sake of experience, which they could not avoid. It was on a calm spring day that they started work. They were dressed in a pair of grey trousers and two white, short-sleeved shirts. Their hair was cut to an average length. Confused, they stood behind the counter. Very quickly, a crowd of customers and onlookers gathered, until half the street was blocked. Hajj Mohsen addressed his sons: "Just do your work, and don't pay any attention to the people."

However, Nasibi was gripped with anger, while Qismati's eyes were soon filled with tears. All of a sudden a press photographer made his way through the crowd and took a lot of pictures of the two brothers. In the afternoon, a representative from the television station arrived, seeking permission to interview the two young men. However, Hajj Mohsen resolutely refused, his voice betraying anger. When the pictures appeared in the morning papers, they drew even more onlookers to the shop, while sales dwindled. Hajj Mohsen was forced to prohibit them

و جاءت امرأة تعيسة الحال والمنظر، نشطوا إلى تغذيتها وتنظيفها لترضى بما يراد بها، وأعقب ذلك سكون ظاهري على الأقل، أما في الواقع فإن نصيبي كان يسيء معاملة المرأة نهاراً كتعويض عن اندفاعه الليلي، وأما قسمتي فبدا كئيباً مشمئزاً، وسأل الآخر:

– ما ذنبي أنا؟

فنهره نصيبي متسائلاً:

– وهل الذنب ذنبي؟!

لم يحر جواباً لكنه تذكر سميحة بقلبه المسلوب، وعواطفه المتأججة المحرومة فتضاعف أساه. والحق أن كليهما شعر بالضياع والهوان، ولكنّ لم يشعر أحدهما بتعاسة الآخر، وعلى العكس اتهمه بأنه المسؤول عن مأساته، وود لو يتخلص منه بأي ثمن. ودعاهما الأب للعمل في الدكان ولو كتجربة لا مفر من ممارستها. كان يوم حضورهما في الدكان يوماً معتدل المناخ من أيام الربيع. تجليا للأعين في بنطلون رمادي، وقميصين أبيضين نصف كم أما شعر رأسيهما فاستوى مشذباً متوسط الطول. وقفا وراء الطاولة مرتبكين. وسرعان ما تجمع كثيرون ما بين زبون ومتفرج حتى ازدحم الطريق إلى نصفه. وقال الحاج موجّهاً خطابه لابنيه:

– استغرقا في العمل ولا تباليا بالناس.

ولكنّ الغضب تملك نصيبي على حين دمعت عينا قسمتي. وإذا بمصور صحفي يشق طريقه بين الجموع ويلتقط العديد من الصور لمحمدين أو قسمتي ونصيبي. وفي النصف الثاني من النهار جاء مندوب من التلفزيون يستأذن في إجراء حوار مع الشابين، ولكنّ الحاج رفض بحزم وبنبرة شديدة الغضب. وبنشر الصور في الصحيفة الصباحية اشتد إقبال الناس وهبط البيع للدرجة الدنيا، فاضطر الحاج محسن خليل لمنعهما من الذهاب إلى الدكان،

from going to the shop. He told his wife, with sinking heart: "So, the business will die with me."

Nasibi exclaimed, in anger: "Why didn't you get rid of us at birth? Why didn't you show mercy on us, and on yourself?"

Hajj Mohsen said, deeply moved: "You will never know hardship, and your inheritance will allow you to lead a decent and dignified existence."

Nasibi shouted: "Money alone has no value; the reality is that we are both dead! How I wish I could work in the business, buy a car and marry four wives!"

Qismati said, in a sad voice: "I could have been a teacher, or gone into politics."

Nasibi looked at Qismati, and said furiously: "*You* are the obstacle in my way."

Qismati rebutted: "It's *you* who's the obstacle."

Hajj Mohsen exclaimed: "Why don't you accept reality and seek your happiness together?"

Qismati said: "If we had been born with a single head and two separate bottom halves, things would have been easy!"

Hajj Mohsen replied, imploringly: "Happiness is not hard to find for those who truly seek it!"

Qismati said, angrily: "This happiness is the reason for our misery!" Then he turned towards Nasibi, and said: "Stop being so arrogant. If you took a leaf out of my book, you'd become the best and happiest of men. If I followed you, prison would be our fate."

Nasibi replied, mockingly: "Nice try! But that will never

وقال لامرأته بقلب محزون:

– سوف تصفى التجارة عقب انتهاء الأجل[٤٩].

وعند ذلك تساءل نصيبي غاضباً:

– لم لم تتخلص منا عقب ولادتنا؟. لم لم ترحمنا وترحم نفسك؟.

فقال الحاج في تأثر شديد:

– لن تعرفا الضيم أبداً. وسترثان ما يحقق لكما الستر والكرامة.

فهتف نصيبي:

– لا قيمة للمال وحده، الواقع أننا ميتان، كم تمنيت أن أمارس التجارة

وأبتاع سيارة وأتزوج من أربع!

وقال قسمتي في حسرة:

– وعندي الاستعداد لأكون أستاذاً، وأمارس السياسة أيضاً.

ونظر نصيبي إلى قسمتي وقال بحنق:

– إنك العقبة التي تسدّ طريقي.

فقال قسمتي بإصرار:

– أنت أنت العقبة.

فتساءل الحاج:

– ألا تسلمان بالواقع وتسعيان إلى السعادة معاً؟

فقال قسمتي:

– لو خلقنا برأس وأسفلين منفصلين لهان الأمر!

فقال الحاج برجاء:

– لن تعز السعادة على من ينشدها بصدق.

فقال قسمتي بحنق:

– هذه السعادة هي سبب تعاستنا!

ثم التفت نحو نصيبي قائلاً:

– تخلّ عن عنجهيتك واتبعني تبلغ أقصى درجات الرفعة والسعادة، أما

لو تبعتك أنا فيكون مصيرنا السجن.

فقال نصيبي ساخراً:

work! We are completely different. I do not love knowledge; as for politics, if you elected a government, I would immediately side with the opposition, and vice versa. I will not follow you, and you will not follow me; the fighting will not subside."

Impatiently, the father said: "Try to live together in harmony again; it's the only way! It's your destiny, as is your union."

Reluctantly, they again attempted to avoid conflict and disagreement as much as they could. Each of them made an effort to put up with the other's presence, despite Qismati's hidden unease and Nasibi's inner scorn.

They seemed like two friends without a friendship, in an alliance without sincerity. They each lived half a life, and had half-hopes. However, age prematurely left its traces on Nasibi's face, revealing that he was rapidly approaching old age, perhaps as a result of his excesses in most things. He started to complain about a loss of libido, an allergy to drink, and indigestion. Neither herbal potions nor conventional medicine succeeded in improving his condition. In his pain, he expressed the suppressed rage he felt towards his brother, accusing him: "You were jealous of me, damn you!"

Qismati murmured, in a conciliatory tone: "May God forgive you!"

He replied: "Don't look down your nose at me! If I die, you'll have to carry my body till the end of your days and you'll turn into a grave!"

Nasibi's health deteriorated to such an extent that he was gripped by a fear of death. Qismati felt sorry for his brother's decline, and tried to cheer him up: "You'll get even better than you were before!"

Nasibi did not care what Qismati said, nor did he believe it. One morning, he woke up early and shouted: "I'm going to the home of the weeping truth!"

Sitt Anabaya rushed to him, realizing that he was dying. She held him close and started reciting the *sūrat al-Ikhlas*. Then he

— محاولة خائبة لن تنجح. نحن مختلفان تماماً، أنا لا أحب المعرفة، أما السياسة فإنك إن اخترت الحكومة اخترت من فوري المعارضة والعكس بالعكس، لن أبعك ولن تتبعني، ولن تهدأ المعركة.

فقال الأب بنفاد صبر:

— ارجعا إلى الوفاق، لا مفر منه، إنه قدر، كما أن اتحادكما قدر...

وعادا كارهين إلى المحاولة تجنبا الخلاف ما استطاعا، وجارى كلّ الآخر رغم تقزز قسمتي الخفي وسخرية نصيبي بعيداً عن عيني صاحبه. بدوا صديقين بلا صداقة، متحالفين بلا إخلاص، فعاش كلّ منهما نصف حياة، وتعلق بنصف أمل. غير أن آثار العمر طبعت في وجه نصيبي قبل الآوان وتوكد أنه يسرع نحو شيخوخة مبكرة. لعله نتيجة لإفراطه في كلّ شيء. وراح يشكو من فتور في الجنس وحساسية من الشرب، وسوء الهضم. ولم تنفعه العطارة ولا الطب. وفي معاناته أعلن ما يخبئ من حنق على صاحبه فاتهمه قائلاً:

— حسدتني عليك اللعنة.

فتسامح معه قسمتي متمتماً:

— سامحك الله!

فصاح به:

— لن تشمت بي، إذا مت فستحمل جثتي إلى نهاية العمر وتتحول من بشر إلى قبر!

واشتد به الضعف حتى ركبه الخوف من الموت. ورقّ له قسمتي في تدهوره فشجعه قائلاً:

— سترجع إلى خير مما كنت!

فلم يحفل بقوله ولم يصدقه. وذات صباح صحا مبكراً وهتف:

— إني ذاهب إلى موطن الحقيقة الباكية!

وهرولت إليه ست عنباية فأدركت أنه يحتضر فأخذته في حضنها وراحت تتلو الصمدية⁵⁰ وانتفض صدره، وبكى قسمتي أيضاً ولكنّ سرعان

stopped breathing.

Qismati wept, but was suddenly gripped by fear and panic at having a corpse joined to his torso. The two parents exchanged a confused look. What could they do with this body that they could not bury? They hastily summoned a doctor, who examined the situation and said:

"This is a very complex issue, but there is no solution except mummification of the body if it's impossible to excise it."

And so Qismati lived on, carrying the mummified body of his sibling. He soon realized that he was going to be half-alive and half-dead, and that the newly acquired freedom he had so often longed for was nothing but an illusion, which had turned into half a life or no life at all. He decided to immerse himself in work now that the obstacle had been removed. However, he discovered that he had become a different person, one who had suddenly been born fully formed, but one whose enthusiasm had dwindled, his inner urges dried up, his zeal abated and his taste for life dulled. He was a person who had relinquished life, worship and innocent daily pleasures, one who lived under a sky surging with dust, devoid of colour, clouds, stars or a horizon.

He said, a deep sadness pervading his very being: "Death is in the universe."

Most of the time he remained silent, withdrawn in a state of lethargy. Then, his mother asked him: "Why don't you entertain yourself and do something?"

He replied: "I'm doing the only thing I can do, which is to wait for death."

He saw the darkness descend upon him, holding out the promise of peace.

ما غشاه الفزع من الموت المزروع في جذعه، وتبادل الوالدان نظرة حائرة. ماذا يفعلان بهذه الجثة التي لا يمكن دفنها؟. واستُدعي طبيب على عجل فتفحص الحال وقال:

– إنها مشكلة تتضمن مشكلات، ولكنّ لا حل إلا تحنيطه إذ لا يمكن فصله.

هكذا عاش قسمتي حاملاً جثة صاحبه المحنطة. وأدرك من اللحظة الأولى أنه سيعيش نصف حي ونصف ميت. وأن الحرية التي حظي بها، والتي طالما تمناها، ليست إلا وهماً، وأنها نصف موت أو موت كامل. أجل قرر أن يهب نفسه للعمل طيلة الوقت بعد أن زال العائق ولكنه اكتشف أنه شخص جديد آخر. وُلد الشخص الجديد فجأة وبلا تدرج. شخص فتر حماسه، وجفّت ينابيعه، وتلاشت همته، وخمد ذوقه. شخص جفا الحياة والعبادة والمسرات اليومية البريئة. شخص يعيش تحت سماء ماجت بالغبار فلا زرقة ولا سحب ولا نجوم ولا أفق. وقال بأسى عميق:

– الموت في الكون.

ورُئي طوال الوقت صامتاً واجماً شبه نائم فسألته أمه:

– ألا تسلي نفسك بفعل شيء؟

فأجابها:

– إني أفعل ما في وسعي، إني أنتظر الموت.

وبدا لعينيه أن الظلام يهرول نحوه واعداً بالسلام.

Language Notes

1. قِسْمَتي ونَصيبي: lit. "my destiny and my fate", this is a common expression of resignation, e.g. الزَواج قِسْمَة ونَصيب, "marriage is a matter of fate". The word قِسْمَة is also sometimes used as a phrase of condolence, e.g. هذه قِسْمَة ! ("such is fate!"), whereas it is also the etymon of the English word kismet (albeit via Turkish).

2. عَمّ: lit. "[paternal] uncle". It is, however, often used as a term of address for an older man; عَمّو is another form of عَمّ.

3. العَطّار: lit. "perfume seller" (عِطْر, "perfume"), this is a grocer who sells herbs and spices as well as traditional herbal medicines.

4. أَجْزَلَ اللهُ لهُ العَطاء فيما يُحبُّ ويَتَمَنّى: lit. "God generously gave him what he likes and hopes for."

5. ذَرَّ> (u), "to scatter"; cf. ذَرَّة, "atom", طاقة ذَرِّية, "atomic energy"). Synonyms include أَطْفال, نَسْل (pl. أَنْسال) and سُلالة.

6. دَهْر: this is also often used in the sense of "time"; cf. الزَمَن.

7. مَعَ مُجاهَدةٍ للنَفْس لتَرضى بِما وَهَبَ اللهُ وبما مَنَعَ: lit. "with exertion of the soul to content oneself with what God has granted and withheld".

8. أُبَّهَة: (ECA) < بَهاء ("beauty, magnificence"); used to refer to respect based on wealth and smart dress.

9. حَباهُ الحظّ: lit. "luck loved him".

10. سِتّ: general term of address used for women (with their first name); it is equivalent to سَيّدة in MSA. The word is also used in the phrase سِتّ بَيت, "housewife".

11. إلى جانب: contracted form of بالاضافة إلى and إلى (كونها).

12. طواجِن: pl. of (1) طاجِن a traditional earthenware cooking pot; (2) a dish made of meat, rice or vegetables. The ingredients vary from one country to another.

13. فَطَائِر: pl. of فطِيرَة , round layered pastries.

14. السابِحَة فِي: lit. "swimming in" (i.e. "soaked with/in").

15. السَمْن البَلَدي: unclarified butter, ghee.

16. شُورَى الأَحِبّة: "seeking the advice of loved ones"; the use of شُورَى ("consultation") in this context has a religious connotation (cf. Qur. 38: سُورَة الشُّورَى).

17. أَهْل الله: lit. "People of God" (i.e. "God-fearing people"); أَهْل is often used as a head in a genitive construction (إضافة) in the sense of "those who are", e.g. أَنْتُم أَهْل الكَرَم) "you are generous people"). It also often means "family" or "kinsfolk". Indeed, it is this latter meaning that is meant in the common greeting أَهْلاً وسَهْلاً (see حكاية القنديل).

18. العارفينَ والواصلين: Sufi terms denoting certain ranks; in this story, however, it means those who know and are connected, e.g. العَارف بالله. Cf. MSA عَرَّاف ("he who knows well"), "fortuneteller".

19. الأَضْرحَة (المُبَارَكَة): pl. of ضَريح, "tomb", "grave". People in Muslim countries traditionally go to these shrines to ask for favours or be granted wishes. In Cairo, the famous shrines include those of السَيِّدة نفيسة, السَيِّدة زينب and الحُسين.

20. يا أَلطاف الله: !اِلطُفك يا رب "Goodness gracious me!"; is often used to express astonishment, or to beseech God's kindness and mercy.

21. وَحَقّ: introduction to an oath, such as وَحَقّ النَبي) "by the Prophet") or وَحَقّ الله) "by God"), which is equivalent to والله ("by God!").

22. سيدي الكُرْدي: a shrine and mosque in Cairo.

23. الوَايْليَّة: a popular district in Cairo (also known as الوايلي).

24. العَبَاسِيّة: a large and popular district in Cairo.

25. مَخاض: "labour pains" (< مَخَضَ (a), "to be in labour"); also آلام الوِلادة.

26. حَكِيمَة: "midwife" (ECA); MSA قابلة, مُوَلّدة. The word حَكِيم (pl. حُكَمَاء) means "sage" or "doctor" (cf. MSA طبيب).

27. تَبَسْمَل: see حكاية القنديل.

28. رَبِنا يَلْطَف بِنا: "may our Lord show mercy on us"; generally used to express astonishment (see also above, يا أَلطاف الله).

29. يُفْتَح الله: lit. "God opens"; in this context it is best translated as "better luck next time".

30. العاهَة: "disability"; cf. عاقَة.

31. مُحَمَّدَيْن: dual of مُحَمَّد. Proper name used primarily in Egypt; cf. حَسَنِين .

32. دُونَ أَنْ يَنْبِس: "without uttering" (short for دُونَ أَنْ يَنْبِس بِنتِ شَفة).

33. أَدَى الفَرِيضَة: lit. "he carried out a divine duty" (pl. فَرِيضة) or فَرْض (lit. "something apportioned, made obligatory") is a religious duty or obligation for which the believer will be rewarded (whereas omission leads to punishment). Performing the annual pilgrimage to Mecca, for instance, is a فَرْض. Islamic law distinguishes between فَرْض عَيْن (individual obligation such as prayer, etc) and فَرْض كفاية (collective obligation such as جهاد).

34. بِقُدْرَة قادر: lit. "by the strength or power of the one who possess power" (القادر is one of the so-called ninety-nine "beautiful names" – الأَسْماء الحُسْنَى – of God). This expression is often used to mean "(as if) by miracle".

35. العَفْرَتَة: ECA عَفْرَتَ< , to behave like an عُفْريت (see صفحة من كتاب الموتى).

36. الأُوَيِّقات: "small period of time"; diminutive of أوقات (pl. of وَقْت).

37. الوَيْل: "woe unto …"; cf. الوَيْل لَنا , "woe us!".

38. إلى ما شاءَاللهُ: lit. "until God wishes"; used here in the sense of "forever", "indefinitely".

39. خَيزُران: "bamboo"; "cane"; "reed".

40. عَلى مَلأ مِن =الجماعة الملأ . "in front of all people";

41. إنهُ بابٌ مُغْلَق: lit. "it is a closed door" (i.e. "the subject is closed").

42. بِقَدَر لا يُسْتَهانُ به: lit. "in an amount that is not to be belittled" (i. e. "not to be sneered at").

43. الرُّكُوع: see حكاية القنديل.

44. السُّجُود: see حكاية القنديل.

45. اللهُ لا يُكلفُ نَفساً إلاّ وسْعَها: Cf. *sūra* 2:286 ("Impose not on us that which we have not the strength to bear!").

46. الرابطة القَدَريّة: "divine connection"; قَدْر, "destiny" (also قَضَاء).

47. بِنتِ الحَلال: lit. "daughter of lawfulness" (also "Miss Right"); cf. أبْن الحَلالِ (also "Mr Right").

48. فُرجَة: ECA "a show", "scene".

49. عُقْبَ انْتهاء الأجَل: lit. "after the end of the appointed time", i.e. after one's death.

50. الصَمَديّة: this is a reference to *sūra* 112 (الإخْلاص, "devotion"), which is commonly known as الصَمَديّة because the word الصَّمَد) "The Eternal One") appears in the first line of the verse.

Ḥanān al-Shaykh

Born in Beirut in 1945, Ḥanān al-Shaykh is one of the leading contemporary women authors in the Arab world. She is known as a novelist, short-story writer, playwright and essayist. Raised in a conservative Muslim family from the Ra's al-Nab'a district, she started writing at an early age, publishing essays in the daily النهار from the age of sixteen. After completing her university education at the American College for Girls in Cairo (1963–66), she returned to Beirut to work as a journalist at the الحسناء magazine and then at النهار.

It was during her stay in Egypt that she wrote her first novel انتحار رَجُل مَيّت (*Suicide of a Dead Man*), which deals with relationships between the sexes and patriarchal control in Middle Eastern societies. It was eventually published in 1970. Five years later she published her second novel, فَرَس الشيطان (*The Praying Mantis*).

In 1976, she fled from Lebanon to Saudi Arabia because of the civil war, and came to international prominence with her next novel حكاية زهرة (*The Story of Zahra*, 1980), which was later translated into English (1994). The novel revolves around the eponymous heroine, a young woman who tries to take advantage of the Lebanese civil war to escape oppression. Banned in most Arab countries, the book was initially published at the author's expense, as no publisher was prepared to do so on account of its controversial subject matter. Not much later – in 1982 – al-Shaykh moved to London, where she still resides.

In 1983, her short story *The Persian Carpet* appeared in the multi-author volume entitled *Arabic Short Stories* (trans. /ed. D. Johnson-Davies), in which she examined the effects of divorce on children. In 1989 she published مسك الغزال (*Women of Sand and Myrrh*), which was also translated into English (1992). Despite the fact that this novel, too, was banned in many Arab countries, it was named as one of the '50 Best Books of 1992' by *Publishers Weekly*. It tells the story of four women in an unnamed Middle Eastern country and their dealings with the patriarchal society in which they live.

In 1992, al-Shaykh published بَريد بيروت (*Beirut Blues*), a collection of ten letters written by the protagonist Asmahān during the Lebanese civil war to various people both dead and alive. The novel, the English translation of which appeared in the same year, received a great deal of critical acclaim in the West. In 1994 she published a collection of seventeen short stories entitled أكْنُس الشَّمْس عَلى السُّطوح (*I Sweep the Sun off Rooftops*), the English translation of which was released in 2002.

The English translation of one of her recent novels, إنّها لندن يا عزيزي (*Only in London*, 2000), was shortlisted for *The Independent* Foreign Fiction Prize. In the novel, Ḥanān al-Shaykh explores the lives of people caught between Eastern and Western cultures and traditions. In the 1990s, she also wrote two plays, which appeared only in English translation – *Dark Afternoon Tea* (1995) and *Paper Husband* (1997). Both deal with the lives of immigrants in London.

The story "Yasmine's Picture" is taken from وَرْدة الصَّحْراء (*Desert Flower*), published in 1982, at the height of the civil war and after the Israeli invasion of Lebanon. The protagonists of the story are a couple who have left their home in the war-torn southern suburbs of Beirut and sought refuge outside the city. Thus displaced, they live in an eerily empty building, where the male protagonist becomes obsessed with the absent character mentioned in the title. The storyline focuses almost entirely on the man, who, like so many men in the author's oeuvre, is rather weak, unable to make any decisions by himself. He married his wife because she chose him; he moved to this new flat, seeking shelter, because his sister-in-law suggested it to him. In an attempt to escape the harsh reality of war, he becomes fixated on the female owner of the flat in which they are staying. He builds up a picture of her in his mind based on her pictures, diaries, letters and record collection. At the same time, he completely ignores his pregnant wife; she is totally on the margins of his thoughts. His escapism means he is living in an imaginary world of his own making. The story is an allegory of the way in which war victims deal with the traumatic events that impinge upon them, and seek comfort wherever they can.

صورة ياسمين

Yasmine's Picture

Once again, he found himself in front of her picture, gazing at those feline eyes, her rising, tanned forehead, delicate small nose and full lips. He looked at her shiny black hair, with wayward wisps like those of a child.

He turned to his wife and asked: "Is she as beautiful as in the picture?"

She replied, raising the bedcover: "I only had a glimpse of her from a distance, when she was with Nawal."

He paused to think while his eyes moved to the bedsheets; even the beauty of her bedsheets was different, as they appeared to have the natural colours of the shells found in all the world's oceans. As he was about to close the balcony door, the peacock feathers in the copper container stirred.

He remembered once seeing his wife breaking peacock feathers in half so as to make them fit into the rubbish bin. The feathers had been a wedding present from the switchboard operator in his office at the Ministry. He had not been annoyed with his wife for not liking them. Indeed, he did not know of anyone decorating their house with peacock feathers, except in the countryside. He had not imagined them looking so beautiful when they were spread out; they gave the bedroom a poetic atmosphere.

He slowly took off his clothes. When he undid the buttons of his trousers, he suddenly found himself looking at the picture on the dressing table. He lay down on the bed; his wife was sitting in front of the mirror, applying creams to her face with cotton wool. He thought of Yasmine, the woman in the picture, and imagined her sitting there instead of his wife. He wondered whether her body was as fine-boned as her face. He closed his eyes and looked at the coral clothes rack, the like of which he had never seen before, except for the black one in his grandfather's house. The rack he was looking at had straw and canvas hats hanging on it, as well as pearl necklaces. When he felt his wife climbing into bed he asked her: "How old is she?" She thought he was dreaming.

They awoke to the sound of explosions disturbing the calm

وجد نفسه أمام صورتها أيضاً. تأمل العينين الشبيهتين بعيني قطة، ارتفاع الجبهة السمراء صغر الأنف الرفيع، اكتناز الشفتين. رأى الشعر الأسود اللامع وقد التفّت خصلاته كشعر الأطفال، استدار إلى زوجته يسألها: ((هل هي جميلة كالصورة؟)) ردت عليه وهي ترفع غطاء السرير: ((لمحتها مرة من بعيد مع نوال)).

فكر. وقد انتقل بعينيه إلى الشراشف، حتى جمال شراشفها يختلف، كانت أصداف بحار العالم كلها، بألوان الصدف الطبيعية. لما اقترب يقفل باب الشرفة اهتزت ريش الطاووس المشكوكة[1] في إبريق نحاسي أحمر. تذكر أنه رأى من قبل زوجته تكسر كلّ ريشة مرتين حتى تستطيع أن تدخلها سلة النفايات، بعد أن قدمها لهما عامل السنترال[2] في مكتبه في الوزارة هدية زواجهما. لم يتضايق من زوجته لأنها لم تحبها، فهو لم ير أحداً يزين بيته بريش الطاووس من قبل سوى في القرى. لم يتصورها أن تكون بهذا الجمال وهي مفرودة الآن، تضفي جواً شاعرياً على غرفة النوم.

خلع ملابسه ببطء، لما فك أزرار بنطلونه وجد نفسه ينظر فجأة إلى الصورة الموضوعة على تواليت الزينة[3]. تمدد في السرير، زوجته خلف المرآة تمسح وجهها بالقطن والكريمات. تصور ياسمين، صاحبة الصورة، تجلس مكانها. فكر في جسمها إذا كان كالوجه دقيق العظام، أغمض عينيه وهو يتفرّس بالمشجب المرجاني الذي لم ير مثله إلا عند بيت جده وكان أسود اللون أما الآن فقد علقت عليه قبعات من القش ومن القماش، عقود من أصداف البحر أيضاً. لما شعر بزوجته تدخل السرير سألها: ((كم عمرها؟)) وظنت أنه يحلم.

استيقظا على صوت انفجارات تقلق سكون الفجر. وجد نفسه يجلس

of dawn. He sat up in bed, saddened and exasperated. How was it possible that the ceasefire was violated after only five days? He cleared his throat and imagined himself today, tomorrow and the day after a prisoner in this flat. He wished he had not taken the advice of his sister-in-law, Nawal, to leave their flat in Chiyah. He wished he had listened to his wife and stayed in their own house, in spite of its dangerous location and the fact that she was eight months pregnant. He would be enjoying the company of the neighbours now, playing cards or backgammon with them and, if necessary, they could take refuge in the shelter with the rest of the people.

In this quiet building, however, he had never seen anyone at the entrance, not even a child playing. He had pretended more than once to be waiting for the lift without ever pressing the button in the hope of meeting one of the inhabitants of the building, so he could introduce himself to them and exchange a few words about current events and the war. Perhaps others could share their hopes or even pessimism with him, it didn't really matter which. He just wanted to hear a voice other than that of the radio or his wife. Even the telephone was cut off. The flat was totally quiet, except for the twitter of the orange canary that started to annoy him, as its chirruping would increase every time it heard gunfire.

He had not heard a single footstep in the clean entrance hall to the building. Despite the sounds of explosions, the pictures of the sea, the mirrors and the fig tree remained still. As he went up to the flat, he remembered that the last time he had talked to anyone in the building was to the guard, who was carrying his son while hurrying his wife along with insults as they got ready to leave for Akar. He'd asked the guard with some anxiety: "Who will guard the building in your absence?" He'd replied: "How can you be afraid when you have a colonel living in the building? You're extremely lucky."

"We're extremely lucky," his wife said, as she opened the

في السرير يفكر في حزن وضيق، كيف تم خرق وقف النار بعد خمسة أيام فقط. بلع ريقه وهو يتصور اليوم والغد وبعده. وهو سجين هذه الشقة. تمنى لو لم يعمل بنصيحة زوجة أخيه نوال، ويغادرا شقتهما في الشياح[4]، تمنى لواستمع إلى زوجته وبقيا في بيتهما بالرغم من خطورة موقعه وكون زوجته حاملاً في الشهر ماقبل الأخير. لكان الآن يزور الجيران مستأنساً يلعب معهم الورق أو الطاولة واذا لزم الأمر يختبئ في الملجأ مع الجميع. بينما في هذه البناية الهادئة لم يلمح عند مدخلها إنساناً، ولاحتى ولداً يلعب، حاول التظاهر أكثر من مرة بأنه ينتظر المصعد دون أن تكبس يده الزر عله[5] يصادف أحداً من سكان البناية فيعرفه على نفسه، ويتبادلان الحديث في الأوضاع والحرب، لربما بث الآخر فيه روح الأمل أوالتشاؤم، لافرق، يريد أن يسمع صوتاً غير صوت المذياع وصوت زوجته. فالهاتف مقطوع. والسكينة تخيم على الشقة، عدا زقزقة الكنار البرتقالي التي أخذت تضايقه لأنه كان يزيد من زقزقته كلما سمع زخات رصاص. لايسمع أية خطوات في مدخل البناية النظيف، رغم أصوات الانفجارات يرى لوحة البحر والمرايا وشجرة البلح الافرنجي[6] ساكنة، يصعد الشقة وهو يتذكر أن المرة الأخيرة التي تكلم فيها مع أحد في البناية كان مع حارسها الذي كان يحمل ابنه ويستعجل زوجته بشتمها، وهما يستعدان للذهاب إلى عكار[7]. لما وجد نفسه يسأل بارتباك: «والبناية من يحرسها بغيابك؟» أجاب الحارس: «الكولونيل[8] في البناية، وخيفان[9]؟» ولك[10] حظك من السما: «حظنا من السما» قالت

kitchen cupboards and looked at the bags of provisions, the tins of food, the crates of water, the pile of flat bread loaves in the fridge and several gas cylinders on the side of the balcony.

"If they were so well prepared, and if their flat was so safe, why did they leave then?" Moments later, he blamed himself for thinking that all people need is food and drink.

He walked around the house, going into every room. He was content with just looking; he opened cupboards and drawers. His wife smiled and told him: "So, what are you up to?" He answered with a lie: "I am looking for a book, a draughtboard – anything to pass the time with."

She said: "When Nawal met Yasmine in Europe and told her that I was pregnant, Yasmine made her swear to make me look for babies' clothes, maternity dresses and anything else that was useful in the flat." She fell silent, then added: "They are, of course, happy that the flat is safe and sound, and that people like us are looking after it."

Annoyed, he replied: "Even so, isn't it in our interest to be here, out of harm's way and close to the university hospital, in case something happens?" She changed her mind and replied while smiling: "Yes, you're right, you're right."

He entered Yasmine's son's room and stopped in front of a wall covered with pictures of the boy, from the day he was born until the age of three. There were pictures of him crying while licking the baking tin of his birthday cake; with his forehead covered in mud; of her hugging him when he was only a few weeks old in front of the white lace-draped birdcage. Her hair came down to her waist, cascading like that of American Indians.

Then he gasped as his attention was drawn by one of the pictures. He paused for a while in front of it. Her tanned complexion was revealed in an ankle-length sleeveless dress, which also showed her cleavage. He examined her face; it appeared sad, despite the yellow and red flower behind her ear. She seemed lost; the picture showed her son holding onto her

زوجتي وهي تفتح خزائن المطبخ وترى أكياس المؤن والمعلبات وصناديق المياه وأرغفة الخبز بالمئات في الثلاجة وعدة قناني غاز تنتظرعلى جهة من البلكون.

«اذا كانت وزوجها مستعدين حتى هذه الدرجة، وشقتهما أمينة لماذا سافرا؟». بعد لحظة لام نفسه لتفكيره بأن الطعام والشراب هو ما يحتاج اليه الانسان فقط.

يتمشى في البيت، يدخل كلّ الغرف. يكتفي بالنظر، يفتح الخزائن، الادراج، وزوجته تقول له وهي تبتسم: ولو[11]، شو[12] صايرلك[13]؟. ردّ كاذباً: «بفتش على كتاب، على طاولة داما، على شيء اتسلى فيه». قالت: «لما نوال شافت ياسمين في أوروبا وأخبرتها أني حامل،حلفتها ياسمين حتى فتش[14] على ثياب صغار وعلى فساتينها الحبل واستعمل كلّ شيء». سكتت وأضافت: «طبعاً مبسوطين[15] انو[16] الشقة بعدها صاغ سليم، وناس مثلنا عم[17] يحرسوها». ووجد نفسه يجيبها متضايقاً: «ولو، مش كمان من مصلحتنا نكون هون بعاد عن الخطر، قراب لمستشفى الجامعة إذا صار ماصار[18]؟» وجدت نفسها تتراجع مبتسمة: «أي معك حق، معك حق». دخل غرفة ولدها، وقف أمام حائط مشكوك بصور ولدها، منذ أن كان عمره يوماً حتى الثلاث سنوات. وهو يلحس قالب كعكة[19] عيد ميلاده ويبكي والوحل غطى جبهته. ثم صورة تحتضنه وعمره أسابيع أمام قفص لعصفور، تونسي[20] أبيض،شعرها في الصورة وصل خصرها. وهبط كشعر الهنود الحمر.

ثم وجد نفسه يشهق لما استوقفته طويلاً صورة لها وقد بدت بشرتها السمراء برونزية، بفستان يكشف عن ذراعيها وأعلى صدرها. طول الفستان وصل حتى كاحلها. تأمل وجهها الحزين، رغم وردة الأركيديا

scarf while running, as she tried to grab hold of him.

This is the most beautiful woman I've ever seen in my life; she's not as thin as I imagined. She really looks like a movie star. He could not stop himself from going through her things and examining them. He was like a thirsty man chasing a drop of water.

After a few days, he noticed that his preoccupation with her pictures and her virtual presence had a soothing effect while the war was raging outside. The quest for her secrets was the only thing that broke the monotony of the long tumultuous days.

His wife was absorbed in her search for baby clothes in all the suitcases and nylon bags, so that she could wash them and get them ready. When she noticed her husband sitting perplexed in front of the photo albums and the thick envelopes with papers, she just said: "Don't forget to put everything back as you found it."

He saw a picture of Yasmine as a child, sitting on a wooden chair beside fig trees in white underpants. In another one, she was clad in a black university graduation gown; it was the only photograph where she was also wearing eye make-up, with her hair cut shoulder-length. And then there was the picture of her as a hippie, with flowers in her hair, heart drawings on her face, jumping high in the air.

He went through her letters, one of which was from her friend Nuha, who wrote:

"Dear Yasmine, I read your sentence which says: 'Write to Zina, tell her to study hard so I can pass my exams.' I couldn't stop laughing; really, you're so wicked."

When he found a diary, his heart skipped a beat. Much to his disappointment, however, it was empty. Then he found another two diaries, in one of which she had written a single sentence: "Is it the multitude of diaries and my desire for writing that is stopping me from writing?"

He closed the diary and sighed with satisfaction. He wondered: "She's beautiful on the inside, too; she's intelligent,

الصفراء والنبيذية خلف أذنها. كانت تبدو شاردة. رغم أن ابنها أمسك
شالها وظهر وهو يركض، وهي تحاول اللحاق به.

أجمل امرأة شاهدتها في حياتي، جسمها ليس ناحلاً كما تصورت،
إنه كممثلات السينما. لم يعد يوقف نفسه عن البحث في أشيائها. أصبح
رجلاً عطشان يعدو وراء نقطة ماء. بعد أيام لاحظ أن فضوله أمام صورها،
ووجودها الغائب كان يرطب من جو الحرب في الخارج، نبش خفاياها هو
الحدث الوحيد يسجله في رتابة الأيام الصاخبة الطويلة. وكانت زوجته
منهمكة أيضاً في البحث عن ثياب الطفل في كلّ الشنط، وفي أكياس
النايلون لتغسلها وتحضرها. لما ترى زوجها مشدوهاً، شارداً أمام الألبومات
والظروف الورقية السميكة وكانت تكتفي بالقول: «اوعى[٢١] تنس، حط
كلّ شغله محلها». رأى صورياسمين وهي طفلة، تجلس في كلسون ابيض
على كرسي من خشب، بجانب أشجار تين وصورة لها تلبس ملابس
روب التخرج الجامعي الأسود، وقد كحلت عينيها لأول مرة في الصور،
وقصت شعرها حتى رقبتها. ورأى صورة لها وقد بدت من الهبيز، الورود
على شعرها. رسمات القلوب على وجهها، تقفز عالياً في الهواء. يفلش
رسائلها، رسالة من صديقتها نهى تقول لها.

«عزيزتي ياسمين، قرأت جملتك التي. تقول: «اكتبي لزينة ان تدرس
لكي أنجح، و لم أتوقف عن الضحك، فعلاً إنك نمرة».

ورأى مفكرة، دق قلبه. لخبطته كانت فارغة، مفكرة أخرى، وأخيرة
كتبت فيها جملة واحدة: «هل تعدد المفكرات وشعوري بأني أريد الكتابة
على كلها يجعلني لا أكتب ؟»

أغلق المفكرة، تنهد بارتياح وهو يفكر: «إنها جميلة من الداخل
أيضاً: إنها ذكية، ونفسيتها تختلف: لماذا لم يقابلها أم يقابل من هي في

with an unusual attitude." Why hadn't he met her or somebody
like her? Instead, he had allowed his wife to choose and marry
him. He should have known and met someone who hangs
paintings like these on the walls – water colour in which the
hues and translucence of the water and sky quicken one's
heart; someone who loves donkeys, and keeps a statue of a
small donkey made out of white gypsum; someone who keeps a
picture of a Persian cat and writes this dedication underneath:
"This is Silver, one who is beautiful of hair and heart".

*Who gave her this book, which had the following dedication: "To
the one and only Yasmine"?*

Then he got to her music collection. He started to look at
the records, which ranged from Sayyid Darwish to Pink Floyd,
from Abdul Muttalib to Vivaldi. He shook his head. "What
strange moods she has." Suddenly he stopped and thought: why
did he assume this was her music collection? What about her
husband? No, upon inspection of her husband's papers and
his engineering books scattered about, it did not seem that he
had time to listen to music, never mind Arabic music. The only
indication of ownership was the drawing of a jasmine flower
on all the books. There was a book about the singer Asmahan,
newspapers cuttings about her and a collection of poetry
books by both foreign and Arab poets. Her touch was visible
on everything in the house, like the bottles of coloured sand
from Petra, pictures of donkeys (always newborn), wind chimes
suspended from the balcony ceiling that produced soft sounds
whenever there was a breeze. After going through her things, he
suddenly felt tired and dozed off in the rocking chair.

Suddenly, he felt someone's presence in the room and heard
Yasmine talking to him; that must be the ring of her soft voice.
He got up from the chair and started looking in the rooms when
he found his wife asleep. He became annoyed; his quest had gone
on for too long. Then, he woke from his sleep, and smiled as he
realized that he had only been dreaming about Yasmine.

مثل شخصيتها، بل جعل زوجته تختاره وتتزوجه. كان يجب ان يعرف من يعلق كهذه اللوحات على الجدران، لوحات مائية، لون وشفافية الماء والسماء فيها تسرع من ضربات القلب. من يحب الحمير، ويضع تمثالاً لحمار صغيرمن الكلس الأبيض. من يحتفظ بصورة قط فارسي ويكتب: «هذا سيلفر، الجميل الشعر، والقلب» من يقدم إليها كتابه ويكتب لها هذا الإهداء: «إلى الياسمينة الوحيدة». ووصل إلى مجموعتها الموسيقية، أخذ يقلب الاسطوانات ويجد من سيد درويش[22]، إلى البينك فلويد، من عبد المطلب[23] إلى فيفالدى. يهز رأسه: «إنها غريبة المزاج» فجأة، يوقف نفسه: لماذا يفترض أن هذه مجموعتها ؟. ماذا عن زوجها. لا. من أوراق وكتب زوجها الهندسية هنا وهناك لا تدل أن لديه الوقت ليسمع وبالتالي الموسيقى العربية. عدا أن زهرة الياسمين بدل الكلمة مرسومة على كلّ كتاب. كتاب عن المطربة أسمهان[24]، أقاصيص جرائد عنها. وكتب شعرية من الأجنبي والعربي. هي في كلّ شيء في هذا البيت. حتى زجاجات الرمل الملون من البتراء. صور لحمير، دائماً في أشهرهم الأولى. مجموعة عيدان نحاسية علقتها في سقف الشرفة تحدث اصواتاً ناعمة كلما حركتها نسمة هواء. وجد نفسه فجأةء يغفو على الكرسي الهزاز من كثرة ما حدق في أشيائها.

كأنه شعر بوجود شخص في الغرفة. سمع ياسمين تحدثه، لا بد أن هذه رنة صوتها الهادئ. نهض عن الكرسي يبحث في الغرف. لما وجد زوجته نائمة، تضايق. طال بحثه، وجد نفسه يفيق من نومه تماماً ويتسم لأنه ظن حلمه بياسمين حقيقة.

The fact of continuously thinking about Yasmine made him more tense and repressed. She did not know him, but he knew her. He knew her secrets; he had read the letters she had sent to her husband before they were married. He had touched her things, seen her perfume bottles (including the empty ones), her towels, clothes, the pressed coloured cotton in a glass jar. He had found the medicine she used for period pains. He knew every little detail about her. He saw the reflection in the mirror of himself hugging her white bathroom robe with the picture of a wild mushroom embroidered upon it. He truly knew her. He loved her.

At night, he slept close to her, in her bed, feeling her tossing and turning, sensing her "fear of the explosions", as she had put it in a letter she wrote to an American friend of hers before leaving, but never got the chance to post.

Should he get her address from Nawal and write to her? Should he wait for her? Or should he travel to London as soon as his wife gave birth? He sipped coffee from her cup while her yellow canary twittered. He got up, and extended his fingers towards the canary, asking it if Yasmine also played with him like this.

He watered her plants, secretly, as people in Beirut had stopped watering their plants. He looked at her pictures for such a long time that one night it was as if Yasmine was looking back at him.

The shelling had stopped for a week. He thanked God when his wife felt labour pains at dawn that morning. He left his wife at the hospital, and returned home, completely worn out. After opening the door, he saw her standing in front of him. He saw suitcases and a coat. Before he could ask what was going on, there she was in front of him, with those large hazel eyes raised like a cat's, the high forehead, fine nose and full lips. She held out her hand, smiling, and said: "Mr...?"

He did not embrace her. Instead, he found himself reaching for her hand, realizing that he did not know her.

تفكيره بياسمين المتواصل زاد من توتره، وأنت فيه الأحاسيس بالكبت. لا تعرفه، لكنه يعرفها. فتح أسرارها، قرأ رسائلها لزوجها قبل زواجها. لمس أشياءها. رأى زجاجات عطرها حتى الفارغة مناشفها، ملابسها، القطن الملون المكبوس في مرطبان[٢٥] زجاجي. رأى دواء يوقف آلام حيضها إنه يعرفها في أدق تفاصيلها رأى نفسه في المرآة يحتضن روب حمامها الأبيض المطرز عليه فطر بري. انه يعرفها،انه يحبها.

في الليل ينام قربها. في سريرها. يشعر بتقلباتها، بخوفها من الانفجارات كما وضعتها في رسالة كتبتها لصديقتها أميركية قبل سفرها و لم ترسلها. هل يأخذ عنوانها من نوال ويكتب لها؟ ينتظرها؟ أم يسافر إلى لندن حالما تضع زوجته؟ هو يحتسي القهوة في كوبها، وكنارها الأصفر يزقزق، ينهض، يمد له إصبعه يسأله إذا كانت ياسمين تداعبه هكذا. يسقي زريعتها، في الخفاء رغم ان كلّ بيروت توقفت عن السقي. كان ينظر في صورها طويلاً، لدرجة أنه شعر ذات ليلة بأنها تنظر اليه أيضاً. لذلك عندما توقف إطلاق النار منذ أسبوع وشكر الله لأن زوجته أحست بآلام الوضع فجر هذا الصباح. وعاد منهوكاً من المستشفى وقد تركها في غرفة العمليات وأدار المفتاح في ثقب الباب. رآها أمامه. رأى حقائب سفر، ومعطفاً، وقبل أن يستفسر، رآها أمامه، عيناها عسليتان كبيرتان مرفوعتان كعيني قطة جبهتها عالية، أنفها دقيق. شفتاها مكتنزتان. مدت يدها مصافحة مبتسمة: حضرتك؟...

لم يعانقها، وجد نفسه يمد يده يصافحها، ويكتشف أنه لا يعرفها من قبل.

Language Notes

1. مَشْكُوك: passive participle (اسم المَفْعُول) of شَكَّ (u), which is used here in the rare meaning of "stick together" (rather than the far more usual "to suspect"). This usage, though attested in CA, is more often used in the colloquial (LCA/SCA).

2. سِنْتْرال: dial. (<Fr. *centrale*), "the telephone exchange (office)".

3. تواليت الزِّينة: dial.; MSA خُوان الزِّينة (pl. - أخاوين/أخْونة).

4. الشِّيّاح: densely populated southeastern suburb of Beirut.

5. بَعَلهْ: dial.; MSA لَعَلهُ (> لَعَل).

6. شَجَرة البَلَح الافْرَنْجي: type of palm tree with a wide trunk and short branches, which does not produce dates.

7. عَكّار: district in the north of Lebanon, with a large coastal plain and high mountains to the east. In 2003, Akkar became a province, with Halba its capital. It is famous for its many Roman and Arab archaeological sites.

8. كولنيل: dial.; MSA عَقيد (pl. عُقَداءُ).

9. خيفان: dial.; MSA هَلْ أنْتَ خائف؟.

10. لَك: "hey, you!"; "oi!". This form is a dialectal clipping of ولك and ولاك (< ultimately to وَلَد). These are normally used as a vocative for both genders and 2nd person sg. and pl. They are used to show contempt for the addressee. Similar forms are in use in Iraqi, for instance: ولَك (masc. sg.), ولِچ (fem. sg., pron. *wilitch*).

11. وَلو: a particle used in Lebanese and Syrian dialects to express astonishment, surprise, disapproval or aversion.

12. شُو: LCA/SCA; MSA ماذا.

13. جَرَى لك: LCA/SCA; MSA صايرلك.

14. حتى أفَتَش: MSA حتى فَتَش; the first-person subject marker ا of the verb فَتَش is elided in the Lebanese and Syrian dialects.

15. مَبْسُوطين: مَبْسُوط, MSA فُرْحان (> "happy") (فَرْحانين). Note that in nearly all colloquials the standard regular plural

ending is ـين (rather than ـون in MSA, where ـين is the plural genitive/accusative form). In some dialects (e. g. Iraqi) مَبْسُوط also means "punched", "hit"!

16. انو: SCA/LCA; MSA is أَنَّهُ (أَنَّ + هُ>).

17. عَم: progressive particle used primarily in Levantine Arabic (Lebanon, Syria, Jordan and Palestine).

18. صار ما صار :LCA/SCA; MSA. حَصَلَ ما حَصَلَ.

19. كَعْكة: this is the unit noun ("one cake"); the collective (i.e. "cake" in general) is كَعْك.

20. قفص لعصفور تونسي أبيض: a particular type of birdcage, tall and narrow, usually draped with lace. It takes its name from the fact that it commonly comes in white and blue, which are the traditional colours of houses in Tunisia.

21. اوعَى: "Watch it" (masc. sg. ; fem. sg. أُوعِي), SCA/LCA; MSA. إِيّاك. (For its use in ECA, see طبلية مَن السماء).

22. سَيِّد دَرْويش: Egyptian composer and singer (1892–1923) generally regarded as the father of modern Arabic music. He liberated Arabic music from the old classical style, and was also a master of new musical theatre. He composed Egypt's national anthem, بلادي، بلادي، لَك حُبِّي وفُؤَادي ("My Country, My Country, My Love and My Heart Are for You"). His songs are still as popular today as when he was alive.

23. عَبْد المُطَّلِب: popular Egyptian singer (1910–80). Among his best and most popular songs are بتسأليني بحَبِّك ليه ("You Ask Me Why I Love You") and رَمَضان جانا ("Ramaḍān Came to Us").

24. أسْمَهان: famous Lebanese-born female singer (1918–44). In her early teens, she, together with her brother, فَريد الأطرَش – the famous lute player and singer – moved to Egypt. She died in a car accident caused, it is rumoured, by the war waged between the secret services in Cairo during World War II.

25. مَرْطَبان: SCA/LCA (also مَرْبَان or برَطمان in ECA); a glass jar with a lid for preserving fruit, jam, etc.

Muḥammad Shukrī

Undoubtedly one of Morocco's most famous, if not infamous, twentieth-century literary figures, Muḥammad Shukrī (Mohamed Shoukri) (1935–2003) was born into a very poor family in Banī Shakīr, a small village in the north of Morocco. Soon after his birth, the family moved to Tangier, which would remain the novelist's home for the rest of his life. Literature came late to Shukrī, who remained illiterate until his early twenties. The extreme hardships of his poverty-stricken childhood are depicted with chilling realism in his first book, الخُبْز الحافي (*Naked Bread*), in which the reader accompanies the protagonist on his forays into crime, drug abuse and prostitution. Though written in the 1960s, its explicitness meant that that it would only be published in 1982 (in Lebanon), and it was another two decades before it became officially available in the author's native land. However, the book already enjoyed fame in the West thanks to a translation in English by the American author (and fellow Tangier resident) Paul Bowles under the title *For Bread Alone* (1973), whereas another novelist and compatriot, Tahar Ben Jelloun published a French translation in 1981. Interestingly enough, Bowles's translation was not based on the Standard Arabic of the original manuscript, as the translator was not familiar with it; instead, the source text was Shukrī's "translation" of his book into the Moroccan dialect (in which

Bowles was proficient). Subsequently, the book was translated into some ten languages. Later on, Shukrī released a second volume of autobiography, زَمانِ الأخْطاء (*The Time of Mistakes*, 1992), which later appeared as الشُّطّار (*Streetwise*, 2000). Shukrī made his publishing debut with a short story, العُنْف عَلى الشّاطىء (*Violence on the Beach*), which appeared in 1966 in a Lebanese literary journal, yet it was not until 1979 that his first book appeared under his own name – a collection of short stories titled مَجْنُون الوَرْد (*Crazy about Roses*, 1979).

Thanks to Bowles's translation, Shukrī's fame spread within the Western literary establishment, many of whose more flamboyant members visited the author in Morocco. Some of these encounters, such as those with Bowles, Jean Genet and Tennessee Williams, were later immortalized by Shukrī in his books جان جنيه في طنجة (*Jean Genet in Tangier*, 1974), تينسي وليامز في طنجة (*Tennessee Williams in Tangier*, 1979) and بول بوولز وعزلة طنجة (*Paul Bowles, the Tangier Recluse*, 1996).

Shukrī's oeuvre also includes such novels as السُّوق الدَّاخلي (*The Inner Market*, 1985), غَواية الشَّحْرور الأبْيَض (*The Seduction of the White Sparrow*, 1998), and the collection of short stories from which the present story has been extracted, الخَيْمة (*The Tent*), which appeared in 1985 amidst the usual controversy and furore that accompanied many of Shukrī's books.

In his work, Shukrī – who may be called a poet of the dispossessed – reveals a fascination with the underbelly of Moroccan society, the trials and tribulations of which he describes graphically, with great poetic force and compassion, devoid of voyeurism.

The following story is by no means an exception, as we follow the nocturnal peregrinations of a young prostitute grappling with life's deceptions.

The Night and the Sea

She began to feel as if the beach was hers alone. In the distance, an old man dressed in rags limped along, throwing pieces of bread to the seagulls. She stopped and looked at the small beach huts, most of them without doors. All the bars were closed. The little old man was leaving the beach, tossing the last crumbs from his basket to the small flock trailing in his wake, his bald head tilted to the left due to disability. Some of the birds still followed him.

She took off her shoes and flung them onto the sand together with her bag. It began to rain. It was a warm rain. The raindrops soaked her hair. She let the waves lap at her feet, raised her head and closed her eyes. The raindrops trickled down into her open mouth. She loved doing that in the shower as well.

She picked up her shoes and bag and continued walking barefoot, contemplating the footprints she left behind. She grew increasingly sad without, however, knowing why. She crossed a small puddle along the long path leading across the beach.

She entered the Atlas Bar, ordered a Bloody Mary and then headed for the toilets to dry her hair. In the corner of the bar a young man and his girlfriend were seated. The woman was sobbing as her boyfriend tried to reassure her, swearing blindly that "Nadia" was just a colleague from work.

"So much rain these days!" said a foreigner to his friend, the English bar owner, who replied: "It's the year of the floods in Morocco."

Widad sat on a bench and looked at the two of them without understanding a single word. She caught the eye of the foreigner, and they both smiled.

The young man put a coin in the jukebox. His girlfriend stopped crying and smiled. He caressed her hair and face, and cupped her hand in his. A record began to play:

الليل والبحر

انبعت فيها شعور بأن الشاطىء صار لها وحدها. بعيداً عنها شيخ
هندي يعرج يرمي الخبز المفروم إلى طيور البحر. توقفتْ. استعرضتْ بيوت
الشاطىء الصغيرة. أغلبها منزوعة أبوابها. الحانات١ مقفلة كلها. الهندي
القصير يبتعد خارجاً من الشاطىء نافضاً آخر فتات سلّته وسرب صغير
يتبعه. رأسه الأصلع مائل على انحراف عاهته اليسرى. بعض الطيور مازالت
تتبعه. خلعت حذاءها ورمته مع حقيبتها على الرمل. بدأ مطر دافىء.
القطرات تخترق شعرها. تركت قدميها تلعقهما ألسنة الأمواج. رفعت
وجهها مغمضة عينيها. القطرات تتسرب إلى فمها المنفغر. تفعل ذلك بلذة
حين تكون تحت المشَنّ٢. التقطت حذاءها وحقيبتها ومشت «حفيانة»٣
متأملة آثار قدميها. تَعَمَّق حزنها، لكنه لا يوحي لها بشيء تدرك معناه في
وضوح. عَبرت بركة مياه هُلامية في الممر الطويل عبر الشاطىء. دخلت حانة
الأطلس. طلبت «بلاديميري». دخلت المرحاض لتجفف شعرها المبتل. في
ركن٤ الحانة شاب صحبة شابة تنتحب في صمت. يدخن ويشرب ويتكلم
بانفعال خافت. يقسم لها بالله العظيم أن نادية ليست إلا صديقة في العمل.
قال الأجنبي، رفيق صاحب الحانة الإنجليزي:
ـ ما أغزر المطر في هذه الأيام !
ـ قال صاحب الحانة:
ـ إنه عام الفيضانات في المغرب.
جلست وداد على المقعد الطويل وتأملتهما دون أن تفهم كلمة من
كلامهما.
تناظرت هي والأجنبي فابتسما.
وضع الشاب القطعة النقدية٥ في شَقِّ الحاكي٦. كَفَّت رفيقته عن النحيب.
باسمها. لاطَف شعرها ووجهها ثم احتضن يدها في يده. بدأت
الأسطوانة:

"Oh God, please don't make her suffer for my wrongdoings ..."

Suddenly, the door was flung open and Zubeida walked in, drunk. Tall, with bulging eyes, she had the kind of body that was always ready to pleasure a battalion of soldiers returning victorious from war. She exchanged kisses with Widad. The barman placed a glass of wine and a sugar bowl in front of Zubeida. She scooped a spoonful of sugar in her glass and stirred it in. Widad thought to herself that Nabil had a similar habit of putting salt in his beer to slow down the effects of the alcohol.

Zubeida said to Widad: "I haven't slept for more than two or three hours over the last three days." She slipped off her shoes and stood barefoot. "It makes me sick. My head's spinning like a top."

Widad's words froze in her throat as she thought of the men she had slept with and whom she didn't love.

She turned to look at the sea. The horizon was cloaked in mist. Night was falling. Rain buffeted the windowpanes. The bar owner and his friend were chatting. A thought like a perfumed flower blossomed in Widad's mind, racked with sorrow about the things she had never had. She couldn't stand an empty glass, and beckoned the barman to top it up. Lightning flashed, followed by crashing thunder. Zubeida trembled. She exchanged an enigmatic glance with Widad. Outside, the sea and the sky were raging.

"I can't stand thunder," said Zubeida.

Suddenly a white cat appeared in the room. It sidled up to Zubeida, looking up at her affectionately, meowing. Zubeida looked at it, horrified.

"Do you like it?" she asked Widad.

Widad answered, surprised: "It's only a cat."

"Not every cat is just a cat. One day, my mother was cleaning a fish and a cat came and meowed innocently around her. When she tried to shoo it away, the cat attacked her, sinking its teeth and claws in her hand. Two days later, the cat returned to

«يا إلهي ! أنا الخاطىء، أما هي، فلا تَدَعها تعاني...».

فُتح الباب بقوة ودخلت زبيدة سكرى٧. لها عينا بقرة. طويلة وجسمها مستعد أن يلذذ فرقة من العائدين منتصرين في الحرب. تَباوست مع وداد. وضع «الحاني»٨ كأس نبيذ٩ والسكرية لزبيدة. ملأت ملعقة وحركتها في كأسها. فكرت وداد: إن نبيل أيضاً يشرب أحياناً البيرة ممزوجة بقليل من الملح حتى لا يشمل بسرعة. قالت زبيدة لوداد :

لم أنم منذ ثلاثة أيام أكثر من ساعتين أو ثلاث كلّ ليلة.

خلعت حذاءها ووقفت عارية القدمين.

– هذا يقيني من القيء. إن رأسي يغلي.

تُحس وداد أن رغبتها في الكلام تنحبس في حلقها. تفكر في هؤلاء الذين تنام معهم دون أحلام.

نظرتْ إلى البحر. الأفق غائم والليل ينزل والمطر يصفع الزجاج. صاحب الحانة ورفيقه يتحدثان. زهرة عاطرة تتبرعم في خاطر وداد الحزينة. إن حسرتها على الأشياء التي أحبتها و لم تمتلكها قط تؤلمها. لم تحتمل كأسها فارغة. أومأت للحاني أن يملأها. بَرْق أعقبه رعد عنيف. انتفضت زبيدة. تبادلت نظره غامضة مع وداد. البحر والسماء يعنفان. قالت زبيدة:

– لا أطيق الرعد.

ظهرت فجأة قطة بيضاء في القاعة. تطلعت إلى زبيدة باستعطاف وماءت. نظرت إليها زبيدة بخوف. قالت لوداد :

– هل ترينها قريبة من القلب؟

اندهشت وداد:

– إنها مجرد قطة.

– كلّ قطة ليست دائماً مجرد قطة. كانت أمي تغسل سمكاً وقطة تموء ببراءة حولها. حين همّت أن تطردها هاجمتها وغرزت أسنانها ومخالبها في يدها. بعد يومين عادت القطة إلى المنزل. وجدت أمي مبرراً لعقابها.

the house. My mother found a pretext to punish the animal by locking it in a small room. After a few days, we opened the door and found a ghostlike creature that could barely move, let alone walk. Its eyes were filled with madness. It was a terrifying sight.

"I told my mother: 'We're going to feed her and give her some water. ' She shouted: 'No, you won't! It will die of hunger. It's possessed by Satan and you have to kill it! Take the animal far away from here, to a place where there's no food. '

"My little brother Mustafa and I put the cat into a basket and took it to a remote, desolate place, and we left her there. I asked my brother to wait with the cat until my return. When he asked me why, I told him that I was going to find the animal something to eat and some water so that it could survive. He said: 'I'll tell Mummy!'

"We left the animal and went back home. My little brother was skipping along and kicking empty cans; I, however, felt quite sad for the cat, which was about to die of hunger. That night, my mother felt the convulsions of the cat. The following morning, my brother and I collected some food and drink and went in search of the cat to give it to her in case she was still alive. We couldn't find her. I tried to convince my mother that somebody must have taken it home with them.

"She said: 'Never! You must have freed her spirit into the ghost that was strangling me the whole night.' For years afterwards, this incident continued to haunt my mother because she never rid herself from the cat's ghost until the day she died."

"And so you waited for the day to take revenge on cats for your mother?"

"Me? Never! Animals don't give me any pleasure anymore."

Zubeida asked the barman to fill up their glasses. Widad thought about Miloud al-Farsi's cat. He was a bachelor who shared his own food with his beautiful cat, whom he bathed and who slept in his bed. When she grew old and sick and her

حبستها في حجرة صغيرة. بعد أيام فتحنا لها الباب. شبح يتحرك بصعوبة. لم تستطع أن تمشي. نظراتها مجنونة. منظرها يخيف. قلت لأمي.

— سنطعمها ونُشْربها.

صَرَخَت أمِّي :

— أبداً. ستموت جوعاً. إنها مسكونة بالشيطان. لابد أن نقتله فيها. اذهبي بها بعيداً حيث لا تجد شيئاً تأكله.

وضعناها، أنا وأخي الصغير مصطفى، في سلة وحملناها بعيداً وتركناها في أرض جرداء. طلبت من أخي أن ينتظرني قدامها حتى أعود. قال لماذا؟ قلت سأبحث لها عن شيء من الأكل والماء عساها تعيش. قال: سأقول هذا لأمي.

تركناها وعدنا. هو يقفز ويقذف العلب الفارغة بقدميه وأنا حزينة على القطة التي ستموت جوعاً. في تلك الليلة أصيبت أمي بتشنج القطة. في الصباح حملنا طعاماً وشراباً أنا وأخي وذهبنا نبحث عن القطة لكي ننقذها إذا كانت ما زالت حيّة. لم نجدها. حاولت أن أقنع أمي بأن أحداً أخذها لِيُعْنى بها. قالت:

— أبداً. لا بد أن تكون قد حلّت روحها في الشبح الذي بات الليل كله يخنقني. عاشت أمي سنوات بعد ذلك الحادث لكنها لم تتخلّص قط من شبح القطة حتى ماتت.

— ولهذا تلحّ عليك أنت اليوم رغبةُ الانتقام لأمك من القطط.

— أنا؟ أبداً، لكنّ الحيوانات كلها لم تعد تفرحني.

طلبت زبيدة من الحاني أن يملأ لهما كأسيهما. تذكرت وداد قطة ميلود الفارسية. كان أعزب. يطعم قطته الجميلة مما يأكله، يُحَمّمها بنفسه، تنام في فراشه. وعندما شاخت ومرضت وبدأ يتساقط شعرها الجميل ملأ حوض

beautiful hair began to fall out, he filled the bath with water, grabbed her by the neck and held her down in the water until she died.

The song continued: "*I was twenty years old when I wasted my time on silly things.*"

He took out his diary and wrote in it: "Hope is fate, assuming that there is goodwill. How many times have I embraced a man I hated, for the sake of a fickle woman we both loved."

He looked at Widad, lovingly. She asked: "What are you writing?"

"*Thoughts and feelings. The night of people and my naked nights. Evil nights. Lonely nights. The nights of two beetles of the same species as I am who are fighting over a dead mouse. Magian nights. The Magians used to like melancholy nights."*

He was sitting close to the window, looking at the stars and writing. Widad was in her nightdress and lay on the edge of the bed, her legs touching the floor. Suddenly he felt a slight irritation, and wrote: "It is man, not God, who causes pain. He doesn't feel sad since He is omniscient. As for people, we are often in pain because we know so little."

He didn't know anymore how to select his thoughts. He took a sip from his glass. Widad felt like an orphan in front him. He had his whole future ahead of him. He would finish his university studies and graduate as a philosophy teacher. He would have another woman, while she would continue to sleep with men she didn't love.

It occurred to her to kick him out and never see him again in her flat. However, her heart began to throb. She changed her mind and looked at him, filled with love, while he was engrossed in writing down his feelings, many of which he did not understand.

Nabil was sitting on the sand as Widad went through her usual rituals to soothe her nerves, walking along the edge of the sea with the water flowing over her feet. Most of her vitality returned. He continued to record his feelings and thoughts in his book without looking up. He thought she was like a flower without a stem. Then he

الحمّام بالماء وأمسكها من قفاها ثم أغرقها ضاغطاً عليها حتى اختنقت.

الأغنية تقول: «كان لي عشرون عاماً حين كنت أُضيّع الوقت في الحماقات».

أخرج مذكرته وكتب فيها: «الأمل هو الصدفة، والافتراض هو حُسن نية. كم من مرات عانقت فيها إنساناً أكرهه من أجل امرأة طائشة نشترك معاً في حبها!».

نظر إلى وداد بحب. سألته:

– ماذا تكتب؟

– خواطر.

«ليل الناس وليلي العاري. ليل وحشي، مهجور. ليل خنفستين من جنس مثلي تتعارك حول كان حول فأرة ميتة. ليل مجوسي. المجوس¹⁰ كانوا يحبون الليل الكئيب».

كان جالساً قرب النافذة يتأمل النجوم ويكتب ووداد، في ثياب نومها، مستلقية على حافة الفراش ورجلاها على الأرض. فجأة شعر بقليل من الضجر فكتب: «إن الناس يتألمون لأن الله لا يتألم. هو لا يحزن لأنه يعرف كلّ شيء، أما نحن البشر فنتألم كثيراً من أجل أن نعرف القليل».

لم يعد يعرف كيف ينتقي أفكاره. رشف من كأسه. وداد تشعر بأنها يتيمة أمامه. هو له مستقبله. سينهي دراسته الجامعية ويتخرج أستاذ فلسفة. ستكون له امرأة غيري أما أنا فسأظل أنام مع رجال لا أحبهم.

خطر لها أن تطرده ولا ولن تراه أبداً في شقتها، لكنّ نبضات قلبها بدأت تضطرب ثم غيرت رأيها ونظرت إليه بحب وهو مستغرق في كتابة خواطره التي لا يفهم أكثرها.

نبيل جالس على الرمل ووداد تقوم بطقوسها المسكنة لأعصابها متمشية على حافة البحر والماء يغمر قدميها.

عادت أكثر حيوية. كان مستمراً في كتابة خواطره على الدفتر. فكر فيها: إنها مثل وردة بلا ساق. ثم كتب لنفسه: إن ليل الغاب أفضل من ليل

wrote to himself: "A forest night with its owls, bats, crickets, frogs and foxes is better than a beach night. Here, everything is buried under the sand and there is no life beneath the waves."

It seemed to them that the sea was split: the green is close, the blue farther away. The horizon forms a string of white flowers, screened by the mist.

He picked up a handful of sand. His eyes were in hers, gleaming with desire. He closed them. He felt her breath warming his face. The grip of his hand on the sand loosened. They hugged. Nakedness always made him yearn for her body.

She turned her gaze towards the faces arranged in a row along the length of the bar. A lone youth was talking to a red flower he held in his hand; the woman sitting opposite him looked on, as he sought her advice on what to say to the flower. Widad felt she was an object of desire to all of them. Samir looked at her, showing his jacket for sale. She imagined them taking turns raping her. The bar was filled with men. Five or six of the women were each drinking with more than one man. She drank her glass there, while other glasses were awaiting her somewhere else. Widad hated herself for being desired in this way. She was afraid that someone other than Nabil would love her. She reflected that in passion there was some love. Her punter was paying good money for her. He was an old married man who was kind to her. However, he did not show up tonight.

Nabil had written in his notebook: "I don't understand Widad except if she is far away from me. I feel as connected to her as I do to my own life, while distance brings out the various dimensions of this connection; I can't even enjoy music unless it comes to me in exquisite vibrations. The natural view appears more inspiring when it is enough for me to look into the abyss, while I am overcome with vertigo that fills my head with hallucinations that haunt me like they do those who are treated with electroshocks in mental hospitals. My true soul stops on the other bank, at the top of the lighthouse whose mad lights reveal what floats on the sea. I am fed up with those who are reasonable towards themselves, as well as with raving madmen."

الشاطىء: البومة، والخفاش، والجدجد، والضفدع، والثعلب. أماهنا فكل شيء مدفون في هذه الرمال وماهو حي تحت الأمواج.

بدا لهما البحر منقسماً على نفسه: اللون الأخضر قريب، الأزرق بعيد. والأفق البحري يشكل حقلاً من الزهور البيضاء المكسوة بالضباب.

قبضت يده على حفنة من الرمل. عيناه في عينيها رغبة متوهجة. أغمضهما. أحس بأنفاسها تدفىء وجهه. تراخت يده القابضة على حفنة الرمل. تعانقا. العراء يغزيه دائماً بدفء جسدها.

ألقت نظرة على الوجوه المصفوفة على طول المشرب[11]. شاب وحيد جالس إلى المشرب يتكلم مع وردة حمراء في يده والمرأة أمامه شاهدة مستشيراً إياها عما يقوله للوردة. أحست وداد أنها مشتهاة من جميعهم. سمير ناظراً إليها عارضاً سترته للبيع. تصورتهم مجانين يتناوبون على اغتصابها. الحانة ملأى[12] بالرجال. خمس أوست منهن تنادم كلّ واحدة منهن أكثرمن واحد: تشرب كأسها هنا وكووس تنتظرها هناك. وداد تكره نفسها حين تكون مشتهاة بهذا الشكل. تخشى أن يحبها أحد غيرنبيل. تعتقد أن في الشهوة بعض الحب. إن زبونها يدفع لها ثمناً. إنه مُسنّ ومتزوج. لطيف معها، لكنه لم يأت هذه الليلة.

وكان نبيل قد كتب في مذكرته: إنني لا أفهم وداد إلا عندما تكون بعيدة عني. إن حياتي لها صلة نفسها بنفسها في البعد الذي يميِّز أبعادها. فحتى الموسيقى لا أتذوق منها إلا ما كان يأتيني على شكل تموُّجات أثيرية، والمنظر الطبيعي يبدو أكثر إلهاماً حين يكفي أن أنظرإلى الهوة السحيقة فيغمرني الدوار ويغسل ذهني من الوساوس الملحة عليّ كما يحدث للذين يعالجون بالصدمات الكهربائية في المصحّات[13] العقلية. إن نفسي الحقيقية تقف فوق الضفة الأخرى على المنارة الكاشفة بمصباحها المجنون عما يطفو فوق البحر. لقد سئمت هؤلاء العقلاء مع أنفسهم والمجانين أكثر جنوناً.

She was still sitting alone when a black Moroccan man walked in, handsome and smartly dressed. He sat down with two others at a table and started to recount how he had saved a girl from drowning on the beach. Suddenly, he said in a loud voice: "I hate ungrateful people."

Widad could not stop herself from looking at him. He stared at her with his left eye, his mouth wide open and his tongue running along his lower lip. She thought to herself: "He's trapped me. If only I hadn't looked at him. I've never slept with a black guy."

A small child entered, holding out her hand into empty space. Widad beckoned her. She grabbed her outstretched hand.

"What's your name?"

"Rahma."

"Where's your mother?"

"She's waiting for me outside."

She gave her a coin, and gently turned her away.

Widad looked at the hand as though it were a crow joyfully alighting on her shoulder. She felt it slipping down her back. This was the first time a black man had touched her. She looked at him in the darkness. He smiled at her, his eyes filled with joy. It seemed to her that nothing could satisfy him. These feelings for a man who longed for her without her having any clear desire were like a dark night to her. She remained calm. Her feelings towards him were blurred. His claws dug into her back, and then he said:

"Are you happy?"

She looked at him silently, as if in a daze. He appeared to her like a child that does not deserve any punishment. He kissed her on the cheek; his nose was warm, his breath heavy with alcohol mixed with a strong fragrance. She had let herself go in worse places. She got up and left amidst the rapacious stares of the drunks. The black man followed her, swaggering.

كانت ما زالت وحيدة عندما دخل زنجي[14] مغربي. كان جميلاً وأنيقاً. جلس مع اثنين إلى طاولة وأخذ يقص كيف أنقذ فتاة من الغرق في الشاطىء. فجأة قال بصوت عالٍ:

ـ إنني أكره الناس الذين لا يعترفون بالجميل.

لم تستطع وداد أن تمنع نفسها من النظر إليه. غمزها بعينه اليمنى تاركاً فمه منفغراً ولسانه ينزلق على شفته السفلى الممتلئة. فكرت: لقد أوقعني في فخ. ليتني لم أنظر إليه. لم أنم قط مع زنجي.

دخلت طفلة مادة يدها في الفراغ. أشارت لها وداد أن تقترب منها. أمسكتها من يدها الممدودة:

ـ ما اسمك؟

ـ رحمة.

ـ وأين أمك؟

ـ تنتظرني في الخارج.

أعطتها قطعة نقدية وصرفتها بلطف.

رأت وداد يداً مثل غراب تحط في مرح على كتفها. أحست بها تنزل على ظهرها. إنه أول زنجي يلمسها. نظرت إليه في غموض. ابتسم لها. عيناه فرحتان. خيل إليها أنها لن تستطيع أن تشبعه في شيء. كان هذا الشعور، أمام رجل يشتهيها دون رغبة منها واضحة، يشكل لديها ليل الأعماق. ظلت هادئة. ومشاعرها نحوه ضبابية. ضغط برأسه على ظهرها ثم قال:

ـ هل أنت مسرورة؟

نظرت إليه دون أن تفوه بشيء. منوّمة. بدا لها كطفل لا يستحق أي عقاب. قبّلها على خدها. أنفاسه الحارة المخمورة ممزوجة بعطر قوي. تخيلت نفسها في أكثر الأماكن وحشية. قامت وخرجت وسط نظرات السكارى المفترسة والزنجي يتبعها في زهو.

Language Notes

1. حانات :sg. حان or حانة, lit. "a place where wine (خَمْر) is sold".

2. مِشَنّ: this is a very uncommon word meaning "bathtub".

3. حَفْيانة: dialectal expression (MCA, but also common in other colloquials, such as Iraqi); MSA: حاف (fem. حَافية); pl. حُفاة.

4. رُكْن: pl. أَرْكان. lit. "a corner", "nook", it generally denotes any semi-closed-off part of a room.

5. قِطْعة نَقْديَّة: (pl. قِطَع نَقْديَّة) < نَقْد ("money"), pl. نُقُود ("change", "coins"). It is synonymous with قطعة من النُّقود or قطْعَة نُقُود.

6. الحَاكي: the basic meaning of this word (indef. حَاكٍ) is "storyteller" (< حَكَى), which has undergone metaphorical extension to mean "record player" ("phonograph"). The word جراموفون (< "gramophone") is also commonly used.

7. سَكْرَى: the feminine form of the adjective سَكْران (pl. سُكَارَى). This is the common paradigm of words of this pattern (e. g. كَسْلان, f. كَسْلا, pl. كسالى – "lazy"). However, in MSA, there is an increasing trend towards a regular feminine, e.g. سَكْرانة.

8. الحَاني: < حان (see above); MSA. سَاقي الحَانة.

9. نَبِيذَ: originally, this was a generic word for various intoxicating drinks, made from barley, honey, etc (which is indeed how it is still used today in Syria). In some countries (e. g. Egypt), نَبِيذ came to be used to mean "wine", alongside the more usual term خَمْر.

10. مَجُوس: mediaeval Arabic historians from the Maghrib and Muslim Spain used this term to refer to both the Normans and the Scandinavian Norsemen, both of whom regularly attempted incursions into western Muslim territories. In the East, however, the term denoted the Zoroastrians.

11. مَشْرَب: this word can either mean "drink" (cf. مَشْرُوب, pl.

مَقْهَى or (مَشاريبُ .or a "drinking place" (pl ,(مَشْرُوبات).

12. مَلأَى: the feminine form of مَلآن (pl. مَلاء).

13. مِصَحَّة: this word is used more in the Maghrib (especially Morocco and Tunisia) than in the East, where مُسْتَشْفَى is more widespread.

14. زَنْجِيّ: also see حكاية القنديل.

Idwār al-Kharrāṭ

One of Egypt's most famous and influential authors, Idwār al-Kharrāṭ (Edwar Al-Karrat) was born into a Coptic family in Alexandria in 1926. Despite taking on the role of sole breadwinner after the death of his father, a small shopkeeper, al-Kharrāṭ nevertheless was able to finish his law studies at Alexandria University.

He began his working life as a journalist, followed by a stint in business before working as a translator and finally devoting all his time to literature, specializing in novels and short stories. Al-Kharrāt made his debut in 1959 with a collection of short stories entitled حيطان عالية (*High Walls*). He was also politically involved, and during his student days he played an active part in the nationalist revolutionary movement (as a member of a far left-wing group), for which he was imprisoned for two years (1948–50).

After his first collection, which was published at the author's expense, it took over a decade for al-Kharrāṭ to release his second book, another collection of short stories entitled سّاعات الكِبْرياء (*Moments of Pride*, 1972). Later he published اخْتناقات العِشْق والصَّباح (*Suffocations of Passion and the Morning*, 1979). At the same time, he concentrated on his translations (from both English and French) and criticism. It was not until 1979 that he published his first novel, the seminal راما والتَّنين (*Rama and*

The Dragon, English trans. 2003), which met with great critical acclaim. Many of al-Kharrāṭ's novels have been translated into English: يا بَنات اسْكْنْدَرية زَعْفران تُرابُها (*The City of Saffron*, 1989), (*Girls of Alexandria*, 1998) and حجارات بوبلو (*Stones of Bobello*, 2005).

Al-Kharrāṭ's work is rich with Egyptian cultural, social and political references, as well as autobiographical elements (e.g. the fact that many of his protagonists are Copts), couched in finely crafted prose in which the author often subverts traditional grammatical conventions. His writing often bathes in an oneiric atmosphere. From his early work (which was marked by a conscious attempt to veer away from the realist school that pervaded so much writing of the time) to the present day, al-Kharrāṭ has continued to remain in the vanguard of contemporary Egyptian and Arabic literature, forever blazing new paths.

The story included here is an excellent example of al-Kharrāṭ's prose and the atmosphere he succeeds in conjuring up so wonderfully and eloquently. The occasion is the death of an iconic Egyptian actress whose name, however, we never learn, whereas the information provided about the mystery lady appears to be a composite of a number of idols of the Egyptian screen and stage. Above all, the story constitutes a journey on the part of the protagonist, to which the reader is party. It also contains some of al-Kharrat's other typical themes such as loneliness, estrangement and alienation, not only from the world around us, but also from loved ones.

At the Theatre

"Masks are the temptations of truth."

That night, Opera Square looked magnificent.

The street lamps were aglow with white, radiant light, while the palm fronds rustled in the night breeze. The statue of Ibrahim Pasha was lit up, proudly showing off its bronze body.

I entered alone.

The marble staircase and the ancient iron gate glistened, while the red carpets muffled all sounds. I noticed that the lowest box, which directly looked out onto the stage, was still empty. My seat was comfortable and alluring. I leaned on the crimson-lined balcony railing, and said to myself: "Why aren't they here yet? It is nearly the appointed time." Then it was as though I had completely forgotten about them.

The murmur of the voices, the movement of feet and the peaceful hubbub rose up to me from the hall, studded with turning lights. The red, plush velvet they lit up added to the impression of luxury. Then the three knocks came; the lights were dimmed, and the din and hum gradually died down.

A man went to the front of the stage, in front of the curtain, taking short, heavy steps. He had a stocky build and was holding a piece of paper in his hand. I heard my neighbour whisper in a clear voice: "Muhammad Bey Sabri, the director."

The opera director stopped in front of the microphone stand, near its large disc. It was only now that I wondered at his presence there. He said:

"Ladies and gentlemen, it is with much regret that I have to announce ... I have to say ... announce ... I have some very sad news ..."

The heavy gilt-embroidered curtain opened with a soft, audible metallic sound.

However, the stage was deserted. The set was that of a

عَ١ المسرح

«الأقنعة غوايات الحقيقة»

كان ميدان الأوبرا٢ ليلتها بهيجاً.

عناقيد المصابيح الكهربية ناضجة بعصارة بيضاء مشعّة، وسعف النخل السلطاني يهمس في نسمة المساء، وتمثال إبراهيم باشا٣ يومض جسمه البرونزي في كبرياء.

دخلت وحدي.

السلالم الرخاميّة والباب الحديدي عريقة تلمع. والسجاجيد الحمراء تمتص الأصوات.

وجدت أن اللوج المنخفض الذي يطلّ على خشبة المسرح مباشرة ما زال خالياً. كان مقعدي وثيراً ومغرياً بالراحة. استندت إلى سياج الشرفة المبطنة العميقة اللون، وقلت: «لماذا لم يأتوا؟ أوشك الميعاد أن يجيء» ثم كأنني نسيتهم تماماً.

كان طنين الكلام وحركة الأقدام واللغط الهادىء يصعد إليّ من القاعة المنشورة بحبّات النور المدوّرة، وكانت حمرة القطيفة المكتومة توحي ببذخ مكتوم.

الدقّات الثلاث، خفتت الأضواء وسقط اللغط والطنين رويداً.

جاء إلى مقدمة الخشبة، من أمام الستار، رجل ثقيل الخطو، قصير، مدموك البنيان، وفي يده ورقة. سمعت جاري يهمس بصوت واضح: «محمد بك؛ صبري المدير."

وقف مدير الدار أمام عمود الميكروفون٥ بقرصه المضلّع الكبير، أنتبهتُ الآن فقط إلى أنه كان هناك، منذ البداية. وقال: سيداتي وسادتي. يؤسفني جدّ الأسف أنعى إليكم...أن أقول. أعلن. عندي نبأ أليم.

انفتحت الستارة الثقيلة المذهبة التطريز بصوت خفيف معدنيّ مسموع. ولكنّ المسرح خاوٍ. ديكور غرفة الاستقبال الأوروبية التقليدية من القرن

traditional nineteenth-century European reception room; it appeared dreary, with faint lights.

At that moment, I saw them, all the actresses, who had lined up on the stage in a single row, with the actors behind them in a second row. The actresses' stage clothes were thick and dignified, old-fashioned; they appeared to be brand new, as though they had never been worn before. The multicoloured satin – blue, green and purple, glistening, heavy, puffed up and riddled with pleats and embroidery – looked stiff. The men's suits, on the other hand, had jackets, wide, flat collars that were tight around their necks and a multitude of buttons.

They were all silent, solemnly standing, motionless. An expectant silence descended upon the theatre.

A tall woman with powerful charisma emerged from the row of actresses. She moved towards the microphone. It was as though the director had disappeared, yet he had, in fact, only taken one step back.

It occurred to me that she had that aura associated with the glory of the theatre in the Twenties, when she was the pin-up of all the students who undid the reins of the horses of her royal carriage and pulled it with their arms tied, vying with one another to tug it from her house in Fouad Street to the theatre in Emad Ed-Din Street.

She was the Sarah Bernhardt of the East, the Small Eagle, Hamlet, Cleopatra, Shajrat al-Durr, Desdemona, Bilqis, the Queen of Sheba, Juliet and Layla, Zubeida the Barmakid, Zizi Hanem and Layla Bint al-Fuqara' all rolled into one – so many living façades, so many lives!

I stopped, alarmed. I had let out a scream without fully realizing what I was doing. Some people from below looked up at me. Two firemen who had been standing next to the stage proceeded towards me as though they were going to stop me from making any movement.

She paused for a moment. Then she said: "Ladies and gentlemen."

الماضي، ويبدو موحشاً، خافت الأضواء.

وعندئذ رأيتهن، كلَّ الممثلات. يقفن صفاً واحداً في الأمام، وخلفهن الممثلون، في الصف الثاني.

ملابس التمثيل النسائية الضخمة الوقور، قديمة الطراز، تبدو عليهن جد قشيبة لم تُلبس من قبل، الفساتين الملوّنة، زرقاء وخضراء وموف، لامعة وثقيلة ومنتفشة٦ ومليئة بالكشكشة والتوشية، راسخة الشكل، والبدل الرجالي ذات الياقات المفلطحة العريضة والفتحات الضيِّقة والأزرار الكثيرة.

كانوا صامتين، جادين في وقفتهم، دون حركة.

نزل على القاعة كلها صمت الترقب.

خرجتْ من بينهم، طويلة، قوية الحضور٧. وتقدّمت إلى الميكروفون، فكأن المدير قد اختفى، مع أنه، فقط، تراجع خطوة واحدة إلى الوراء.

طاف بذهني أنها ما زالت تحتفظ بهالة من مجد مسرح العشرينات، عندما كانت معبودة الطلبة، فكوا لجام جوزالخيل من عربتها الحنطور الملاكي وجرّوا العربة بأذرعهم المتكاتفة ثم تسابقت حشودهم إلى حمل العربة حملاً، من بيتها في شارع فؤاد إلى المسرح في عماد الدين٨.

سارة برنار الشرق، النسر الصغير٩، هاملت، كليوباترا، شجرة الدر١٠، ديدمونة، بلقيس١١، ملكة سبأ، جوليت وليلى١٢، زبيدة البرمكية١٣، زيزي هانم وليلى بنت الفقراء١٤، معاً، كم من أقنعة حيّة. كم من حيوات!

ووقفتُ مروَّعاً، كنت قد صرختُ دون أن أعي تماماً ما أفعل، ارتفعت بعض الأنظار إليَّ من تحت، اتجه إليَّ اثنان من شرطة المطافىء، الذين كانوا على جانبي خشبة المسرح، كأنما ليمنعاني من الحركة.

ووقفتْ صامتة لحظة.

وقالت: سيداتي، سادتي.

Her voice was trembling, revealing the heavy burden that stirred the hearts. It was as if an invisible spark was spreading throughout the entire hall.

After seemingly collecting her wandering thoughts with great difficulty, she continued:

"Ladies and gentlemen ... It pains me to stand here in front of you in this hallowed place and announce to you the demise of a magnificent flower of the theatre, a star of the art, our dazzling ... and brilliant actress ..."

Her voice broke once again as she uttered the name of the deceased.

As if mustering what remained of her strength, she added: "A short time ago, we lost ... despite our calling upon the most experienced doctors and raising our hands to the sky ... We immediately took her to a doctor ... but God decided otherwise ... we've lost her ... may God have mercy on her soul."

Then, she completely broke down in tears, the sobbing reverberating throughout the silent hall in a strange echo.

Everyone in the theatre gasped unconsciously upon hearing the name. People rushed to their feet, and everywhere there was sobbing and crying, interspersed with the short shrill cries of women. All the lights came on, and the doors were opened.

In a space next to the wings near me I saw fake Roman columns made from light wood; an ancient triumphal stone arch, which was actually plywood; splendid, green, glistening ceramic vases made out of cardboard; huge oak and cypress forests that seemed to run until the distant horizon, in which a fiery, red sun went down on a dusty panel; Louis XIV chairs piled on top of one another; black marble tables; walls of country dwellings made of short tree stumps, surrounded by elegant gardens with tulips and violets; cemeteries stretching out in Coptic churchyards; a bridge across a small ditch opposite a country coffeehouse; tall minarets and walls of mosques streaked with yellow and dark brown; imposing staircases

كان صوتها يرتعش، محمّلاً بشحنة هزّت القلوب، وكأنما أنتفض شرر النار غير المرئيّ في جو القاعة كلها.

ثم كأنما استجمعت نفسها المشتتة بجهد جهيد، وهي تقول:

— سيداتي، سادتي، إنه ليحزنني وأنا أقف بين أيديكم على هذا الهيكل المقدّس، أن أنعى إليكم سقوط وردة المسرح اليانعة، نجمة الفن الساطعة، ممثلتنا الباهرة...الزاهرة.

تكسّر صوتها مرّة أخرى وهي تنطق اسمها.

قالت كأنها تستجمع آخر ما في وسعها من تشدد:

— سقطت من بيننا منذ قليل، استدعينا لها نُطس الأطباء، ورفعنا أيدينا إلى السماء. نقلناها فوراً في كنف الأطباء... لكنّ أمر الله نفذ... وفقدناها. يرحمها الله.

ثم أجهشت بالبكاء الصريح الذي كان له الآن صدى غريب في القاعة الصامتة.

كانت القاعة قد شهقت، كأنما من غير وعي، عند سماع الاسم. الآن هبّ الناس واقفين، انفجر النشيج والبكاء وصرخاتٌ نسوية قصيرة ثاقبة، أضيئت الأنوار كاملة وانفتحت كلّ أبواب الخروج.

نظرت عَرَضاً إلى جانب الكواليس القريب مني، الأعمدة الرومانية المتقنة الصنع معمولة من الخشب الخفيف، أقواس النصر عتيقة الحجر، من الأبلاكاش[15]، فازات هائلة خضراء خزفية اللمعان، من الكرتون، غابات السرو والبلوط[16] شاسعة حتى الأفق البعيد الذي تغرق فيه شمس متوهّجة الحمرة على لوحة متربة، كراسي لويس الرابع عشر مكوّمة فوق بعضها بعضاً، الموائد الرخامية السوداء، أسوار البيوت الريفيّة من الشجر القصير المجذوذ تحيط بجناين مونقة بالتيوليب والبنفسج، الجبّانات الممتدة في ساحات الكنائس القوطية، الكوبري[17] على الترعة الصغيرة أمام القهوة الفلاحي، المآذن السامقة وجدران الجوامع المخططة بالأصفر والبنيّ القاتم، السلالم الضخمة العريضة الدورات تصعد إلى شرفات داخلية مسوّرة

with wide banisters rising towards balconies, their ironwork railings inlaid with bunches of flowers; the square in front of Cairo Central Station; ancient statues with broken noses; wooden platforms and estrades; gas lanterns perpetually lit in streets glistening with rain; large pulleys with thickly knotted ropes; towering stepladders; and thick, dangerously dangling cables. All this paraphernalia was dimly lit by yellow lights, which went out and then faintly appeared again in the narrow passageways. The wind suddenly rushed along the painted cloth and cardboard, gently shaking the pillars, forests and edifices, softly stirring the fabric. The smell of the dust in the wings rose to my nostrils.

She was standing there, alone.

She was staring at me, as though she did not see me.

I knew she was dead, and that my love would not die.

There was nobody who saw her there, nobody who heard my cries. Did I call her?

It was as though the shadow of a smile was engraved on her lips. I knew that she would be in great pain, not of her doing and not for herself, but for me, or perhaps for all of us.

I said: "What caused you this pain?"

She said: "Nothing, perhaps a burning desire, just like that. Until I say so."

I said: "Why the pain?"

She said: "An unresolved crisis in the soul has consumed me with grief and sorrow ... pride stood between the two of us – is it because I was only free here?"

I said: "Is there no other salvation ...?"

She said: "To refrain completely from seeing each other."

I said: "Should anyone be required to carry this heavy burden?"

She said: "This is a deserted place. There is no one here."

I said: "Neither a procession of celebrants, nor three Maries?"

بحديد مشغول ترتمي عليه خصل الزهور، فناء محطّة مصر، وتماثيل عريقة ملقاة على وجوهها مكسورة الأنف، المنصّات والبراتيكابلات[18] الخشبية، فوانيس الغاز مضيئة أبداً في شوارع مبلّلة بالمطر، بكرات ضخمة من حبال متورّمة الفتيل وسلالم نقاليّ شاهقة وكابلات متدلّية وسميكة منذرة بالخطر، والأنوار الصفراء تتخايل بين هذه الركامات، تخبو وتشتعل بضعف من جديد في ممرات ضيّقة. يهبّ الهواء فجأة على القماش المرسوم والُورق المقوّى فتهتزّ الأعمدة والغابات والبنايات بخفّة وبترقرق نسيجها. صعدت إليّ رائحة تراب الكواليس.

وهي، وحدها، واقفة هناك.

كانت تحدِّق إليّ، وكأنها لا تراني.

أعرف أنها ميّتة، وأن حبّي لا يموت.

لم يكن أحد يراها هناك. لم يسمع أحد صرختي. هل ناديتها؟

وكأنما ارتسم على شفتيها ظل ابتسامة.

وعرفت أنها تتألّم ألَماً عميقاً لا برء منه. لا لنفسها، بل لي، وربما لنا كلنا.

قلت: ما الذي يدعو إليك هذا الألم؟

قالت: لا شيء. ربما نزعة حارقة، هكذا، إلى أن أقول.

قلت: لماذا الألم؟

قالت: أزمة معقودة في النفس. ترمضني. الكبرياء تحول بينها وبيني، هل لأن حريتي الوحيدة هنا؟

قلت: أما من خلاص آخر . ؟

قالت: امتناعٌ كامل للوصال.

قلت: أحتم أن ينوء بالواحد كلُّ هذا الثقل؟

قالت: هذه ساحة موحشة. ليس فيها أحد.

قلت: ولا موكب المحتفلين. ولا المريمات الثلاث[19]؟

She said: "And torturing soldiers with swords or spears."

I said: "This is not because of you, but because of them."

She said. "They're not there." Then she said: "Also because of you. Did you know this?

I said: "This burden I carry inside of me is deep-rooted, as am I. Is there no path to take?"

She said: "It is as if I haven't spoken. Nobody's heard me. It's as if everything I've done doesn't exist." Then she said: "They don't want what I give them. I give them my desires, my exclamations of joy, my cries of love and torments, and fragments of the soul. Nobody pays attention to me. They don't want to ... they don't want to."

I then said: "One is the same as all. I, for one, hear you, my love. Me, I want you. Even if there's only one."

She said: "Still, the plain of Golgotha is deserted. Lonely."

I said: "Masks are the temptations of truth."

She said: "My tears are for you; you who don't see."

I said to myself: "The light is totally dark. Of course. What were you waiting for?"

She told me: "My mother's village in Sharqiyya province was razed to the ground, as if it was a dark ominous cloud heavy with harmful rain. When it actually rained, its roads changed into deep rivulets of clay, the cattle leaving deep, successive grooves in the soaked soil. I would say to her: 'You'll get electricity from the dam, television, porno videos, chickens from the co-op and subsidised bread at 10 *piastres*.'"

She said: "Their lives revolved around the daily rituals: sleeping on the oven during winter, and on the bench perched against the outside wall in summer. Friday night was the time for lovemaking and recreation, whereas other nights were spent in the mercy of God. The rest of the time was spent chopping away at the soil with the hoe and plough; praying at the mosque; smoking the *gooza*; chatting at the coffeehouse and gossiping about whoever came and went; writing petitions

قالت: ولا جنود التعذيب، بالسيوف والرماح.

قلت: ليس من أجلك. بل من أجلهم.

قالت: ليسوا هناك.

ثم قالت: ومن أجلك أيضاً. فهل عرفت؟

قلت: مريرٌ حمل هذه الأثقال في داخلي، أنا أيضاً. وما من طريق.

قالت: وكأنني لم أقل. لا أحد سمعني. كلّ ما فعلت كأنه لم يكن.

ثم قالت: لا يريدون مني ما أعطيه لهم. أقدّم لهم أشواقي وهتفاتي، صيحات حب وعذابات، جذاذات الروح. ما من أحد يصغي. لايريدون. لايريدون.

قلت أنا: واحدٌ هو الكل. أسمعك أنا يا حبيبتي. أريدك أنا. ولو واحد فقط.

قالت: ما زالت ساحة الجلجثة موحشة. وحيدة.

قلت: الأقنعة غوايات مُقيمة.

قالت: دموعي لكم. أنتم لا ترون.

قلت لنفسي: النور ظلمةٌ كاملة. طبعاً. ماذا كنت تنتظر؟

قالت لي: كانت قرية أمي في الشرقية مرميّة على أرض كأنها سحاب مربدّ منذر بالمطر الوبيل. وعندما تمطر الدنيا فعلاً تتحوّل طرقاتها إلى أوحال عميقة الطين، وتترك البهائم حفراً غائرة متتالية في الأرض المعجونة بالبلل.

سوف أقول: ستأتي لهم كهرباء السد، والتليفزيون[20]، وأفلام البورنو في الفيديو، وفراخ الجمعية، والعيش المدعوم أبو عشر قروش[21].

قالت: الطقوس اليومية كانت محور حياتهم. النوم على الفرن شتاء وعلى المصطبة[22] صيفاً، مضاجعة النسوان ليلة الجمعة المفترجة[23] وكل ليلة أخرى عند فَرَج الله[24]، عناق الأرض بالفأس والمحراث، الصلاة في الجامع، الجوزة وطقّ الحَنَك ع القهوة ونَتْف فروة الرايح والجاي، كتابة العرضحال[25] والشكوى الغفل من الأمضاء، أُكلة البِتاو[26][27] بالمِشّ[27] والجُعْضيض كلّ يوم.

and anonymous complaints. The food consisted of *pitta* bread, fermented cheese and sow-thistle every day, added with meat for religious festivals. And then there were the visits to the shrines of saints for *baraka*, requests for intercession from Imam Shafi'i, Sayyida Zeinab and every member of the Batniyya court for the Prophet's blessing, noughts and crosses and quarterstaff fencing, ancient rituals going back until the beginnings of time, taken to heart without thinking, without formality."

Then she said: "Daily ugliness is a mask; it's deep and contains primal poetry."

I said: "There is nothing that can forgive ugliness, illness and oppression – or poetry, for that matter."

"What has happened to us, and to them? Egypt stinks with the rotting smell of oil and money from the Gulf, with that of our dead. Bring the shovel and the mattock. They fell victim to the attack of electronics. Yet, they continued to say: 'God gives unto those who are calm, righteous and sound asleep, unaware of what is going on'."

The big projector emitted its glowing light, which was reflected on the stage and shone through the curtains of the wings, leaving wide, deep-black shadows on the ground resembling thick, iron bars. The bright ray of light blinded the view into the darkness of the wings.

The centre of the beam shone on her.

She appeared small but tender-skinned, her plump, liquid limbs in the middle of the stage, her face radiant with bliss. Her voice and gestures revealed this freedom, this showing off, the fact that she'd given herself to the audience, voluntarily and unstintingly.

It was as though she had originally not put on those clothes that skilfully and deceitfully hung from her moving body, which made it seem as though she was returning to original innocence and no longer needed covering or nakedness like the wild bodies that looked around to ambush her, true to their nature.

والزَفَر أيام المواسم والأعياد، زيارة الموالد[28] والتبرّك بالقديسين وأولياء الله[29] الصالحين وطلب الشفاعة من الإمام الشافعي[30] والسيدة زينب[31] وكل أعضاء المحكمة الباطنية[32] ببركة الرسول، السيجة والتحطيب، طقوسيّةٌ عريقة متحدرة من غورٍ بعيد، مأخوذة إلى القلب دون تفكير، وليست شكلية.

ثم قالت: والقبح اليومي قناع. وفيه شعر أولّي وعميق.

قلت: ما من شيء يغفر القبح والمرض والظلم. ولا الشعر.

وسوف أقول: ماذا حدث لنا، ولهم؟ خُمّت مصر برائحة النفط وفلوس الخليج. خمّت بموتانا، هات الرفش والمعول. سقطوا تحت سطو الاليكترونات. لكنهم يظلّون يقولونَ: يرزق الهاجع والناجع والنايم[33] على صماخ ودانه[34].

كانت البروجكتورات الضخمة تلقي بأضوائها الساطعة فتنعكس من على خشبة المسرح وتنفذ من بين أستار الكواليس الجانبية تلقي خطوطاً عريضة حالكة السواد كأنها قضبان حديدية غليظة نائمة على الأرض، وخطوطاً ناصعة النور تغشى البصر في العتمة الجانبيّة. وكانت البقعة الدائريّة الرئيسيّة من النور تنصبّ عليها.

تبدو صغيرة القدر لكنّ بضّة، مليئة، سيّالة الجوارح في وسط ساحة المسرح، وجهها مشرق وسعيد.

في صوتها وإيماءاتها هذه الحرية، هذا التبذل، عطاء الجسد للجمهور طواعيةً دون ضنّ.

وكأنها لا ترتدي، أصلاً، تلك الملابس المقطوعة المسدلة بمكر وحذق على جسمها المتحرِّك الذي يبدو كأنه يعود إلى براءة حسيّة بدائيّة فلم يعد بحاجة إلى غطاء أو عراء مثل الأجسام الوحشيّة تجُوس وتتربّص بصيدها الطبيعي في عنصرها الطبيعي.

I asked: "Which is one of them is a mask? ... Is not the truth hidden behind a mask? What does the mirror say?"

Who said that whatever comes out of a deep-rooted natural disposition is nothing but a mask? Who said that she would not go, here and there, or anywhere her passion took her?

She told me: "He wanted me to belong to him, in the bedroom, as I belonged to all of you on the stage. That was impossible, entirely. What could I do?"

I asked her: "Who are you?"

He was waiting for her by the door, pale-faced, angry. He had a chiselled jaw and a thick, Stalin-like moustache. She began to run towards him from the door. He was waiting for her, a grim look on his face. They both got into an old Volkswagen with a broken bumper. The car disappeared around the corner of Abu'l-Ala Bridge.

All that remained was complete emptiness. The dream had suddenly left me. There was nothing left, not even a single image. Yet, a strange feeling emanated from the darkness.

قالت: أيهما القناع؟

قلت: أليس الحق كامناً في القناع؟ ماذا تقول المرآة؟

من يقول إن هذه التي تنطلق عن سجية عميقة فيها ليست إلاّ قناعاً؟ من يقول إنها لا تمشي. هنا والآن، حقاً، على بَرِّ هواها.

قالت لي: كان يريدني أن أكون له، في غرفة النوم، كما أنا، لكم جميعاً، على خشبة المسرح. ذلك مستحيل. تماماً. ماذا باستطاعتي أن أفعل؟

قلت لها: من أنت؟

كان ينتظرها على الباب، شاحب الوجه، غضوباً، له فكٌّ مضلَّع وشارب كثيف على طريقة ستالين. وانطلقت تجري إليه من على الباب، كان ينظر إليها بعبوس، دخل معها العربة الفولكس واجن القديمة ذات الرفرف المكسور. مضت السيارة إلى ناحية كوبري أبو العلا.

كان الخواء كاملاً. الحلم قد أفرغ فجأة من كلّ محتواه، ليس فيه ولا صورة واحدة. بل ظلامٌ يهبّ فيه هواء غريب.

Language Notes

1. (المَسْرَح) عَ : ECA; a contracted form of the preposition عَلَى.

2. ميدان الأوبرا: square in Central Cairo, near the former opera house that burned down in 1988 (the same year that the new opera house was opened on Geziga Island in المْرَكَز القَوْمِيّ الثَّقافيّ – "The National Cultural Centre"). The old Opera House was built by اسْماعيل باشا, who also hired Giuseppe Verdi to write an opera – *Aida* – to inaugurate the building.

3. إبراهيم باشا: Ibrāhīm Pasha (1789–1848), the son of the founder of modern Egypt, مُحَمَّد عَلِي باشا (Muḥammad ʿAlī, d. 1849), took over from his father when the latter, after a reign that lasted for half a century, became medically unfit to rule. Unfortunately, Ibrāhīm died a few months into his own reign. He was succeeded by one of Muḥammad ʿAlī's grandsons, ʿAbbās Ḥilmī (1813–54). The equestrian statue of Ibrāhīm Pasha at Opera Square was erected in 1872 and is the work of the French sculptor Charles-Henri-Joseph Cordier.

4. بك: (ECA) despite its spelling in Arabic, this word is commonly pronounced *bey* (the colloquial pronunciation being reflected in the alternative spelling بيه). Originally a Turkish honorary title for high-ranking officials, today it is often used in Egypt as a term of address indicating respect, flattery or sarcasm. In other countries (e. g. Syria, Lebanon and Iraq), the form بيك is the most common form.

5. الميكروفون: MSA مُكَبِّر الصَّوْت.

6. مُنْتَفِشة: (ECA) it is used here in the sense of "fluffed out" (اتَنَفَشَ <); the MSA انْتَفَشَ denotes "puffed up", "ruffled (feathers, hair)".

7. الحْنْطُور: (pl. حَناطيرُ) a horse-drawn cab, also referred to as a *calèche*.

8. عِماد الدِّين: a major thoroughfare, which runs from 26th of July Street to Bab El Hadid Square (near Cairo's Central Station). It was famous for its cabarets.

9. النَّسْر الصَّغير: lit. "the little eagle". A reference to the play *L'Aiglon* (1905) by the French author Edmond Rostan, and translated into Arabic by عَزيز عيْد and السَّيِّد قَدْري. It was also one of the first successes of the Egyptian actress فاطمة رُشْدي (1908-96) In it, she played the same part that Sarah Bernhardt had made her own on the Paris stage, which earned her the sobriquet "the Egyptian Sarah Bernhardt".

10. شَجَرَة الدُّر: the only female sultan of Egypt (May–July 1250). Renowned for her beauty, Shajrat al-Durr (d. 1259) was a Circassian (or Turkoman) slave purchased by Sultan صالح أَيُّوب. She gained mythical status through her organization of the Egyptian army to deter the invading French troops led by Louis IX (Saint-Louis) while she acted as regent in the absence of the sultan. Her remains are kept in the mosque that bears her name.

11. بلقيس: this is the name by which the Queen of Sheba (of Biblical fame) is usually known in the Arab tradition.

12. لَيْلى: the female protagonist in the legendary ill-fated love affair with the pre-Islamic (*Jāhiliyya*) poet قَيْس بن المَلوَّح, also known as مَجْنُون ("mad"). The story goes that Qays and Laylā fell madly in love with one another, but could not marry as her father had promised her to another man. Upon hearing this news, Qays lost his mind, and began to wander the desert, living among the animals. It is, allegedly, during his more lucid moments that he composed the verses that are some of the most famous love poetry in Arabic.

13. زُبَيْدة البَرْمَكية: a reference to the wife (and queen-consort) of the famous 'Abbāsid caliph, هارُون الرَّشيد (d. 809). The adjective بَرْمَكيَّة refers to her relation to the بَرامكة (Barmakids), a Persian family of ministers in the 'Abbāsid caliphate (a dynasty that ruled from 750–1258 and takes

its name from its founder, العَبَّاس بن عبد المُطَّلب بن هاشم, the Prophet's uncle).

14. ليلى بنت الفقراء: famous Egyptian film (1945) directed by أنْوَر وَجْدي, who also played one of the leads (alongside the hugely famous actress and singer لَيْلى مُراد, to whom he was also married for a while).

15. الأَبْلاكِاش: ECA (< Fr. *plaçage*); MSA: خَشَب مُصَفَّح.

16. البَلُوط; (ECA) MSA: سِنْديان.

17. الكُوبْري: ECA (< Tu. *köpru*); MSA: جِسْر (pl. جُسُور).

18. البراتيكابلاتَ: ECA pl. of براتكابل (< Fr. *praticable*). MSA مِنَصّة.

19. المَرْيَمات الثَّلاثة: according to the Gospels, the Three Maries (i.e. Holy Women) discovered Christ's empty tomb after the Resurrection. Except for Mary Magdalene, the identities of the women have never been ascertained.

20. التليفزيون: reflects the usual colloquial pronunciation both in Egypt and in most other Arab countries; MSA تلفزيون or الشّاشة الصّغيرة (lit. "the small screen"), by contrast with الشّاشة الكبيرة ("the big screen"), which refers to the cinema.

21. أبو عشر قروش: expression denoting possession: cf. e.g. أبو نظارة, "the one who wears glasses" (lit. "the father of glasses").

22. المَصْطَبة: (pl. مَصاطِب or مَصاطِب) this word can also denote a type of ancient Egyptian stone tomb (mastaba).

23. ليلة الجمعة المفترجة: lit. "Friday night, the night of relief". This highlights, of course, the special status Friday enjoys in Muslim culture.

24. فَرَج الله: lit. "God grants relief". This is an expression of reassurance, the implication being that God will make everything alright.

25. العَرْضَحال: (ECA > Tu. *arzıhal*); MSA: الْتِماس or عَريضة (pl. عَرائِض).

26. البتّاو: (ECA) bread made from sorghum (دُرة عَويجة).

27. المِشّ: (ECA) seasoned lumps of fermented cheese in a thick

liquid.

28. المَوالدُ: sg. مَوْلد (lit. "birthplace" or "birthday"); in Egypt, it denotes a popular religious festival celebrated on the birthday of a religious figure, usually near the shrine or place with which that figure is associated. Cf. المَوْلِد النَّبَوِيّ, the Prophet's birthday.

29. القديسين وأولياء الله: both (sg. قدِّيس and sg. وَلِي) mean "saints"; the former refers to Christian saints, whereas the latter is reserved for Muslim saints.

30. الإمام الشافعي: famous legist (d. 820), and founder of a religious "school" (*madhhab*).

31. السَّيِّدة زَيْنَب: granddaughter of the Prophet Muḥammad and daughter of 'Alī b. Abū Ṭālib (the fourth of the so-called 'Rightly Guided' caliphs). Sayyida Zeinab is the Patron Saint of Cairo. She has also given her name to a large working-class area (around the homonymous mosque).

32. الباطنيَّة: the name of a working-class district (between the Citadel and al-Azhar mosque), which used to be known as a centre for the hashish trade.

33. النايم: this form reflects ECA pronunciation (and, indeed, that in many other dialects of the MSA نائم.

34. ودانه: ECA plural of وِدْن; MSA: أُذْن, pl. آذان.

Salwā Bakr

Salwā Bakr (b. 1949) is one of the most distinguished female Egyptian authors and is known as a novelist, short-story writer and playwright. In 1972 she graduated from 'Ayn al-Shams University in Cairo, where she studied Economics and Business Management. Afterwards, she also studied for a degree in Theatre Criticism.

After working as a civil servant (1974–80), she became a respected film and theatre critic as well as working as a journalist. In 1985 she became a full-time author, and to date she has published seven collections of short stories, seven novels and a play. Her works have been translated to different languages. Among her short story collections are زينات في جَنازَة الرَئيس (*Zinat at the President's Funeral*, 1986); عَن الروح التي سُرِقَت تَدريجياً (*Of the Soul which is Gradually Stolen*, 1989); and عَجين الفَلاحَة (*The Peasant Women's Dough*, 1992).

The major themes in Bakr's work are her preoccupation with the plight of the poor and downtrodden in Egyptian society, especially women, who not only are subjected to social and political injustice but also suffer cruelty inflicted upon them by men. To endure this harsh world, women must be strong and learn to become survivors; by empowering themselves, they are able to subvert their men's so-called strength and break the circle of dominance and subjugation. In many of Bakr's stories, the male characters tend to be weak in comparison with the women.

Bakr's most recent work is the novel سَوّاقِي الْوَقت (*Waterwheels of Time*, 2003), in which the author investigates the changes in an individual's life as a result of political, social and economic changes.

In the following story, taken from the collection (2003) that bears the same name, the word شُعُور ("hair") is used as a metaphor, with the hair connecting the two women at once inseparable and weak. The bond that exists between the two leading female characters is vividly described as being as strong as an umbilical cord, and yet as weak as a spider's web.

On the surface, the story deals with the urban life of two women who seemingly lead a humdrum existence on the margins of the society, with very few distractions. In fact, they represent two different generations with different pasts, values and expectations. The older character is fulfilled, living in a past she cherishes, adamantly refusing a new life in the West with her sons. She is content with what she has, clinging to her heritage and past through her "ancestral" hair, photos and belongings. The younger woman, for her part, has no past to cherish or lean on. She lives with the uncertainties of life, burdened with the responsibilities of caring for a disabled child, in constant fear of the unknown.

The story is also about interpersonal relationships with others. While on the surface the reader observes a conventional, rather superficial relationship in which the two women seemingly only have the *narghile* in common, the story also addresses the issue of single mothers in Muslim society, complicated in this case by the fact that the child is disabled.

One may also adumbrate a contrast in language registers, with an elevated vocabulary and formal Arabic prose juxtaposed with colloquial Egyptian.

Ancestral Hair

Sometimes she seemed to me to be a weird genie who hung her braid from on high for me to climb to the summit of her tower. I then lost myself in her maze as though caught in the invisible thread of a spider's web. What else could have tied me to this sixty-year-old woman with her six teeth? She could barely read a newspaper, and moved with the grace of a turtle. I sometimes blame time, that wretched thief that seizes the days of our lives and mercilessly denies us the opportunity to reflect upon ourselves, or others. Other times, I blame the savage geography of this ageing city we are destined to live in, for casting us onto one of its growing protruberances, like a fungus on its old, flabby body.

It occurred to me that what tied us together was my exclusion from society as a divorcée confined by a twenty-four-year-old son with Down's Syndrome who had a wild body but the mind and innocence of a nine-year-old child.

As far as she was concerned, her vision became clearer with age. She had left her two sons, who had settled in the New World some time ago, after she had tried to comply with their wishes and live with them. However, she preferred to return to her old world, to life in Cairo, with whatever was there.

I would always spend my free evenings with her. My mornings did not start until I crossed the ten steps separating her door from mine, so that I could ask her before leaving the building: "I am off to work now. Do you need anything?"

Was it perhaps the *narghile* that tied me to her? I had grown addicted to smoking it with her, despite the fact that I had never even smoked cigarettes before. We would place the *narghile* between us on our balcony at sunset, with the man-child sitting in front of us. We would exchange puffs, causing bubbles in the water that punctuated the topics of conversation, amputated

شعور[1] الأسلا ف[2]

أحياناً، تبدو لي كجنيّة[3] مستحيلة، تُدلي ضفيرتها من شاهق، لأتلقّفها صاعدة إلى علياء قلعتها، فأغيب في متاهاتها وقد رُبطتُ بحبل سرّي[4] من نسيج العنكبوت[5]، وإلا، فما الذي يربطني بهذه العجوز ذات الأسنان الست، والسنين الستين، تطالع الجريدة بالكاد وتتحرك برشاقة سلحفاة. أقول مرات: إنه الزمان السرّاق المغتصب لأيّامنا، فلا يرحمنا بفسحة نتأمل فيها أنفسنا، وكذا الآخرين. مرات أخرى، أدين الجغرافيا المتوحشة لهذه المدينة الشائخة[6] التي قدرعلينا العيش فيها، فلفظتنا إلى نتوء من نتوءاتها النامية كفطر على جسدها المترهل المترهل القديم.

أهجس: إن ما بيني وبينها هو استبعادي كمطلقة مغلولة بطفل منغولي[7] له جسد مستوحش في السادسة والعشرين، وعقل براءة التاسعة. من ناحيتها، قد تتضح الرؤيا بكونها موجودة، هجرت ولديها اللذين سافرا واستقرا منذ زمن في الدنيا الجديدة، بعد أن جربت أن تسايرهما وتكون معهما مرة، لكنها آثرت الإياب إلى دنياها القديمة، والعيش في أم الدنيا[8]، على كلّ الذي هناك.

إن أمسياتي المتاحة معها دوماً، صباحاتي لا تتحقق إلا إذا عبرت الخطوات العشر الفاصلة بين بابها وبابي لأقول لها قبل أن أهبط إلى الشارع: «أنا نازلة[9] للشُغل عاوزة[10] حاجة[11]؟»

هل النرجيلة هي ما يربطني بها؟ لقد أدمنت تدخين النرجيلة[12] معها، علماً بأنني ما دخنت السجائر يوماً. نضع النرجيلة بيننا في شرفتنا وقت الغروب، والرجل الطفل قبالتنا، نتبادل أنفاساً تدغدغ ماء قارورتها فتتكركر مالئة فراغات زمن جملنا المتبادلة. جمل مبتورة بلا رجاء أو مستقبل،

sentences without hope or a future, with a single purpose – to affirm our presence as living beings.

"It's been quite humid these past couple of days."

"Umm Khalil, the caretaker, cleaned the building skylight last night."

"Careful, my darling Mamdouh, the coal could burn your hand."

Yet, I told myself that the *narghile* could not be the only thing that tied me to her. It was possible that I was affected by some kind of despair, and for good reason. I looked as if I was a widow over fifty, while I was only approaching forty. Should I not get on with my life with a son who is my disability, like a bird whose feathers have been clipped so it cannot rise or fly? How often did I not wish I had had another man, rather than the one who had placed this yoke around my neck and ran off with another woman, who gave him boys and girls that had come into the world with sound minds, growing and flourishing with the passing of time, like the rest of God's creatures.

What man would want me with this huge burden that shackles me and increases my isolation from other people and from life. I never venture out except to go to work, while my home is where I escape from the world; it is the only refuge I have, where she and I could smoke the *narghile*. Meanwhile, my son would sit in front of us, with a vacuous gaze like a master circus clown playing possum to make people smile.

All we knew about each other were tall stories and inexplicable mysteries, despite being neighbours for many years. When we first met, she had told me the trite story of her life, which had gone unnoticed and would probably end in the same way. Whenever I looked at her, I felt that her face befitted her life story. Anyone looking at it would not remember any of its features, for the very simple reason that they would not bother to take another glance in order to store the details in their memory.

وكأن غرضها الإعلان عن وجودنا كأحياء فقط: «الرطوبة عالية من اول
امبارح[13]».«أم خليل البوابة مسحت منور العمارة بالليل».«حاسب[14]
يا ممدوح يا حبيبي الفحم يحرق يدك». لكنّ أقول إن الترجيلة لا تكفي
لتكون سبباً، ربما أكون مصابة بنوع من اليأس، و لم لا؟! ألست أبدو كأرملة
تجاوزت الخمسين، بينما سنوات عمري لم تزل تزحف نحو الأربعين،
ألست أمضي في الحياة، بهذا الابن العاهة[15] كطير قص ريشه، فلا سبيل له
إلى الارتفاع والتحليق ؟! ألا أتمنى ألف مرة أن يكون لي رجل آخر، بدلاً
من ذلك الذي وضع النير في رقبتي ومضى إلى أخرى منحته صبياناً وبناتاً
جاؤوا إلى الدنيا بعقول تنمو وتزدهر بمرور الأيام كبقية مخاليق الله[16] ؟ من
الرجل هذا الذي يرغبني بهذا النتوء الضخم الرابض على عنقي، والمكبل
لخطواتي، والذي يدفعني يوماً بعد يوم للانزواء والعزلة بعيداً عن الناس
والحياة فلا أخرج إلا لعملي فقط، ولا أعود لبيتي إلا لأحتمي بسقفه هاربة
من الدنيا إلى ملكوتي[17] الوحيد المتاح، حيث الترجيلة بيني وبينها، والولد
أمامنا يرقبنا بنظرات ميتة كمهرّج ضخم في سيرك، يتصنع الموت ليبعث
البسمات على الشفاه.

ما أعرفه عنها وتعرفه عني هو ضرب من التهويمات وهالات غموض،
رغم سنوات جيرتنا الممتدة، فقد كشفت لي عند بداية تعارفنا منذ سنوات،
عن سيرة ذاتية خابية، لن يلحظها أحد، وستكتمل دون ما يمكن التوقف
عنده، حتى وجهها بت أظن كلما تأملته أنه موائم تماماً لسيرة من هذا النوع،
فالمرء إذا ما تطلع إليه مرة، لن يجذر في الذاكرة أياً من تفاصيله، لأنه ببساطة
لن يحاول الالتفات متطلعاً إليه مرة أخرى، باحثاً عما يجود به على أرشيف
هذه الذاكرة.

However, I started to look at her in a different way since that day I paid her an unexpected visit. I went to see her in the morning of one my days off, while my son was asleep in bed like a beached whale. I wanted her to lend me some yarn:

"Have you got some green thread I could use to sew my olive-green skirt? It's torn along the side and I can't be bothered to go out and buy a whole skein for that!"

She replied, seemingly engrossed in something else: "Come here, and look in my sewing basket."

I said: "No, no ... I left the flat door wide open, and Mamdouh is inside, in bed. When you find it, bring it over, in your own time."

"Do come in for a moment!" she said, while beckoning me to follow her inside. Then she added: "Come in, take the basket and look for the thread in *your* own time."

I followed her into the only bedroom of her small flat, which was big enough for an old, lonely woman like her. She opened the wardrobe so as to give me the sewing basket, which was made out of wicker. She noticed my raised eyebrows as I stared at the enormous pile of hair on the white bedsheet, which was lit by the morning sun and revealed a tapestry of interwoven colours – black, purple and silver.

She sighed: "Look! I opened my pillow before I got the door. I thought I'd better air the stuffing at once in the sunlight, as the pillowcase is worn out and torn. I intend to make a new one."

I looked at the long, loose braids on her back, in amazement: "Oh ... the pillow is entirely filled with hair."

"Yes, my mother's hair. It used to be her pillow. Each time she combed her hair with her ivory comb after her bath, she used to gather whatever hair had come out, and put it in a coarse cotton bag until it became a pillow. Look, this is the black hair from when she was young; that's the red from the time she started to dye it with henna after she turned grey. When she grew older, she kept her hair in its original colour.

غير أنني في ذلك اليوم الذي دخلت عليها فيه فجأة، بدأت أراها على نحو مختلف، فلقد ذهبت إليها في صبيحة يوم إجازتي، بينما كان رجلي الطفل، يرقد على سريره كحوت ميت دفعت الأمواج به إلى شاطئ من الشطآن. كنت أود أن تعيريني خيطاً فسألتها:

– عندك[18] فتلة[19] خضراء أخيط بها جونلتي[20] الزيتية[21] لأن جنبها انفتق، وأنا مكسّلة[22] أنزل أشتري بكرة ؟!

قالت وقد بدت منهمكة للغاية في أمر من الأمور:

– تعالي، دوري في مرجونة الخيط.

قلت :

– لا. لا. أصلي[23] تركت باب الشقة على آخره، وممدوح جوه على السرير. لما تلاقيها هاتيها لي على مهلك.

– الله. تعالي لحظة. قالت وهي تشير إلى أن أتبعها. ثم أضافت:

– تعالي خدي المرجونة معك، ودوري على الخيط فيها براحتك[24].

دخلت وراءها غرفة النوم الوحيدة بالشقة الصغيرة الوافية بالنسبة لعجوز وحيدة مثلها، فتحت الدولاب لتعطيني سلة الخيط المصنوعة من القش، وإذ لاحظت حاجبيّ المرفوعين فوق عينيّ المحدقتين في كومة الشعر الهائلة فوق ملاءة السرير البيضاء، وقد تساقطت عليها أشعة شمس الصباح، فبدت خيوطها تشابكات من الأسود والأرجواني والفضي، قالت وهي تتنهد:

– شوفي[25]. فتحت مخدتي قبل ما أفتح لك الباب، وقلت أهوّي الشعر بالمرة[26] وأحطّه[27] في الشمس. أصل كيسها قدم وانفتق. ناوية أعمل لها غيره جديد.

تساءلت بدهشة، وأنا أتأمل ضفيرتها الطويلة المنسدلة على ظهرها:

– ياه. المخدة كلها شعر.

– آه شعر أمّي. المخدة كانت في الأصل مخدتها، كلّ ما تسرّح شعرها بعد الحمّام بالمشط سنّ الفيل[28]، تلم النازل منه وتحطّه في كيس دمور[29] لحد ما صار مخدّه. شوفي شعرها الأسود لما كانت شابّة والأحمر لما صارت تحنّيه بحنّة حمراء بعد ما الشيب طقطق فيه، فلما شاخت تركته على لونه. كان

"She used to have a plait like silver thread. Unfortunately, when she died, I was in hospital. They stopped me from attending her funeral, as I'd just given birth and they said it would be bad for me, that I could lose the milk in my breasts. If I had been at her deathbed, I would have cut her braids and taken them. May God have mercy on her soul. Thank God, I have a bunch of her hair in the pillow. I also kept two molars and an incisor, which she took out before her death; I keep them in an old satin purse."

"Ah ... two molars and an incisor. Oh, my word!" I exclaimed, as I grabbed the sewing basket and rushed back to my flat.

Was this incident a watershed in the way I viewed Mounira Fathi? I don't know. All that happened afterwards is that I kept thinking about her, with the picture of the hair on her bedsheet imprinted in my mind. When I was back in my flat trying to thread the green yarn through the eye of the needle, my mind remained with her mother's red, black and white hair glistening in the light.

I had mixed feelings towards her after that day. I no longer thought of her as an ordinary woman who goes unnoticed as a matter of course. In some way, she had become a mysterious old lady with peculiar idiosyncrasies. Since that day I started to think about her world, something I had not done before. Whenever I entered her flat after that, to smoke the *narghile* or drink coffee, I would pause to look at the many pictures that covered every wall of the flat. I soon discovered that she had not only hung her and her family's pictures on the wall, but also that her family's history was to be found in every corner of her flat.

The pictures were not of herself at all; each told a story about the life that this woman had once lived. Even her small kitchen had a picture of her mother and aunt on the wall above the old, round marbletop table in the corner. It showed her mother

عندها ضفيرة كما سلوك[30] الفضة. يا خسارة لما ماتت كنت في المستشفى، ومنعوني من حضور خرجتها[31] لأني كنت نفساء[32]، وقالوا حرام، وخافوا الحليب يضيع من صدري. لو كنت جنبها ساعة طلوع الروح[33] كنت أخذت ضفيرتها، قصيتها، ألف رحمة[34] تروح لها، لكنّ الحمد لله عندي منها كومة الشعر في المخدة، وضرسين، وسن، كانت خلعتهم قبل موتها، محتفظة بهم في كيس أطلس[35] قديم.

– آه ضرسين وسن. يا سلام !؟ قلت، وأنا آخذ منها سلة الخيط وأندفع آفلة إلى شقتي.

هل كانت هذه الواقعة لحظة انقلاب في رؤيتي لمنيرة فتحي؟. لا أعرف، كلّ الذي حدث بعد ذلك هو أنني ظللت أفكر فيها، وقد انطبع مشهد الشعر المهوش على السرير، شعر أمها الباقي وهو يلتمع بألوانه الحمراء والسوداء والبيضاء، بينما أحاول تسديد الخيط الأخضر في خرم الإبرة بعد عودتي مرة أخرى. لقد تخالطت مشاعري تجاهها بعد ذلك اليوم، فلم تعد بالنسبة لي هي المرأة العادية، التي لا تلحظ عادة، بدت على نحو من الأنحاء عجوزاً غامضة، لها تعقيدها المثير، وأظن أنني منذ ذلك اليوم بدأت التوقف لتأمل عالمها الذي لم أكن أتوقف عنده من قبل، فصرت كلما دخلت إلى شقتها بعد ذلك، لشرب النرجيلة[36] أو القهوة، أتلكأ قليلاً أمام الصور العديدة المرصعة لكل حيطان بيتها[37] تقريباً، لقد اكتشفت أنها لا تعلق صورها وصورعائلتها على الحائط فقط، بل إنها تنشر تاريخها العائلي في كلّ ركن من أركان بيتها، فالصور لم تكن شخصية أبداً، بل كانت بمثابة حكايات ناطقة بحياة عاشتها هذه المرأة ذات يوم، حتى مطبخها الصغير، حظي بصورة لأمها وخالتها علقت على الحائط فوق المنضدة ذات القرص الرخامي القديم المكونة،

cutting up a huge fish while her aunt enthusiastically held onto its tail.

Everywhere there were pictures of her uncles, her sons, her deceased husband and his family at the seaside, the zoo, at a school and at the pyramids. The only personal picture was one of her as a bride, or so it seemed. It showed her as a radiant young woman in a white silk dress holding an ostrich feather fan, the sides of which touched the upper part of her tightly-wrapped chest emerging from the wide opening of her garment.

Her short, clipped sentences no longer sounded ordinary to me; rather, they filled the blank spaces that the pictures failed to reveal:

"My father, may he rest in peace, used to smoke the *narghile* after his afternoon nap. Would you believe it? The first time I smoked it was with him! I used to draw one or two puffs from it at first, until I made sure it was fine. At the time we used to buy dried tobacco and soak it in water. My mother used to prepare it and cut it for my father to use."

She did not speak about her parents except in passing, when telling me a story about her past, which was the only certainty by which she had lived her entire life. I myself began to look for a certainty of my own, which has pained and tormented my soul.

"The postman brought me a letter from Sami, my eldest son, just before the noon call to prayer. I was busy dusting the silver cake tray that belonged to my aunt, may God have mercy on her soul. She gave it to me on my wedding day.

"My son Fouad phoned me from America last night. His eldest daughter is intending to come to Egypt. She is a brunette, because her mother is originally from Italy. But she has the dark skin of my uncle Hussein, may he rest in peace."

"Oh, how lucky she is!" I would say to myself sometimes. She was content with everything in the world. I, on the other

بدت الأم فيها منهمكة في تقطيع سمكة ضخمة بينما الخالة تمسك بذيلها في حماس. في كلّ مكان صور لأعمامها وأخوالها وأبنائها وزوجها الميت وأهله في البحر، في حديقة الحيوان، داخل مدرسة، عند الهرم؛ الصورة الوحيدة الشخصية، كانت لها وهي عروس على ما يبدو إذ ظهرت فيها شابة نضرة بفستان من الحرير الأبيض، تمسك بيدها مروحة من ريش النعام، وقد لا مست أطرافها لحم صدرها المشدود المنبثق من فتحة ثوبها الواسعة.

جملها القصيرة المقتضبة، لم تعد عاديّة بالنسبة لي، إنها تملأ فراغات عجزت الصور عن الإفصاح عنها:

— النرجيلة. بابا الله يرحمه، كان مزاجه يدخنها بعد القيلولة[38]، تصدّقي أول مرة دخنتها كان معه ! كنت أسحب منها نفساً أو نفسين في الأول، حتى أتأكد أنها سالكة. كان التمباك[39] أيامها[40] نشتريه وهو ناشف ونبلّه وننقعه في المياه، وأمي كانت تقصه وتوضّبه[41] وبابا يسحب منه على الجاهز.

إنها لا تتحدث عن والديها إلا عبوراً[42]، لحكاية من حكاياتها عن يقينها القديم، ذلك الذي تعيش فيه دوماً وأبحث من خلاله عن يقيني، يقين يقيني آلام الروح وعذاباتها.

— جاب لي[43] البوسطجي[44] جواب[45] من سامي ابنى الكبير قبل آذان الظهر، وأنا كنت مشغولة بشيل التراب[46] من شيّالة الكعك الفضية، كانت لخالتي الله يرحمها وقدمتها لي يوم دُخلتي[47].

— فؤاد ابنى كلمني بالتليفون من أمريكا بالليل. ابنته الكبيرة ناوية تزور مصر. طالعة سمراء لأن أمها أصلها من إيطاليا. لكنّ سمارتها طبق الأصل سمارة عمي حسين الله يرحمه.

يالحظها! أقول لنفسي مرات، ما كلّ هذا الرضا عن الدنيا والعالم. أنا

hand, am consumed by fear a thousand times every day. I am so frightened I could scream sometimes. I am scared to lose my job and income (what would my son and I do for food?). I am afraid that the old building we live in could collapse suddenly, like so many these days (where would we live if it actually happened?). I am frightened that my life will continue unchanged, with no hope of finding a man to be at my side and share the trials of everyday life, or give me some joy now and then.

However, my greatest and deepest fear, one that increases by the day, is that I might wake up one morning and not find my only certainty in this world, that is, my old neighbour Mounira Fathi, the beacon of tranquillity amidst my spiritual anxieties and the key to my life. I am scared she might suddenly die and leave me deprived of my daily dose of spiritual stimulation, which gives me the hope to live the next day.

What is death? I often wondered about that when I was having thoughts like these while feeling lonely at night, observing my sleeping whale and his snorting that would go into a never-ending crescendo. I would ask myself: Is death like an absence? If so, of what? The absence of outward appearance, features and body, the absence of the spirit or the absence of a shared moment? I searched for the true definition of death. This remained my obsession for a long time. Whenever I got off work, I would play a game with the computer.

One day, after inputting some data, I asked about death and got astonishingly naive answers: the decomposition of the body and its passing away, the disappearance of a person, the cessation of heartbeats, the stopping of blood circulation, the end of brain function, etc.

However, does death not have two sides? On the one hand, there is the person who dies and, on the other, the person who is shocked by the death of the one who dies. How do we evaluate death from the point of view of one party and not the other? Hence what is the assessment of death from the standpoint of the other party?

يأكلني الخوف كلّ يوم ألف مرة. أخاف إلى درجة الرغبة في الصراخ أحياناً. أخاف أن افقد وظيفتي وأصبح بلا مصدر للدخل (من أين نأكل انا وابني؟). أخاف أن تنهار العمارة القديمة التي نسكن فيها مثلما تنهار عمارات عديدة هذه الأيام (أين نسكن لو حدث ذلك بالفعل ؟). أخاف أن تستمر حياتي هكذا، لا أمل في وجود رجل إلى جانبي يشاركني قسوة الأيام، أو يمنحني فرحاً ما في بعض منها.

لكنّ خوفي الأهم والأعمق، والذي كان يتزايد يوماً بعد آخر، هو أن أصحو من نومي ذات صباح لأجد الدنيا ليس بها يقيني الوحيد.

جارتي العجوز منيرة فتحي، تميمة السكينة لهواجس روحي ومفتاح حياتي.

كنت أخاف أن تموت فجأة وتتركني، فأفقد تلك الجرعة اليومية المنشطة لروحي، والمانحة الأمل لي في إمكانية العيش ليوم آخر.

ما هو الموت؟ كنت أتساءل عادة عندما أصل إلى هذا الحد من التفكير، بينما أبقى وحيدة في الليل، أتأمل حوتي النائم وقد علا شخيره دون انقطاع.

أقول لروحي: الموت هو الغياب؟ غياب ماذا؟ غياب الشكل والملامح والجسد؟ أم غياب الروح، أم غياب لحظة المشاركة ؟ أريد تعريفاً مقبولاً للموت ؟ ظل ذلك هاجسي لفترة طويلة، حتى أنني كنت عندما أفرغ من عملي ألعب اللعبة مع الكمبيوتر أسأله بعد أن أغذيه بقدر من المعلومات؛ وقد قدم لي إجابات مدهشة في سذاجتها: تحلل الجسد وفناؤه. اختفاء شخص. توقف ضربات القلب. هبوط الدورة الدموية. إنتهاء وظائف المخ... الخ.

ولكنّ أليس في الموت طرفان، الذي يموت، والذي يصدمه موت من يموت؟ كيف نعرف الموت بحالة طرف دون الطرف الآخر؟! إذن ما تعريف الموت بالنسبة للطرف الآخر؟.

I again put the question to the computer, with amazing results:

"The eye does not see. The ear does not hear. The mouth does not kiss. The hand does not touch ..."

My dear neighbour's answer was more accurate than that given by the computer, and with a speed I was not expecting at all. One day, she came to see me after midnight. She had been knocking on my door persistently. When I awoke from my sleep and opened it, thinking that a catastrophe had befallen my child, I found her standing in front of me, looking very faint. She said she felt very sick. I quickly drew her into my flat and made her lie down on my bed. I ran to the kitchen to get her some water, as she complained her mouth was dry. Soon after, I ran to the telephone and called her a doctor from the nearest hospital. Then I rushed back to her and found her lying on the bed, motionless, with her head slumped on the edge of my pillow so that her braid was dangling on the floor – a silver braid that reflected the scarce light from the lamp that hung beside the bed.

I just stood there, nailed to the floor. I wanted to scream, but a reassuring feeling engulfed my soul and filled me with a calm I had not experienced before.

What I had dreaded for so long came to pass, yet there I was – calm and reassured; I realised that life was possible. In the last moment I spent with my neighbour, there was no *narghile* between us, and no man-child sitting in front of us.

"Here is death, expressing a tangible definition, a tactile object; it is the regret for a past we do not wish to end," I said to myself as I gazed at her wizened face, upon which death had drawn an eternal expression.

In spite of that, I felt regret, whereas her death caused an overwhelming sense of ambiguity and confusion; when I was confronted with her death, it struck me that it defied all definitions and understanding. I felt that I had been robbed of

رحت أعاود سؤال الكمبيوتر مرة أخرى، الإجابة كانت مذهلة: العين لا ترى. الأذن لا تسمع. الفم لا يُقبّل. اليد لا تلمس.

جارتي العزيزة، قدمت لي إجابة أكثر دقة مما قدمه الكمبيوتر، وبسرعة لم أكن أتوقعها أبداً فقد جاءتني مرة بعد منتصف الليل، تدق بابي دقاً متلاحقاً، فلما فتحت وقد هببت من النوم، أظن أن مصيبة قد حلت بطفلي. وجدتها أمامي في حالة إعياء واضحة، قالت إنها متعبة جداً، سحبتها بسرعة لداخل شقتي، مددتها على سريري، جريت إلى المطبخ لأناولها شربة ماء طلبتها لأن ريقها جاف، وما إن فعلت حتى جريت إلى الهاتف لأطلب لها طبيباً من أقرب مستشفى.

عندما عدت إليها بعد ذلك مسرعة، وجدتها ممددة على السرير بلا حراك، وقد مال رأسها على طرف مخدتي لتتدلى ضفيرتها باتجاه الأرض، ضفيرة فضية تتكسر عليها الشعاعات الشحيحة للمصباح المعلق بجوار السرير.

وقفت متسمرة، رغبت في الصراخ، لكنّ شعوراً مطمئناً مطمئناً بدأ يجتاحني مغلفاً روحي بسكينة لم تعهدها من قبل.

اذن. لقد دخلت اللحظة التي طالما خشيتها، لكنّ ها أنا فيها، هادئة، مطمئنة، وقد أدركت أنها ممكنة وليست مستحيلة، إنها اللحظة/النهاية مع جارتي التي كانت، لا نرجيلة بيننا ولا طفل رجل قبالتنا.

«الموت. ها هو يفصح عن تعريف ملموس، محسوس له، إنه الحسرة على ماض نتمنى ألا يكتمل»، قلت لنفسي وأنا أتأمل وجهها الشائخ، وقد رسم الموت عليه تعبيراً أبدياً لا نهاية له.

ورغم ذلك، فقد شعرت بحيرة ونوع من الغموض تجاه تصادم ذلك الموت معي، لقد بدا لي أنه منفلت من كلّ تعريف، منفلت من كلّ مفهوم. أشعر أنني سُرقت، شيء ما، غالٍ وثمين سُرق مني، وخُطف عنوة.

something, something dear and precious that had been wrested from me by force.

Dazed, I quietly went to my wardrobe and took out the scissors. I walked up to her and briefly stood there looking at her once more, before my hand grasped her thick soft braid and cut it resolutely. There were a few black hairs that had withstood the passage of time.

I headed towards the mirror and looked at myself as I placed the braid on my head, like a garland. My soul grew increasingly calm as I declared to myself a certain victory, while the shrill sound of the ambulance siren penetrated my ear.

بدون أن أدري سرت بهدوء إلى دولابي لأخرج منه المقص، وأمضي
بثبات إليها، ثم أقف قليلاً أتأملها مرة أخرى، قبل أن تمسك يدي بضفيرتها
الناعمة الغزيرة فأقصها بحزم، وقد استبانت بها شعيرات سوداء شحيحة
صارعت الأيام.

توجّهت إلى المرآة، نظرت نفسي وأنا أثبت الجديلة إكليلاً على رأسي،
كانت روحي تزداد سكينة، وأنا أعلن لنفسي إنتصاراً ما، بينما سيارة
الإسعاف تعلن عن مقدمها بأصوات حادة تخترق أذنيّ.

Language Notes

1. شُعُور: this word serves both as a little-used plural of شَعْرَة, "hair" (though more commonly شَعْر) and "feelings".

2. أَسْلاف :pl. or سَلَفَ < سلْف (u), "to precede"). Note also the adverb سَلَفًا ("beforehand"); other words for "ancestors" include الآباء (pl. of أب, "father") and الأَجْداد (pl. of جَدّ, "grandfather").

3. جِنِّيّة: sg. of جِنِّيات , "female *jinn*" (see حكاية القنديل).

4. حَبْل سُرِّي: "umbilical cord" (cf. سُرَّة, "bellybutton"; حَبْل, "rope").

5. خُيُوط العَنْكَبُوت :نَسِيج العَنْكَبُوت (pl. أَنْسِجة). Variants include: and بَيْت العَنْكَبُوت. Note that نسيج also means "textile", "fabric" and "tissue" (biology). The spider's web has many religious connotations in Islam. It is said, for instance, that when the Prophet Muḥammad fled with Abū Bakr (one of his companions) and hid in the cave of al-Harrā', a spider built a web around the entrance to the cave so that the enemies of Islam would think the cave was inhabited. There is even a *sūra* (44) in the Qur'ān that is named after the spider.

6. المَدِينَة الشائِخَة: lit. "ageing city"; the connotation is clearly negative, with شائِخ being derived from the verb شاخ (i) ("to age"). The use of this adjective in this context is rather unusual, as one would have expected عَتيق or قَدِيم, which have a more neutral connotation, e.g. المَدِينة القَدِيمة ("the old city") or المَدِينَة العَتيقة ("the ancient city").

7. الطفل المَنْغُولي: lit. "mongoloid child" (originally a calque from the term formerly used in English).

8. أمّ الدُّنْيا: lit. "the Mother of the World", an epithet usually used for Cairo (and attributed to the famous fourteenth-century Tunisian historian Ibn Khaldūn [1332–82], who has been called "the father of modern sociology").

9. أنا نازْلَة: ECA and many other dialects; MSA أنا خَارْجَة ("I am going out"), نزل ("to descend" or "come down from stairs"), but it is used in many dialects as "to go out".

10. عَاوزة: (ECA) fem. active participle (of عازَ, "to be in need/want of"), which may stand alone or in nominal sentences (جُمَل اسْميّة). It is the usual construction to express that one wants something (where MSA uses a verb like أرادَ, "to want" or أوَدَّ, "to like"), e.g. عايز كتاب ("I'd like/want a book"). It is inflected for gender and number: عاوِز (f. عَاوْزة; pl. عاوْزين), with the variant عايْز (m.), عايْزة (f.), عايْزين (pl.).

11. حاجة: though this word is also used in MSA in the sense of "need", its semantic field in ECA is much wider and, in fact, corresponds to MSA شيء ("something"): e.g. عايز أي حاجة؟ ("Do you want anything?").

12. نَرْجِيلة: originally a Turkish word, the more common term in Egypt for the hookah or hubble-bubble is شيشَة .

13. البارِحة: أول امبارح "the day before yesterday" (ECA < CA, "yesterday"), cf. MSA أوَّل أمْس or يَوْم قَبْل أمْس.

14. حاسب: ECA; MSA أُحْذر.

15. الابْن العَاهَة: lit. "the disability child". In this context, the disabled child has become a disability to his mother.

16. مَخْلوق الله: "God's creatures"; مخاليقُ is the pl. of مَخْلوق (alongside مَخْلوقات), the passive participle of the verb خَلَقَ [u], and thus lit. "(the) created".

17. مَلَكوت: "Cosmos", "universe"; unlike similar words such as العالَم or الدنيا this has a more mystical and religious connotation in that it denotes the hidden world of spirits and souls (cf. Qur. 23:88, 36:83).

18. عَنْدَكَ؟: common across Arabic colloquials; MSA هَلْ عندَكَ؟. In spoken Arabic, the interrogative particle is normally deleted, its function supplanted by a rising intonation. Also note that in most dialects, the second-person sg. gender-marking final vowel (ـك and لك) is elided.

19. فْتلة: ECA; MSA خَيْط.

20. جُونَلَّة: ECA (> It. gonnella, "skirt"). In Iraq, Syria and Lebanon, the commonly used word for a woman's skirt is تَنُّورة.

21. زِيتِيّ "olive-green"; cf. زَيْت, "olive (oil)" (pl. زَيْتُون).

22. مْكَسَلة: ECA; MSA كَسلانة.

23. أَصْلي: ECA, "the fact is, because"; MSA لأَنِّي / لأَنني.

24. بِراحْتَك: ECA; MSA عَلى راحَتِك, from راحة ("comfort", "rest").

25. شُوفي: ECA, imperative (sg. fem.) of the verb شاف (u), "to see", which is a common cross-dialectal equivalent of the MSA رَأى.

26. بالمَرة: ECA; MSA في نَفْس الوَقْت .

27. حَطّ (u): ECA ("to put", "place"); MSA وَضَعَ.

28. سِنّ الفيل: lit. "elephant tusk"; here, it, of course, means "ivory".

29. دْمور: a type of cheap, coarse cotton material traditionally used for upholstery.

30. سُلُوك: ECA. MSA أَسْلاك pl. of سلْك .

31. خَرْجَة: ECA; MSA جَنازة "funeral procession".

32. نَفْساء: (pl. نَوافِسُ) refers to a woman who has recently given birth (cf. نِفاس, "childbirth").

33. سَاعَة طُلوعَ الرُوح: lit. "the hour of the rising of the soul"; cf. الاحْتِضار or ساعَة الاحْتِضار.

34. أَلْفْ رَحْمة تَروحَ لَها: lit. "one thousand mercies for her". The word أَلف ("one thousand") is often used in Arabic for emphasis, e.g. أَلْفْ شُكر ("a thousand thanks").

35. أَطْلَس: ECA ("satin"); MSA ساتان.

36. شُرْب الَنَرجيلة: in ECA, one does not "smoke" a *narghile*, one "drinks" it (this is, of course, a reference to the fact that it is filled with water). Interestingly enough, this usage has also been extended to other things such as cigarettes; e.g. تَشْرب سيجارة, "do you want to smoke a cigarette?". In other Arabic dialects, دَخَّن ("to smoke") is the usual verb, as it is in MSA ("No smoking", for instance, translates as مَمْنُوع التَّدْخين).

37. بَيْت: (pl. بُيُوت), can mean either "house" or "home" (e. g. في البَيْت, "at home"). In the story, the protagonist does not live in a house, but in a flat (شَقّة, pl. شُقَق).

38. القَيْلُولة: "nap", "siesta" (also قائلة <قال (i).

39. تِمْبَاك: ECA (> Tu.); MSA تَبَغ.

40. أيَّامُها: cf. في ذلك الأيّام، في تلْك الأيّام.

41. عُبُوراً: عَبَرَ > (u), "to pass by".

42. تِوَضِّبُه: ECA; MSA تُجَهِّزُه from جَهَّزَ, "to make ready", "prepare".

43. جابُ لِي: ECA; MSA احْضَرَهُ لِي, "he brought it to me".

44. بُوسْطَجى: ECA; MSA ساعي البَريد.

45. جَوَاب: ECA "letter" or "reply"(!); MSA, respectively, رِسالة and جَواب (or رَدّ, pl. رُدُود).

46. بِشيل التُّراب: "to dust", ECA; MSA أزال الغبار / أزال التراب .

47. يَوَم دُخْلتِي: ECA "my wedding day" (دُخْلة, "wedding"); MSA يَوَم زواجِي or يَوَم عُرسِي.

Fu'ād al-Takarlī

Fu'ād al-Takarlī was born in 1927 in the Bab al-Sheikh area in the heart of Baghdad. He graduated from law school at the University of Baghdad in 1949, and began working for the Ministry of Justice. He became a judge in 1956, before being appointed head of the Court of Appeals in Baghdad. In 1963 he went to Paris to study law for two years, after which he returned to his native Iraq.

In 1983 he resigned from his post to devote his time to writing. Although he had begun writing short stories in 1947 and published a few of them in 1955 in the Beirut-based literary journal الأديب, his first collection of short stories, entitled الوجه الآخر (*The Other Face*), saw the light only in 1960. His first novel, الوجه الآخر (*The Long Way Back*), was published in Beirut in 1980, and has been translated into French and English (2001). His other novels include خاتم الرَّمْل (*The Seal of Sand*, 1995) and المَسَرَّات والأوْجاع (*Joys and Heartaches*, 1998). In 1990, al-Takarlī took up residence in Tunis, which would remain his home until 2003, when he moved to Syria. Two years later, he went to Amman, where he passed away in February 2008.

The following story is excerpted from his collection خَزين اللامَرْئيات (*Tales from the Invisible World*), and focuses on the way people deal with change, on the fine line between being content with one's circumstances and submitting to them.

The narrator, who is also the protagonist of the story, adapts himself to hardship following the death of his father, with his mother and three sisters forced to eke out a meagre existence on the father's paltry pension. This reversal of fortune forces the family to move to a smaller house, while at the same time shattering any dreams of his obtaining a university education.

The death of the narrator's father has not only made him the family's sole breadwinner but, as the only male in the family, also the guardian of its moral reputation. He is, however, abruptly awakened from his usual lethargic state by a chance encounter with his childhood sweetheart, who has climbed the social ladder by marrying the head of the company he works for. Throughout, the narrator's state is one of fecklessness: too weak and self-pitying to make decisions of his own, he allows himself simply to be carried with the tide, which presents the least effort.

A Hidden Treasure

Inside some people – not everyone – there is a store of contentment and satisfaction which can overflow and, in time, make the pressures and bitterness of life bearable. This abundance of contentment transforms the curse of poverty into an acceptable situation, and deprivation into something that can be changed or forgotten.

When my father was still alive, my mother, sisters and I used to have a modest lifestyle: we were well fed and adequately clothed. We were descendants of what could be called a noble and respectable family, which had more than once witnessed reversals of fortune. As a result, it had gradually lost its wealth and social status. My father grew old, and we had to make do with his small pension.

I and my three younger sisters were born to my father and his second wife – my mother – when he was in his fifties, which was something he neither wished for himself nor for his wife or children. However, it is impossible to predict when children will be born in a marriage, and it was only after ten years that the Almighty had mercy on my parents and they had us. On the one hand, we were a comfort to them in their loneliness, but, on the other, we added to their financial burden.

My three sisters and I never felt the pressures of hardship, except when my father passed away after succumbing to an illness he could not ward off for long. I was only sixteen at the time, and for reasons unknown to us, our world was shattered and destiny treated us harshly.

I was in my third year of secondary school, eagerly awaiting the day I would complete my university studies. However, I was not determined enough, nor was I able to resist the distractions that surrounded me. When the landlord of our house in Ra's al-Chol on the outskirts of the Bab El-Sheikh quarter came to ask

خزين¹ اللامرئيات²

في ثنايا بعض النفوس، لاكلها، خزين من أحاسيس القناعة أو الرضا، يفيض فيحيل، مع الزمن، مرارة الحياة وضغوطها الشديدة إلى حال مقبولة وغير مؤذية. فمع هذا الفيضان يصير العوز المادي اللعين عادة لاضرر منها كبيراً، والحرمان أمراً قابلاً للاستبدال والنسيان.

حين كان أبي حياً، تعودنا – أنا وأمي وشقيقاتي³ – على العيش .بمستوى متوسط، يضمن لنا طعاماً جيداً ولباساً لائقاً وخدمة متواضعة. كنا من سلالة عائلة كريمة كما يقولون، خانها الدهر⁴ عدة مرات ففقدت ثروتها تدريجياً ونزلت درجات في سلم المجتمع. بقي لنا، وقد شاخ أبي، أن نقتات على راتب تقاعده الضئيل.

كنا أربعة أطفال؛ أنا وثلاث بنات أصغر مني، رزق بنا أبي من زوجته الثانية والدتي، وقد جاوز الخمسين. لم يكن ذلك ماكان يريده لنفسه أو لزوجته أولأبنائه؛ غير أن مالايمكن الرهان عليه حين الزواج، هو وقت ولادة الأولاد. وهكذا، بعد عشر سنوات من عقد قران والدي، فتح الله عليهما باب الرزق⁵ فجئنا نؤنس وحدتهما ونزيد من ثقل المسؤولية على كتفي أبي.

إلا أنا وشقيقاتي الثلاث، لم نشعر بوطأة العوز علينا مطلقاً، إلا حين تُوفي والدي فجأة بعد مرض لم يستطع مقاومته طويلاً. حينذاك، وكنت في السادسة عشرة من عمري، هبطت بنا الدنيا⁶ وجار علينا الزمن⁷ لغير سبب مفهوم.

كنت في الصف الثالث المتوسط، أتشوق بحماس لإنهاء دراستي الجامعية، غير أني لم أكن صلب الروح ولاقادراً على مقاومة الشر المحيط بي في العالم؛ فحين جاء صاحب الدارالتي كنا نسكنها في «رأس الجول»⁸ بأطراف محلة «باب الشيخ»⁹ وطالبنا بأجرة الشهرين الماضيين، لم أستطع

us to pay him the two months' rent we owed him, I was unable even to apologise to him in an appropriate manner, and for some reason I did not react to the rough and rude way he spoke to me. My eyes were filled with tears when I told my mother what had happened, and how that lowlife landlord had shown no respect for my father's memory or our family's reputation.

She embraced me tenderly, and said: "May God forgive him! You're right, my son, your family is honourable ... your family may not have a lot of money ... that's not right, and no one should be expected to bear this. Come on, let's get our act together."

We did indeed organize our affairs by moving into a smaller and cheaper house, while I quit my studies when my uncle found me an apprenticeship at a technical college to study petrochemical engineering in oil refineries. I was able to earn money during my studies.

My illiterate but commonsensical mother did not remember the glory days she had experienced with my father, nor did she much regret what we had lost; instead, she lovingly and naturally focused her attention on what we had now, being her daughters and a son who was earning an honest living.

She possessed this rare store of contentment and satisfaction. She celebrated my first wages when I was still in my mid- to late teens. She gathered us in the evening around a small table, on which she had placed a nice cake with one candle. She switched off the light and addressed us all: "Look at yourselves! Look how beautiful you are! Such lovely fresh young faces! Let's forget everything and celebrate what we have – our health and good looks!"

It was a wonderful evening; my sisters and I would remember it for the rest of our lives. After that, we just had to accept whatever hardships, joys and troubles came our way. I did not graduate easily from the Institute of Petrochemical Engineering, and I resigned myself to the fact that I had to repeat the year.

حتى أن أعتذر له بشكل ملائم، وسمحت له، لأدري لماذا، بأن يسمعني كلمات فظة وغليظة لم أرد عليها.

واغرورقت عيناي بالدموع وأنا أروي لوالدتي ماجرى لي وكيف أن هذا المالك الوضيع الأصل لم يحترم ذكرى والدي ولاسمعة عائلتنا. احتضنتني بحنان وقالت لي:

ـ ليغفر الله له؛ ولكنّ اسمع ياولدي، عائلتك كريمة... هذا أمر صحيح؛ عائلتك لاتملك مالاً. هذا أمر لايصح ولايقبله أحد. تعال ندبر حالنا.

وتدبرنا حالنا بالفعل، فانتقلنا إلى دار أخرى أصغر وأرخص أجراً، وتركت دراستي بعد أن وجد لي خالي مكاناً في معهد صناعي أدرس فيه المكننة في مصافي النفط وأتناول أجوراً أثناء الدراسة.

لم تتذكر والدتي الأمية المتزنة في تفكيرها، أيام العز[10] التي عاشتها مع والدي ولا تحسرت كثيراً على مامضى، بل ركزت اهتمامها بتلقائية محبة على مانملك الآن. هي وبناتها وابنها الذي يشتغل ويكسب نقوده بشرف. كانت تملك ذلك الحزين النادرمن مشاعر القناعة، فعملت على جعلنا نحتفل بأول راتب استلمته وأنا ما أزال بين سني المراهقة والشباب. جمعتنا، في المساء، حول مائدة صغيرة، وضعت عليها كعكة جميلة تعلوها شمعة واحدة ثم أطفأت الضوء الكهربائي وخاطبتنا:

ـ انظروا إلى أنفسكم، انظروا ماأجملكم! ماأحلى هذه الوجوه الشابة النضرة!

لننس كلّ شيء، غير مانملك من صحة وجمال.

كانت أمسية رائعة، رسخت في أذهاننا أنا وشقيقاتي، طوال العمر.

ولا محيص بعد ذلك من أن تمضي الأيام بنا وتجلب معها ماتجلب من منغصات ومسرات ومتاعب. لم أتخرج بسهولة من معهد المكننة البترولية ذاك، وقبلت برحابة صدر، أن أعيد سنة دراسية أخرى؛ فقد كانت في

My mother had little doubt that there was great benefit to be had from repeating a year.

When I graduated I got a job straightaway in one of the oil refineries not far from Baghdad. Our circumstances improved, both materially and psychologically, and we were the envy of many people. We did not move from our modest house, nor did we accept handouts from anyone. The passing of time did not affect family harmony or our close bond with a woman who overwhelmed us with love and understanding. I did not envy my sisters when they continued their studies. Quite the contrary, I was happy for them. I was twenty-five years old when one of my sisters married. Although at the time I did not think about marriage, I did discuss the idea quietly, with my mother reaching the happy and optimistic conclusion that it was not too late for me.

After the revolution, I was put in charge of managing the service department at the Doura oil facility. Although my salary increased, my ambitions did not. I had the same kind of feelings of contentment my mother had, and I felt comfortable. I was not philosophical about life. I thought that life, or rather the material possessions it offered, did not force people to pursue them, nor did it tempt them to do so; the fact of the matter is that people instil in themselves a desire and love of ownership and control, committing crimes under the guise of legitimate ambition. I discussed this with my mother, who as I have said was illiterate; she appreciated my way of thinking and realized its implications. She was so touched by it that she came over to kiss me, praying God to keep me in good health.

My mother and I lived by ourselves in our small house after my sisters got married, but we did not feel despondent as it was normal in our society for women to marry, live in their husbands' houses and lead their own lives. That day was the start of autumn. I was twenty-eight years old. I was busy at work, not doing anything in particular, when Dr Ahmed

الإعادة، حسب رأي والدتي، فائدة كبيرة لاشك فيها.

تخرجتُ ونُسبتُ مباشرة للعمل في أحد المعامل للتصفية البترولية يقع في ضاحية غير بعيدة عن بغداد. كنا نعيش بتوازن مادي ونفسي نحسد عليه. لم ننتقل من دارنا المتواضعة و لم نقبل مساعدة من أحد؛ كما لم ينفرط، مع الزمن، تآلفنا ولاالتمامنا حول تلك المرأة الفياضة بالمحبة والفهم؛ ولم أحسد أخواتي حين استمررن في دراستهن، بل غبطتهن. وكنت في الخامسة والعشرين من عمري حين خطبت إحدى شقيقاتي وتزوجت. لم أفكر آنذاك بالزواج. ناقشت الفكرة، بهدوء، مع والدتي فانتهينا إلى نتيجة مرحة ومشرقة هي أن القطار لم يفت بعد عليّ[11].

كنت أصبحت، بعد الثورة، مسؤولاً عن إدارة قسم التصليحات في منشآت «الدورة»[12] النفطية، فزاد راتبي لكنّ طموحي لم يزد. كان لدي بعض الخزين من أحاسيس القناعة الذي تملكه والدتي، وكنت مرتاحاً. لم أكن فيلسوفاً، غير أني وجدت الحياة أو، إذا أردنا الدقة، معروضاتها، لاتترصد للإنسان ولاتسعى إليه كي تغريه، بل الحقيقة الخفية هي أن الإنسان بذاته، الذي يحرض نفسه على التمني والاشتهاء، وعلى حب التملك والسيطرة وارتكاب الجرائم باسم الطموح المشروع. هذه الخاطرة قلتها لوالدتي، الأمية التي لاتعرف القراءة ولاالكتابة، ففهمتها وأدركت أبعادها وتأثرت بها، فقامت لتقبلني وتدعو الله ليحفظني. كنا لوحدنا في دارتنا الصغيرة، بعد أن تزوجت شقيقتاي الأخريان خلال العام الماضي، لكننا لم نكن نشعر بالوحشة، فقد كانت سنة المجتمع[13] البشري أن تتزوج الشقيقات، وأن يمضين إلى بيوت أزواجهن ليعشن حياتهن الخاصة. ذلك النهار، بداية الخريف، كنت في الثامنة والعشرين من عمري وكنت منكباً على العمل، غير منشغل بشيء، حين طلبني الدكتور أحمد راغب المدير العام لمؤسسة

Raghib, the general manager of the refinery laboratories, sent for me. I went to wash my hands and change my clothes for the meeting with him. I did not wonder about the reasons for this somewhat strange invitation; I was not particularly bothered. I sat waiting for a few minutes in the reception area and was then shown into his grand office. He was a forty-something, sullen, well-dressed man with a sharp eye.

He welcomed me, somewhat reservedly, and stood up to shake my hand: "Come in, Mr Abdul Rahman. Be seated."

I had often heard about his integrity and managerial acumen. I speculated that, perhaps, he was going to ask me to move to a different plant. The matter did not concern me much. As it turned out, his request was far simpler than that. He knew about my practical experience repairing machines, and asked me to take a look at the oil heating system at his official residence before he started using it. It had been damaged the year before, and had not been repaired properly. He added that the house he lived in was owned by the state, and he feared that if he asked an ignorant worker to fix the system, he might do more damage than good. I concurred with his argument, and smiled. I asked him politely when he would like me to start. He told me he would like me to get to it straightaway, if possible. Then he called his secretary and asked her to tell his driver to take me to his house and bring me back afterwards.

The general manager's house was not far from the plant; it only took ten minutes by car before the driver pointed to a grand, white house with two floors, which appeared at the end of a clean tarmac road. It was surrounded by extensive gardens, with green trees seemingly glistening under the September sun. My arrival had been announced. The gardener was waiting near the outside door, while the housemaid stood on the balcony facing the main entrance. The maid showed me to the boiler room at the back of the house. She was a polite young lady in clean clothes, well versed in the art of addressing the likes of me with contempt.

معامل التصفية، فذهبت أغسل يدي وأبدل ثيابي استعداداً لمقابلته، دون أن أتساءل عن أسباب هذه الدعوة الغريبة بعض الغرابة. لم أكن قلقاً، هذا هو كلّ شيء. جلست منتظراً في غرفة السكرتيرة دقائق قليلة، أدخلوني بعدها إلى مكتبه الفخم. كان في حوإلى الأربعين، جهم الطلعة، أنيق الملبس، حاد النظرات، تلقاني بترحيب متحفظ:

ـ تفضّل سيد عبدالرحمن. تفضل اجلس.

ثم قام يصافحني.

كنت سمعت مراراً عن استقامته وصلابته الإدارية، فخمنت أنه، ربما، يريد أن ينقلني إلى معمل آخر برضاي. لم يهمني الأمر كثيراً؛ إلا أن طلبه كان أبسط من ذلك. رجاني، بسبب مايعرفه عن خبرتي العملية بالمكائن وتصليحاتها، أن ألقي نظرة على جهاز التدفئة النفطي في داره الحكومية قبل أن يبدأ بتشغيله، فقد أصابه عطب في السنة الماضية و لم يتم تصليحه كما يجب. ثم أضاف أن داره هذه من ممتلكات الدولة، وأنه يخشى أن يستقدم عاملاً جاهلاً فيفسد الجهاز بدل أن يصلحه. أيدته في أقواله مبتسماً وسألته بأدب متى يفضل أن أبدأ العمل فأجاب: حالاً إن أمكن؛ ثم كلم السكرتيرة ورجاها أن تخبر سائقه أن ينقلني إلى بيتهم ويعود بي بعد ذلك.

لم يكن مسكن السيد المدير العام بعيداً عن المعمل؛ إذ لم تمض إلا دقائق عشر حتى أشار السائق إلى دار فخمة، بيضاء بطابقين، لاحت لنا في نهاية طريق مقير نظيف.

كانت محاطة بحديقة واسعة، بدت لي أشجارها الخضراء تتلامع تحت شمس أيلول؛ وكانوا على علم بمجيئي، إذ رأيت البستاني ينتظر قرب الباب الخارجي والخادمة واقفة في الشرفة مقابل المدخل الرئيسي. دلتني على قسم من الجهاز نصب في الجهة الخلفية من الدار. كانت شابة مؤدبة بثياب نظيفة، تتقن الكلام باحتقار مع أمثالي.

I spent some time carefully examining the main boiler and discovered it had a simple fault as a result of some ignoramus tinkering with it. I had no trouble repairing it. As I wanted to examine the rest of the system inside the house, I called the housemaid and requested that she inform the lady of the house and take me inside. It only took me a few minutes, and I did not find anything wrong with the rest of the internal heating system. I thought it would be a good idea to switch on the entire system and verify that it worked properly, and told the housemaid of my intention so that she could carry the message to the lady of the house. She hesitated for a moment, then asked me to wait outside on the balcony while she informed her mistress. My hands were grimy from the black grease of the boiler, so I started to wipe them with a paper tissue. As I stood waiting on the balcony, I looked at the vast garden extending seeming endlessly, its tall, swaying trees screening the horizon. I heard a familiar, warm voice before I could turn around.

"Excuse me, is there really a need for ..."

She stood in the doorway, looking radiant in a light-blue outfit. She looked at me as I turned towards her.

"Oh ... Abdul Rahman! Mr Abdul Rahman? Is that you?"

She raised her heavily beringed hand in front of her mouth.

Throughout my life, I've always believed that calm is never followed by a storm, and that it is possible to leave the past behind and to live a slow and easy life until the end. I was not ready to change my mind about this, but my mother disagreed.

She said: "How could you forget Khadija? It wasn't so long ago that she left us all of a sudden! But ... how silly of me! It's been ten years ... no ... it must be twelve, or perhaps more. Oh, God! It's as if it's been only hours! Did you say that she is very keen to see me?"

I shook my head.

Now and then, she used to come to our house, accompanying her mother; she was thirteen years old then ... a striking-looking girl with

قضيت بعض الوقت أفحص بدقة المحرك الأساسي، فاكتشفت فيه خللاً بسيطاً ناتجاً عن عبث من قبل ناس جاهلين. أصلحته دون عناء كبير، ثم أردت أن أفحص بقية التأسيسات داخل البيت فناديت على الخادمة وطلبت منها أن تخبر السيدة بذلك وترشدني إلى الداخل. تم الأمر خلال دقائق، و لم أعثر على أي خلل في الآلات الداخلية، فخطر لي أن أشغل الجهاز بأكمله لأتأكد من أنه يعمل بانتظام. أخبرت الخادمة بفكرتي كي تعرضها على سيدتها. ترددت قليلاً ثم رجتني أن أنتظر في الشرفة الخارجية ريثما تخبرها. كنت ملطخ اليدين ببعض دهونات الجهاز السوداء، فأخذت أمسحها بمنديل ورقي. بدت لي الحديقة من الشرفة، شاسعة لانهاية لحدودها، وأشجارها العالية المتمايلة تخفي خط الأفق. سمعت الصوت الدافئ الأليف قبل أن ألتفت.

ـ العفو سيد، هل تجد ضرورة...

كانت في بدلة خروج زرقاء فاتحة، تقف، مشعة بألوانها، في إطار الباب. رأتني حين استدرت إليها.

ـ آه، عبد الرحمن! سيد عبد الرحمن؟ أنت؟

ورفعت يدها، المغطاة بالخواتم، إلى فمها.

كان في ظني، طوال حياتي، أن الهدوء لاتعقبه عاصفة، وأن من الممكن أن يستمر النسيان والبطء والتراخي في المعيشة حتى النهاية؛ و لم أكن مستعداً لتغيير رأيي هذا، غير أن والدتي لم تقبل هذا الرأي مني.

قالت:

ـ كيف استطعت أن تنسى ((خديجة)) واسمها، و لم يمض وقت طويل منذ تركتنا فجأة؟ ولكن... ما أغباني! إنها عشر سنوات، لا بل اثنتا عشرة سنة وربما أكثر. يالله. كأنها ساعات! تقول إنها تريد بإلحاح أن تراني؟

فهززت لها رأسي.

كانت تأتي إلى دارنا برفقة والدتها بين الحين والآخر؛ صبية في الثالثة عشرة من عمرها. متألقة، سوداء العينين والشعر، ناصعة بياض الوجه؛

black eyes, black hair and a pale white complexion. Her mother used to leave her with us. I never knew why. She used to help my mother and sisters with the household chores. Khadija openly showed her fondness for me, never refused me anything and was always eager to please me. I, on the other hand, was at that wild age of fourteen, reserved, shy and too proud to pay any attention to young girls. Khadija would throw dazzling glances at me, her rosy cheeks blushing whenever I talked to her or asked her for something.

My mother added: "How can you ask who she was? But ... don't you know? She's the daughter of Ali Asghar, a sergeant-major in your uncle's outfit and his aide. Her poor mother was very fond of me, and used to come and visit us and leave Khadija with us so that she could help me out around the house and play with the girls until her mother finished the housework at your uncle's house. How destiny can change things! Did you say that she's the wife of your managing director? Talk about a reversal of fortune!"

Afterwards, I needed to restore the hidden balance of the simple and unexciting life I had always wanted. Unfortunately, the memories would not allow me to do so.

We were free as birds that summer holiday. My sisters, Khadija and I fooled around and played in our large house to our hearts' content, with the innocence of childhood. The game we used to play most was hide-and-seek. It was an exciting game, full of cunning, and we preferred it to all others. As we played it so often, it happened once that Khadija and I were hiding in a dark corner behind a pile of bedding in one of the rooms. We were wedged together next to the wall, hunching in fear of being spotted by my youngest sister, when I suddenly felt the combined heat of our young bodies. Next to her, I felt my shoulder brushing up against her heaving bosom. Her shining eyes radiated with delight, framed by the black hair that cascaded around them. I was shaking, subconsciously wanting to move closer to her and put my arms around her. I felt deliciously dizzy and drew her close to my chest; I started pressing myself strongly against her, feeling the curves of her body while she gave herself over to me.

وتركها والدتها لدينا، لا أدري لماذا، فتأخذ بمساعدة أمي وشقيقاتي في
شؤون الدار؛ وكانت شغوفة بي بشكل مكشوف، لاتعصي لي أمراً أبداً،
وتسعى لخدمتي بكل الطرق. إلا أنني لم أكن أعيرها اهتماماً، وكنت في
عمري الموحش ذاك، الرابعة عشرة، منعزلاً خجولاً متكبراً على الفتيات
الصغيرات؛ وكانت «خديجة» تتابعني بنظراتها الساطعة، وخدودها الوردية
تزداد احمراراً كلما كلمتها أو خطر لي أن أطلب منها شيئاً.

تابعت والدتي حديثها:

ـ تقول من كانت؟ ولكنها. ألا تعلم؟ ابنة رئيس العرفاء[14] «علي أصغر»
الذي كان تحت إمرة خالك ومرافقاً[15] له، وأمها المسكينة كانت تأتي
تزورني محبة بي، وتبقيها عندنا كي تساعدني وتلعب مع البنات ريثما تكمل
هي خدمتها في بيت خالك. ياللقدر[16]! تقول إنها زوجة مديركم العام؟
ياللقدر!

كان عليّ، بعد ذلك، أن أعيد التوازن اللامرئي لحياتي التي أردتها، دائماً،
بسيطة ومسطحة. ولكنّ الذكريات لم تترك لي أن أنجح في هذه المهمة.

كنا أحراراً كالطيور، في تلك العطلة الصيفية، أنا وشقيقاتي وخديجة،
نمرح ونلعب في بيتنا الكبير كما نشاء ونشاء البراءة والعبث واختلاط الأمور.
وكانت تلك اللعبة «الختيبة»[17] الجميلة والمراوغة، هي التي تجذبنا أكثر من
الألعاب الأخرى. ومعها وبازدياد اختلاط الأمور بيننا، صار، مرة، أن
تواجدنا، أنا وهي، مختبئين في غبش زاوية ضيقة وراء كومة من الأفرشة
في إحدى غرف البيت. التصقنا ببعضنا حذو الجدار، خشية أن ترانا
أختي الصغرى، والتحمت حرارة أجسادنا الفتية على حين غفلة[18]. كنت
بجانبها؛ أحس بكتفي يمس صدرها والارتفاع الخجول لنهدها؛ وكانت
عيناها براقتين تشعان بهجة، وخصلات الشعر الأسود تلتف حولهما،
وكنت أرتجف. وددت، لاإرادياً، أن أندس بها أكثر وأكثر فأحيطها بذراعي.
تملكني دوار لذيذ فضممتها إلى صدري ورحت أضغط بشدة وأتحسس
جسدها ومنحنياته وكانت مستكينة إليّ.

Memories do not vanish from a person's mind for no reason. Indeed, they can be a source of misery if one is not careful.

I was in the middle of something, concentrating on my work, when I was once again summoned by the general manager.

"Thank you so much, Mr Abdul Rahman. We turned on the heating yesterday, and it's working fine. Of course, this is all thanks to you." All the while, he was busy opening his desk drawer, and never looked up at me. "Were you and my wife neighbours some years ago?"

I told him we had been, and he raised his head, holding a parcel in his hands. I didn't like his look. He offered me the parcel: "This is a small gift as a token of my deep appreciation. I hope you'll accept it from me as a sign of friendship."

I was embarrassed, and began to stammer. As he got up, he added: "Today you'll be taken back to your house by my driver, so that he learns where it is, as my wife would like to visit your mother tomorrow. That is, if it's okay with you, of course?"

Afterwards, my mother gave me a full account of the visit: "She leaped at me and started to shower kisses on me, on my hands, cheeks, shoulder and hair. I was even afraid she might drop her young son, who she was holding in her arms. She'd called him Abdul Rahman, out of affection for you. Do you see?

"I was saddened by the difficult times they'd had, and the terrible hardships they'd endured after her father retired, and, later on, after his death in their Turkmen village near Kirkuk. She told me how her mother, may she rest in peace, wanted to return to Baghdad, to us ... However, she became disabled through illness.

"Finally, she got married five years ago. Now she's settled here. She asked about anyone who was in some way connected with Bab El-Sheikh. She was on the verge of tears when she said that her heart had nearly stopped when she saw you in front of her, in worker's overalls and your hands all grimy. She really is a genuine person! If only you could see how many presents she brought me and your sisters."

لاتختبىء الذكريات عن وعي الإنسان دون سبب؛ فهي مصدر شقائه إن لم يأخذ حذره؛ وكنت، في غمرة العمل، أحذر نفسي وأدعوها إلى اليقظة، حين أرسل السيد المدير العام بطلبي:

ـ شكراً سيد عبد الرحمن، ألف شكر. شغلنا جهاز التدفئة أمس وكان على أحسن مايرام، والفضل في ذلك يعود لك بالطبع. قل لي. ولم يرفع نظره، بل بقي منشغلاً بفتح درج في مكتبه:

ـ أكنتم جيران أهل زوجتي قبل سنوات؟

أجبته بالإيجاب؛ فرفع رأسه وهو يمسك بلفافة بين يديه. لم ترقني نظرته. قدم لي اللفافة:

ـ هذه هدية بسيطة لك تعبيراً عن عميق شكري. أرجو أن تقبلها مني عربون صداقة بيننا.

خجلت من تصرفه وتلجلجت في الكلام بشكل مزعج. أردف وهو يقف:

ـ اليوم سيعود بك سائقي إلى بيتكم ليستدل عليه، فزوجتي تروم أن تزور السيدة والدتك غداً، إذا سمحت بذلك.

حدثتني والدتي:

ـ ارتمت علي ملهوفة وأخذت تقبلني قبلات لاتنتهي؛ في يدي ووجنتي وكتفي وشعري، حتى خشيت أن يقع ابنها الصغير من بين ذراعيها. سمته عبد الرحمن تيمناً باسمك. أترى؟ أبكتني الحال الصعبة التي مروا بها، وكيف ذاقوا[19] الأمرين بين تقاعد أبيها ووفاته وهم في قريتهم التركمانية[20] بنواحي كركوك[21]. تقول كم أرادت أمها، يرحمها الله، أن تعود إلى بغداد. إلينا، إلا أن المرض أقعدها. ثم جاءها النصيب[22] أخيراً فتزوجت منذ خمس سنوات واستقرت بها الحياة هنا. كانت تسأل عنا كلّ من له صلة بمحلة ((باب الشيخ)) إلا أنها لم تصل إلى نتيجة ما. تقول وهي على وشك البكاء. وقع قلبها إلى الأرض حين رأتك أمامها، واقفاً ملطخ اليدين بثياب العمال. فتاة أصيلة حقاً! لو ترى ماجلبت لي ولشقيقاتك من هدايا.

I did not know what to do with the memories that subsequently began to besiege me wherever I went, other than conjuring them up over and over again. Perhaps they would end up being consumed, their effect eradicated from my mind.

It turned out that during our chance encounter she was more versed in the relations and delights that can exist between a man and a woman than I was. As soon as I hesitantly put my lips on her cheeks to kiss her, I could feel her arms around me, her hot lips seeking my mouth and grabbing it. It was a gentle, yet burning kiss. It completely threw me, and took us away from the world. We were not discovered, and, in the end, we left our hiding place to rejoin the game, intentionally making a lot of noise. Not a trace of my kisses remained on her hot, shiny lips as she ran her tongue along them.

After the meeting, I did not know what had happened to my universe. I had fallen victim to a constant state of bewilderment, which worried me more than it did my mother. I was certain that nothing new had happened, so what caused my apathy at work and an unusual loss of interest in the machine world around me? Everything was normal, and had been in its place since time immemorial, except that this heart of mine was continuously agitated.

She invited all of us, by way of her important husband, to her grand house for dinner – all of us … all of us: my mother, my three sisters with their husbands and children, and I … *"All of you … all of you should come and visit us."* Faced with this overwhelming desire, we could not but gratefully accept the invitation.

Our moment of seclusion and kisses, which appeared to me to be engraved on my forehead and in the sky, raced through my mind, conjuring up images of other passionate encounters. I remembered my hunger for her – a special kind of hunger that consumes the mind and body and everything in between. I could not bear to be away from her, except for the briefest of moments, and I did all I could to spend time just with her. It

لم أجد ما أعمله مع الذكريات التي أخذت تحاصرني حيثما حللت، غير أن أستعيدها وأستعيدها، لعل هذه الاستعادات المتكررة تستهلكها وتزيل آثارها من نفسي.

كانت أعلم مني آنذاك، في اتحادنا الصدفي، بما بين الأنثى والذكر من صلات ولذاذات؛ فما إن وضعت شفتي على خدودها أقبلها بتردد، حتى شعرت بذراعيها تحيطان بي وبشفتيها الحارتين تنشدان فمي وتطبقان عليه. كانت قبلة ناعمة مشتعلة رقيقة؛ أخذت بلبي وذهبت بنا بعيداً عن العالم، ولم ننكشف وخرجنا، بعد لأي، راكضين نعاود اللعب بضوضاء مفتعلة؛ ولم تفتني صورة شفتيها الحمراوين المضيئتين من أثر قبلاتي وهي تمر بلسانها عليهما.

لم أدر، بعد ذلك، ما الذي جد في هذا الكون، وجعلني مملوكاً لحالات ذهول مستديم، كانت تقلقني أكثر مما تقلق والدتي. لم يحصل أمر جديد بالتأكيد؛ فما سبب هذا التباطؤ في العمل والابتعاد اللامألوف عن عالم المكائن المحيط بي؟

كل شيء كان معروفاً منذ زمن، كان موضوعاً في مكانه من الزمن الأزلي، سوى أن هذا القلب بين الضلوع لا يني يضطرب ويضطرب.

دعتنا، كلنا، عبر زوجها المرموق المركز، لزيارتها في دارتها الفخمة ولتناول طعام العشاء؛ كلنا. الوالدة وأنا والشقيقات الثلاث وأزواجهن وأطفالهن. كلكم، تأتون إلينا. ولم يكن لنا، أمام هذا الحنين الجارف، غير أن نقبل شاكرين.

خلوتنا الأولى تلك وقبلتنا، التي خيل إلي أنها انطبعت على جبيني وعلى صفحة السماء، تداخلت في ذهني وأعادت لي صور اللقاءات المجنونة الأخرى بيننا. تذكرت ذلك العطش[23] إليها، عطشاً من نوع خاص، يمتلك الروح والجسد وما بينهما. لم أعد قادراً على فراقها إلا هنيهات قليلة، كنت أعمل جهدي بعدها كي أنفرد بها. لم يكن ذلك متاحاً طوال الوقت؛ وما

was not always possible, and as soon as she left me, my hunger for her returned with a vengeance, burning my chest and my entire being.

We had to be careful as we walked along the garden path towards the entrance of their house. Autumn had arrived and surrounded us, like the evening and sky with its poignant blue shades. I walked beside my mother, trying hard to control myself and to act the way I normally did at home. The dinner party was a festival of emotions, sad memories, never-ceasing yearning, bright lights, cheerful noises and children's music. She appeared to be in harmony with her husband and her beautiful child.

She only occasionally addressed me. Yet she would drop everything and hang onto my every word whenever I spoke. At times I noticed her looking at me with our usual glance, even if it did not last for more than one second, if that. She stood in front of the glass shelves in a black suit, embroidered with shiny pearls, looking at me with a contemplative, radiant look that was marred by a touch of hidden sadness. Whenever our eyes were about to meet, she elegantly moved to the other side of the room. It was the same look she used to have all those years ago.

It was on that noisy, joyful morning that we stole priceless moments from time; or perhaps it was fate twisting the arm of time so that it would grant those golden moments, against all odds. We quickly went up to the small room we used to call "the Kafshkan". We did not speak much, especially her. We rushed behind a wardrobe, in a narrow corner, locked in an eager embrace. My hunger for her, this amazing girl, was at its peak. The kisses drowned us in a sea of obliviousness to the world, and I was eager to remove her clothes with my trembling hands. She gave in to my every movement, compliant, silent, kissing me ardently and drowning herself in my eyes. Very soon we were naked and kissing, in no doubt that we were about to perform the wondrous act of creation, when suddenly I was gripped with an unprecedented fear as I looked into her eyes and saw a hidden terror and deep sadness ...

أن تفارقني حتى يعود العطش حاداً يحرق صدري وكياني كله.

كنا مضطرين بتعقل ونحن ننحدر سائرين عبر ممر الحديقة إلى مدخل دارهم. كان الخريف هناك، يحيط بنا؛ والمساء والسماء ذات الزرقة المؤسية؛ وكنت أسير جنب والدتي، جاهداً أن أضبط إيقاع نفسي مع الجو العائلي المألوف.

كانت دعوة العشاء مهرجاناً من العواطف المتبادلة والذكريات الشجية والحنين الذي لم يخمد، والأضواء والصخب المرح وموسيقى الأطفال؛ وكانت مع زوجها وطفلها الجميل، تبدو على أعلى درجات الانسجام. لم تكن توجه إلي الحديث إلا لماماً، غير أنها كانت تقطع انشغالها بأي شيء لتصغي بالانتباه لما أقول. ولمحتها مرة؛ جمعتنا نحن الاثنين لمحة هي لمحتنا. لم تدم إلا ثانية واحدة أو جزءاً منها؛ كانت واقفة أمام رفوف الزجاجيات في بدلة سوداء مطرزة باللآلئ المشعة، تنظر إلي نظرة متأملة، متلامعة، تشوبها مسحة من حزن لا يبين. ولم تدع لي أن ألتقي معها بالنظر، وتحركت بخطوها المتزن إلى جهة أخرى. تلك النظرة نفسها هي التي ماتزال تحملها في عينيها الجميلتين في سنوات العهد البعيد. عهدنا.

في ذلك الضحى المتوثب بالضجة والمرح، حين سرقنا من الزمن لحظات لا تثمن؛ أم لعله القدر العجيب، هو الذي لوى ذراع الزمن فمنحنا، على غير عادته، تلك اللحظات الذهبية. صعدنا بسرعة إلى الغرفة الخشبية الصغيرة التي كنا ندعوها ((كفشكان))[24]؛ لم نتكلم؛ لم نكن نتبادل الكلام، لا كثيراً ولا قليلاً، خاصة هي. انحشرنا بلهفة وعجلة، خلف دولاب للملابس، في زاوية ضيقة. كنت في قمة تعطشي لها، لهذه الصبية، لهذه الأنثى المذهلة. أغرقنا القبل في بحر من الغياب عن العالم، رأيت نفسي فيه أتشبث بنزع ملابسها بأيد مرتجفة. كانت مستسلمة لكل بادرة مني؛ مستكينة، صامتة، تقبلني بشراهة وتغوص بنظرها في عيني. وخلال ثانية، وجسدانا عاريان، ونحن مقبلان، لا شك، على استكمال عملية الخلق العجيبة، هاجمني رعب لا مثيل له وأنا أهم بها وأبادلها النظر وأرى في عينيها معنى خفياً من الروع والعمق العميق... العميق.

It was that same look she exchanged with me at the party, standing at a distance, behind the sparkling glassware. What is the link between these two looks, so remote in time? I did not know then, and I still do not know today.

At that moment, I pulled away from her, in a flash. I remember it well ... Oh, how well I remember the warmth of her abdomen and her bosom, her tenderness and our intertwined limbs. The storm passed peacefully. Unfortunately, my mental state, like other aspects of my life, took a turn for the worse thereafter.

The dinner ended as all great feasts do, with the exchange of presents and telephone numbers, kisses and promises of further visits. We were quite happy as we returned to our respective homes.

I simply wanted to ignore what had happened, and was determined to draw from my store of contentment and satisfaction in order to achieve this, if it had not been for another look from her. She was enthusiastically writing down her telephone number for my mother before we left, when she stopped writing as though she had forgotten something and raised her eyes, for a moment, towards me. Her face was radiant, and the way she looked at me revealed a hidden and obscure desire I was able to decipher despite my bewilderment.

When we spoke on the telephone, she said, in her warm voice: "Thank you for this call, Abdul Rahman. Thank you very much. I wanted to talk to you, and you've made it easy for me. If only you knew how happy I was to see you all."

"To see us all?"

"You don't know what you all mean to me and how I value you all; you above everyone else, and, of course, the rest of your family. Forgive me, Abdul Rahman, that I won't be able to see you. I'm indebted to you for everything."

"To me? I don't know what you mean."

"Oh, how could you say that? Don't you remember? You didn't ruin me, though you could have done. Don't you

تلك كانت نظرتها نفسها التي رمتها عليّ قبل حين وهي تقف على مبعدة، خلف الزجاجيات المتألقة مثلها. أية دلالة تجمع بين هاتين النظرتين المتباعدتين في الزمان؟ لم أعرف، ولا أزال.

إلا أن النكوص عنها بدأ آنذاك. في تلك البرهة الزمنية بالغة القصر. أتذكر جيداً. آه. كم أتذكر جيداً حرارة بطنها وصدرها ونعومتها، وتلاقي أعضائنا وأفخاذنا. ومرت العاصفة بسلام، لكنّ أموري النفسية وغيرها، انتكست بي بعد ذلك كما يجب.

انتهى مهرجان العشاء كما تنتهي المهرجانات الكبرى. بالهدايا والقبل وبالوعود بزيارات أخرى وتبادل أرقام التلفونات؛ وكنا سعداء ونحن عائدون إلى بيوتنا.

كنت أريد أن أهمل كلّ ماحصل بهدوء، مصمّماً على الاستعانة بخزيني من أحاسيس القناعة لإنجاز هذه المهمة، لولا نظرة أخرى من عينيها. كانت، بحماس، تسجل رقم تليفونها لوالدتي قبل أن نغادر، حين توقفت عن الكتابة كأنها نسيت أمراً ما، ورفعت عينيها، لحظة، وتطلعت إلى جانب حيث أقف. كان وجهها صقيلاً، رائعاً، وانعطافتها البسيطة نحوي توحي برغبة غامضة مستترة، استطعت رغم اضطرابي، أن أفهمها.

قالت، عبر الهاتف، بصوتها الدافئ:

ـ أشكرك ياعبد الرحمن على مخابرتك هذه. أشكرك كثيراً، كنت أريد أن أحدثك، فسهلت لي ذلك. لو تعلم كم سعدت برؤيتكم.

ـ رؤيتنا؟

ـ أنت لاتفهم معناكم عندي ومعزتكم. أنت أولاً وآخراً وبقية العائلة. لاتؤاخذني عبدالرحمن لأني لا أستطيع رؤيتك، ولكني مدينة لك بكل شيء.

ـ أنا؟ لا أفهم شيئاً مما تقولين.

ـ آه، كيف تقول هذا؟ ألا تتذكر؟ أنت لم تكسرني. كنت قادراً على ذلك. ألا تتذكر؟ لقد حفظتني. حفظت لي حياتي، ولم أنسَ ذلك. لن

remember? You spared me. You spared my life, and I can never forget that. You're the one who granted me the life I'm living now. Anyway, how are you? Do you know what happened to me when I saw you ... that day ...?" She stopped talking for a moment, evidently struggling to continue the conversation. "Your mother told me that you're happy with her. Is that true, Abdul Rahman? Tell me you are happy. Aren't you happy?"

"To some extent; to be more precise, I'm content with my circumstances. I have an ample store of such feelings."

"Is that enough? Is that enough for you?"

"What else can I do?"

I heard her sigh."Can I help you in any way ... as a friend?"

I did not respond. An embarrassing silence passed.

She asked me: "Are you still ill? I mean, you know ..."

"More or less. I'm of no use to anyone."

"Really? Oh, God! Our happy times didn't last for long."

The next day I sought refuge in that store of feelings I had proudly told her about. I only found hunger, misunderstanding and hollow echoes, which rang out the name of "Khadija".

أنساه مطلقاً. أنت الذي منحتني حياتي هذه. ولكن. كيف أنت؟ هل تعلم ماحصل لي وأنا أراك. رأيتك ذلك اليوم. وصمتت؛ وكانت تغالب نفسها، كما يبدو، كي تستمر في الكلام:

ـ قالت لي الوالدة أنك سعيد معها. أليس كذلك ياعبد الرحمن؟ قل لي أنك سعيد. ألست سعيداً؟

ـ إلى حد ما. أنا بالأحرى قانع بما أنا فيه. لدي خزين من هذه المشاعر.

ـ وهل تكفي هذه؟ هل تكفيك؟

ـ ومالعمل إذاً؟

سمعتها تتنهد:

ـ أأستطيع مساعدتك. كصديقة؟

لم أجبها. مرت بيننا فترة صمت محرج. سألتني:

ـ ألا تزال مريضاً؟ أعني أنت تعلم.

ـ تقريباً. لا فائدة مني كبيرة.

ـ حقاً يا إلهي. لم تدم أوقاتنا السعيدة طويلاً.

استنجدت، في اليوم التالي، بذلك الخزين الذي حدثتها عنه بافتخار، فلم ألقى إلا العطش وسوء الفهم والأصداء الجوفاء. كان اسمها ((خديجة)).

Language Notes

1. خَزِين: "storage" (> خَزَنَ (i), "to store").

2. لا مرئيات: (لا + مَرْئِي >: ("not" + "seen"); cf. الْمَرْئِيات, "the
   visible world"). The use of the particle لا is a common
   feature in MSA, where it is joined with a noun or adjective
   to render the English "un/in-" or "non-": e.g. لامَرْكَزِي
   ("decentralized"), لامادِّيّة ("immaterialism"). Note that
   if the article is added, there are two لـ, e.g. اللامَسْؤُولية
   ("irresponsibility"). The Arabic words غَيْر and عَدَم can be
   used in a similar sense: e.g. عَدَم الاسْتِحْياء ("shamelessness"),
   غَيْر مَعْقُول ("unreasonable").

3. شَقِيقة: (pl. شَقِيقَات; m. شَقِيق, pl. أشِقّاءُ, أَشِقّة); a blood-sister
   (i. e. same father and mother) as أُخْت can be used for
   "stepsister", "half-sister" or even as a form of address for an
   unrelated female.

4. خانَها الدَهْر: lit. "Time has betrayed (the family)."

5. فَتَح الله عَلَيهُما باب الرزق: lit. "God opened the door of
   livelihood to both of them"; in this context, however, it
   means that God had mercy on them.

6. هَبَطَتْ بِنا الدُنيا: lit. "the world descended on us", i.e. things
   declined in material terms.

7. جار الزمان بنا: lit. "time was cruel to us"; جار (u), "to
   tyrannize", "to commit an outrage" > جَوْر, "oppression",
   "injustice".

8. رأس الجول: (pronounced *ra's al-chōl*) a suburb of Baghdad
   at the end of Bab El-Sheikh (see next note). Note that the
   Iraqi dialect (like some Gulf dialects, as well as Palestinian)
   has the sound "ch" (as in "Charles"), which is usually
   represented in writing by the so-called "three-dotted *jīm*",
   i.e. چ. This letter is originally Persian, which has provided
   other letters to render "European" sounds: پ (for "p")
   and گ (for "g"). Note, however, that in Egypt ج is used

to denote "j" (as in "genre"); cf. جراچ, "garage" (since ج is pronounced "g" in ECA). In Morocco "g" is represented by a three-dotted *kāf*, ݣ as in the place-name أݣادير.

9. باب الشْيخ: one of the densest populated areas, situated in the heart of Baghdad. Literally meaning "the door of the Shaykh", it refers to Shaykh 'Abd al-Qādir al-Gaylānī, (1077-1165), whose tomb is in the Mosque that is named after him, and which attracts thousands of visitors each year. Fu'ād al-Takarlī was born in Bab El-Sheikh.

10. أيّام العْز: lit. "days of glory".

11. القطار لْم يَفتْ بَعْد عَلىَّ: lit. "the train has not passed me by yet", i.e. there is still time for me to get married.

12. الدُورَة: a small town some twenty kilometres outside Baghdad, known for its oil refineries.

13. سُنّة المُجْتَمَع: lit. "law of society", meaning customary procedure. In another context السُنّة or سُنّة النَبي refers, of course, to the *Sunna* or conduct of the Prophet Muhammad.

14. رَئيس العُرَفاء: this military term corresponds to رقيب أوَّل (pl. رُقَباء) in many other countries (Egypt, Syria, Lebanon). The word عُرَفاء is the plural of عَريف, which is, variously, a "sergeant" (Iraq) or a "corporal" (e. g. in Egypt, Syria).

15. مُرافق: this term is restricted to Iraq; in many other Arab countries, the term مُلازم is used.

16. يا للقدر: on the use of the vocative particle (with لِ) in this exclamatory phrase, meaning: "Oh, what a (strange) fate!", see كتاب الموتى.

17. الخْتِيبَة: another common term in ICA for this game is الخْتيلة or الغماية (in Egypt it is known as أسْتُغُمّاية).

18. فجاءةً = حين غفلة.

19. ذاقُوا الأمرين: lit. "they tasted the two bitter things" (ذاقَ (u), "to taste").

20. قريتهم التركمانية: "their Turkmen village"; most of the populations of the villages around the city of Kirkuk

are Turkmen (a Turkic ethnic group found also in areas around Arbil and Mosul) and Kurdish.

21. كَرْكوك: an oil-rich city in the north of Iraq.

22. جاءَهَا النَصيب أخيراً: lit. "fate came to her eventually", i.e. she got married in the end.

23. العَطْش: note that in this figurative expression, the Arabic refers to "thirst", whereas in English it is "hunger".

24. كَفُشْكان: an old name for a room built inside another room in some traditional Iraqi houses, where the ceiling of the room is very high. Access is provided by a wooden staircase. In some cases, it is simply an attic. It is usually used for the storage of furniture, etc. It is also known as الكِنْجينَة.

Laylā al-'Uthmān

Born in Kuwait in 1945, Laylā al-'Uthmān (Leila Othman) is a well-known novelist and short-story writer. She began writing at a very early age while still at school, and published articles in many local periodicals on social and literary issues. She is regarded as one of the most prominent female fiction writers of the Arabian Peninsula. Her collections of short stories include اِمْرَأَة في إناء (*A Woman in a Vessel*, 1976), الرَّحيل (*The Departure*, 1979) and الحُبُّ لهُ صُور(*Love Has Many Images*, 1982). Her novels include المَرأَة والقطة (*The Woman and the Cat*, 1985) and وَسُميّة تَخْرُج من البَحْر (*Sumayya Comes Out of the Sea*, 1986). Her most recent novel, المَحاكمة (*The Trial*, 2000), portrays the various political and social conflicts she has experienced in her native country.

In her fiction, al-'Uthmān deals with conflicts between men and women and with the outside world, often concentrating on specifically Arab themes and on the position of women in Middle Eastern society. Many of her works have been translated into a number of European languages (e. g. Russian, German and Swedish).

The following story deals with the aspirations, dreams and frustrations of two women belonging to entirely different social and economic backgrounds. At the same time, it also affords the reader a glimpse into the complex social fabric of a society in flux, inextricably bound up with the theme of guest workers.

Night of Torment

With yearning eyes, she looked at the perfume bottle that had been left behind, next to one of the washbasins. She felt a strong urge to grab it, open it and spray a little on her rough palm, in which she was grasping a quarter *dinar* note given to her earlier by the owner of the perfume on her way out. She thought: "What if I took the bottle and sprayed it all over my body, so my enticing fragrance could spread like that of all other women?"

Before she could give in to the urge, however, the owner of the bottle returned to the washroom, marched towards the bottle, put it in her handbag and gave her another quarter *dinar*, as if to reward her for finding the bottle in its place. Then she quickly left, her fragrance lingering in the air.

Her veins seemed to extend like fingertips, gathering the smallest particles of the fragrance that made its way from her nose to her lungs, which were saturated with the toilet odour. However, soon after, the smell of disappointment dispelled every whiff of the fragrance.

Since she had started her humble job as an attendant in the ladies' room at the airport, she had been inhaling the black nauseating air that flowed into her windpipe, soothed only by transitory fragrances.

She was sitting in her plastic chair, taking in the daily arrivals with languishing eyes: women attired in colourful, elegant clothes, girls squeezed into tight jeans and short blouses, all of whom were in a hurry to relieve themselves. Her ears registered the rustling sound of women's clothes sliding down their bodies, followed by trickling bladders and murmuring bowels, and then the waterfall of the flush expelling the waste, leaving only the odour in the air.

When the women left the cubicles, they gathered at the

ليلة القهر ١

عيناها تغازلان الزجاجة المنسية قرب المغسلة، رغبة عنيفة تحثها أن تندفع إليها، تفتحها، ترش قليلاً على كفها الخشن الذي يصكّ على – ربع الدينار٢– كانت صاحبة الزجاجة قد أسقطته إليها قبل أن تخرج. فكرت: «ماذا لو أخذت الزجاجة كلها أرشها على جسدي فتفوح رائحتي شهية ككل النساء؟».

قبل أن تحملها صهوة الرغبة اقتحمت المرأة المكان، اتجهت نحو زجاجتها التقطتها، دستها في حقيبة يدها، واستلت ربع دينار آخر كمن يكافئها على وجود الزجاجة في مكانها، ثم غادرت بسرعة بعد أن نشرت عطرها في الفراغ.

امتطّت كلّ أوردتها مثل أنامل رقيقة تجمع ذرات العطر المنتشرة وتسري بها من الأنف إلى الرئتين المتخمتين بروائح المراحيض٣، لكنّ ريح الخيبة بصدرها بددت كلّ العطر.

منذ أن بدأت عملها المتواضع– ناطورة لحمّام النساء في المطار– وأنفها يتنشق سواد الهواء المعتل ويدلقه في قصبات صدرها فلا ترطّبه غير ذرات العطور القادمة والمغادرة.

تجلس على كرسيها البلاستيكي، وبعينيها الذابلتين تتابع المشهد اليومي: نساء يدخلن بملابسهن الأنيقة الملونة، فتيات ببنطلونات الجينز الضيقة والبلوزات القصيرة، كلهن عجولات للتخلص من (حَشرهنّ٤) تلتقط أذناها حفيف ملابسهن وهي تنزلق عن أجسادهن، يتبعها خرير (المثانات ومخزون الأمعاء٥)، ثم ينفلت (السيفون٦) بشلاله ليجرف البقايا ويترك الروائح منتشرة.

يخرجن من المراحيض ليتزاحمن على المغسلة، يشطفن أكفهن المزينة بالخواتم، يتأملن وجوههن في المرايا، يصبغن الشفاه، يوردن الخدود، يخرجن

washbasins to wash their beringed hands, examine their faces in the mirror, put on lipstick, apply blush to their cheeks, and do up their tousled hair with colourful combs. Finally, they would douse themselves with fragrance from see-through bottles, and rush out in response to the announcements made over the public address system: "All passengers going to ... please make your way to Gate Number ..."

She started work by picking up the pieces of paper scattered on the floor and those left on the lids of the bins. Then she checked the white washbasins, cleaned the scum left on the sides with a brush and poured a little Dettol down the plughole, tidied up the loose toilet rolls and generally readied the washroom for the hasty passengers. She would return to her chair, hopefully awaiting the generosity of some of the women – a quarter *dinar*, half a *dinar* or some coins, maybe. Many of them, however, left without even noticing either her or her constant dreaming, and she would be left whispering to herself every time: "One day, I'll own a bottle of perfume like that."

When she went out into the street after work, the combined smells of exhaust fumes, people and food rushing into her nostrils were sweeter to her than those she endured in the public washroom. As soon as she opened the door to the wretched annex where she lived, she smelled the suppressed odours rushing towards her like gaping maws, dispelling the street smells and thus leaving only the lavatory odour on her body and clothes.

At night, she would be engulfed in grief and besieged by images of women and their expensive accessories and fashionable clothes. She would slowly exhale in an attempt to catch the slightest whiff of the ladies' perfumes. However, they soon clashed with the smell of her snoring husband, lying next to her. She filled her lungs with the oily smell of *sambousak* and potato *kibbeh*, which her husband had eaten in the Indian restaurant where he works. She would suppress her overwhelming grief: "Surely he must smell the toilet odours on me."

أمشاطهن الملونة، يسوين خصلات شعرهن المتناثرة. وآخر اللمسات تلك الرشات المتتالية من عطور الزجاجات الشفافة يخرجن بعدها مسرعات مليبات للنداءات المتكررة: «على جميع المسافرين المتجهين إلى ... التوجه إلى بوابة رقم ....)».

تبدأ عملها بالتقاط الأوراق المتناثرة على الأرض، وتلك المكومة فوق أغطية سلّات المهملات، تنظر في الأحواض البيضاء، تكشط بالفرشاة ما علق بجوانبها تصب قليلاً من الديتول، تمسح الأطراف تسوّي الرولات المتهدلة، مهيئة بذلك المكان لقادمات آخريات مستعجلات. تعود إلى كرسيها مؤملة بكرم بعضهن، ربع دينار، نصف دينار. أو فكات معدنية. وكثيرات يخرجن غير مكترثات بوجودها ولا بحلمها الذي لا يهدأ ولا يبور فتهمس لنفسها كلّ مرة: «ذات يوم سأمتلك زجاجة عطر)».

حين تخرج إلى الشارع بعد إنتهاء عملها، تتراكض إليها روائح السيارات والبشر والأطعمة متمازجة، لتتراكم داخل أنفها، فتحسها أشهى من رائحة نهارها الطويل داخل الحمّام. وحين تفتح باب الملحق البائس الذي تسكنه، تحس روائحه المكبوتة تهب إليها كأفواه مفتوحة تنفخ ريحها لتطرد روائح الشارع فلا تبقى سوى رائحة الحمّام اللاصقة بجسدها وملابسها.

في الليل يسيّجها قهرها. تحاصرها صور النساء بزينتهن وموديلات ملابسهن تكتم آهة، وتستل شهيقاً لعلها تصطاد ولو ذرة من روائح عطورهن. لكنها تصطدم برائحة زوجها الشاخر بقربها تعبئ رئتيها برائحة دهن (السمبوسك[7] وكبة البطاطا[8]) التي يتشبع بها حيث يعمل في المطعم الهندي. تتحرق وتكبت أفواه حسرتها: «بالتأكيد هو يشم بي رائحة المراحيض)».

She was carried away by her desire, imagining herself holding a perfume bottle, making her most hidden dream come true: "If I spray some of this fragrance on me, all our bad smells will vanish, and we will embrace each other tightly." She went to sleep and in the corridors of her dreams found herself chasing tens of winged perfume bottles flying around.

The day you dropped a dinar *in the toilet attendant's palm, you thought you gave her a fortune, but she gave it back to you and surprised you by saying: "I want your bottle of perfume."*

You wanted to remind her of her situation as you once again held out the dinar: *"The* dinar *is more useful to you than the perfume."*

However, she continued to refuse, requesting the perfume instead. You could not tolerate the naivety of her warped aspirations as you examined her shabby clothes and her scarf that was frayed at the edges. A perfume like yours would not suit her. She sensed your contempt. She slowly rubbed her clothes while staring at your elegant outfit. You wanted to remind her of things other than the clothes. With a circular movement of your hand, you indicated the size of the restroom and raised your voice, in an attempt to suppress her lustful desire for the perfume: "What use is the perfume to you while you are here?"

She smiled at you, feebly trying to curry favour, and then begged you, tears choking in her throat: "I'd spray it on myself at night to attract my husband."

Overcome with astonishment and sadness, you felt the pangs of regret that were about to mollify your heart. You did not hesitate. You got the small bottle out and gave it to her. She joyfully leaned forward to kiss your slender palm, but you quickly pulled it away and ran off when you heard your flight being called.

In reality, you were running away from a memory, its moss embedded in the lake of your life. At that moment, those difficult years that had been heavier to bear than a millennium exploded in front of you. The toilet attendant had unintentionally brought back memories, just as you finished fastening your seatbelt on the plane.

You closed your eyes and cast your mind back to those painful

تمتطي حصان التمني، تتخيل أنها ممسكة بزجاجة عطر فيبرق حلمها المكنوز: «حين أرش منها على جسدي ستطرد كلّ روائحنا. سنلتصق ببعضنا أكثر». تنام وفي دهاليز الأحلام تجد نفسها تطارد عشرات من الزجاجات ذات الأجنحة.

ذات يوم أسقطت في كف امرأة الحمّام – دينارك – تصورت أنك وهبتها ثروة لكنها ردته إليك وفاجأتك:

– أريد زجاجة عطرك.

قصدت أن تنبهيها لحال واقعها وكفك تمتد ثانية بالدينار:

– الدينار أفيد لك من العطر.

لكنها أصرت على رفضه والتمسك بطلب العطر، لم تحتملي سذاجة تطلعها الأعوج وعيناك تسريان على ثيابها الرثة، وغطاء رأسها ذي الحواف المنسولة، حال لا يناسبه عطر كعطرك. شعرت بإحساسك المرصود ضدها، مسحت على ملابسها بهدوء مقصود وهي تركز على ثيابك الأنيقة، أردت أن تذكريها بشيء غير الملابس، بحركة دائرية من كفك أشرت لمساحة الحمّام، أطلقت صوتك قاصدة أن تكبتي رغبتها الشبقة إلى العطر:

– ماذا يفيدَك العطرَ وأنت هنا.

ابتسمتْ لك بتودّد بارد نثرتْ كلماتها بتوسل لا يخلو من رغرغة دمع مكتوم:

– أرشه في الليل ليجذب زوجي.

أسقطتك في دائرة الدهشة والحزن. شعرت دبابيس الندم تغتال لدانة قلبك لم تترددي. أخرجت زجاجتك الصغيرة ومنحتها لها، انحنتْ بفرحها إلى كفك الرشيق لتقبله لكنك عاجلت بجذبه وفررت ملبية نداء الرحلة. وكنت في الواقع تفرين من ذكرى تعشبت طحالبها في بحيرة حياتك. والآن تفجرت أمامك تلك السنوات التي كانت بمرارتها أثقل من ألف عام.

دفعتك امرأة الحمّام غير قاصدة أن تفكي أحزمة ذاكرتك في اللحظة التي أنهيت ربط حزام الأمان في الطائرة. أسبلت جفنيك، وشرعت تستعرضين ليالي القهر الموجعة التي كانت تمضي وأنت مركونة في زوايا الفراش،

nights that went by as you lay cowering in the corner of the bed, after having endured his daily rage. He ignored you, even though you were sweeter than an apple and fresher than a rose. He ignored you, yet he longed for you and desired you. You had been warned that he was a "womaniser", "drinker", "selfish" and "bad-tempered". Yet your mind was set. You had been smitten by his good looks and sweet talk, which drew you towards his deceitful, shallow exterior. Your conceit was another reason: "With my beauty and intelligence, he will prefer me above all other women and I'll keep him on the straight and narrow."

Early on, your life changed and your dreams were shattered; you did not captivate him, nor did he surrender. You smelled other women's perfumes on his clothes and washed off the traces of their make-up. You imagined what they looked like, wondering whether they were better looking or smarter than you. The worst was the moment you discovered his affair with your closest friend, whose face, body and voice were so familiar to you.

That particular night stretched in front of you unlike any other night, as he came home highspirited and drunk; unlike him, he was carrying a parcel in a coloured wrapping. You were suddenly filled with a joy that touched the deepest of your dashed hopes, and you wondered: "Did he remember me and buy me a present?"

You waited until he went to bed and started snoring. Your overwhelming curiosity made you open the parcel. To your amazement, it contained a luxurious bottle. You opened the pink card and read his sweet dedication to your treacherous friend: "Your favourite perfume that makes my head spin and makes me your slave forever."

Your deepest hopes were crushed as though they had been ground by a thousand millstones and turned into frantic grains of dust besieging you, inflaming your innermost jealousy and stinging your soul with a stupid hope: "What if I captivated you with it tonight?"

You went into the bathroom and rubbed your soft body, which had been untouched for more than two months, and put on a diaphanous sky-blue nightdress. You held the perfume bottle and poured half its

مغموسة بسوائل غضبه اليومية. يعوفكِ وأنت أشهى من تفاحة وأنضر من زهرة. أنت التي تشتهاها وتمناها ورغم كلِّ الذي تناهى إليك عنه: «إنه زير نساء، عاشق للشراب أناني وعصبي المزاج». إلا أنكِ تشبثت برأيك. همتِ بوسامته وعذوبة لسانه. جذباك نحو لجينه⁹ الشفاف المخادع. غرورك هو الآخر أغواك: «بجمالي وذكائي سأختصه دون كلّ النساء وسأعدل ضلوع حياته العوجاء».

سرعان ما اعوجّت أيامكِ وتكسرت أحلامكِ، لم تأسريه وتستأثريه، كنت تشتمين عطورهن في ثناياه، تغسلين آثار المساحيق البائته على ثيابه، تتخيلين أشكالهن ولا تعرفين إن كن أجمل منكِ أو أذكى. لكنّ فجيعتكِ كانت لحظة اكتشافك علاقته بأقرب صديقة إليك تلك التي تعرفين وجهها، تفاصيل جسدها، ورنة صوتها.

اشرأبت أمامك دون كلِّ الليالي. تلك الليلة التي دخل بها البيت منتشياً بخمرته. لكنه على غير عادته يحمل في يده رزمة ملونة. فاجأك فرح مسّ عروق آمالك المسحوقة ترنّم سؤال بداخلكِ: «هل تذكر وجودي فاشترى لي هدية؟»

انتظرته حتى ولج الفراش وعاط شخيره، استحوذك فضولك الشرس أن تفتحي الهدية. أذهلتكِ الزجاجة الفاخرة. فتحتِ الورقة الوردية قرأتِ إهداءه العذب لصديقتك الخائنة:

«عطرك المفضل الذي يدوّخني ويجعلني أسيرك دائماً».

تهاوت عروق أملك. طحنتها ألف رحى فصارت مثل ذرات غبار أهوج حاصرك، أشعل فتائل غيرتكِ الخامدة، ولسع روحكِ بأمل غبي: «ماذا لو أسرتك به أنا الليلة؟».

دخلت الحمّام. دعكت جسدك البض المهجور لأكثر من شهرين، ارتديت قميصاً سماوياً شفافاً. أمسكت بالزجاجة وسكبتِ نصف عطرها – الآسر– على أنحاء جسدكِ حتى أصابع القدمين. اندسستِ تحت

enticing content all over your body, up to your fingertips. You sneaked under the duvet and moved close to him, reducing the distance that usually separated you, your body tingling with desire. You had hardly settled in when he started and awoke from his deep sleep, as though he'd been stung. Your heart fluttered and your hope grew: "He'll water me after the drought and cull my ripe fruit. This perfume is truly magic."

You were terrified by his savage reaction as he ripped the sky-blue nightie with his hands, screaming: "How dare you wear her perfume?!" His outburst was like that of a thousand volcanoes. He threw the perfume away, and the only thing left were noxious fumes. He pushed you out of the bed and kicked you along the floor, while you called out for help against the pain in your heart. He spat on you, cursed you and dragged you to the bathroom. He threw you into the tub and emptied the box of washing powder and any other detergents he could get hands on over you. He started to drown you with the hot shower water in order to remove all traces of the perfume from your body, while you flapped about helplessly like a fish.

The door slammed shut, and you spent a night that was worse than a thousand torments, in the tub, drowned by liquids and the torture. How much time has gone by since you snatched your soul from his brackish lake, the thick curtains of oblivion cloaking the smell of your former torment?

She went from the restroom into the street, elated, her nose prepared for the onslaught of perfume and the mixture of the usual smells. It was a day unlike other days, and an eagerly anticipated night that would not be like other nights. She felt a great debt to that woman. She did not regret refusing a *dinar* she greatly needed. Instead, she was holding something that was far more precious and coveted. She was on cloud nine, and dreams are not bothered by busy traffic. If it had not been for the sound of the horn from a speeding car, she would have been run over. She held on tight to her worn bag, where she kept the bottle that she guarded as closely as her heart. She reached the bus stop and sat down in the shelter. She pulled the

اللحاف، تعمدت تجاوز المسافة الفاصلة بينكما، وفي جسدك تستثار براعم الرغبات. ما كدت تستقرين حتى أنتفض من نومه الثقيل كالملدوغ. رفرف قلبك وفاحت أمنيتك: «سيرويني بعد القحط ويقطف ثماري الناضجة إنه لعطرٌ ساحرٌ حقاً».

أرعبتك ردة فعله المتوحشة، إنهالت كفاه تمزقان السماوي، وترضان مرمرك المكشوف وصراخه: «كيف تجرأت على عطرها؟» صراخ فلق ألف بركان، أطاح بالعطر فما عدت تشمين غير سموم الدخان. قذفك من الفراش. دكك بقدميه على الأرض التي استغاثت من الألم قبلك، بصق، شتم، وسحلك إلى الحمّام. قذفك بقلب البانيو[10] أفرغ عليك علبة مسحوق الغسيل وبعض ما طالته يدك من سوائل التنظيف. أخذ يغرقك بماء الدش الحار ليزيل عن جسدك كلّ أثر للعطر، وأنت مثل سمكة تنازع في حوض ماء خابط.

صفق الباب. وأمضيت ليلة القهر الأصعب من ألف قهر داخل البانيو غارقة بسوائلك والعذاب. كم مضى الآن منذ أن انتزعت روحك من بحيرته الآسنة هادلة ستائر النسيان السميكة على روائح قهرك القديم؟

خرجتْ من الحمّام إلى الشارع، فرحتها أوسع من مداه، أنفها المهيأ لشم العطر يذري مزيج الروائح المعتادة هو نهار غير كلّ النهارات، وليلة منتظرة ستكون غير كلّ الليالي. شعرتْ بامتنان كبير لتلك المرأة. لم تندم أنها رفضت ديناراً هي بحاجته. إنها الآن تقبض على الحاجة الأثمن والأشهى. تطير وتحلم غير عابئة بزحام الطريق. ولولا أن زعق بوق السيارة المندفعة لكانت العجلات داستها بالأسفلت. شدت على حقيبتها المهترئة حيث تلبد الزجاجة وكأنها قلبها الذي خشيت عليه الموت. وصلت موقف الباص، جلست تحت مظلته، واستخرجت كنزها الثمين تناجيه: «تلك الزجاجة! آه

precious treasure out of her bag, and whispered to it: "Oh, how I've dreamed of this bottle!" She stared at it, played with it. She took off its golden top and held the atomizer to her nose. Just as she was about to spray some perfume on her, the bus arrived and a mob of Asian workers like her, as well as those from other parts of the world, jostled to board.

The bus filled with the odour of summer sweat on the exhausted workers' bodies, mixed with the scent of coconut oil they treated their hair with, malodorous feet and pungent breath, heavy with the customary aroma of spices and *ash*. All of them invaded her nose, normally filled with the smell of the airport lavatory that stuck to her clothes and skin. She thought of the treasure in her bag, took it out and cupped it in her palms, like a mother cradling her child's head. She got off, smiling, lovingly staring at the bottle, filled with a desire to open it. She wetted the tip of her finger with the perfume and put some on the tip of her nose in order to subdue the smells in the bus.

The man next to her moved in the seat. His elbow collided with her arm, jolting it; she closed her palms, fearful for the bottle, and clutched it to her chest so that it appeared she was reciting some sacred prayers.

She entered her flat, and for the first time she felt that something valuable had come in with her. She rushed to take the bottle out of her bag and kissed it repeatedly, her heart filled with a hitherto unknown joy. She began to flirt with the bottle, praising it: "Finally, my love, you are mine, and my body will know no smell other than yours. Ah … thank you, generous lady." She danced with the bottle in the narrow room, dreaming of a night other than the ones she knew.

How could she know the secrets of the perfume, its meaning and how to treat it? She did not even know how to celebrate its arrival in her home, the smell of the first spray on her fragrance-free body. It did not occur to her to bathe first in

كم حلمت بها)) تأملتها. داعبتها. رفعت غطاءها الذهبي، ألصقتها بأنفها، كادت تضغط الرأس المستدير لترش منها لولا أن أقبل الباص وتدافع إليه أمثالها من العمال الآسيويين وغيرهم من جنسيات أخرى.

اكتظ الباص بروائح التعب وعرق الصيف المبيت في الأجساد المنهكة متمازجاً بروائح شعور مدهونة – بالحل – ومن الأقدام التي اختزنت حشواتها الحامضة، من أفواه تزفر جوف المعدات التي ألفت التوابل[11] والآش[12] والكاري. كلها تقتحم أنفها المعبّق أصلاً برائحة ثيابها وجلدها المعجونين برائحة حمّام المطار. فكرت بكنزها المحفوظ في الحقيبة استخرجته أرقدته بطن كفيها المتلاصقين، بدت مثل أم تحضن رأس وليدها. انفجرت ابتسامتها وهي تتأمل الزجاجة بحنان مشبع بالرغبة أن تفتحها. تبلل طرف إصبعها بالعطر وتمسح أرنبة أنفها لتحجب عنها رائحة الباص.

تحرك الرجل الملاصق لها في المقعد. اصطدمت كوعه بذراعها فاهتزت، أطبقت كفيها خوفاً على الزجاجة وألصقتها إلى صدرها فبدت وكأنها تتلو صلوات مقدسة.

دخلت ملحقها[13] ولأول مرة تشعر أن شيئاً جديداً غالياً يدخل معها، سارعت باستخراج زجاجتها، أشبعتها بالقبلات، وصدرها يكبر بفرح لم تعهده، نثرت تسابيح صوتها تغازل الزجاجة: ((أخيراً يا حبيبتي امتلكتك وسيعرف جسدي رائحة غير رائحته. آه. شكراً لك أيتها المرأة الكريمة)). دارت في المكان الضيق تراقصها تغني حالمة بليلة غير تلك الليالي.

من أين لها أن تعرف سر العطر ومعناه وأصول التعامل معه؟ هي تجهل حتى كيفية الاحتفاء بخطوته الأولى إلى بيتها، وبرشتها الأولى الأكثر شبقاً وهي تصب على جسد بكر من أي عطر. لم يخطر ببالها أن تستحم لتكشط

order to remove the various odours, nor, for that matter, to change her time-worn, kitchen-stained clothes, reeking of the airport lavatory. She did not comb her hair, thick with stale, greasy lotions, or put make-up on her face, which was well used to the dust and the bus exhaust. She was overwhelmed with immense joy and her longing dream.

The moment she decided to put on the perfume, the bottle she was holding in her hands turned into something resembling an insect spray pursuing the buzz of a dull fly; she became the fly whizzing around and spraying herself randomly, not caring what she sprayed, whether it be parts of her body, her hair or her garments. The sound of the atomizer spray mixed with her laughter, singing and the sighs of incipient delight. She emptied the entire bottle, apart from a little bit that remained at the bottom and could not be reached by the siphon. She was determined not to leave a single drop; with a pestle she broke the bottleneck, extracted the last drops and applied them to her hair and cheeks, oblivious to the small pieces of broken glass that were scratching her.

She decided not to do any work. She made herself comfortable on the cotton bed and relaxed in the knowledge that tonight he would not turn over, claiming he was tired. Tonight, the gulf of perfume would draw him to her hungry body, which would be cured from the pain of waiting. This magical fragrance would make him empty his hidden rain and spray his stored seeds.

When he slipped into bed, he as usual began to snore from exhaustion. She felt his head twisting and turning, like someone chasing away silly ideas. He kicked with his legs as though pushing away a mouse or a cockroach that had climbed onto them. Then she heard him sniffing – fast, repetitive sniffs – like someone trying to ascertain the source of a particular smell. She realized that he had discovered a new smell. She was under the illusion that he was aroused by her. In her conceit, she moved close to him and grabbed his back; he shook, but

عن جسدها أنواء روائحه المتراكمة، ولا أن تغير ثوبها الملطخ بعثرات الأيام، وروائح الحمّام ودبق المطبخ. لم تمشط جدائل شعرها الملبدة بدهنها القديم، ولا أن تزين الوجه الذي اعتاد غبار الطبيعة ودخان الحافلات. فرحها المشدوه وحلمها الملهوف استلباها. وفي لحظة القرار بالتعطر تحولت الزجاجة بين يديها إلى ما يشبه مبيداً حشرياً يلاحق طنين ذبابة ثقيلة الظل، صارت هي الذبابة تدور وترش نفسها بعشوائية لا تفرق بين مناطق الجسد والشعر والثوب. صوت الرشيش السريع يتمازج بضحكاتها، غنائها، وتنهدات فرحها الأول. أفرغت كلّ الزجاجة بقي في القاع قليل لا يصل إليه الأنبوب الساحب أصرت ألا تترك نقطة منه أحضرت يد الهاون كسرت عنق الزجاجة وتلقفت النقط الأخيرة لتمسح بها شعرها وو جنتيها غير عابئة بذرات من فتات الزجاج المكسور تخدشانهما. قررت أن لا تقوم بأي عمل. وارتاحت على فراشها القطني مؤملة النفس أنه لن يستدير عنها بحجته الليلة «أنا متعب» الليلة سيجرفه تيار العطر إلى جسدها الجائع ستداويه من ألم الصبر والانتظار. وبهذا العطر الساحر ستجعله يفرغ مطره المكتوم ويرش بذاره المخزون.

حين اندس في الفراش يشخر من التعب كعادته شعرت برأسه كمن يطارد أفكاراً عبثية ويرفس بقدميه وكأنه يدفع بفأر أو صرصار تسلق عليهما. ثم سمعته ينشق نشقات متتالية سريعة كمن يبحث عن مصدر رائحة ما! أدركت أنه اكتشف رائحة جديدة. اغترّت أنها استثارته وبكل غرورها اقتربت منه التصقت بظهره فاهتز ولم يستدر. نطت عليه، قابلته

did not turn towards her. She pounced on him, her body on top of his, confident that he would reciprocate, attracted by her perfume and lusting for her body. Instead, he sighed twice and rolled over to the side she had vacated. He was restless, while his breathing came close to sneezing. She started to have doubts about the perfume: "Is it possible that no one other than the person wearing the perfume can smell it, or has he got a cold?"

Suddenly he turned towards her; her heart sang, her body shuddered and her hunger grew, but in that brief moment, her smile evaporated as her dream shattered and his scream hit her like the plague: "You smell horrible tonight, I can't stand it! Go and wash!"

She felt as though her body was falling into a deep well, from which rose the stench of filled lavatories. The smells from the soles of her feet swept to the rest of her body, removing any traces of the perfume and taking its place.

بكل جسدها وتصورها الواثق أنه سينط عليها مجذوباً لعطرها وولهان لجسدها. لكنه زفر زفرتين واستدار إلى الناحية التي أخلتها. وظلت حركته غير مستقرة وتنشقاته وصلت حد العطاس. شكّت في أمر العطر: «هل يمكن ألا يشمه أحد غير الذي تعطر به أم تراه مصاباً بالزكام؟» فجأة استدار نحوها. وفي لحظة مخطوفة لا مساحة لها من الزمن. اللحظة التي زغرد فيها قلبها. تهيأ جسدها. ارتعش جوعها. انفلشت ابتسامتها وصدح حلمها، جاءت صرخته لتنزل عليها كالبلاء:

– رائحتك الليلة كريهة لا أطيقها. قومي اغتسلي.

شعرت بكل جسدها يهوي إلى جب عميق. تفوح منه روائح حمامات غير مهجورة. تسللتها الرائحة من أخمص قدميها إلى كلّ الجسد. جرفت كلّ أثر للعطر. واحتلت مكانه الشاغر.

Language Notes

1. قَهْر: verbal noun (مَصْدَر) of the verb قَهَرَ (u); "to cause" or "to force", as well as "to defeat" (e. g. قَهَرَ الجيشُ عَدوَّهُ, "the army defeated its enemy").

2. دِّينار: the local currency in various Arab countries, e.g. Jordan, Iraq, Tunisia, Algeria and Libya. Its plural (دَنانير) is sometimes used in the sense of "money" (cf. فُلوس).

3. مَراحيض. pl. of مِرْحاض: "Toilet", "urinal". Other terms for "lavatory" or "restroom" include بَيْت الرَّاحة (lit. "the house of rest"), بَيْتُ الخَلاء (lit. "the room of emptiness") and the borrowing تواليت.

4. حَشَرَهُنَّ : < حَشَرَ (i, u), "to press", "squeeze".

5. مَخْزُون الأَمْعاء: lit. "the store of the bowels".

6. سيفون: colloquial (> Fr. *siphon*); MSA ثُجَّاجة المِرْحاض.

7. سَمْبُوسَك: a common snack in many South Asian countries. It consists of a fried, triangular-shaped pastry shell stuffed with, for instance, onion, peas and potato. Depending on the stuffing, it can be either savoury or sweet.

8. كَبّة البَطاطا: a small, round, savoury snack of mashed potatoes, meat and spices, deep-fried in oil.

9. لُجَيْن: very formal word for "silver" (cf. فِضّة).

10. بانْيُو: colloquial (> It. *bagno*); MSA حَوْض الأَسْتِحْمام.

11. تَوابِل (pl. of تابِل), "spices"; cf. بَهارات.

12. الآشَ: Iranian thick vegetable soup.

13. مُلْحَق (pl. مُلْحَقات or مَلاحِقُ); a reference to the fact that in the Gulf states, the servants' quarters are usually located in an annex to the house or building they work in. In some cases (e. g. in Saudi Arabia), the word also denotes an extra floor to a house.

Yūsuf Idrīs

Yūsuf Idrīs (1927–91) is considered the undisputed master of the Egyptian short story. Originally trained as a doctor at the University of Cairo, he briefly worked at the famous Qaṣr al-'Aynī hospital in central Cairo. During his student days he was also, like so many of his contemporaries (e. g. Idwār al-Kharrāṭ), active in the nationalist movement, and was imprisoned by the British authorities. Idrīs's involvement in politics would remain a constant throughout his life. As with most Arab intellectuals, the Arab-Israeli war of 1967 was a watershed moment, and until his death Idrīs remained a staunch champion of the Palestinian cause.

As an author, Idrīs's career was extremely varied, spanning novels, criticism, journalism (he, for many years, had a column in Egypt's leading daily, الأهرام) and plays, as well as short stories. In addition to eleven collections of short stories, Idrīs wrote nine plays, the most famous of which is undoubtedly الفَرافير (al-Farafeer).

His stories invariably deal with social issues affecting the nation's poor and dispossessed, without, however, descending into maudlin social realism or pessimism. Idris's protagonists battle against the odds, and always manage to rise to the challenges with which they are faced.

In terms of style, Idrīs was a trailblazer in that he was one of the few to mix Standard Arabic with the Egyptian colloquial in the dialogue of the villagers whose lives he portrayed with such imagination and sensitivity; the Egyptian dialect even shines through in the Standard Arabic passages. Though this practice was condemned by some of his fellow literati – not least by Najīb Maḥfūẓ, who continued to use Standard Arabic for both narrative and dialogue – it made Idrīs all the more popular among the Egyptian reading public.

In addition to individual stories, the following works by Idrīs have been translated into English: أرْخَص ليالي (*The Cheapest Nights and Other Stories*, 1978); الحرام (*The Sinners*, 1984); *Rings of Burnished Brass* (1992); and *City of Love and Ashes* (1999).

He died of heart failure while in London for medical treatment.

The story that is presented here is culled from the collection entitled حادثة شرف (*An Incident of Honour*), which was published in 1961. It is a delightful example of Idrīs' 'house style': witty – even comical at times – yet never condescending; socially committed, yet devoid of meretricious soapbox antics. The story is set in a sleepy fictional village (even though it shares its name with several others, the biggest being in Dakahlia province, near the mouth of the river Nile), with the events surrounding the protagonist serving as a prism through which the author deals with a number of serious issues, such as poverty, solidarity, tradition and belief. As usual, the prose is polished and the dialogues wonderfully vivid and evocative; this is Egypt's master story teller at his best.

طبلية من السماء

A Tray from Heaven

If you see someone running along the streets of Munyat al-Nasr, that is an event. People rarely run there. Indeed, why should anybody run in a village where nothing happens to warrant running? Meetings are not measured in minutes and seconds. The train moves as slowly as the sun. There is a train when it rises, one when it reaches its zenith and another one at sunset. There is no noise that gets on one's nerves, or causes one to be in a hurry. Everything moves slowly there, and there is never any need for speed or haste. As the saying goes: "The Devil takes a hand in what is done in haste."

If you see someone running in Munyat al-Nasr, that is an event, just as when you hear a police siren you imagine that something exciting must have happened. How wonderful it is for something exciting to happen in such a peaceful and lethargic village!

On that particular Friday, it was not just one person who was running in Munyat al-Nasr; rather, it was a whole crowd. Yet no one knew why. The streets and alleys were basking in the usual calm and tranquillity that descended upon the village after the Friday noon prayers, when the streets were sprinkled with frothy rose-scented water smelling of cheap soap; when the women were busy inside the houses preparing lunch and the men were loitering outside until it was time to eat. On that particular day, the peace and tranquillity were broken by two big, hairy legs running along the street and shaking the houses. As the runner passed a group sitting outside a house, he did not fail to greet them. The men returned the greeting and tried to ask him why he was running, but before they could do so he had already moved on. They wanted to know the reason, but, of course, were unable to find out. Their desire to know compelled them to start walking. Then one of them suggested they walk faster, and suddenly they found themselves running. They were not amiss in greeting the various groups sitting outside the houses who, in turn, also started running.

أن ترى إنساناً يجري في شارع من شوارع منية النصر، فذلك حادث، فالناس هناك نادراً ما يجرون، ولماذا يجرون وليس في القرية ما يستحق الجري، المواعيد لا تُحسب بالدقائق والثواني... والقطارات تتحرك في بطء الشمس. قطار إذا طلعت، وآخر حين تتوسط السماء، ومع مغيبها يفوت واحد. ولا ضجيج هناك يثير الأعصاب ويدفع إلى التهور والسرعة. كلّ شيء بطيء، هادىء، عاقل، وكل شيء قانع مستمتع ببطئه وهدوئه ذاك، والسرعة غير مطلوبة أبداً، والعجلة من الشيطان'.

ان ترى واحداً يجري في منية النصر، فذلك حادث. وكأنه صوت السيرينة' في عربة' بوليس النجدة'. فلا بد أن وراء جريه أمراً مثيراً. وما أجمل أن يحدث في البلدة الهادئة البطيئة أمر مثير.

وفي يوم الجمعة ذاك، لم يكن واحد فقط هو الذي يجري في منية النصر، الواقع أنه كانت هناك حركة جري واسعة النطاق. ولم يكن أحد يعرف السبب. فالشوارع والأزقة تسبح في هدوئها الأبدي، وينتابها ذلك الركود الذي يستتب في العادة بعد صلاة الجمعة حيث ترش أرضها بماء الغسيل المختلط بالرغوة والزهره° ورائحة الصابون الرخيص، وحيث النسوة في الداخل مشغولات بإعداد الغداء والرجال في الخارج يتسكعون ويتصعلكون إلى أن ينتهي إعداد الغداء. وإذا بهذا الهدوء كله يتعكر بسيقان ضخمة غليظة تجري وتهز البيوت. ويمر الجاري بجماعة جالسة أمام بيت فلا ينسى وهو يجري أن يلقي السلام، ويرد الجالسون سلامه ويحاولون سؤاله عن سبب الجري ولكنه يكون قد نفذ. حينئذ يقفون ويحاولون معرفة السبب، وطبعاً لا يستطيعون. وحينئذ يدفعهم حب الاستطلاع إلى المشي، ثم يقترح أحدهم الإسراع فيسرعون ويجدون أنفسهم آخر الأمر يجرون، ولا ينسون أن يلقوا السلام على جماعات الجالسين، فتقف الجماعات ولا تلبث أن تجد نفسها تجري هي الأخرى.

However obscure the motive, it was bound to be known in the end, just as it is inevitable that people quickly start gathering at the scene of an accident. It is a small village. There are thousands of people who will give you directions. You are able to run its length and breadth without running out of breath.

It did not take long before a crowd began to gather near the threshing floor. Everyone who was able to run had arrived; only the old and aged remained scattered in the street. They preferred to saunter, as village elders do, and to leave a space between them and the youngsters. However, they were also hurrying, intent on arriving before it was too late and the incident became news.

Like other towns, Munyat al-Nasr was superstitious about Friday, and any event that took place on that day was viewed as a sure catastrophe. The people of the village were, however, excessively superstitious. They were opposed to any work being done on that day for fear it would end in failure, and thus they postponed all work until Saturday. If you asked them why they were so superstitious about it, they would tell you it was because Friday is a day of misfortune. It was, however, clear that this was not the real reason; rather, it was merely a pretext enabling the farmers to put off Friday work until Saturday. And so, Friday became the day of rest. The word "rest" was considered ugly among the farmers, as well as an insult to their toughness and to their extraordinary ability to work indefatigably. Only townspeople needed rest, that is, those who had fresh meat and worked in the comfort of the shade, and in spite of that, still ran out of breath. Weekly rest was a heresy. So, Friday must surely have been a day of bad luck. As a result, work had to be postponed until Saturday.

It is for this reason that people expected that the running meant a grave misfortune had befallen one of them. But when they arrived at the threshing floor they did not find a flat-nosed cow, a raging fire or one man killing another. Instead they found Sheikh Ali standing in the middle of the floor. He was in

غير أنه مهما غمض السبب، فلا بد قي النهاية أن يعرف. ولا بد أن يتجمع الناس في مكان الحادث بعد قليل. فالبلدة صغيرة. وألف من يدلك، وقبل أن تلهث تكون قد قطعتها طولاً وعرضاً.

وهكذا لم يمض وقت طويل حتى كان قد تجمع عند الجرن عدد كبير من الناس. كلّ من في استطاعته الجري كان قد وصل، ولم يبق مبعثراً في الطريق غير كبار السن والعواجيز الذين آثروا التمشي حتى يبدوا كباراً في السن وحتى يبدو ثمة فرق بينهم وبين الشبان الصغار والعيال. ولكنهم كانوا أيضاً يسرعون وفي نيتهم أن يصلوا قبل فوات الأوان وقبل أن يصبح الحادث خبراً.

ومنية النصركغيرها من بلاد الله الواسعة تتشاءم من يوم الجمعة، وأي حادث يقع فيه لابد أنه كارثة أكيدة. ليس هذا فقط، بل إنهم، مبالغة في التشاؤم، لا يجرؤون على القيام بأي عمل في هذا اليوم،بالذات، مخافة أن يصيبه الفشل، وعلى هذا توئجّل الأعمال كلها إلى يوم السبت. وإذا سألت لماذا هذا التشاؤم، قالوا لك لأن في يوم الجمعة ساعة نحس. ولكنّ الظاهر أن السبب الحقيقي ليس هذا، والظاهر أن ساعة النحس هذه حجة ليس إلا، ووسيلة يستطيع بها الفلاحون أن يؤجلوا عمل الجمعة إلى السبت، وبهذا يصبح يوم الجمعة راحة، ولكنّ الراحة كلمة بشعة عند الفلاحين. الراحة إهانة لخشونتهم وقدرتهم الخارقة على العمل التي لا تكل. الراحة لا يحتاجها إلا أبناء المدن فقط ذوو اللحوم الطرية الذين يعملون في الظل، ومع هذا يلهثون. الراحة الاسبوعية بدعة، اذن ألا يكون يوم الجمعة شوئماً وفيه ساعة نحس، وحينئذ فقط من الجائز أن تؤجل الأعمال لتتم في يوم السبت.

ولهذا كان الناس يتوقعون أن يكون سبب حركة الجري هذه مصيبة كبرى حلت بأحد. ولكنهم حين يصلون إلى الجرن لا يجدون بهيمة فطسى ولا حريقاً قائماً. ولا رجلاً يذبح رجلاً.

كانوا يجدون الشيخ علياً واقفاً في وسط الجرن، وهو في حالة غضب

a fit of anger, and had taken off his *jilbab* and turban. He was holding his stick and shaking it violently. When people asked what was going on, the ones who had arrived first replied: "The sheikh will blaspheme God."

At that moment people began to laugh. This was undoubtedly another of Sheikh Ali's jokes. In fact, he himself was regarded as a joke. His head was the size of a donkey's, whereas his eyes were as wide and round as those of an owl, except that his were bloodshot in the corners. His voice was hoarse and loud, like a rusty steam engine. He never smiled. When he was happy, which was rare, he would laugh boisterously. When he was not happy, he would scowl. A single word that he did not like was enough to make his blood boil to the extent that it would be turned into fuel, and he would swoop down on the one who had uttered the word that had caused offence. He might even bear down on this person with his fat-fingered hands, or his hooked, iron-tipped stick, which was made out of thick cane. He was very fond of it and cherished it, calling it "the commandant".

Sheikh Ali's father had sent him to al-Azhar for his education. One day, his teacher made the mistake of calling him "a donkey", to which Sheikh Ali, true to type, had retorted: "And you are as stupid as sixty donkeys." After he was expelled, he returned to Munyat al-Nasr, where he became a preacher and *imam* at the mosque. One day he mistakenly performed the prayers with three genuflections. When the congregation attempted to warn him, he cursed all their fathers, gave up being an *imam* and stopped going to the mosque. He even gave up praying. Instead, he took up playing cards, and continued to play until he had to sell everything he owned. At that moment, he swore he would give that up too.

When Muhammad Effendi, the primary schoolteacher in the district capital, opened a grocery shop in the village, he suggested to Sheikh Ali that he should keep the shop open in the morning, which he accepted. However, this only lasted for

شديد وقد خلع جلبابه٦ وعمامته وأمسك بعصاه وراح يهزها بعنف. وحين يسألون عن الحكاية. يقول لهم السابقون: الشيخ ح يكفر٧. وكان الناس حينئذ يضحكون، فلا ريب أن تلك نادرة أخرى من نوادر الشيخ علي الذي كان هو نفسه نادرة. فرأسه كبير كرأس الحمار، وعيناه واسعتان مستديرتان كعيون أم قويق٨، وله في ركن كلّ عين جلطة دم. وصوته إذا تكلم يخرج مبحوحاً مكتوماً كصوت الوابور٩ إذا انكتم نفسه وشحر. ولم تكن له ابتسامة، فقد كان لا يبتسم أبداً. إذا انبسط ونادراً ما ينبسط، قهقه، وإذا لم ينبسط كشّر. وكلمة واحدة لا تعجبه يتعكر دمه حتى يستحيل إلى مازوت وينقض على قائلها. قد ينقض عليه بيده ذات الأصابع الغليظة كالصوامع. أو قد ينقض عليه بعصاه، وعصاه كان لها عقفة، وكانت من خيزران غليظ. وكان لها كعب من حديد. وكان يحبها ويعزها ويسميها الحكمدار١٠.

أرسله أبوه ليتعلم في الأزهر١١، وهنا أخطأ شيخه مرة وقال له: أنت بغل. فما كان من الشيخ علي إلا أن رد عليه وقال: أنت ستين بغل. ولما رفدوه وعاد إلى منية النصر عمل خطيباً للمسجد وإماماً. ونسي ذات يوم وصلى الجمعة ثلاث ركعات١٢، ولما حاول المصلون وراءه تنبيهه لعن آباءهم جميعاً وطلق من يومها الامامة والجامع. ولأجل خاطرهم طلّق الصلاة. وتعلم الكوتشينة وظل يلعبها حتى باع كلّ ما يملكه، وحينئذ حلف بالطلاق١٣ أن يطلها. وكان محمد أفندي١٤ المدرس بالمدرسة الابتدائية في البندر فاتحاً دكان بقالة في البلدة، عرض على الشيخ علي أن يقف في الدكان ساعات الصباح فقبل، ولكنه لم يعمل إلا ثلاثة أيام، وفي اليوم الرابع كان محمد أفندي

three days. On the fourth day, Muhammad Effendi could be seen standing in front of his shop, dripping with *halva*. Sheikh Ali had discovered that Muhammad Effendi had put a piece of metal in the scales to doctor them. Sheikh Ali had told him: "You're a crook." No sooner had Muhammad Effendi said: "How dare you, Sheikh Ali! Shut up if you want to keep your job!" than the sheikh hurled a handful of *halva* at him. From that day onwards, nobody ever dared to give Sheikh Ali any work. But even if anybody had dared, it would not have mattered as Sheikh Ali himself was no longer interested in working anyway.

Sheikh Ali was also a very ugly man as well as irascible and unemployed, and yet nobody in the village really hated him. Quite the contrary; most of the villagers loved him and liked to exchange funny stories about him. Their greatest joy was to sit around him and arouse his anger, much to everyone's merriment. When he got angry and his features darkened, unable to speak, it was impossible for any of the bystanders to control themselves and not collapse with laughter. They kept on egging him on, while he grew angrier and angrier. They would laugh until the end of the gathering. Everyone would utter: "What a character you are, Sheikh Ali!" They would then leave him alone to vent his anger on "Abu Ahmad", which is what he called his poverty. He considered Abu Ahmad his arch-enemy. Sheikh Ali spoke about his poverty as if it were a person of flesh and blood standing in front of him. Usually, the tirade would be sparked if someone asked him:

"So what has Abu Ahmad done to you today, Sheikh Ali?"

Sheikh Ali would fly into a real rage at that moment, because he did not like anyone to talk about his poverty when he was talking to it. And whenever people talked about his poverty he would be driven to rage. Sheikh Ali was, in fact, quite shy, despite his stern features and words. He preferred to go for days without smoking, rather than ask any of the villagers to roll

واقفاً أمام الدكان يتصبب حلاوة طحينية°¹. فقد اكتشف الشيخ علي أن
محمد أفندي يضع قطعة حديد في الميزان ليطب، وقال له الشيخ علي: أنت
حرامي. وما كاد محمد أفندي يقول: لايمها يا شيخ علي واسكت وخليك
تأكل عيش، حتى قذفه الشيخ علي بكتلة الحلاوة الطحينية. ومن يومها لم
يجرؤ أحد على أن يعهد للشيخ علي بعمل. وحتى لو كان قد جرؤ، فالشيخ
علي نفسه لم يكن متحمساً لأي عمل.

وكان هذا الشيخ علي قبيحاً. ضيق الصدر، لا عمل له، ومع هذا لم يكن
في البلدة من يكره. كان الجميع يحبونه ويعشقونه ويتداولون نوادره، وألذ
ساعة هي تلك التي يجلسون فيها حوله يستفزونه ليغضب، وغضبه كان
يضحكهم. كان إذا غضب، واربدت ملامحه، وانكتم صوته. كان الواحد
منهم لا يتمالك نفسه ويموت من الضحك؟ ويظلون يستفزونه ويظل هو
يغضب. ويضحكون حتى ينفض المجلس. وعلى كلِّ لسان كلمة: الله
يجازيك¹⁶ يا شيخ علي، ويتركونه وحيداً ليصب جام غضبه على (أبو
أحمد) فقد كان يسمي الفقر (ابو أحمد) وكان يعتبره عدوه الوحيد اللدود.
ويتحدث عنه كما لو كان آدمياً موجوداً له اسم ولحم ودم. وكانت مجالسه
تبدأ حين يسأله أحدهم:

– أبو أحمد عمل فيك ايه¹⁷ يا شيخ علي النهارده¹⁸؟

وكان الشيخ علي يغضب حينئذ غضباً حقيقياً. ذلك لأنه لم يكن يحب
ان يحدثه أحد عن فقره، إذا تحدث هو به أما أن يتحدث الناس عن
فقره فذلك شيء يدفع إلى الغضب. فالشيخ علي كان خجولاً جداً رغم
قسوة ملامحه وكلامه. وكان يفضل أن يبقى أياماً بلا دخان على أن يطلب
من أحدهم أن يلف له سيجارة. وكان يحمل معه على الدوام إبرة وفتلة لرتق

him a cigarette. He always carried a needle and thread about his person in order to mend his *jilbab* in case it became torn. When his clothes got dirty, he would go far away from the village in order to wash them, and would remain naked until they were dry. Because of this, his turban was cleaner than any other turban in the village.

So it was only natural that the people of Munyat al-Nasr laughed at this new drollery on that particular day. However, in this case the laughter soon died down and people fell silent, tongue-tied with fear. The word blasphemy was a terrible one to use, especially in a village that, like any other, lived in peace and tranquillity. Its people were good people, who knew nothing except their work and family. Just like any other village, there were petty thieves stealing corncobs, big thieves raiding cattle pens and snatching the excess cattle with hooks; big and small tradesmen; known and unknown loose women; honest folk and liars; spies; sick people; spinsters and righteous people. However, you found them all in the mosque when the *muezzin* called the faithful to prayer. You would not find a single one of them breaking their fast during Ramadan.

There are laws and guiding principles of life that everyone must abide by: a thief does not steal from another thief; no one blames anyone for his profession; and no one dares to talk about things that would offend public feelings. And there was Sheikh Ali blasphemously talking to God in this way without hindrance. The villagers were laughing a little, but as soon as they heard what he was saying, they were dumbstruck.

Sheikh Ali's head was bare, and his short-cropped white hair glistened with sweat. In his right hand, he clutched his stick. His eyes were glowing like embers, while a look of fierce and senseless anger had settled on his face.

He said, addressing the sky: "What do you want from me? Can you tell me what is it that you want from me? I left al-Azhar because of some sheikhs who act as if they are the sole

جلبابه إذا تمزق، وإذا اتسخ ذهب بعيداً عن البلدة وغسل ثيابه وظل عارياً حتى تجف. ولذلك كانت عمامته الوحيدة أنظف عمامة في البلدة.

كان حرياً إذن بأهل منية النصر أن يضحكوا من هذه النادرة الجديدة. ولكنّ الضحكات كانت تموت في الحال... والألسن تتراجع خائفة إلى الحلوق وكأنما لدغتها عقارب. فكلمة الكفر كلمة بشعة. والبلدة مثل غيرها من البلاد تحيا في أمان الله، فيها كلّ ما تحفل به سائر البلاد. الناس الطيبون الذين لا يعرفون إلا أعمالهم وبيوتهم. واللصوص الصغار الذين يسرقون كيزان الذرة. والكبار الذين ينقبون الزرائب ويسحبون البهائم من أنوفها بالخطاطيف، والتجار الذين يتاجرون بالمئات. وتجار القروش، والنساء الملعبات غير المعروفات وأولئك المعروفات على نطاق البلدة كلها، والصادقون والكاذبون والخفراء. والمرضى والعوانس والصالحون: فيها كلّ ما تحفل به سائر البلاد. ولكنّ الجميع تجدهم في الجامع إذا أذّن المؤذن للصلاة، ولا تجد واحداً منهم فاطراً في رمضان. وثمة قوانين مرعية تنظم حياة الكل ويسمونها الأصول، فلا يتعدى اللص على لص، ولا أحد يعيِّر أحداً بصنعته ولا يجسر واحد على تحدي الشعور العام. وإذا بالشيخ علي يقف ويخاطب الله هكذا بلا احم ولا دستور.

كانوا يضحكون قليلاً ولكنهم ما يكادون يسمعون ما يقوله حتى يتولاهم وجوم.

كان رأسه عارياً وشعره القصير يلمع بالعرق وبالشيب والعصا الحكمدار في يمينه وعيناه تنفثان حمماً، وفي وجهه غضب أحمق شديد، وكان يقول موجهاً كلامه إلى السماء:

ـ أنت عايز١٩ مني ايه. تقدر تقول لي أنت عايز مني ايه؟ الازهر وسبته٢٠ عشان٢١ خاطر شوية٢٢ المشايخ اللي٢٣ عاملين٢٤ اوصياع الدين: ومراتي٢٥

guardians of the faith. I divorced my wife, sold my house, and out of all people you chose me to inflict Abu Ahmad on. Why me? Who don't you send down your anger, oh Lord, on Churchill or on Eisenhower? Or is it because you can only do it to me? What do you want from me now?

"So many times in the past you made me hungry, and I endured it. I would tell myself: 'Imagine it's the month of Ramadan, and you're fasting. It's only one day, and it'll pass. ' But, this time, I haven't eaten anything since yesterday afternoon, and I haven't had any cigarettes for a week. I haven't touched hash for ten days. And you're telling me that in Paradise there is honey, fruit and rivers of milk, yet you don't give me any of it! Why? Are you waiting for me to die of hunger and go to Paradise before I can partake of your beneficence? No way! Save it! Let me live today and after that, take me wherever you like.

"Come on, man, why don't you get this Abu Ahmad off my back? Why don't you send him to America? Is he my destiny? Why do you torture me? I have nothing, except this *gallabiyya* and this stick. What do you want from me? You either feed me right now, or take me now! Are you going to feed me, or not?"

As Sheikh Ali uttered these words he was in a state of extreme fury; he actually began to froth at the mouth and became soaked with sweat, while his voice filled with fierce hatred. The people of Munyat al-Nasr stood motionless, their hearts almost frozen with fear. They were afraid Sheikh Ali would continue and become blasphemous. But that was not the only thing that scared them. The words spoken by Sheikh Ali were dangerous ... they would cause the wrath of God the Almighty, and it would be their village that would pay the price when His vengeance struck everything they owned. Sheikh Ali's words threatened the safety of the entire village, and so he had to be shut up. In order to do this, some of the village elders began shouting placatory remarks from afar with a view to making Sheikh Ali regain his

وطلقتها. والدار وبعتها، وابو احمد وسلطته علي دونا عن بقية الناس. هو
ما فيش²⁶ في الدنيا دي كلها إلا اني. ما تنزل غضبك يا رب على تشرشل
ولا زنهاوز... مش قادر²⁷ إلا علي اني؟ عايز مني ايه دلوقت²⁸؟ المرات
اللي فاتت كنت بتجوعني يوم وباستحمل... واقول ياواد كأننا في رمضان،
وأهو يوم وينفض المرة دي²⁹ بقالي ما كلتش³⁰ من أول امبارح³¹ العصر،
وسجاير ممعييش سجاير بقالي اسبوع. ومزاج³² حد الله ما دقته بقالي عشرة
أيام، وأنت بتقول فيه في الجنة عسل نحل وفواكه وانهار لبن. ما بتدنيش³³
منهم ليه. مستني أما أموت من الجوع علشان³⁴ أروح الجنة وآكل من
خيرك؟ لا يا سيدي يفتح الله. احييني النهارده وابقى بعد كده³⁵ وديني
مطرح ما توديني. يا أخي ما تبعد عني ابو احمد ده³⁶. ما تبعته امريكا.
هو كان انكتب علي. أنت بتعذبني ليه³⁷. آني ما حلتيش إلى الجلابيه دي.
والحكمدار عايز مني ايه. يا تغديني دلوقتي حالا. يا تاخدني حداك على
طول. ح اتغديني والا لأ³⁸.

كان الشيخ علي يقول هذا بانفعال رهيب، حتى لقد تكوم الزبد فوق
فمه، وطماه العرق، وامتلأ صوته بحقد فاض عن حده. وأهل منية النصر
واقفون وقلوبهم تكاد تسقط من الرعب. كانوا خائفين أن يسوق الشيخ
علي فيها ويكفر. ولم يكن هذا فقط مبعث خوفهم. فالكلمات التي يقولها
الشيخ علي خطيرة... قد تغضب الله سبحانه و تعالى، وقد تحل ببلدهم من
جراء ذلك نقمة تأتي على الأخضر واليابس. كان كلام الشيخ علي يهدّد
البلدة الآمنة كلها، وكان لا بد من إسكاته. وعلى هذا بدأ العقلاء يطلقون
من بعيد كلمات طيبات³⁹ يرجون فيها من الشيخ علي أن يعود إليه رشده

senses and hold his tongue. For a while, Sheikh Ali turned away from the sky and directed his gaze towards the onlookers:

"Why should I be quiet, you miserable wretches? Should I be quiet until I die of hunger? Why should I keep quiet? Are you afraid for your houses, women and fields? It is only those who have something to lose that are afraid! As for me, I don't have anything to be scared of. And if He is annoyed with me, let Him take me! In the name of my religion and all things holy, if someone were to come and take me, even if it was Azrael, the Angel of Death, himself, I'd bash his skull in with my stick. I'll not be silent unless He sends me a table laden with food from heaven, right now. I'm not worth less than Maryam, who was only a woman after all; but I'm a man. And she wasn't poor. I, on the other hand, I've had to suffer at the hands of Abu Ahmad. By my religion and everything I hold dear, I'll not be quiet until He sends me a dining table right now!"

The sheikh once again turned to the sky: "Send it to me right now, otherwise I'll say whatever's on my mind. A dining table, right now! Two chickens, a dish of honey and a pile of hot bread – only if it's hot – and don't you dare forget the salad! I'll count up to ten. And if the dining table's not sent down, I'll not stop at anything."

Sheikh Ali began to count, and the people of Munyat al-Nasr silently counted ahead of him, but they became increasingly nervous. Sheikh Ali had to be stopped. One of them suggested they get the strongest youths of the village to throw him to the ground, gag him and give him a thrashing he would not forget. However, one look at Sheikh Ali's fiery, rage-filled, mad eyes was enough to forget the proposal. It would be impossible to knock Sheikh Ali down before he lashed out once or twice with his stick. Every youth was afraid he would be the one to be struck, and that instead of Azrael's head being splattered, it would be one of theirs. For this reason, the proposal foundered.

One of them said, impatiently: "You have been hungry all your life, man, why pick today?"

ويسكت، وترك الشيخ علي السماء قليلاً والتفت إليهم:

– اسكت ليه يا بلد دون. اسكت لما أموت م'[٤] الجوع. اسكت ليه.
خايفين على بيوتكم ونسوانكم وزرعكم. اللي حداه حاجه يخاف عليها،
انما أنا مش خايف على حاجه[٤١]. ان كان زعلان مني ياخدني، انما وديني وما
اعبد ان ايجه حد ياخدني انشا الله يكون عزرائين[٤٢] لمدشدش[٤٣] على رأسه
الحكمدار. وديني ماني ساكت إلا أما يبعت لي مائدة من السما حالاً. أنا
مش أقل من مريم. هي مهما كانت حرمة، انما أنا راجل[٤٤]. وهي ماكنتشي[٤٥]
فقيرة، انما انا ابو أحمد طلع ديني. وديني وما اعبد ماني ساكت إلا أما يبعت
لي حالاً مائدة.

والتفت الشيخ علي إلى السماء وقال:

– هه. ح تبعتها حالا دلوقتي والا ما أخلي ولا أبقي حدايا إلا ما اقوله
مائدة حالاً. جوز[٤٦] فراخ وطبق عسل نحل ورصة عيش ساخن. على شرط
عيش[٤٧] ساخن. واوع[٤٨] تنسى السلطة. وديني لعادد لغاية عشرة وان ما
نزلت المائدة ماني مخلي ولا مبقي[٤٩].

ومضى الشيخ علي يعد، وقلوب منية النصر تعد معه مقدماً. والأعصاب
قد بدأت تتوتر، وأصبح لابد من عمل شيء لإيقاف الشيخ علي عند حده.
واقترح أحدهم أن يلتف جماعة من شباب البلدة الأقوياء حوله ويوقعوه
أرضاً، ويكمموا فاه، ويعطوه علقة لا ينساها. غير أن نظرة واحدة ألقاها
الشيخ علي من عينيه المشتعلتين بالغضب المجنون أذابت الاقتراح. فمن
المستحيل أن ينالوا الشيخ علي قبل أن يخبط هو خبطة أو خبطتين برأس
الحكمدار. وكل شاب قد قدر أن الخبطة ستكون من نصيبه. والذي يهدد
بدشدشة رأس عزرائين كفيل بدشدشة رأس الواحد منهم، وعلى هذا ذاب
الاقتراح.

وقال أحدهم في فروغ بال:

– ما أنت طول عمرك جعان[٥٠] يا راجل اشمعنى[٥١] النهارده.

Sheikh Ali's fiery gaze bored down at him, as he replied: "This time, Abd al-Jawwad, you weakling, my hunger has lasted longer."

Somebody else shrieked: "Alright then, man, if you were hungry, why didn't you tell us? We would have fed you instead of listening to your nonsense!"

Sheikh Ali then set upon him: "Me, ask you something? Am I going to beg to you, a village of starving beggars? You're starving more than I am! Beg *you*? I have come to ask Him, and if He doesn't give it to me, I'll know what to do!

Abd al-Jawwad said: "Why didn't you work so that you could've fed yourself, you wretch?"

At that point, Sheikh Ali's anger reached its peak. He flew into a temper, quivering and quaking, alternately directing his harangue towards the crowd gathered at a distance, and at the sky: "What's it to do with you, Abd al-Jawwad, son of Sitt Abuha?! I'm not working! I don't want to work! I don't know how to work. I've not found work. Is what you do work, you bovine prat?! The work that you do is donkey's work, and I'm not a donkey! I can't bust my back all day long; I can't hang around on the field like cattle, you animals. To hell with all of you! I'm not going to work! By God, if I was meant to die of hunger, I still wouldn't do the work that you do! Never!"

In spite of the sheikh's anger and the terrifying nature of the situation, people started laughing.

The sheikh was shaking, and said: "Ha! ... I'll count to ten and, by God, if I don't get a dining table, I'll curse God and do the unspeakable."

It was clear that Sheikh Ali was not going to change his mind, and that he intended to go ahead with his intentions, which would have unimaginable consequences.

As Sheikh Ali started to count, droplets of sweat poured down people's foreheads, and the noon heat became intolerable.

وأصابته نظرة نارية من الشيخ علي، وأجابه:

- المرة دي يا عبد الجواد يا معصفر[٥٢] الحكاية طالت.

وزعق فيه آخر:

- طب[٥٣] يا أخي لما أنت جعان مش تقول لنا واحنا[٥٤] نوكلك بدل الكلام الفارغ اللي أنت قاعد تقوله ده.

وهبّ فيه الشيخ علي:

- اني اطلب منكم، اني اشحت منكم يا بلد جعانة، دا أنتو[٥٥] جعانين أكتر مني، اقوم أشحت منكم، اني جاي[٥٦] أطلب منه هو، واذا ما ادانيش[٥٧] ح اقدر اعرف شغلي.

وقال له عبد الجواد:

- ما كنت تشتغل يا أخي وتاكل. يخفي وجهك.

وهنا بلغ الغضب بالشيخ علي منتهاه، وتزربن وراح يهتز ويصرخ ووزع كلامه بين الجمع المحتشد عن بعد وبين السماء:

- وانت مالك يا عبد الجواد يابن ست أبوها[٥٨]. مانيش[٥٩] مشتغل، مش عايز اشتغل. ما بعرفش اشتغل. مش لاقي شغل. هو شغلكو ده شغل. يا عالم بقر. دا شغلكو[٦٠] ده شغل حمير، واني مش حمار. اني ما اقدرش يتقطم وسطي طول النهار. ما اقدرشي اتعلق في الغيط زي البهيمة. يا بهايم يلعن ابو كوكلكو مانيش مشتغل. والنبي[٦٢] لو حكمت اموت م الجوع ما اشتغل شغلكو أبداً.

وكان غضبه شديداً إلى الدرجة التي جعلت الناس تضحك بالرغم منها وبرغم الموقف الرهيب الذي كانوا فيه.

وانتفض الشيخ علي أنتفاضة عظيمة وقال.

- هه. ح أعد لغاية عشرة والنبي ان ما بعت لي مائدة لكافر وعامل ما لا يعمل.

وكان واضحاً أن الشيخ علي حقيقة لن يتراجع، وأنه ينوي أن يلبخ[٦٣]، ويحدث حينئذ ما لا تحمد عقباه.

وبدأ الشيخ علي يعد، وبدأت نقاط العرق تنبت على الجباه، وأصبح حر

Some started to whisper that the vengeance of God had begun to unfold itself, and that this terrible heat was but the beginning of a terrible conflagration, which would consume all the wheat and crops.

One of them made the mistake of saying: "Why don't any of you get him a morsel of food, so he'll come down?"

Although Sheikh Ali was counting loudly, he heard these words and turned around, towards the gathering: "What morsel, you louts? A piece of your rotten bread and stale cheese that has all been eaten by worms? You call that food? I'll only be quiet if a dining table arrives here, with two chickens on it."

There was a lot of grumbling in the crowd. Suddenly, one of the female bystanders said: "I've got a nice okra stew; I'll bring you a plate of it."

Sheikh Ali shouted at her: "Shut up, woman! What's this okra nonsense, you …! Your brains are like okra, and the smell of this village is like that of acid okra!"

Then Abu Sirhan said: "We've got some fresh fish, Sheikh Ali, which we've just bought from Ahmad the Fisherman."

Sheikh Ali roared: "What's this miniscule fish of yours, you bunch of minions! Do you call that a fish? Damn it, if He doesn't send me two chickens and the other things I ordered, I'll continue cursing – and hang the consequences!"

The situation became unbearable. It was a question of either remaining silent and losing the village and everyone in it, or of shutting up Sheikh Ali by any means possible. A hundred people called out to invite him for lunch, but he refused each time.

Eventually, he said: "I can't continue with this poverty, people. For three days, no one has offered me even a morsel. So, leave off with the invitations now. I won't shut up until you give me a dining table full of food sent by the good Lord."

الظهر لا يطاق، حتى أن بعضهم تهامس أن النقمة لا بد قد بدأت تحل، وأن ذلك الحر الفظيع إن هو إلا مقدمة الحريق الهائل الذي سوف ينشب ويأتي على كلّ القمح الواقف والمحصود.

وأخطأ أحدهم مرة وقال:

– ما تشوفولوا لقمة يا ولاد يمكن يهبط.

ويبدو أن الكلمة وصلت إلى أذن الشيخ علي مع أنه كان يعد بصوت عالٍ مرتفع، فقد استدار إلى الجمع قائلاً:

– لقمة أيه يا بلد غجر. لقمة من عيشكو المعفن وجبنتكم القديمة اللي كلها دود، وده أكل، وديني ماني ساكت إلا أما تنزل لي المائدة لغاية هناه وعليها جوز فراخ.

وسرت همهمة كثيرة في الجمع وقالت ولية من الواقفات:

– اني طابخة شوية بامية حلوين يا خويا اجيب لك صحن.

وصرخ فيها الشيخ علي:

– اخرسي يا مرة. بامية أيه يا بلد كلها قرون. دا عقولكو بقت كلها بامية وريحة بلدكو زي ريحة البامية الحامضة.

وقال أبو سرحان:

– حدانا سمك صابح يا شيخ علي شاريينه لسه٦٤ من أحمد الصياد.

وزأر فيه الشيخ علي:

– سمك أيه بتاعكو٦٥ ده اللي قد العقلة يا بلد (صير).

هو ده سمك، وديني ان ما بعت جوز فراخ والطلبات اللي قلت لك عليها لشاتم وزي ما يحصل يحصل.

وأصبح الوضع لا يحتمل، إما السكوت وضياع البلدة ومن فيها، وإما إسكات الشيخ علي بأي طريقة، وانطلقت مائة حنجرة تعزم عليه بالغداء، وانطلق صوته مائة مرة يرفض، ويصر على الرفض ويقول:

– ماني قاعد على اللضي يا بلد، بقى لي تلات ايام٦٦ ماحدش عزم علي بلقمة، حليت العزومة دلوقتي، وديني ماني ساكت إلا أما تيجي المائدة من عند ربنا.

Heads turned around to enquire who had cooked that day, as not everyone cooked daily; indeed, it would have been highly unlikely for anyone to have meat or chicken. Finally, at Abd al-Rahman's house they found a *ratl* of boiled veal, and they took it to Sheikh Ali on a tray together with some radishes, two loaves of crisp bread and onions. They told the sheikh:

"Is that enough for you?"

Sheikh Ali's eyes alternated between the sky and the tray; when he looked at the sky his eyes gleamed with fire, whereas every time he looked at the tray his anger grew. The onlookers stood by in silence.

Eventually, Sheikh Ali said: "All along I wanted a dining table full of food, you useless lot, and you bring me a tray? And where's the packet of cigarettes?"

One of the villagers gave him a packet of cigarettes. He stuck out his hand and took a large piece of the meat. He wolfed it down, and said: "And where's the hash?"

They told him: "How dare you? That's rich!"

Indignantly, Sheikh Ali said: "Right, that's it!" Then, he left the food, took off his *jilbab* and turban and once again started brandishing his stick, threatening that he would start blaspheming again. He would not be silent until they brought him Mandur the hash dealer to give him a lump of hashish.

Mandur said: "Take it. Take it, Sheikh, you deserve it! We didn't see, we didn't know you'd be embarrassed to ask. People sit with you and they seem happy, but then afterwards they're not interested anymore, and leave you. As for us, we have to see to your comfort, Sheikh. This is our village, and without you and Abu Ahmad it would be worthless. You make us laugh, and we have to feed you … What do you say to this?"

Sheikh Ali again launched into a raging fury, at the height of which he lunged at Mandur, shaking his stick at him and almost hitting him over the head with it.

"Laughing at me? What is so funny about me, Mandur, you donkey brain? Damn you, and your father!"

واستدارت الرؤوس تسأل عمن طبخ في هذا اليوم، إذ إن كلّ الناس لا يطبخون كلّ يوم، وأن يكون لدى أحدهم (زفر) أو فراخ يعد حادثاً جللاً، وأخيراً وجدوا عند عبد الرحمن رطل لحمة (بتلو) مسلوقاً بحاله، فأحضروه على طبلية... وأحضروا معه فجلاً، جوزين عيش مرحرح، ومخ بصل، وقالوا للشيخ علي:

– يقضيك ده.

وتردد بصر الشيخ علي بين السماء والطبلية وكلما نظر إلى السماء قدحت عيناه شرراً وكلما نظر إلى الطبلية احتقن وجهه غضباً، والجمع يغمره السكون، وأخيراً نطق الشيخ علي وقال:

– بقى[67] اني عايز مائدة يا بلد غجر، تجبولي طبلية، وفين[68] علبة السجاير.

و أعطاه أحدهم صندوق دخانه.

ومد يده وتناول قطعة كبيرة من اللحم، وقبل أن يتاويها في فمه قال:

– وحتة[69] المر[70] فين؟!

فقالوا له: حقة إلا دي.

وهاج الشيخ علي وقال: طب هه. وترك الطعام، وخلع جلبابه وعمامته وراح يهزّ عصاه ويهدّد بالكفر من جديد. و لم يسكت إلا بعد أن أحضروا مندور تاجر المر، وبلع له فصا، وقال له:

– خد[71]. خد يا شيخ مش خسارة فيك. أصلنا ماحدناش نظر، وما كناش[72] عارفين[73] انك بتنكسف[74] تطلب، الناس تقعد وياك وتنبسط وبعدين تدلدل ودانها وتمشي وتسيبك، واحنا لازم نشوف راحتك يا شيخ. هي بلدنا من غيرك أنت وابو احمد تسوي بصلة. أنت تضحكنا واحنا ناكلك. ايه رأيك في كده؟!

وغضب الشيخ علي غضباً شديداً، وطار وراء مندور وهو في قمة الغيظ ومضى يهز الحكمدار وهو يكاد يهوي بها على رأسه ويقول:

– انا أضحكوا. هو اني مضحكة يا مندور يا ابن البلغة[75]. امش داهية تلعنك وتلعن أبوك.

Mandur was running in front of Sheikh Ali, laughing. The bystanders were watching the chase, laughing. Even when the sheikh came after all of them, reviling and cursing them, they kept on laughing.

Sheikh Ali remained in Munyat al-Nasr, and things still happened to him every day. He was still short-tempered, and people continued to laugh at his bouts of anger. However, from that day on they made allowances for him. When they saw him standing in the middle of the threshing floor, taking off his *jilbab* and turban, grabbing hold of his stick and starting to shake it at the sky, they understood that they had been oblivious to his problem, and had left Abu Ahmad alone with him for longer than was necessary. Before a single blasphemous word left his mouth, a tray would be brought to him with everything he asked for. Occasionally, he would accept his lot, with resignation.

وكان مندور يجري أمامه وهو يضحك، وكان الناس يتفرجون على المطاردة وهم يضحكون، وحتى حين طار الشيخ علي وراءهم جميعاً وهو يسبهم ويلعنهم كانوا لا يزالون يضحكون.

ولا يزال الشيخ علي يحيا في منية النصر، ولا تزال له في كلّ يوم نادرة، ولا يزال سريع الغضب، ولا يزال الناس يضحكون من غضبه. غير أنهم من يومها عرفوا له، فما يكادون يرونه واقفاً وسط الجرن وقد خلع جلبابه وعمامته وأمسك بالحكمدار في يده وراح يهزّها في وجه السماء، حتى يدركوا أنهم نسوا أمره وتركوا (ابو احمد) ينفرد به أكثر من اللازم، وحينئذ، وقبل أن تتسرب من فمه كلمة كفر واحدة تكون الطبلية قد جاءته، وعليها ما يطلبه، وأحياناً يرضى بما قسم وأمره إلى الله.

Language Notes

1. العَجَلة من الشيطان والصَّبْر من :part of a saying: العَجَلة من الشَّيْطان الرَّحْمن ("haste is of the Devil, patience is divine").

2. السِّرينة: "siren" (ECA); MSA نَفير تَنْبيه.

3. عَرَبة: "car" (ECA); MSA سَيارة. Note that this word also means "cart" (both in ECA and MSA), whereas the usual word for "car" in ECA is عَرَبيّة.

4. بوليس النجدة (النَّجْدة): بوليس: "police" (ECA); MSA شُرْطة. The (lit. "emergency police") may be compared to the civil defence in that it is a special section of the police force on hand to help in case of emergencies. Note that النجدة...النجدة means "Help! Help!".

5. الزَّهْره: (ECA) a blueing agent (for laundry). Cf. ECA زَهْريّ, "blue". The word زَهْرَة can also, of course, mean "rose" (as it does in MSA).

6. جلباب: (pl. جَلابيبُ) a loose, robe-like garment. Interestingly enough, the author chooses to use this term rather than the ECA جَلابية (pl. جَلابيا, جَلابيبُ), as it is this quintessentially Egyptian male dress the protagonist is presumably wearing.

7. حَ يكفر: "he will think" (ECA); cf. MSA سَوْف يكفر or سَيكفر. In ECA, the prefix ح (راحَ>, "to go") is added to the imperfect (المضارع) to denote the future aspect (often implying intention). It is also used interchangeably with راح or رايح (which has the feminine and plural forms رايْحة and رايْحين), e.g. رايحين نكتب، راح نكتب، حَنكتب all mean "We're going to write".

8. اُمّ قُوَيْق: "owl" (ECA); cf. MSA بُوم (coll.). In contradistinction to European lore, the owl is associated with highly negative symbolism (stupidity, untrustworthiness) in Arab culture, and it is referred to as غُراب اللَيْل ("night crow").

9. الوابُور: (< It. *vapore* or Fr. *vapeur*, "steam") in ECA, as in a number of other dialects, this word can have a variety of meanings, e. g. "steam engine" (MSA مُحَرِّك بُخاري), "steamship"

(قاطِرَة MSA) "locomotive" (بَواخِرُ .pl ,باخِرِة MSA).

10. الحُكُمْدار: (ECA < Turkish *hükümdar*, pl. حكمدارية) denotes anyone in executive authority (e. g. chief of police, school prefect).

11. الأَزْهَر: one of the most ancient universities and undoubtedly the most famous mosque-university in the Islamic world.

12. ثَلاث رَكَعات: this refers to the number of genuflections (also see حكاية القنديل) the faithful have to perform in prayer. In this case, as it is the Friday prayers (i. e. the prayers performed in the mosque at midday), it should have been two (whereas it is four for ordinary midday prayers performed at home).

13. حَلَفَ بالطَلاق: (lit. "to swear by divorce"); a strong oath, the use of which is not restricted to marital issues! It reflects the highly negative connotation attached to divorce in Muslim culture.

14. أَفَنْدي: (pl. أَفَنْدية) originally an Ottoman title and honorific for various dignitaries, in Egypt it is a term/reference of address used for all persons with a certain standard of literacy.

15. الحَلاوة الطحينية: a sweetmeat made of honey and containing sesame seeds, nuts, rosewater, etc. (the English word "halva" is, of course, derived from the Arabic حَلاوة, "sweetmeat").

16. اللهُ يُجازيك: variants of this expression include جَزاك اللهُ كلَّ خَيْر (lit. "May God reward you with everything that is good") and رَبِّنا يجْزيك (lit. "May our Lord reward you").

17. ايه: (pronounced eeh,) "what" (ECA < CA أَيّ, "what", "which"); MSA ماذا.

18. النهارده: "today" (ECA); cf. MSA اليَوْمَ. The ECA word is derived from النَّهار ("day", as opposed to "night") and the demonstrative دَه ("this").

19. عايِز: see شعور الأسلاف.

20. سِبْتُه: "I left it" (ECA < ساب, "to leave") MSA تَرَكْتُهُ .

21. عشَان: "because" (ECA < CA عَلى شَأن, "on those grounds"); cf. MSA لأنَّ.

22. شُوَيَّه: "a bit, more or less" (ECA < CA diminutive of شيء, "thing"); cf. MSA قَليل.

23. اللي: the invariable relative pronoun in ECA (and indeed in the overwhelming majority of colloquial varieties). It

corresponds to the MSA الَّذِي (masc, sg.) الَّتِي (fem. sg.), اللَذان (masc. dual nom.), اللتان (fem. dual nom.), اللَّذَيْن (masc. dual gen. /acc.), اللتَيْن (fem. dual gen. /acc.), الذِينَ (masc. pl.), اللواتي/اللاتي (fem. pl.).

24. عامْلِين: active participle (عَمَل >، "to work"): عامْلة (f.), عامِلَين (pl.).

25. مراتي: "my wife" (ECA = CA إمْرأتِي, "my woman"); cf. MSA زوْجَتِي.

26. ما فِيش: "nothing" (ECA < CA ما+فِيه شَيء, "not in it a thing"), cf. MSA لا شَيْء.

27. مِش (قادر): (ECA negating particle < CA ما + شَيْء, "not a thing"), cf. MSA, ما, لم or لا (with verbs), and لا with nouns. The ECA particle can be pronounced مِش or مُش.

28. دِلوَقْتِي: "now" (ECA < CA هذا الوَقْت, "this time"), MSA الآن. Note also that in ECA ق is pronounced as a glottal stop.

29. دي: "this" (ECA feminine demonstrative); cf. MSA هذه. Note that the ECA demonstrative comes after the noun, whereas in MSA it precedes it: e.g. ECA العَرَبيّة دي = MSA هذه السّيارة ("This car").

30. ما كَلْتْش: "I haven't eaten", ECA split negative construction ما + ش + أكلت; cf. MSA لم آكل. The split negative is an alternative to مُش (see above) in that it can also be attached to prepositions and even pronouns: e.g. ما عَنْدِيش ("I don't have any …"), مَنْتاش ("Aren't you [m.] coming with us?").

31. أول امبارح: see شعور الأسلاف.

32. مَزاج: "hashish" (ECA); MSA حَشِيش. It is interesting to note the reference to drugs in combination with an oath involving God (حد الله)! Note also that in ECA (and in Omani Arabic) ج is pronounced as "g" (as in the English "go").

33. بِتَدْنِيش: "you're giving me" (ECA: ب+تدني+ش). The particle ب is used in ECA with imperfect verb forms to denote a continuous or habitual action (there is no equivalent in MSA). MSA: تَعْطِينِي.

34. عَلَشان: (ECA < CA عَلَى شأن, "for (what) matter", a variant of عشان (see above).

35. بَعْدَ كَدَه: "afterwards" (ECA كده, pronounced kedah < CA

(كَذا, cf. MSA بَعْدَ ذَلِكْ. Also note the expression مش كده؟ "isn't that so?" (مَش < MSA أَلَيْسَ كَذلكَ). In the affirmative (كده) it simply means "not like that".

36. دَه: "this" (ECA masculine demonstrative); cf. MSA هَذا.

37. ليه: "why?" (ECA, pronounced lēh); MSA لِماذا.

38. وَالا لأ: (ECA < CA وَالّا, "otherwise") MSA أَوْ لَا.

39. كلمات طَيِّبات: "nice words"; this is an example of a sound fem. pl. in ECA for inanimate things, which corresponds to a fem. sg. in MSA: كلمات طيبة("nice words").

40. م: (ECA) abbreviated form of مِن.

41. حاجة: see شعور الأسلاف.

42. عزرائِين: "Azrael"; corrupted form of عَزْرائيل. This substitution of "n" for "l" is not uncommon in ECA, e.g. فِنْجال (for MSA فِنْجان, "cup"), بُرْتُقان (for MSA بُرْتُقال, "oranges").

43. بِمُدَشْدَش "smashing", ECA (دَشْدَشَ >, "to smash, shatter"); MSA حَطَّمَ.

44. راجِل: "man" (ECA) MSA رَجُل.

45. ما كَنْتْشِي "you weren't"; ECA split negative (> ي+ش+كانت+ما); MSA لَمْ تَكُنْ.

46. جُوز: "two", "a pair" (ECA) MSA زَوْج ("couple", "set of two"). This is an example of metathesis, i.e. the swapping around of consonants.

47. عَيش: "bread" (ECA), MSA خُبْز.

48. اوْع: "watch it, you!"; masc. imperative of وَعَى ("to heed", "bear in mind"). Cf. MSA اِحْتَذِر or اِنْتَبِه.

49. ماني مخَلِّي ولامبَقِي: (ECA) MSA لَن أَتْرُك ولَنَ أَبْقَى شيءً.

50. جُوْعَان: "hungry" (ECA); MSA جُعَان.

51. اشمعْنَى: "why" (this one and not another one) (ECA); MSA: لِماذا.

52. مُعَصْفَر: lit. "dyed in safflower".

53. طَب: "right" (ECA); MSA طَيِّب.

54. اِحْنا: "we" (ECA); MSA نَحْنُ.

55. أَنْتو: "you", m. pl. (ECA); MSA أَنْتُم.

56. جاي: "coming"; ECA present participle or جاء >, "to come"; cf. MSA جِئْتُ.

57. ما ادانيش: "he didn't give me"; ECA split negative

. لَمْ يُعْطني :MSA (ما+أدى+ني+ش)

58. ستّ َ أبُوها: a typically Egyptian name (associated especially with the Upper Egyptian countryside), which literally translates as "Mrs Her Father"!

59. مانيش: ECA split negative (see above), involving the first person singular pronoun (ما+أنا+ش) and meaning "I don't have".

60. (شُغْلُكُم) بِكو :("your" – m. pl. (ECA); MSA كُم (e. g. شُغْلِكُم)

61. أبوكُم كُلُّكُم (= آباوُكُم) :"all your fathers" (ECA); MSA أبُوكُو كَلكُو (جَميعاً).

62. والنَّبي: an oath (lit. "by the Prophet"), with variants such as وَالله, وَحَياتي.

63. لَبَخ: "to perplex" (ECA); MSA شَوَّشَ, أذْهَلَ (u), حَيَّرَ, رَبَكَ.

64. لسَّه: "not yet" (ECA < CA); MSA لَيْسَ بَعْدُ (=لَيْسَ).

65. بتاعكو: "yours" – m/f. pl. ; ECA possessive particle بتاع (CA > تَبَع, "to belong to") with the second person pl. morpheme كو (MSA كُم), i.e. "yours".

66. تلات ايام: "three days" (ECA); MSA ثلاثة أيام. Note the absence of so-called gender polarity for numerals in ECA. The word تلات also reveals the common pronunciation of ث in ECA as ت (or sometimes س).

67. بَقَى: "so, then"; ECA invariable particle (not to be confused with the verb بَقِيَ, "to stay"!).

68. فين : "where" (ECA); MSA أيْنَ.

69. حَتَّة: "piece", "morsel" (ECA, pl. حتَت); MSA: قطْعة (pl. قطَع).

70. مُرّ: "hashish" (ECA); MSA حَشيش. Also see note above on مزاج.

71. خُد: "take" (ECA); MSA خُذْ (imperative). The ECA form reflects the common pronunciation of ذ as د (or ز) in Egypt.

72. ما كناش: "we weren't" (ECA split negative); MSA . لَمْ نَكُنْ

73. عارفين: active participle (عَرَفَ > "to know"): عارفة (f.), عارْفين (pl.).

74. بتنْكسف: ECA تنكسف + the continuous particle بِ.

75. أَبَنَ البُلغة: lit. "son of a slipper".

Bibliography

The Authors

Bakr, Salwā (2003): *Shu'ūr al-aslāf*, Cairo: Maktabat Madbūlī

al-Faqīh, Aḥmad Ibrāhīm (1976): *Akhtafat al-najm wa ayna anti?*, Tunis: al-Dār al-'Arabiyya li-l-Kitāba.

Idrīs, Yūsuf (1981): *Ḥāditha sharaf*, Beirut: Dār al-Ādāb.

al-Kharrāṭ, Idwār (1990): *Makhlūqāt al-ashwāq al-ṭā'ira wa maḥaṭṭat al-sikka al-ḥadīd*, Beirut: Dār al-Ādāb.

al-Madanī, 'Izz al-Dīn (1982): *Ḥikāyat hādhihi 'l-zamān*, introduced by Samīr al-'Iyādī, Tunis: Dār al-Junūd li l-Nashr.

Maḥfūẓ, Najīb (1982): *Ra'aytu fīmā yarā al-nā'im*, Cairo: Dār Miṣr li 'l-Ṭibā'a.

al-Shaykh, Ḥanān (1982): *Wardat al-ṣaḥrā'*, Beirut: Mu'asassat al-Jāmi'iyya li 'l-Dirāsāt wa 'l-Nashr wa 'l-Tawzī'.

Shukrī, Muḥammad (2003): *al-Khayma*, Casablanca: Maṭba'at al-Najāḥ al-Jadīda.

al-Takarlī, Fu'ād (2004): *Khazīn al-lāmar'iyyāt*, Damascus: Dār al-Madā.

Tāmir, Zakariyyā' (1973): *Dimashq al-ḥarā'iq*, Damascus: Manshūrāt Maktabat al-Nūrī.

al-'Uthmān, Laylā (2005): *Laylat al-qahr*, Cairo: Dār Sharqiyyāt li 'l-Nashr wa 'l-Tawzī'.

al-Zafzāf, Muḥammad (1980): *al-Shajra al-Muqaddasa*, Beirut: Dār al-Ādāb.

References

'Abd al-Raḥmān, Y. (2003): *Mawsū'at al-'āmiyya al-Sūriyya: Dirāsa Lughawiyya Naqdiyya*, Damascus.

Arabic Language Academy (2004): *Al-Mu'jam al-Wasīṭ*, Cairo, 4th edn.

al-Buzurkān, Rif'at Ra'ūf (2000): *Mu'jam al-alfāẓ al-dakhīla fī 'l-Lahja al-'Irāqiyya al-Dārija*, Baghdad: al-Dār al-'Arabiyya li 'l-Mawsu'āt.

Elias, Elias A. and Edward E. Elias (1994): *Elias' Modern Dictionary, English-Arabic*, Cairo.

Encyclopaedia of Islam, 2nd edn, Leiden/London (E. J. Brill), 1960–.

al-Fīrūzābādī, Muḥammad b. Ya'qūb [n. d.]: *al-Qāmūs al-muḥīṭ*, 4 vols, ed. M. M. b. al-Talamīd al-Turkuzī al-Shinqīṭī, Cairo: al-Maṭba'a al-Yamaniyya.

Hinds, Martin and El-Said Badawi (1986): *A Dictionary of Egyptian Arabic. Arabic-English*, Beirut: Librarie du Liban.

Ibn Manẓūr, Jamāl al-Dīn (1299/1881–1308/1890–1): *Lisān al-'Arab*, 20 vols, Būlāq.

Pickthall, Mohammed Marmaduke (1996): *The Meaning of the Holy Qur'ān*, London: UBSPD.

Wehr, Hans (1994): *Arabic-English Dictionary*, 4th edn, Urbana, IL: Spoken Language Services Inc.

al-Zabīdī, Abū Muḥammad Murtaḍā (1306–7/1888–90): *Tāj al-'arūs min sharḥ jawāhir al-qāmūs*, 10 vols, Cairo.